KU-755-210

HELEN GRANT

The GLASS *Demon*

PENGUIN BOOKS

PENGUIN BOOKS

Published by the Penguin Group
Penguin Books Ltd, 80 Strand, London WC2R ORL, England
Penguin Group (USA) Inc., 375 Hudson Street, New York, New York 10014, USA
Penguin Group (Canada), 90 Eglinton Avenue East, Suite 700, Toronto, Ontario, Canada M4P 2Y3
(a division of Pearson Penguin Canada Inc.)
Penguin Ireland, 25 St Stephen's Green, Dublin 2, Ireland (a division of Penguin Books Ltd)
Penguin Group (Australia), 250 Camberwell Road, Camberwell, Victoria 3124, Australia
(a division of Pearson Australia Group Pty Ltd)
Penguin Books India Pvt Ltd, 11 Community Centre, Panchsheel Park, New Delhi – 110 017, India
Penguin Group (NZ), 67 Apollo Drive, Rosedale, North Shore 0632, New Zealand
(a division of Pearson New Zealand Ltd)
Penguin Books (South Africa) (Pty) Ltd, 24 Sturdee Avenue, Rosebank,
Johannesburg 2196, South Africa

Penguin Books Ltd, Registered Offices: 80 Strand, London WC2R ORL, England

penguin.com

First published 2010
1

Set in 10.6/14.85 pt Sabon LT Std
Typeset by Palimpsest Book Production Limited, Grangemouth, Stirlingshire
Made and printed in England by Clays Ltd, St Ives plc

British Library Cataloguing in Publication Data
A CIP catalogue record for this book is available from the British Library

ISBN: 978-0-141-32576-7

www.greenpenguin.co.uk

For Iona

PENGUIN BOOKS

The GLASS *Demon*

Helen Grant was born in London. She read Classics at St Hugh's College, Oxford, and then worked in marketing for ten years in order to fund her love of travelling. In 2001 she and her family moved to Bad Münstereifel in Germany, and it was exploring the legends of this beautiful town that inspired her to write her first novel. She now lives in Brussels with her husband, her two children and a small German cat.

Praise for *The Vanishing of Katharina Linden*:

'A feast of treats and creeps . . . wonderful' – *Guardian*

'A richly textured, effortlessly written novel'
– *Sunday Telegraph*

'For something so chilling, it is terrific entertainment'
– *Sunday Times*

'An impressive debut from a writer to watch'
– *Daily Mail*

'Gripping stuff . . . not for the faint-hearted' – *Carousel*

'Remarkable' – *Independent*

T 00 909455 04

Books by Helen Grant

The Vanishing of Katharina Linden
The Glass Demon

CHAPTER ONE

If anyone were to ask me, 'What is the root of all evil?' I would say not 'Money' but 'Food'. It was food – specifically the lack of it – that killed my sister, or at least assisted at the death. And the old man that day in the orchard in Niederburgheim was the only person I have ever seen who died of eating an apple.

He was lying in the long grass, and all we could see of him at first was a checked shirt and the worn knee of a pair of blue overalls. We all thought he was asleep.

'Just nip out of the car and ask that man in the grass,' said Tuesday.

'I think he's asleep,' I said doubtfully.

'I'm sure he won't *mind*,' she replied in a severe voice. 'And shut the door when you get out, will you? It's windy and I don't want my hair –'

I slammed the car door, cutting her off in mid-sentence, and waded through the tall grass. It was the end of a long hot summer and the grass was dry and brittle, with a pleasant smell like hay.

'*Entschuldigen Sie bitte?*' I called, peering at the recumbent figure.

There was no reply. I could almost feel Tuesday's impatient gaze pecking at my back.

'*Entschuldigen Sie bitte?*' I repeated, a little more loudly.

For a moment I thought I saw movement, but it was only the wind ruffling the grass. A fat bumblebee buzzed past close to my face and instinctively I put up a hand to ward it off. I took a step closer to the supine figure in the grass. He was a very sound sleeper, whoever he was; perhaps he had had too much beer with his lunch. I could see part of the lunch lying close to his outstretched hand – a large, rosy-looking apple with a bite mark standing out palely against its reddish skin. I took another step closer.

Behind me, the car door opened. 'What are you *doing*?' called Tuesday irritably.

I didn't reply. I was standing there with the dry ends of the grass pricking my bare legs and the breeze lifting the ends of my dark hair, my mouth dry and my eyes round with shock. I was looking at the corpse at my feet. At the *corpse*. Grey-blue eyes iced over with Death's cataracts, blindly staring at the summer sky. Mouth gaping open, although its owner clearly had nothing to say, ever again. And at the side of the close-cropped head, a dent, an obscene crater in the smooth curve of the skull. Red on the stalks of the yellow grass. Blood. I was nearly standing in it.

There was a *clunk* as the car door closed again, and I heard Tuesday picking her way towards me, cursing to herself. Vegetation crunched under her feet. As she came up behind me I heard her draw breath to speak and then suddenly hold it. A hand clutched my shoulder; Tuesday was hanging on to me, her other hand clamped over her mouth.

'Oh, my *God*,' she squeaked out eventually. 'Is he *dead*?'

My throat seemed to have constricted; I tried to speak but no words came. Instead I just nodded.

'Should we take his pulse or something?' said Tuesday in a choked voice.

'I don't think there's much point,' I managed to say.

I looked again at the red on the grass, and then down at my bare toes in their sandals. I took a step backwards, Tuesday staggering back with me. Her nails were digging into my shoulder.

'What do we *do*?' she croaked.

'Get Dad,' I suggested.

I had to resist the temptation to push her off; the nails were hurting. I felt oddly numb looking down at the body. It didn't seem real, more like some sort of strange tableau, an illustration for an accident-prevention poster. An apple tree with a wooden crate sitting underneath it. A ladder pushed up against the tree trunk. The red apple with the scalloped white bite mark on it. And sprawled in the grass, the body. Already my imagination was making patterns out of the scene. The old man – he looked about seventy to me – had been picking apples. Maybe he'd forgotten that he wasn't as young as he used to be. He'd clambered up the ladder and started work, reaching up among the leafy branches to twist the apples off their twigs. Then he'd seen that red apple – the one now lying on the ground – and hadn't been able to resist. He'd plucked it, taken one big bite, and then – either because he only had one hand free or because he was savouring the apple too much to look what he was doing – he had overbalanced and fallen off the ladder. Thump. Straight on to the hard earth. One clumsy dive on to a log or a hard stone: lights out. So much for the benefits of healthy eating.

Tuesday let go of my shoulder and staggered back towards

the car. My father had opened his own door by now and was shouting something to her. I watched her veer from side to side, as though she had had one too many cocktails. She put up a hand as if trying to ward him off. I hoped she'd have the good sense to tell him to make Polly and Ru stay in the car.

I glanced back at the man lying in the grass. Again that feeling of unreality swept over me. It seemed so incongruous, him lying there stone dead with the apple just a few centimetres from his outstretched hand, as though he might suddenly sit up and take another bite. My gaze slid reluctantly back to that terrible dent in the side of his head. I thought of the force required to crack someone's skull like that, and for a moment I thought I would throw up my service-station sandwiches. I turned my head away, and as I did so something caught the light and winked brightly at the edge of my vision.

In spite of my rising nausea I couldn't resist taking another look. At first I saw nothing at all, but then the breeze stirred the lower branches of the apple tree, and with the shifting of shadow and light I saw something flash in the grass. At first I did not understand what I was seeing, but then I realized it was glass – all around the lifeless body of the man, the earth was sparkling with broken glass. I couldn't make sense of it at the time, and anyway my mind was full with the enormity of seeing a dead person lying there in front of me. It was only later, when I remembered the tale of Bonschariant – the Glass Demon – that I began to wonder.

CHAPTER TWO

I was still standing at the same spot, watching the shards of glass winking in the sunlight, when my father came up beside me.

'Did you touch anything?' was the first thing he said.

I shook my head, shuddering at the thought of touching those lifeless hands or, worse, that battered head. *You've got to be joking.*

'Let's go, then.'

I gaped at him. 'What?'

'Get in the car, Lin.'

He had already turned and was starting to walk away.

I glanced at the figure on the ground once more before half-running after my father. 'Dad? Are we going to find a police station, then?'

'No.'

I stopped short. 'But we have to.'

He paused and shot me an uncompromising look. 'No, we don't.'

'But – there's a dead body.'

'I know there's a dead body.'

'Don't we have to report it or something?'

'Someone has to report it. But it isn't going to be us.'

'But, Dad –'

'Look, Lin,' said my father grimly, 'we didn't kill the old boy, did we? He probably just fell off his ladder, had a heart attack or something. There's nothing we can do for him, otherwise of course we would go for help. But he's dead, and if we get involved we're going to be spending hours, maybe days, in some German police station. So just come and get in the car, will you?'

'What if it wasn't an accident?' I blurted out.

My father stared at me. 'Of course it was an accident. What else could it be? Someone's hardly going to come and mug an old man when he's halfway up a tree picking apples, are they? Now, *get in the car.*'

As we reached the car he opened the rear door and held it for me. 'Come on, move. I want to get away from here.'

Reluctantly I climbed in.

'That was the worst thing that's ever happened to me,' Tuesday was saying, huddled in the front seat with a tissue clamped to her nose.

It was the worst thing that ever happened to that old man too, I thought as the car pulled away from the roadside with a screech of tyres. I twisted round to look through the back window, trying to catch a glimpse of the figure lying in the grass by the tree, but we were already too far away for me to make out the blue-clad knee or the checked shirt.

I slumped back in my seat. I tried to work out how I felt about what we had just seen and done. I had just seen a dead person – a corpse. I had been close enough that I could have touched it. *Him*, I reminded myself. *Him*, not *it*. I felt strangely detached. Perhaps a reaction would come later. Or perhaps,

I thought, listening to the sobs from the front seat, Tuesday was having the hysterics for both of us.

Neither she nor my father had noticed the glass lying glittering around the old man's body like some unearthly and unseasonal frost. After a while I put it from my mind too, believing – wrongly, as it turned out – that it had nothing to do with us at all.

CHAPTER THREE

We should not even have been in Germany that afternoon – not if things had gone the way my father had intended them to. Instead of standing there in the orchard at Niederburgheim, gazing queasily down at the corpse of an elderly German farmer, I should have been back in England, enjoying one of the hottest summers on record. I might have been with my friends, lying on the grass in the big park near our house, swigging iced tea from plastic bottles and soaking up the sunshine. We might have nagged someone who already had their licence to drive us somewhere – the coast, maybe. Seventeen was not too old to think that summer wasn't summer without the wheeling and screeching of seagulls and the whisper of the surf.

Instead, we were facing almost an entire year of being stuck in an obscure part of Germany neither I nor my friends had even heard of, near a town with a name most of them couldn't pronounce. And all because someone else was being made Professor of Medieval Studies instead of my father.

It was not enough for him that he was employed by one of the most famous and most ancient universities in the world. I doubt that even if he had been made professor it would have been enough for him. His ambition was a monstrous thing, a rampaging bull elephant upon which he rode like an ineffectual mahout, while the rest of us ran alongside like street children, trying to keep up yet afraid of being trampled.

What he really wanted was to be not only the Professor of Medieval Studies but a media star. My father had the good looks of a Hollywood actor – straight nose, square jaw, a thick head of dark hair. When he smiled he went from being good-looking to being swooningly handsome. In his imagination he saw his good looks displayed to advantage on the screen; he saw himself dressed in tight jeans and an open-necked shirt, standing in front of a crusader castle or a medieval palace, dispensing soundbites about fourteenth-century history and the culture of the Middle Ages. He liked to tell Tuesday that he wanted to make medieval politics sexy, but actually what he wanted was to be Heinrich Schliemann or Allan Quatermain or Indiana Jones.

His more sober-minded colleagues watched his progress rather as crows perched on a gable might regard the strutting of a peacock on the lawns below. Still, he was the obvious candidate for the professorship, and he probably would have got it, had it not been for the matter of the dean's brother's book. The book was an earnest and densely written volume about eroticism in medieval literature, with a plain cover and printed in an eye-wateringly small type. It was published simultaneously with my father's own book on the same topic, which had a painting of Lancelot and Guinevere kissing on the cover and the word SEX in the title. My father's book outsold the dean's brother's by thousands to one. The affront was still in the mind of the dean and his peers on the selection committee when my father's name came before them.

The moment my father realized that events were going

against him was towards the end of a Friday afternoon, late in the summer term. Closeted in my room, the first I knew of his arrival home was the cataclysmic slam of the front door, which made every window in the house rattle. His progress down the hall was tempestuous; it sounded as though a wild animal had got into the house and was wrecking everything. There was a tremendous thump as the leather case he carried his papers in was flung into a corner of the hall, followed by a crash that was my father kicking the door. A series of four-letter words, the ones which Tuesday was always primly telling us not to use, came pouring out, mercifully muffled by the closed door between us. Then I heard the distinctive sound of breaking glass. I guessed that the statue which normally stood on the hallstand, a rearing horse with a silvery glaze, had met its end on the tiled floor.

A door opened downstairs and I could hear Tuesday's voice floating up. I could not hear what she was saying but it was evidently something soothing. To no avail; my father crashed up the stairs with a mighty stamping tread which shook the floor, and then, like an echo of the thunderous slam of the front door, I heard his study door shut with a bang which reverberated through the entire house.

I didn't see my father again that night. The first we saw of him was the following morning. Tuesday was wandering around the kitchen, ineffectually trying to make some filter coffee for herself. I was chewing a muesli bar which I had found in the back of the kitchen cupboard and staring out of the window at the overgrown front garden. I was wondering what would happen if neither my father nor Tuesday ever got around to mowing the lawn, whether it would keep growing until the grass blocked out the light.

The kitchen door opened and I turned in time to see my father stroll in, rubbing his hands and smiling that jaw-droppingly handsome smile, the one which had once led one of the assistant librarians at the history faculty to compare him to George Clooney. I caught Polly's eye but neither of us dared react; we waited to see what there was to react to.

My father waited until he had all our attention. Then he did that irresistible smile again. 'Well,' he said, and his tone was almost jovial, 'how would you like to live in Germany?'

CHAPTER FOUR

When my father had made up his mind, there was no changing it. All the same, I tried. I would be taking my A levels in the next academic year; I could not imagine how we would reconcile that with moving to a remote part of rural Germany. Besides, I had friends in our hometown, I had a life. I had no intention of giving any of it up without a fight.

My father was implacable. 'You can do the German *Abitur* exam,' he said. 'You spent the whole of last summer in Germany, didn't you? You can cope with the language.'

This was perfectly true. Tuesday had a cousin who had married a German some ten years before. 'Uncle Karl', as we called him – although he was not really our uncle – had organized the trip for me. I had spent the holidays near Trier with some friends of his who owned an organic farm. The farm was the attraction, since I was hoping to study earth sciences, but my German had come on amazingly. I changed tack.

'The syllabus will be different. I'll never catch up, even if I can understand it.'

'But you can perfect your German,' said my father airily. 'After a year, you'll be completely fluent.'

'What's the point?' I almost screamed. 'I don't want to read *German* at university! I want to be a *scientist*!'

'Lin –'

'Why can't I stay here?'

'Because you're only seventeen. You need someone to look after you.'

If I had not been so angry I would have laughed myself sick over *that*. Tuesday's attempts at domestic duties were sporadic and inefficient; if I had not learned to cook beans on toast myself by the age of eight I would probably have starved by now. And my father was always too heavily involved in academic work to notice things like an empty fridge or children in too-small shoes.

I tried to involve Polly in the fight but without success; in the face of my father's eloquence and shifting arguments she was defenceless. Besides, she had much less to lose; she had already agreed a gap year with my father and Tuesday, and would be stuck in Baumgarten no longer than a couple of months before she left to spend the rest of the year in Italy with friends of Tuesday. It would not have been in Polly's nature to backpack around India for a year or teach English in China; she was seemingly quite content to stay with someone Tuesday knew, and to study the arts, just as everyone in our family always did – everyone, it seemed, except me. I adored my gentle, non-combative sister, but she was useless as an ally in battle.

In the end there was nothing to do but admit defeat. I stormed upstairs to my room and slammed the door shut with an almighty bang. I would have thrown a few things too, except for the sudden unpleasant realization that I was behaving exactly the way my father had the evening before. I put down the china rabbit I had been about to hurl against the wall and flung myself on to my bed.

My woes, had I known it, flowed from a single document which sealed all our fates, as surely as if it had been a letter ordering our executions. What the writer could not have known, as he sat in his study some six hundred kilometres away, carefully inking the name *Heinrich Mahlberg* at the bottom of it, was that he was signing his own death warrant too. When he wrote my father's name on the front of the envelope in his careful hand, he was firing a bullet that would bury itself in his own brain. Yet still he might have escaped, had his letter remained undisturbed in the lower strata of my father's overflowing in-tray.

The day my father stumped back from the history faculty filled with the righteous fury of one who has been denied his birthright, he had stormed into his study, kicked the filing cabinet and swept the mountain of papers on his desk on to the floor. It was only when he had calmed down a little that he noticed Herr Mahlberg's letter, which had fluttered out from the scattered heap of documents and was lying open on the polished floorboards.

To my father, this was a decisive moment, akin to the moment when an apple fell on Sir Isaac Newton's head or Archimedes leapt out of his bath and ran stark naked through the streets of Syracuse shouting 'Eureka!' He picked up the letter and read it through again several times. When Herr Mahlberg had written to him months before, telling him that he believed he knew where the lost glass of the Allerheiligen Abbey was to be found, my father had hardly taken him seriously. The Allerheiligen glass was a kind of Holy Grail to medievalists, a five-hundred-year-old masterpiece of stained glass whose history had ended in darkness. It was probably a wild-goose chase; bits of very inferior stained glass were always turning up here and there, and now and again some local historian or over-enthusiastic young research fellow would make a fool of himself with half-baked claims that it had come from the legendary abbey.

Now, however, Herr Mahlberg's letter appeared in the light of a lifeline. Let the university's chosen candidate, the soon-to-be Professor Goodwin Lyle, enjoy his moment of triumph; my father would not be there to see it. If Herr Mahlberg's claim had any truth in it, and my father were the first expert to see the glass, it would mean a well-needed boost to his career. If not, then he would return to the university after a suitable interval and quietly devote himself to making Professor Lyle's life as difficult as possible.

Against the persuasive lure of these ideas, it was impossible for me or Tuesday or Polly to dissuade my father from his chosen course. I stormed, Tuesday sulked and Polly simply looked quietly sad, but he was not to be swayed. The house was put up for rent, the tickets were bought and, shortly after Polly's A-level results came in, we set off for Germany.

CHAPTER FIVE

If I were a believer in Fate I would have thought that our first introduction to a citizen of our new home – a dead one, lying so horribly still among the crushed grass and fallen apples – was an evil omen. But as we drove away from the orchard, it was my father's unfeeling attitude towards the dead man which was occupying my thoughts – that, and the riddle of the broken glass.

For a while we drove on in silence, punctuated by the occasional sniffle from Tuesday. Reuben had started to grizzle, with all the misery and frustration of an eighteen-month-old confined for hours to a car seat. Tuesday didn't seem to notice, so Polly eventually hauled his baby cup out of his bag and offered it to him. I was determined not to say anything to Tuesday or my father. Furious thoughts were still racketing around my brain like wasps in a jam jar.

Undeniably the old man was dead, and there was nothing we could have done for him; it was just as certain that we would have spent hours with the authorities, while Reuben howled and Tuesday had theatrical hysterics and I tried to translate for everyone with my imperfect German. It would have been grisly, that was true. But I couldn't help fretting about what would happen if someone found out that we had discovered the body and failed to report it, and, even worse, I wondered what would happen if nobody else found the body at all. How long would it lie there, with the blood drying to dark brown on the grass and the cold flesh stiffening and eventually – horrible thought – starting to decompose? I imagined rain slanting down on to the still face, splashing into the sightless eyes and filling the open mouth; I imagined days and weeks passing, and the flesh dropping from the bones. Tendrils of plants would grow up around it, perhaps even push their way up through the empty eye sockets and the terrible dent in the skull. I started to feel distinctly sick.

'Can you stop the car?' I croaked.

'What?' said my father distractedly.

'I'm going to be sick.'

The car swerved to the side of the road. I opened the door and just managed to stick my head out before the remains of the sandwiches finally came up.

'Are you OK, Lin?' I heard Polly say in an anxious voice.

'No.' Cautiously I lifted my head.

'Why don't you get out for a minute, Lin?' I heard Tuesday say.

I had a strong suspicion that she was more concerned about whether I would throw up again inside the car than about my health. I clambered out of the car, feeling a strong desire to get away from her and my father. I wondered whether the old man was still lying there alone in the orchard, or whether he was already surrounded by a group of wailing relatives, cradling his head and weeping on to his checked shirt.

'What does that sign say?' called my father from the front seat.

I went over to it and had a look.

'Niederburgheim.'

'I've found it,' Tuesday was saying as I climbed back into the car. Evidently she had recovered from the worst thing that had ever happened to her with admirable speed. She had a road map spread out in front of her and was poring over it, twisting a hank of yellow hair absent-mindedly with her fingers. 'But there are at least three castles in this bit.'

'We passed something with a tower,' said Polly. 'Back in the little town. It could have been a castle.'

'Why didn't you say so?' said my father irritably, not seeing how his tone stung Polly.

She caught my eye and looked away, but she said nothing. My father put the car into gear and we drove slowly back the way we had come.

'There,' said Polly suddenly as we passed a side street.

My father reversed up and we all gazed down the street.

'Wow,' I said.

'Didn't you say it was in woodland?' said Tuesday, running one lacquered fingernail ineffectually across the map.

My father shrugged. 'There's plenty of woodland around here. Maybe Karl meant it was *near* woodland.'

Winding down the window, Tuesday sniffed the air and said, 'There's certainly plenty of *countryside* around here.'

As the car edged down the street we gazed open-mouthed at the castle. A massive stone wall rose straight out of a little moat crossed by a humpback bridge. Further on was a huge square tower topped with an onion-shaped dome tiled in grey slate. All the windows were framed by shutters painted in a red-and-white geometric design.

Even with my mind still occupied with what we had seen in the orchard, I was impressed. The castle looked like something out of Grimms' fairy tales. I couldn't wait to send my friends a snap of it; they wouldn't believe it.

'Typical of the area and period,' my father was saying in his best history-programme voice, but nobody was listening to him.

'It's *gorgeous*,' said Tuesday raptly.

As soon as the car stopped we scrambled out, Polly carrying Ru in her arms.

'Karl has excelled himself,' my father said to Tuesday.

We crossed the little stone bridge and stood at the iron gates, gazing into the courtyard beyond.

'There's a *red carpet*,' said Polly in awe.

We all stared at it. She was absolutely right; the place looked as though it had been decorated for the arrival of visiting dignitaries. The red carpet stretched from the gates to a little canopy covering the castle doors. It was lined on either side with enormous candles in heavy black ceramic holders, creating a rather funereal effect, as though the castle were awaiting the arrival of Count Dracula.

'Let's go in,' said my father, but we had hardly taken a couple of steps across the red carpet when the castle door opened and a man stepped out.

My first impression was of a tall, broad-shouldered figure clad entirely in black. Then I saw the flash of white at his throat and realized that he was a Roman Catholic priest wearing an old-fashioned soutane. As soon as he saw us he strode towards us in a brisk manner which hinted at unfriendliness. As he approached I was struck by a new impression; if he had not been so old (I thought he must be about thirty) he would have been incredibly handsome.

Tuesday evidently thought so too, because she threw her shoulders back and began to toy with the strings of beads dangling down the front of her blouse.

'*Guten Abend. Was kann ich für Sie tun?*' said the priest to my father in a distinctly cold tone. He ignored Tuesday completely.

Close up, he was almost impossibly good-looking, with a strong-featured face, sleek jet-black hair and bold dark eyes. I found myself staring at him as though mesmerized.

'*Ich bin . . .*' My father's German suddenly dried up. He was more used to poring over academic texts than actually speaking the language. He looked around for me. 'Lin?'

Heart thumping, I stepped forward and found myself withering under the priest's disapproving gaze.

'This is my father, Dr Oliver Fox,' I said in German.

'Are you on the guest list?'

'The guest list?' I was thrown for a moment. 'No – I don't think so . . .'

'The castle is not open to the public,' said the priest.

'No, we *live* here,' I started to say, then changed it to, 'We are *going* to live here.'

'It's not a holiday house,' said the priest severely.

'I know.' I was floundering. 'My uncle Karl booked it – he knows someone . . .'

I dried up altogether, realizing that I did not know how to say *on the forestry commission*. The physical proximity of the priest was like looking into the sun – you could feel your brains beginning to boil. Even the German word for *forest* skittered away out of my grasp.

'I think you have the wrong place,' said the priest eventually.

'What's the castle called?' I asked my father helplessly in English.

'The Kreuzburg,' he said.

A flicker of interest crossed the priest's face. '*Die Kreuzburg?*' He looked at my father, as though reassessing him. Then he said very carefully, in slightly accented English, 'You are the professor who is researching the Allerheiligen glass?'

'Yes,' said my father firmly in a now-we-are-getting-some-where tone. I think he thought that the priest would stand back and hand him the keys to the castle. If so he was disappointed.

'This is not the Kreuzburg,' said the priest. 'There is a –' he thought carefully – 'a funeral party here today.'

'Well, can you tell us how to find the Kreuzburg?' asked my father.

He was audibly disappointed. I dared not look at Tuesday.

'You have a map?'

My father handed it over.

'Here. You see?' I watched the priest's long slender hands with fascination as he turned the map over. 'Here is Niederburgheim. There is a way through the woods – here – but I think it is closed, except for the *Forstverwaltung*, the forest workers. If you can't go through here you will have to go here – and here – through this village.'

Tuesday tried to peer round my father's shoulder at the map. The point upon which the priest's index finger was resting was a tiny square in the middle of a clump of green.

'It's really in the middle of the forest,' she said.

'Yes.'

'Well,' said my father heartily, as he folded up the map, 'I suppose it will be perfect for walking, won't it?'

The priest looked at him seriously. 'No,' he said. 'I cannot recommend it.'

CHAPTER SIX

Despondently we climbed back into the car. Tuesday had the piqued expression of someone who is not used to being ignored. She did not look back as the car moved off, but I did. The priest had already disappeared into the castle.

We left Niederburgheim, mercifully not passing the orchard, and drove out into countryside bounded with pine forests. Feeling tired and distinctly grubby, I stared out of the car window without really taking anything in. My mind kept sliding guiltily back to the priest, to the sleek black hair and dark eyes. I rubbed my face with something like irritation. *You'll never see him again*, I told myself. *And anyway, he's old.* I shifted uncomfortably in the confined space and sighed.

It was very late in the afternoon when we finally reached the Kreuzburg. Ru, who had wailed and struggled for most of the journey from England, suddenly fell asleep two minutes before the car drew up outside the castle. We left him unconscious in his car seat and climbed out to look.

'But it's a ruin,' said Tuesday.

I could tell what she was thinking: *Bring back the other castle. That was the one I wanted.*

'Not completely,' said my father, but he looked crestfallen too.

We gazed out over the lake. I think it had once been a neat moat encircling the castle walls, but it seemed to have leaked out into the surrounding land. Untidy tufts of vegetation clogged the water's edge. The castle itself had an uncompromising squareness about it. It was ringed with massive rough-hewn stone walls, golden in the fading sunlight but still unromantically solid and heavy. At the north end rose a tall square tower. If my eyes were not deceiving me there was a young tree growing from the top of it. Everywhere the masonry was under siege from plants of all kinds. It did not look like a place where anyone could possibly live.

'Is it habitable?' asked Tuesday, echoing my thoughts.

'How are we going to keep Ru out of the lake?' said Polly.

'What the hell was Karl thinking of?' said my father.

I could imagine the complaints, the recriminations and the downright hysterics on Tuesday's part which were going to erupt. I felt something close to panic myself when I looked at the ruinous state of the castle, and the forest closing in on every side. Spend a whole year here? We might as well have moved to the Gobi Desert.

I thought that if I had to listen to Tuesday making a scene I would lose control completely. I left them all to it and wandered off by myself. There was a dirt path which appeared to run right round the Kreuzburg. On the inside of the path there was moat; on the outside there were woods. There was nothing else to be seen at all. I stood at the side of the path and stared into the woods. It was dark under the towering pine trees. There would be animals in there, foxes and badgers and deer and wild boar. When night fell it would be utterly dark and the only sounds would be the surreptitious rustling of night creatures moving about in the undergrowth. My mind skipped back to the old man in the orchard and I wondered if he would still be lying there when the darkness came. Hastily I tried to push the thought away – instead I tried to think about my hometown, about the cinema and the cafes and the brightly lit streets. My friends would be sitting in one of those cafes, eking out a coffee or Coke each, texting their boyfriends, discussing plans for the last week of the holidays. At this very moment someone might be saying, 'I wonder what Lin is doing.'

I groaned inwardly. The thought of being confined in a castle in the middle of the German Eifel, with nothing to look at but trees, was terrible. Ten times worse was the thought of being shut up there with Tuesday, who would have nothing to do but look at trees either.

I turned to go back to the others and almost jumped out of my skin. Someone was standing behind me, only a metre away. The shock was so great that for a moment I could not even scream. Then he beat me to it.

'I'm sorry – I'm sorry – don't scream!' he said in hurried German.

I felt like telling him that there was no chance anyway, because I was having a heart attack. Then I felt like thumping him. It wasn't the Ghoul of the Woods, or the Mad Axeman of Niederburgheim, it was just a boy, about my age or a little older, dressed in jeans and a faded sweatshirt, dark hair flopping untidily over his eyes. Nothing scary there. Just a boy. A boy who any minute now was going to start laughing his head off and pointing at the stupid English girl who'd just made a total idiot of herself. I tried to catch my breath and let my heartbeat slow to a gallop. In the meantime I glared at him, just to let him know that if he started smirking I would blow my top.

'You understand German?' he said suddenly in English. Perhaps he had seen our car, with the British number plates.

'Of course I do, *Vollidiot*,' I snapped back in German. I put my hands on my hips. 'I suppose you think that was funny, sneaking up on me like that?'

'I'm sorry,' he said for the third time, reverting to German. I wasn't mollified.

'What are you doing here anyway?' I demanded.

'I live here,' he said.

'What, here?' I said, turning round to glance at the crumbling castle walls.

'Well, over there, at the farm,' he said, gesturing vaguely.

I was reluctant to show too much interest, but I looked anyway and could see absolutely nothing apart from more pine trees.

'Really?' I said as coolly as I could. 'Well, you still haven't said what you're doing *here*.'

'It's not forbidden to come here,' he replied, starting to sound a little defensive. 'The ruined part of the castle is open to the public.'

'We're not in the castle,' I pointed out. 'And I don't like people sneaking up on me.'

'Are you English?' he asked suddenly.

'No,' I said with heavy sarcasm. 'I'm Swedish.'

'Really?'

I gave a sigh of exasperation. 'No, I'm English.'

'Is your father the professor?'

'Sort of,' I said.

'Is it true that he is going to find the Allerheiligen glass?'

I racked my brains but could not come up with the German for *Mind your own business*. In the end I settled for, 'Who said that?'

'My friend's next-door neighbour's aunt, Frau Kessel.'

I looked at him incredulously. He was staring at me with an expression of avid interest which I found faintly irritating. His eyes were the colour of mud, I noticed.

'I have to go,' I said.

'I'm Michel,' he said, as though he had not heard me.

'OK,' I said, not proffering my own name. 'Michel, I have to go.'

'Your father – he won't find the Allerheiligen glass,' said Michel suddenly. 'Not on his own.'

'I have to go,' I said again, and walked off, leaving him standing there. It didn't occur to me at the time to wonder what he meant by that: *Not on his own*.

CHAPTER SEVEN

The Allerheiligen glass, I thought in disgust, as I walked back to the castle. Was everyone obsessed with it? *I* was sick of the sound of it already. This was unfair; if it had not been for the glass, my father would have found some other reason for escaping from our hometown. I wished he had taken it into his head to research something which was not hidden in the obscurest part of the back of beyond. But that was the point, wasn't it? The odious Goodwin Lyle could be made President of the United States and Supreme Commander of the Galactic Empire to boot, and we wouldn't hear about it, marooned out here in the sticks.

If I hadn't been so cross it might have been intriguing. Even as a medievalist's daughter I knew that most people weren't remotely interested in ancient stained-glass windows, yet the first two people we had spoken to since arriving clearly knew what it was and why we were here.

I knew what the Allerheiligen glass was, of course; I had heard my father talking about it ever since I was tiny. It was a lost series of stained-glass windows, nearly five hundred years old, that had come from the abbey of the same name. Unlike Polly, who gallantly tried to take an interest in everything my father told us about his studies, I was determined to turn my back on it, I, who was going to study earth sciences and confound the entire family tradition of studying the arts. All the same, the Allerheiligen glass was one of those topics which you were not likely to forget, even if you had absolutely no interest in medieval art, for two very simple reasons: first, that if the glass were still in existence it would be worth a fortune, and second, the windows were haunted by a demon.

I didn't believe in demons; I ranked them with ghosts and vampires and werewolves, as products of a fevered imagination, or phenomena with a perfectly rational explanation. I did not realize yet, that summer when I was seventeen, and my sister Polly was still alive, when the sun was shining and even the wind was warm, and my whole body was restless, that there are worse things than being stuck in a small town for a year. There *are* demons, and they are more terrible than we can imagine.

CHAPTER EIGHT

'There you are,' said Tuesday in a reproving voice when I reappeared. 'We've found the way in.' She gestured towards the castle. 'There's a bridge. They've left us some food, though I don't know what it is.'

I followed her over the bridge and through a large green wooden gate set into the stone wall. Inside was a little courtyard and – I was relieved to see – a stone-built house with small white-framed windows, obviously of a much more recent date than the rest of the castle buildings. There was even a kitchen garden, though it was terribly overgrown, and a tumbledown outhouse with a peeling door fastened with a simple latch. I peeped inside but there was nothing of any interest: simply piles of old agricultural tools and what looked like a mixture of rusting pikes and wooden staves propped up in the far corner. Everything had an abandoned look and I guessed that the house had been empty for some time. Tuesday did not give me any more time to look around; she shepherded me into the house. The front door led directly into a large, shabby-looking room decorated in an outmoded style and dominated by a big scrubbed-pine dining table. On the table were a collection of jars and packages and a note. I picked up the note. 'Welcome to the Kreuzburg,' I read aloud. I picked up one of the jars and studied the label: '*Eifeler Bärlauchschmalz*'. It was lard.

'Well, what is it?' asked Tuesday.

'Low-fat spread,' I said, putting the jar down. I opened one of the paper packages and looked inside. 'And here's some bread.'

'Good,' said my father, who had just come in with his arms full of books and papers. 'Has anyone found the fuse box yet?'

There was no light; I flicked the switch up and down but nothing happened. None of us could find the fuse box so that night we settled down to eat by the light of some of Tuesday's scented candles. The smell of vanilla was over-powering. I would have taken my supper outside but it was dark now. As I stood at the door I could hardly make out the bulk of the castle walls and the forest beyond. When I came back to the table, Polly had taken Ru upstairs to bed, though I wondered how he would sleep if he had to lie there in a miasma of French vanilla. My father had found a little bottle of herb liqueur among the groceries and he and Tuesday were sipping glasses of it rather tentatively.

'So,' said my father, 'what do you think of the castle, Lin?'

'It's very dark,' I said. 'I can't see anything at all out there. There's not a single light anywhere. There is a farm around here somewhere, though,' I added. 'I met someone from it.'

'Really?' said Tuesday in a bored voice.

'Yes. He asked if I was the professor's daughter,' I said, looking sideways at my father.

'I suppose you said no?' said my father. There was a slight edge of bitterness to his voice.

'I said, sort of.' I thought about it. 'He seemed to know

all about us. He wanted to know if you were really looking for the Allerheiligen stained-glass windows. He said you'd never find them.'

'He did, did he?' said my father. Now he sounded rather interested in spite of himself. 'That's intriguing.' He took another mouthful of the liqueur and grimaced. 'He probably means he doesn't *want* me to find them. There are all sorts of superstitions about those windows. Who was he, this person you met?'

'Just a boy.'

Tuesday raised her eyebrows. I ignored her.

'What are the superstitions?' I asked, hoping to draw attention away from myself.

My father put down the glass on the pine table. 'The demon Bonschariant,' he said.

'Bonschariant?' repeated Tuesday in the faintly complaining tone she used when she suspected that everyone else was in on the joke. 'What sort of a name is that?'

I didn't listen to the rest. It meant nothing to Tuesday, but for me hearing the name again for the first time in years was like raising my head to the breeze and scenting smoke on the air, the sulphurous smoke of a distant conflagration. I remembered very clearly the first time I heard it.

I suppose I was about seven or eight at the time; at any rate I remember having to look up at the big arched window on the upstairs landing of our house, a window I can now look through without having to stand on tiptoes. It was raining so heavily that the water was running down the glass in sheets, turning the world outside into a greyish blur. I think it had been raining like that for days; the memory is tinged with a feeling of restlessness and disappointment.

I turned from the window and wandered along the landing to my father's study. If the door was closed, none of us was allowed to disturb him, but now the door was open a little way. I supposed that I might look inside without a telling-off.

'Dad?'

I stood on the threshold, peering in. When there was no reply, I pushed the door gently, and it swung back until I had a clear view of the whole room. My father was not there. Cautiously I entered the study, taking care not to tread on the second floorboard from the door, the creaky one which squealed like an angry sow if you trod on it.

The study was littered with items which would have given most children sleepless nights, such as the tortured St Sebastian statue on the corner of the desk, looking like a pincushion, so stuck full of arrows was he, and the print of St Lucy with her eyes on a plate which hung over the fireplace. For a child of my age I had considerable nerve, being used to the gruesome examples of medieval art dotted around the house, so they were not the reason I was being cautious; it was more the fear of detection. There was no actual rule that we children were not allowed in the study when my father was not there, but I was old enough to know that this was unlikely to be a sufficient defence if I were caught poking about.

The lamp on my father's desk was on, creating a pool of golden light in the gloom caused by the rain lashing the windows. It was natural that I should gravitate towards it, and, as I did so, I saw the book sitting in the middle of the desk, as though under a spotlight. Treading carefully, I went round the desk until I was standing in front of my father's big oak chair, and peered at the book.

It was a large, thick, hardback volume, the corners a little worn with age. I don't think there was a title on the front cover – it had probably been printed on the dust cover, long since tattered to pieces – and I didn't think to look on the spine. I simply opened the book.

The first thing I saw was a rather rough and simplistic black-and-white illustration – woodcut, I think they call it – showing what appeared to be the frame of a large arched window, the sort you see in very old churches, with a cluster of smaller diamond-shaped spaces in the top part of the arch. But there was no glass to be seen; instead the frame was filled with a figure who appeared to be climbing *out* of the window, a figure so grotesque that it gave me nightmares afterwards. It corresponded more or less to the shape of a man; it had four limbs and a head, and stood upright, but there the resemblance ended. It had a thick, muscular, scaly body studded with nodules or crusts which gave it a foul, diseased look, and the hands which clutched the window frame looked more like talons. The nails were long and curving and wickedly sharp. But it was the face that frightened me most. It was something between a dragon and a wild boar, bristling all over with rough scales, and with jagged tusks protruding from the slobbering mouth. The eyes, which were set deep within the ridged brows, showed no white at all, seeming to be nothing but gleaming black pupil. The thing was grimacing and the misshapen jaws were open, as though it would have liked to step right out of the picture and sink its fangs into me.

I might have been used to gruesome medieval art, but something about that crude illustration struck me with a dumb horror. I looked at the picture steadily for about a minute while my skin crept and the thumping of my heart seemed to fill my ears, and then I slammed the book shut so violently that it slid to the floor, and ran from the room, careless of the thunder of my feet on the floorboards.

My father met me at the head of the stairs; he was carrying a large cup of coffee that he had brought up from the kitchen.

'Whoa,' he said, smiling at me. 'Where are you going in such a hurry?'

To my shame I burst into tears. After that it was impossible not to tell him the whole story. At first I was afraid he would be angry with me for poking about in his study without permission, but in fact he seemed more amused than anything. He took me by the hand and led me back to the study. If anyone else had tried to make me go, I would have refused, but I idolized my father. All the same, I clung to his hand as he opened the book at the page with the illustration and tried to make me look at it again.

'It's a legend, quite an *interesting* legend,' he said. 'Look.'

I didn't look.

'His name is Bonschariant,' said my father.

'Why's he climbing out of that window?' I asked, trying to keep the tremble from my voice.

'He's supposed to haunt the glass,' said my father. He turned the book back to himself and studied the picture.

'He's broken it, though,' I objected.

'He's not really broken it,' said my father. 'He's supposed to appear *through* it, but I don't think the artist could think of a better way of showing that. He's done it this way to make Bonschariant look more threatening – see?' The annoyance about my treatment of the book had subsided, and now he was enjoying telling me about it. Medieval studies was the one topic he would talk to us children about for hours, if we could be induced to listen; I suspect he was practising for future audiences of non-academics.

'But why?' I asked him.

'It's a sort of warning. The window is supposed to represent one of the windows of the Allerheiligen Abbey in Germany. The man who designed the windows – his name was Gerhard Remsich – did such an astonishing job, and the pictures were so realistic, especially the ones of the Devil, that people said he had been helped by a demon.'

'And was he?' I wanted to know.

'Of course not. But in those days people thought it was a bad thing to take too much praise for yourself if you created something like that. They thought everything came from God –'

I don't remember the rest of the discussion. When my father drifted off into the field of medieval theology, he lost my interest at once. I remembered the picture, though, and although I occasionally looked at one or other of my father's books over the years if there was really no other amusement available, I took care not to open that one again.

Of course, all that seemed rather pitiable now. It was surprising to think that superstitions surrounding the glass could still have any weight with the local population. I reflected dismally that there must be even less to do in this part of Germany than I had hitherto suspected if they amused themselves by scaring each other with tales like that. Or perhaps they reserved such stories for outsiders like us. I imagined them sitting in the local *Kneipe*, the German version of a pub, clad in lederhosen and those funny little green hats with a thing like a shaving brush on one side, slapping their hefty knees and laughing themselves hoarse over the things they had told the credulous foreigners.

Polly had reappeared at the bottom of the stairs. Evidently she had managed to coax Ru to sleep. My gaze slid to Tuesday, who had not moved from her place at the table. In spite of the grimaces she had made when she first tasted it, she was pouring herself another glass of the liqueur. I felt a familiar mixture of affection and annoyance at Polly – why did she allow Tuesday to let her do all the work? If Ru had started calling Polly 'Mummy' I should not have been at all surprised.

'There you are, Polly,' said my father, seeing an opportunity for widening his audience. 'I was just about to tell Lin about the local superstitions.'

It was as well that he did not see the face I pulled. Polly had no thought of escape, however; she sat down on one of the uncomfortable wooden chairs drawn up to the pine table and prepared herself to listen. She dipped a finger thoughtfully into the jar of *Bärlauchschmalz* and scooped out a tiny glob of it, which she tasted absent-mindedly.

Tuesday leaned across without saying a word and slapped Polly's fingers. I think I was the only one who saw the glances Polly and Tuesday exchanged, the way Tuesday's gaze flickered casually up and down Polly's figure, telegraphing a reproach. My father was too impatient to continue with his story to notice any restlessness among the listeners. He plunged on heedlessly.

'The glass that I came here to research, the Allerheiligen glass, came from an abbey, oh, I suppose about thirty kilometres from here. The abbey is gone; it was closed down about two centuries ago, and most of the stone was carted off to build other things. There's nothing to see there. But the glass . . .' My father leaned forward, his eyes bright with excitement. 'The glass might have survived.'

'How?' I asked, intrigued in spite of myself. It was impossible to think that anything so fragile could have survived the destruction of the window frames it was set into.

'It could have been removed. Packed. Hidden.' My father shrugged. 'Other windows survived it. The windows from the abbey at Steinfeld, for example. They vanished for a century and then turned up in the chapel of a manor house in Hertfordshire.' He sat back. 'The Steinfeld windows were partially created by the same master craftsman who did the Allerheiligen glass, Gerhard Remsich. They were auctioned in the 1920s and sold for the equivalent of about eight hundred thousand pounds in today's money.'

For the first time since the beginning of the conversation I saw Tuesday sit up and take notice. 'So these other windows . . .' she began slowly.

'Would be worth over a million pounds, yes,' said my father.

There was a moment's reverential silence as he and Tuesday considered this marvellous fact.

'Then why . . .' began Tuesday eventually.

'Why isn't everyone out looking for them?' finished my father. He picked up his glass again and swilled the evil-looking liquid about in it. 'That's the point. They're unlucky. They said that the artist was inspired by the Devil when he made them, that the scenes with demons in them were drawn *from the life*. They said that if you were to walk through the cloisters late at night you would see a dark shape on the other side of the glass, keeping pace with you, and if you were to turn and look directly at it, you would see him glaring at you through the window. Bonschariant. The Glass Demon. And, at that moment, your heart would stop.'

I could not suppress a shudder. My father saw it and smiled. In the dancing candlelight his face had a mocking, saturnine look: he could have been a miser gloating over gold, or a misanthrope delighting in the death of a relative. I looked away.

'Herr Mahlberg, the local historian who wrote to me, told me that these superstitions persist,' continued my father. 'He is a rational person; he was frustrated by it. He thought that he knew where the glass was located, but nobody would cooperate with him. And that,' said my father thoughtfully, taking a sip of the liqueur and wincing, 'is significant, don't you think?'

Polly and I looked at each other and then back at my father.

'Why?' said Polly.

'Because,' said my father, 'if the locals believe the glass no longer exists, then why are they trying to stop anyone finding it?'

CHAPTER NINE

The next morning I was woken at five thirty by the lights suddenly going on. I sat up in bed, blinking at the sudden glare. Polly's bed was empty, the covers thrown back. I got up and staggered out on to the narrow landing, rubbing my eyes. When I went down into the kitchen, Polly was already there. She was dressed in a baggy track suit and was lacing up her running shoes.

'The lights are on!' she said cheerfully.

'I know. They woke me up.'

'Sorry. I found the fuse box – it was behind the front door.'

'What are you doing?' I groaned. 'It's still the middle of the night.'

'Going for a run – what do you think?'

I cocked my head to one side and studied her. I thought I knew what this was about. 'Polly, don't take what Tuesday says so seriously.'

Polly gave a tremendous yank on her laces. 'She's right. I ought to get fitter.'

'Polly, it's *five thirty* in the morning.'

'So?'

'So *Tuesday* wouldn't get out of bed at five thirty.'

'She doesn't need to.'

'She's a lot less fit than you are,' I retorted. 'The nearest thing she comes to exercise is walking round the shops and lifting her credit card on to the counter.'

'Yeah, well, she's skinny,' said Polly, straightening up.

'*Polly!*' I was exasperated. 'She looks like a stick insect.'

'Don't make such a fuss, Lin. I'm just going for a run, I'm not having liposuction or anything.'

I watched her go over to the front door and twist the key. It was an old one and the lock was stiff, so I had already turned away when she got the door open. A moment later I heard her make an exclamation.

'Lin! There's something here!'

I turned back. She was just outside the door, treading up and down on the spot as though she were standing in something sticky.

'There's something all over the ground!'

'What, has a wild boar come out of the woods and crapped on the doorstep?' I asked facetiously.

'No – it's something crunchy. Can you put the light on?'

I went over and flicked the switch, shivering as the cool outside air wafted around my bare legs. 'So, what are you standing in? Maybe it's snails.'

'Yuck. No, I think it's –' She stopped.

'It's what?'

'It looks like broken glass, but there's something in it.'

Curious, I went to the doorway to have a look.

'Get out of it, can't you? I can't see what it is.' I peered at the ground. 'Someone's dropped a bottle of something, I think. It looks like . . . ' I hesitated.

The glass shards were smeared and streaked with a red-brown substance. Ketchup? Fruit juice? Possibilities flashed through my mind. *Blood?*

'I don't think we should touch it,' I said hastily. 'Not with our bare hands anyway.'

Polly was peering at the ground.

'It looks like blood.'

'It can't be,' I said, trying to convince myself. 'Who would be carrying a bottle of blood around with them?'

'Maybe someone broke a bottle and cut themselves,' suggested Polly.

She lifted a foot and examined the sole of her training shoe with disgust.

'There's too much of it, if it's blood,' I pointed out. 'We would have noticed if one of us had cut ourselves that badly.'

'It must have been the last people, then, or the person who left the food.'

'Then it would've been there last night when we arrived,' I said. 'It definitely wasn't, though. We couldn't all have stepped over it dozens of times and not noticed it.'

We stared at each other. Polly looked pale, I noticed. My gaze slid past her to the open gateway and the strip of forest which was visible through the arch. Under the densely clustered pine trees tendrils of early-morning mist were curling through the cool air. It looked very dark under the canopy of foliage. The night before, the forest had seemed wild but not threatening, the domain of foxes and badgers. Now it looked somehow sinister. Anyone could be standing in the darkness under the pine trees, unseen by us but watching our every movement. I shivered.

'Polly, don't go running this morning.'

'Why not?'

'I don't know,' I said. 'Something's not right.'

'Don't be silly. You're giving me the creeps,' said Polly nervously.

'Can't you just stay here?'

I found myself staring at that dark space under the trees, looking for any sign of movement. There was nothing, or at least nothing that I could pick out among the shadows. Still I had that feeling of being watched.

'We'll have to clear up this mess before the others get up. Supposing Ru steps in it?'

Polly sighed. 'OK. But I'm definitely going tomorrow morning.'

I stepped back to let her into the house. 'If you go later I'll come with you. But I'm not getting up at five thirty.'

Polly rummaged through the cupboards, looking for a dustpan and brush. I fetched a pair of tongs from the kitchen drawer and picked up the larger shards of glass with those. I held up one particularly big piece and studied it. Whatever the reddish-brown liquid was, it had dried on to the glass in blotches and smears reminiscent of brush strokes. *Funny*, I thought. *It looks just like stained glass.*

CHAPTER TEN

School did not start until the following week, so later that morning my father recruited me as interpreter for his initial enquiries. He did not put it like that, of course; that would have meant admitting to the deficiencies in his own spoken German.

'It might be interesting for you, Lin,' he said.

'Thanks, Dad, but . . .' I struggled to think of a convincing excuse for not accompanying him.

'Ten minutes,' he said breezily, before I had time to come up with anything.

I had already opened my mouth to argue when a thought occurred to me. Why not go along and make some enquiries of my own? I thought I would feel very much better about the events of the afternoon before if I knew for certain that someone had found the body of that poor old man in the orchard – and that nobody had seen us stopping there. Perhaps then I would feel less bad about leaving him there, without even closing his eyes. Certainly I would feel much happier if I reassured myself that the local papers were not running the headline BRITISH CAR SPOTTED AT DEATH SCENE.

The other advantage of going with my father was that I

would no longer have to listen to Tuesday complaining about the fact that her mobile phone would not work in the middle of the woods. I had watched her at the chaotic eating relay that passed for breakfast in our household; she had kept switching the phone on and off and pressing the buttons, and eventually she had even tried shaking it. She had reacted to the discovery that there was no signal much in the way that an extraterrestrial of an advanced race would have reacted if he had crash-landed here in the Stone Age. I thought that going with my father would be preferable to staying at the castle and listening to her complaints, even if he were going to ask me to translate words like *rood screen* and *gargoyle*.

I did my best to smile helpfully at my father. 'How long will it take to get . . . wherever we're going?'

'Baumgarten,' said my father. 'That's where Herr Mahlberg lives. Ten minutes and we'll be there.'

Nearly an hour later, we were still not there. My father had printed directions that Uncle Karl had sent him, together with a map, but we missed a turn somewhere and found ourselves on the other side of Baumgarten, looking at the factory chimneys of Nordkirchen. We doubled back, and this time I tried to use the map, but I was hampered by the large scale; we seemed to pass dozens of tiny roads that were not marked. Eventually by sheer luck we found ourselves on Adlerstrasse, a road which was mentioned in the directions; we turned off it on to the side road where the local historian lived, but then we couldn't find his house.

'His name is *Heinrich* Mahlberg,' said my father. 'I haven't got a house number but you can look at the names on the gates.'

There were only six houses on the street and we stopped outside each of them. I had to get out of the car each time and read the little name over the bell; at the first five there was a name other than Mahlberg, and at the sixth there was no name at all. The house looked well kept and the garden was tidy, but the roller blinds were down on all the front windows and a free newspaper was sticking out of the letter box. I peered at the little glass box over the bell, but there was no name in it at all – not even a piece of paper from which the letters had faded out. I tried ringing the bell anyway, but there was no reply. Eventually I knocked on the door too, feeling rather foolish and wondering what I would say if someone other than the elusive Herr Mahlberg were to open the door. In the event the house remained silent and nobody came to answer.

I went back to the car.

'It's empty.'

We debated what to do, and decided to return to the centre of Baumgarten and ask. My father drove back with a stormy look on his face, muttering to himself. Karl should have given us better directions, or got hold of Herr Mahlberg's telephone number – what we were supposed to do?

I didn't say anything. I thought Uncle Karl had done more than most people would have. I could have wished, however, that he had not been quite so free with information about my father's research. Judging by the handful of people we had already spoken to, everyone within a ten-kilometre radius knew that my father was here to research the Allerheiligen glass. Quite illogically, I had a feeling that this was a bad thing. Seeing the house which possibly belonged to Herr Mahlberg shuttered and deserted did nothing to dispel this feeling.

Chapter Eleven

We drove back to the centre of Baumgarten, parked and went to look for the post office. It was late morning by now and the little town was becoming busy. When we walked into the post office my father groaned; it was packed out.

We took our places in the line, behind a little old lady dressed unseasonably in a green woollen coat with a large and very ugly edelweiss brooch pinned to the front of it. I noticed the brooch because she turned round and gave us both a very hard stare. As she turned back my father rolled his eyes at me.

The queue was moving at a snail's pace. Eventually there was only the little old lady in front of us, but by then one of the post office workers had come out and hung a 'closed' sign on the front door. I shuffled my feet uncomfortably. The old lady was taking forever. There was something about the way she moved, slowly but deliberately, that made me suspect that she was taking her time on purpose. My father kept looking at his watch.

At last she had finished and my father, almost beside himself with impatience, virtually shouldered her aside to get to the counter.

'*Ich suche ... diese ... Adresse ...*' I heard him say, pushing the piece of paper with the directions to Herr Mahlberg's house under the glass. 'Mahlberg . . . Heinrich.'

He glanced round, looking for me. Reluctantly I went up to the counter. I noticed that the old lady had packed her things into her bag, but that she was in no hurry to leave. Unless my eyes deceived me, she was listening in to the conversation between my father and the clerk with avid interest.

'*Das kann ich nicht sagen,*' the clerk was saying.

'He says he can't say,' I translated helpfully.

'I know that,' snapped my father. 'But does that mean he doesn't know or he won't tell me?'

I leaned over the counter. 'We just want to confirm the address,' I said in German, but the man was already shaking his head. He had one hand up ready to pull down the little blind at his window. I could see he was dying for us to go so that he could get to his bratwurst roll.

'Try at the town hall,' he said brusquely, and the blind came down with a tight little snap.

'Damn it!' exploded my father.

I saw the old lady's eyebrows go up so far and so fast that I thought they might dash like fleeing field mice into the thick white bush of her hair. I gave her a tentative smile. It was not returned. Instead the old lady's gaze moved steadily from my face right down to my feet and back up again, as though she were scanning me for concealed weapons. Her gaze snagged on my jeans and for a moment the thought *Would look so much better in a dress* passed through her mind so visibly that she might as well have inked it on her forehead in gigantic letters.

'Come on, Lin,' snapped my father. 'We're wasting our time here.'

I dragged my gaze away from the old lady's basilisk stare and half-turned to go.

Suddenly a skinny claw shot out and grabbed me by the upper arm. The old lady was surprisingly strong – and the collection of rings that adorned her gnarled fingers like a knuckleduster was digging into my arm. I started to protest and found myself looking at close range into a pair of very intense grey eyes, alarmingly magnified by her spectacles.

'You are the English professor and his daughter? The professor who is looking for the Allerheiligen glass?'

'Ye-es,' I stammered.

'Herr Mahlberg cannot help you,' she said with grim satisfaction. 'Herr Mahlberg is *dead*.'

'*Tot*? What did she say? Did she say Herr Mahlberg was dead?' my father asked me.

I frowned. 'I think so. That can't be right.' I stared at the old lady. 'We're looking for Herr *Heinrich* Mahlberg. We're supposed to be meeting him.'

'No mistake,' said the old lady sharply. 'Herr Heinrich Mahlberg, he's definitely the one who's dead. I should know. It was my cousin's cleaning lady who found him.'

There was a snap behind us as the clerk on the other side of the glass panel lifted the blind again. He said nothing but looked at us balefully and indicated the door. The old lady gave him the kind of look that would have made a barracuda swim in the opposite direction, and marched us out of the post office.

Once out on the pavement I found that she had deftly situated herself with her back to the bright sunshine, so that my father and I were blinded by it, which only enhanced the sense of being interrogated.

'You don't have his address?'

'We have the street name,' I said, unfolding the directions. 'But we don't have the number, and we couldn't find his name on any of the gates.'

The old lady gave a condescending glance at the papers I was clutching. '*Doch*, *doch*, you have the right street. It's the big house with the red roof and a birch tree at the front.'

'We tried there. There wasn't any name and nobody answered the doorbell.'

'Of course not. Didn't I tell you Herr Mahlberg was dead? How should he answer the doorbell?' came the acid reply.

'But – we have a *meeting* with Herr Mahlberg,' said my father.

'The only meeting Herr Mahlberg is having is with his Maker,' she told him brusquely.

My father looked dumbfounded. 'What happened?'

'It is a very long story,' said the old lady severely. She pushed back her green woollen sleeve and consulted her watch. 'Really, I should be getting back to Münstereifel . . .' she began.

My father was enough of a politician to know that this was the moment at which some offering must be laid out if we wanted any more information. He glanced about him. 'Look, there's a coffee shop over there.' He raised his eyebrows knowingly. 'Lin?'

Obligingly I began, 'Would you come and have a cup of coffee with us, Frau . . .?'

'Kessel,' supplied the old lady.

'We're inviting you,' I added hastily, observing her expression of doubt.

'Well, I suppose I might spare a quarter of an hour,' said

51

Frau Kessel, with the air of one granting an enormous favour.

For someone so full of doubt she was across the road, through the coffee-shop door and installed in the best seat by the front window in double-quick time. My father ordered a coffee for himself and a soft drink for me; Frau Kessel ordered not only a large coffee but also an enormous slice of apple strudel with a great frosting of cream on it. I watched her attacking it with a sort of horrid fascination; it was like watching a lion rending a dead antelope.

Kessel, I thought. Hadn't the German boy, Michel, mentioned someone called Frau Kessel?

'So what happened to Herr Mahlberg?' I asked eventually, when she was licking the last of the cream from her lips.

She looked at me, patting her lips carefully with her napkin. 'Drowned.'

'Drowned?' I repeated. 'I thought you said – it was someone's cleaning lady who found him . . .'

I had a sudden crazy vision of Herr Mahlberg and the cleaning lady going swimming together in the river we had seen flowing through Niederburgheim. Or perhaps she had been passing by on her way to a job, laden down with mop, bucket and kitchen spray, and had seen him from the bridge as he struggled in the water. She might have extended the mop handle to him in the hopes of saving him, but –

'He drowned in the bath,' said Frau Kessel with grim relish.

'*What?*' said my father.

'He drowned in the bath,' I repeated in English. 'What happened?' I said to Frau Kessel in German.

Frau Kessel took a sip of coffee. 'Nobody knows exactly.

He went to a meeting the night before it happened; he was giving a little talk to the Eifel Club – something about local churches, I think.' She shook her head, as though asking herself why anyone in their right mind would want to occupy their time with such things. Then she went on: 'He seemed perfectly well when he gave the talk; a good friend of mine was there, you know, and she saw him. A bit dried-up-looking, she said – that's what comes of living in the past – but no sign of illness, nothing at all. These bookworms, they can go on forever as long as they have their dusty old books to occupy them.

'Well, my friend said the talk was quite interesting *if* you like that sort of thing, and afterwards there were questions, so I suppose Herr Mahlberg would have got home quite late. Nobody knew anything was amiss until ten o'clock the next morning when the cleaner went in. She had her own key – I must say, Herr Mahlberg was very *trusting*,' said Frau Kessel with a sniff. 'She called for Herr Mahlberg but there was no reply, so she thought he must be out. She didn't even go upstairs for the first hour; she was busy on the sitting room and the kitchen. Herr Mahlberg, being a bachelor, had simply no idea how to keep a kitchen tidy; she said it always took her ages to get it sorted out. Greasy pans on the stove and empty bottles in the sink, can you believe it? These bookish types are always the worst – *excuse* me, Professor,' she added, giving my father a ghastly smile.

'Anyway, after she'd finished the downstairs she went up to do the bathroom. The door is opposite the top of the stairs, and the very first thing she noticed when she got to the top was that it was only ajar, not open as it normally was. She could see a shoe on the floor, a man's outdoor shoe, and it suddenly occurred to her that perhaps Herr Mahlberg was actually in the bath and hadn't heard her come in. Of course it would be *dreadful* if she barged in and he was in the bath, but she couldn't really see her way to *knocking*. In the end she went and did the bedrooms first. She said she took as long as she reasonably could, and made a bit of noise on purpose with the broom, in the hopes that Herr Mahlberg would hear her and make himself decent. Still, she didn't hear a sound from the bathroom, not even a splash.

'Finally, when she'd finished every other room in the house, she went and stood on the landing outside the bathroom and said, "Excuse me, Herr Mahlberg." There was no reply. She looked through the gap in the doorway and she could still see the shoe, and on the other side of it there was a *puddle of water*. *That* was when she started to think that something had happened. It wasn't just a *little* puddle, the sort you make if you get out of the bath and you've forgotten to put the bath mat down; there was a positive *lake* on the bathroom floor. The other thing she noticed was that it was quite cold standing there – you'd expect warm air to be coming from the bathroom if someone had just run a hot bath, wouldn't you? But she couldn't see any steam at all. She started to feel a little worried about Herr Mahlberg. Still, she didn't like to go in.

'She tried calling him again, but there was still no reply. In the end she knocked on the door and it swung open. Not completely, but enough that she could see a leg – Herr Mahlberg's leg, hanging motionless over the side of the bath. It was horribly pale. She said she just screamed out his name, and he didn't move, so she knew it was an emergency and she just ran into the bathroom.

'He was lying in the bath, dead. The water was nearly up to the top and Herr Mahlberg was lying there with his head right under the water and his dead eyes staring up at her through it. She said she just about screamed the place down – fit to wake the dead, you might say, though much good it did Herr Mahlberg – and then she pulled herself together and tried to haul him out of the bath. She couldn't get him right out, but she managed to get his head above water. It was no use, though,' said Frau Kessel, with unmistakable satisfaction. 'He was as stiff as a board and stone cold, with his mouth and his eyes open, staring at her. She said she could hardly bear to touch him – it was like trying to haul up a sack of wet cement – but she had to try. Anyway, it was clear she couldn't do anything to help him, so she had to let him go so that she could go and call the police.

'It was then she realized that she was bleeding. She was wearing house shoes – the open-toed sort – which she always did when she was cleaning, and a bit of glass had got into one of them and cut her on the big toe. She'd been so shocked by what she'd seen that she hadn't even noticed it. She was standing in a pile of broken glass. It was all over the floor. She had to cover the cut up before she could go downstairs to the telephone, otherwise she would have bled all over Herr Mahlberg's rug, not that he would have cared at that point, poor man,' added Frau Kessel with grim relish.

'Glass?' I said.

Thoughts whirred in my head like a flock of birds. For a split second I was back there, in the orchard in Nieder-burgheim, looking down at a corpse surrounded by glittering shards of glass – a corpse we had abandoned, which was perhaps lying there now, at the mercy of the elements. I could feel my face burning and prayed that I was not actually blushing. I had the unpleasant feeling that if the old lady noticed anything was wrong she would be able to reach right into my brain with those bony fingers and remove the guilt-soaked memory for examination like a pathologist lifting an organ from the thorax of a dead body. Surely she could *see* what we had done?

Thankfully for me, my father stepped in. He seemed to have recovered from the initial shock of discovering that his main contact here in Germany had died without imparting his knowledge to a wider audience than a backbrush and a rubber duck. Still, he wanted to probe for information, to be sure he had understood what had happened.

'And what would glass . . .' he began in his faltering German.

'Be doing on the bathroom floor?' supplied Frau Kessel, wagging a forefinger at us. 'That is the question, isn't it?' Abruptly she drew back the finger and leaned towards us, like an elderly eagle straining forward on its perch. 'Gin,' she hissed.

My father and I looked at each other.

'They say he had a bottle of gin in there with him,' said Frau Kessel.

She sat back and looked at us expectantly.

'He was drinking in the bath?' I ventured.

'He was drinking *everywhere*,' retorted Frau Kessel. 'Berta – that's my friend who was at his talk that night – saw him drink two glasses of schnapps, saw it with her own eyes. He went home and started on the gin. Couldn't even have a bath without taking the gin up there with him. Drank too much and drowned. It's obvious. The bottle fell out of his dead hand and broke on the floor,' she added dramatically.

'So . . .' began my father.

'So,' she supplied triumphantly, 'as I told you, you cannot meet Herr Mahlberg, *Herr Professor*. Nobody can meet him at all.'

CHAPTER TWELVE

We drove back to the Kreuzburg in silence. My father glared ahead at the road, his face set. I stared out of the window, fidgeting and not daring to say anything in case it provoked an explosion. My father had spent the short walk back to the car ranting about his 'evil luck' – first the professorship had slipped from his grasp, and now this had happened, the sudden death of his best contact in Germany. He wasn't sorry for Herr Mahlberg; he was *mad* with him. I felt a hollow pit in my stomach. Was this going to mean another move? My father's post at the university was being kept open for him, but we still had the rest of the sabbatical year to get through.

I hadn't managed to scan any of the local headlines either. I tried to console myself with the thought that had there been any reports of British families heartlessly leaving dead bodies lying in orchards, Frau Kessel would have been the first to tell us.

The car made a sharp turn on to the track which led into the woods. As we passed beneath the trees I thought I saw something move in the undergrowth – a bulky brown shape. A deer? My eyes were still adjusting to the reduced light under the overhanging trees. I could not make out what it was. I twisted in my seat, but whatever it was had gone.

'Can you hear something?' said my father suddenly.

He reached down and switched off the air-conditioning. We strained our ears, listening.

'No-o-o . . .' I began, and stopped. There *was* something, a sound which was growing in volume and urgency. Sirens.

My father glanced in the rear-view mirror. 'Shit.' Abruptly he pulled over on to the side of the track. I turned just in time to see the gleaming red bulk of a fire engine bearing down on us. A moment later it had thundered past, making the car vibrate with the rumbling of its passing. My father and I looked at each other.

'Does this track go anywhere else but the castle?' I asked, with a rising feeling of dread.

'I don't think so.'

My father didn't say anything else, just put the car into gear and gunned the engine, so that the car leapt forward out of the space, throwing up clods of earth and bits of broken plants. I clung to the door handle as the car roared along the track, bouncing over potholes and skidding slightly on the gravel. There was what seemed like an age of suspense as we followed a long straight section of track through the forest, then suddenly we had turned a corner and come out into the open area in front of the castle. I was relieved to see that there was no black column of smoke rising from it anywhere. The fire engine was parked at an angle in front of the castle gate.

The moment my father had stopped the car we both ripped the doors open, leapt out and ran for the gate. My father wasn't fit, and I made it to the gate first.

The first thing I saw, to my relief, was Tuesday, with Ru in her arms. Polly was standing next to her, barefoot and

59

with one of my father's jumpers on; I guessed she'd had to leave the house suddenly. My gaze moved from Polly to the house.

'Oh no,' I breathed.

It was clear what had happened. A small tree standing very close to the corner of the house had caught fire; the tree itself was a blackened skeleton, and a great sooty patch spread over the stone wall beside it, as though a dark fungus were trying to consume the house. I had a dim recollection that the tree had been a dead one; the branches and twigs had been brittle and leafless. No doubt it had burned magnificently, and the house could easily have gone up too. The wooden frame of the little window nearest to the conflagration was already brown and scorched.

Firemen were moving about in the courtyard; as my father went over to speak to Tuesday I watched one of them kicking through the ashes under the remains of the tree. Then I noticed someone else, standing a little way from Tuesday and Polly. The boy from the farm – Michel – the one with the mud-coloured eyes. I heaved a sigh.

'*Sprichst du Deutsch?*' said someone. It was one of the firemen, hulking in a heavy jacket and helmet.

'Yes,' I said in German, and was rewarded with a grunt which might have been approval.

'It's safe,' he said. 'They can go back in.'

'Fine.'

I didn't trust myself to say any more. I trudged over to where my family were standing in a little huddle, looking sorry for themselves. Tuesday had handed Ru to Polly and was clinging to my father. Unlike Polly, she had managed to evacuate the house in a coordinated outfit and matching lipstick. I gave Michel a cursory nod and went straight up to Polly.

'What happened?'

Polly looked at me helplessly. 'I don't know, Lin. Tuesday was upstairs looking for something and I was in the kitchen making Ru a drink. He was sitting on the rug, just playing. I kept thinking I smelt burning but I couldn't see any smoke or anything. I thought maybe I'd burned Ru's milk or there was something sticking to the ring on the stove top. I lifted the pan up but there wasn't anything. I went back into the living room to call Tuesday and ask her if she could smell anything, and then *he* burst in.' She indicated Michel.

'What, *him*?' I gave a sideways glance towards Michel.

He saw me looking and began to blush furiously. I looked away; a horrid suspicion was beginning to rise in the pit of my stomach like a wave of nausea. I'd seen the way Michel looked at me. I did not even want to contemplate that he might have had something to do with starting the fire, so that he could rush in and play the hero.

Polly didn't notice my confusion. 'Yeah, he just burst in through the front door, yelling something – it sounded like *fire* –'

'*Feuer*?'

'Yeah, that's it. He picked Ru up off the rug and then he grabbed me by the arm and started trying to drag me to the door. I didn't know who he was – I thought he was mad or something and I started yelling, so Tuesday came downstairs to see what was going on, and then she smelt the smoke too. I just grabbed Dad's jumper – couldn't find any shoes – and we ran outside.' She turned to look at the smoking remains of the tree. 'That whole tree was on fire. It was like a bonfire.

That window frame started smoking too. We thought the whole house was going to burn down. Tuesday was going crazy – she kept trying to call Dad on her mobile phone but she couldn't get a signal. She was swearing her head off and then she threw it at the wall.' Polly raked her hands through her sand-coloured hair. 'Then Michel – that's what he said his name was – said he'd run back to the farm and call the fire brigade.' She glanced at him. 'He speaks really good English.'

'Hmm.' I tried not to look at Michel. 'Did he say what he was doing here in the first place?' I said in a low voice. It was not low enough; he heard me.

'I came to ask if you want to come to school with me,' he said in English. 'You know – a lift.'

I shook my head. 'No, thanks. It's nice of you, but . . .'

'There's no bus from here,' said Michel. He was giving me that look again.

'My parents will drive me,' I said firmly.

I didn't give him the opportunity to argue; I turned away and walked over to look at the charred remains of the tree, hoping he would take the hint.

It was a pitiful sight, brittle and blackened. A phrase I had read in a story once ran through my head: *It's a case of cremation*. The thought made me feel rather sick. I did not want to think what might have happened if the entire house had gone up.

The ground around the tree was a mess of ash and scorched wood. If I had not stood there for so long, my back resolutely turned to Michel, I might not have noticed it. Glass. You could hardly see it at first – it was not glittering, like the glass which had frosted the earth in the orchard, it was dull and discoloured. Gazing at the jagged shards, their gleam dulled to an opaque glaze by the fire, I was irresistibly reminded of teeth. No; not teeth – *fangs*. Fangs of glass.

CHAPTER THIRTEEN

Lunch was a miserable affair. My father was thrown into despair over the death of his main contact, Herr Mahlberg. Tuesday claimed to have lost her appetite because of the mere thought of what might have happened; Polly certainly lost hers once Tuesday told her not to be a pig and eat all the tomatoes. Ru was fractious and badly behaved after having waited so long for something to eat and drink. I did my best to push away the feeling of dread which had come over me when I saw the scorched glass outside, and had even managed to appear relatively cheerful, right up until the moment when Tuesday asked why Michel had come to the castle in the first place.

'To see if Lin wanted a lift to school,' said Polly.

'Great,' said my father.

'I said no,' I cut in hastily.

'You said *what*?' snapped Tuesday.

'I said I thought you or Dad would be driving me,' I said, with a sinking feeling.

'But school starts at eight fifteen,' Tuesday pointed out. 'If Michel's family are prepared to take you, I don't see why *I* have to get up that early too.'

'We hardly know them,' I tried, but it was no use.

'How can you say that?' demanded Tuesday. 'He practically saved all our lives.'

I looked down at my plate. The rye bread and smoked ham, not particularly appetizing in the first place, now looked inedible. 'Well, he's gone anyway,' I said.

'Lin.' A note of steel had entered Tuesday's voice; this was *important* – this was an extra hour in bed in the morning that we were talking about. 'He says he lives in the farm in the woods, doesn't he? You're not doing anything this afternoon. Why don't you go for a walk and see if you can find the farm? Then you can tell Michel and his parents that we'd *love* to take them up on their offer of a lift.'

It was on the tip of my tongue to tell her that this would be outright lying, but I suppressed it. 'OK,' I said with a sigh. Perhaps the farm would be impossible to find; I hoped so anyway.

As it happened, the expedition into the woods was put off. Just as we were finishing lunch, someone knocked at the front door.

Tuesday froze with her cup of coffee halfway to her lips. 'I hope that's not the landlord wanting to know what we've done to his tree,' she said.

We looked at each other. The knocking sounded again. Reluctantly I got to my feet.

To my relief, it was not Michel standing outside on the stone step. In fact I didn't recognize our visitor at all. He was a rather chubby man of about sixty, not much taller than I was, with a pudgy-looking face framed with greying hair which curled on to his collar. He was dressed in a dark suit in an out-of-date cut, with a dark shirt underneath it and no tie. He looked to me like the sort of person whose elderly mother still picked out his clothes and his thick-soled unfashionable shoes for him. I took in the pursed lips and the fussy way he held his hands clasped in front of him, and guessed that this was someone you would not want to be cornered by at a social event – the sort of person who grabs you by the arm to stop you getting away while they bore you to death with their one feverishly nurtured obsession, whether it be stamp collecting or steam trains. The only thing about him that didn't spell anorak was his eyes. They were very blue, very alert, and they were fixed on me.

'Fräulein Fox?' said the man. His voice was just the way you would expect it to be: clear and a bit prissy.

I stared at him, undecided how to respond. He didn't look like anything dangerous, a policeman or a journalist from the local paper. All the same, the memory of the body we had left lying in the orchard weighed heavily on me. I was not sure whether I should admit to being Fräulein Fox or not.

'I can speak English if you like,' said the man when I didn't reply. 'I am looking for Dr Oliver Fox.'

I heard my father's chair scrape on the flagstones as he stood up. 'I'm Oliver Fox.' He strolled over to where I stood, still holding on to the door. He and the visitor made an incongruous pair – the would-be media star and the geek.

'Hermann-Joseph Krause,' said our visitor, and extended a hand, which my father shook rather gingerly. I could see he was wondering who this person was.

I, on the other hand, was thinking, *Who has a name like Hermann-Joseph? And who admits to it if they do?* I would love to have turned and shot Polly a glance, but dared not.

'It's good to meet you,' said Hermann-Joseph Krause to my father. His English accent was excellent but there was a stiffness about the way he spoke. 'You are researching the Allerheiligen windows, I believe.'

'Well . . .' My father hesitated. I wondered if he was starting to feel as I did, somewhat exasperated at the fact that everyone in the entire area seemed to know why we were here.

Herr Krause was undeterred by my father's reluctance. He pressed on.

'I have come to offer you my assistance.'

'You're offering help?' said my father cautiously.

I could tell that he was sceptical, though the fact probably passed Herr Krause by; my father was very good at producing expressions of earnest and sincere interest, and Herr Krause didn't look like the sort of man who was often on the receiving end of them.

'Of course. May I come in?'

As my father showed Herr Krause in, I briefly entertained the idea of making my escape before I was dragged in to translate as the conversation ran aground on some piece of obscure vocabulary. But where would I go? I certainly didn't intend to go looking for Michel's house until it was absolutely unavoidable, and there was nothing else apart from forest for kilometres all around. While I was still debating the merits of claiming a sudden irresistible interest in pine trees, Herr Krause had established himself in one of the dining chairs and was surveying the room with ill-disguised interest. I went and stood by Polly, who was still pushing her lunch around her plate, and gave her a surreptitious nudge in the shoulder with my elbow. *Look at this guy!*

'This must be your mother,' said Herr Krause to me, smiling hopefully at Tuesday.

She didn't return the smile; she had seen those shoes too.

I didn't smile either. It was on the tip of my tongue to tell him that she wasn't my mother, but I knew what my father would say if I did.

'This is Tuesday,' said my father.

He might have made some further introduction, but he saw the look on Tuesday's face and thought better of it. Tuesday would have forgiven a serial killer or an evil despot all his crimes if he were charming and beautifully dressed, but she would have turned her back on St Peter himself if he had been wearing shoes like those. I almost felt sorry for Herr Krause.

'So,' said my father, placing his hands palm down on the pine table with an air of brisk attentiveness. 'You have an interest in the glass?'

'Yes.' Herr Krause was nodding. 'I have studied the history of the Allerheiligen Abbey for years.'

He paused deliberately, as though waiting for a response, and patted his chubby thighs with his fingers. His trousers were shiny at the knees, I noticed.

My father didn't reply. I could see that Herr Krause had failed to impress him, with his flabby indefinite face and worn-out suit. He smiled gently but he let the silence stretch out a little too long, hoping to make Herr Krause uncomfortable so that he would get to the point.

'I don't mean to publish anything myself,' said Herr Krause, aiming for a self-deprecating tone but unable to keep the hint of self-importance out of his voice. 'I intend to put all my notes at your disposal, Dr Fox.'

My father's smile grew wider and more tigerish at this; I guessed he was thinking the same as I was, that Herr Krause's notes would all be in German, probably handwritten or printed out laboriously on some antiquated typewriter, and about as much use to him as an Assyrian's shopping list stamped out in cuneiform. Still, my father's main contact in Germany having gone to present his findings to a higher authority, my father had to make do with whatever leads he had.

As I unwillingly listened to Herr Krause's fastidious and rather pompous voice rambling on, an uncomfortable thought occurred to me. There seemed a definite danger that Herr Krause would represent more of a hindrance than a help. Perhaps this was the point. I remembered Michel's parting words to me the first time we had met, outside the castle: *Your father – he won't find the Allerheiligen glass – not on his own.* Clearly there was some feeling among the local people that it would be better if we left well alone, that the glass – if indeed it still existed – should be left in obscurity. The inhabitants of Baumgarten had drawn up their ranks to resist us, and Herr Krause was the champion they had sent out to engage in single combat with my father.

This idea was confirmed a minute or two later when I came out of my reverie just in time to hear Herr Krause say, 'Of course, the glass itself no longer exists, that is for certain.'

This pronouncement did not alarm my father as much as it might have done. He was a veteran of the academic world, in which epic battles could be fought and won over whether one particular word of medieval Latin had originally appeared on a palimpsest or not. The truth was a largely irrelevant bystander to these battles; in the absence of absolute proof one way or another, the laurels went to whoever could present the most convincing argument.

Herr Krause was saying that the Allerheiligen glass no longer existed. Herr Mahlberg had claimed that it most certainly did. This was familiar territory to my father.

'It is by no means certain, Herr Krause,' was his opening salvo. 'Other local *scholars* –' I saw him hand the word over reluctantly – 'believed not only that it exists but that it can and should be located.'

Herr Krause shook his head pityingly. 'You are referring to Herr Mahlberg?' He sighed heavily. 'Let me tell you something, Dr Fox. Herr Mahlberg, he was a good man with a real interest in local history. But, you know, he didn't come from here, from Baumgarten.'

I saw a look of real irritation cross my father's face at this.

'He had some ideas about the glass, yes,' continued Herr Krause, 'but he was wrong about this. I know for a fact that the glass was destroyed in the early nineteenth century by the French troops.'

'How do you know this?' interjected my father.

'There was a letter in the archive in Trier,' said Herr Krause. 'I had an uncle who was also interested in the glass and he saw this letter, before the war. It was a letter from the last abbot, whom the French turned out when the abbey was closed, describing the ransacking of the abbey buildings and the destruction of the windows.'

This was quite a serious blow, but my father attempted to parry it. 'And have you personally seen this letter?'

'Actually, no,' said Herr Krause primly. 'The letter, like many other documents, was destroyed when the archive was bombed during the war.'

My father maintained his expression of calm interest. I doubt Herr Krause noticed the infinitesimal pucker which appeared at the corner of his mouth, but I saw it and knew my father didn't believe what Herr Krause was telling him.

Herr Krause was shooting my father what was intended to be a sympathetic glance; he reminded me of an old sheep, rolling its eyes at us over a fence. Evidently he took my father's silence to mean that he was crushed by this piece of news, since he hurried on, 'But I am sure a history of the glass would be of great interest, even though the glass itself no longer exists. Here is my card.' He fumbled open a little card case and handed the card over. 'Please, do visit me at any time. My notes are mostly handwritten –'

I knew it! I thought.

'But I think you will find them of great use. You read German, of course?'

'Of course,' said my father drily.

'Well,' said Herr Krause, getting to his feet. 'I must go.'

I heaved a mental sigh of relief and wondered whether I could slip away somewhere while he was taking his leave; anything rather than go looking for the farm. But Herr Krause had not quite finished. He stopped halfway to the door.

'I see you have had a fire,' he said to my father.

'Yes,' said my father.

'You should be careful,' said Herr Krause. 'The woods can be very dry at this time of year.' His gaze shifted from my father to Tuesday and then to Reuben, who was sitting in his high chair apparently attempting to finger-paint with a little pot of fromage frais. 'I hope no one was hurt,' he said.

Suddenly I had a strong conviction that Herr Krause was

really here to represent the town, that he was going to go back and report to them like a chubby fifth-columnist. Would they be pleased or disappointed that none of us had been hurt?

'We're all fine,' I said loudly, winning myself a startled look from Tuesday.

Herr Krause's gaze was suddenly on me instead of Ru, and I found myself reflecting that he did not remind me of a sheep after all so much as a plump little pig, rooting for truffles in the rich loam of our private lives. A second later I felt guilty – he was smiling at me with such genuine concern.

'*Gott sei Dank*,' he said in a low voice; *thank God*. Then he made a little gesture of farewell to my father, something halfway between a nod and a bow, and he was gone.

'What a dreadful man,' said Tuesday when the door had barely closed behind him. She looked at my father. 'Did he say the glass was *destroyed*?'

Tuesday rarely took a very close interest in my father's studies; in fact it was probably something of a mystery to his university colleagues that he was married to her at all. I sometimes conjectured that he had chosen her for her decorative qualities; certainly she stood out at faculty parties among the other wives, who were habitually swathed in artistic draperies of no particular form or shape and garlanded with hideous ceramic pendants. Tuesday would have looked good at an awards ceremony or a magazine photo shoot, and never mind that she could not tell a Holbein from a Jackson Pollock.

Now, however, she was not only interested, she was anxious. She understood the value of the stained glass perfectly well; a million pounds was not something she was likely to forget.

'Oliver?' she said. 'Do you think –'

'No, I don't,' said my father shortly. He scowled.

'He's left something behind,' said Polly suddenly.

She picked it up; it was the silver card case with a handful of cards in it.

I held out my hand. 'I'll run after him.'

Anything rather than give him an excuse to come back. I took the card case and went to the door. The courtyard was empty; he must have made a quick start. I ran over to the gate and looked out. There was no sign of a car, and no sign of Herr Krause. *Funny*, I thought. I wandered out into the open area in front of the castle and peered down the tracks in all directions but I could not see anyone, either on foot or in a car. Herr Krause had apparently vanished into thin air.

CHAPTER FOURTEEN

To my dismay, the topic of the lift to school had not been forgotten, and after Polly and I had cleared away the lunch things Tuesday insisted that I set off to look for the farm. I started from the spot where Michel had surprised me the first time we met, setting off in the direction of his vague wave. There were two possible tracks, both of them nothing but packed earth with a sprinkling of gravel here and there. At the side of the tracks were drainage ditches which were overgrown with brambles and ferns, and beyond them the dark damp undergrowth overhung with trees. On impulse I took the right-hand track. After about two hundred metres it split, the main track continuing ahead and a smaller, muddier track leading off to the right. In the fork of the intersection there was an object which I recognized as a shrine – a thing like a little glass-fronted hut on a red stone plinth. Behind the glass was a relief carving of a man and a stag. My gaze dropped to some lettering cut into the stone plinth. ST HUBERTUS, I read. I peered at the figure again. Someone had put a candle in a red plastic holder into the shrine, but it had long since burned down, giving the shrine a rather forlorn look.

'Well, St Hubertus – which way do I go?' I muttered.

The carved figure was facing right, his outstretched hands pointing towards the stag as though blessing it. I decided to take the right-hand turn again.

It was rather hard going and my shoes were quickly caked in mud. Still, I was hopeful that the track might take me to the farm; I could see the marks of other shoes in the mud. This was somehow comforting, as it meant that other people had passed this way and might even be close by. There was no doubt about it, the forest made me feel distinctly uncomfortable, though it was hard to say why. I had not seen a single living thing since I left the castle, and certainly not a dangerous wild boar or the intimidating bulk of a stag. It was silent apart from the rustle of leaves in the wind and the occasional distant chirp of a bird high up in the treetops. I scanned the undergrowth but could see nothing moving.

'Idiot,' I whispered, hugging myself.

I went on, trying to keep to the side of the path where the ground was drier. Ahead, the path continued in a straight line for about a hundred metres and then seemed to curve away to the right. I looked down at my filthy shoes, looked back up again, and a dog had appeared on the track up ahead. I jumped, then relaxed; it was just a dog after all. No. It was not *just* a dog – it was a very large, very powerful and aggressive-looking dog, and it had seen me. For a second it paused, its great muzzle snuffing the air, scenting the presence of an intruder. Then it leapt forward and bounded down the track towards me.

'Shit . . .'

Instantly adrenalin was shooting through my veins, a toxin so swift and powerful that I thought it would stop my heart.

I sucked in a breath but the air seemed thin, the inadequate atmosphere of a strange planet; my ears were buzzing and I was getting no oxygen. *It's going to rip my throat out.* I took a step back on legs that felt as though they would hardly support me for a moment longer. My head turned wildly as I scanned the trees and bushes around me, looking for something to climb, something to put between me and the dog. To my horror I realized there was nothing. The trees were all pines, with no lower branches capable of supporting anything bigger than a squirrel; for the rest, there was nothing but bushes, and a hound that size would come through those like a chainsaw.

I looked back down the track. The dog was closing on me very fast. It was bounding along, muscles clenching under its brindled hide, jaws agape. Its teeth looked gigantic; already I could imagine them grinding my flesh into ribbons. Sick with terror, I stooped and caught up a stick from the ground. It would be all but useless as a weapon to bludgeon the dog, but I had some faint hopeless idea of wedging it into the creature's jaws.

Instantly there was a piercing whistle which made my ears ring. The dog skidded to a halt and stood there panting, every muscle rigid with tension, its eyes fixed on me. Its powerful flanks were heaving, and saliva was hanging from its mouth in gleaming threads. I still clutched the stick like a talisman, my knuckles white, though my palms were slick with perspiration and I doubted I could wield the thing to any useful effect.

Gradually I became aware that someone was shouting. I looked away from the dog, further up the track. A man was running towards me. I thought he was about fifty, old enough to be my father at any rate, craggy-faced, with messy dark hair shot through with grey. He was dressed in some sort of scruffy-looking green coat and ancient brown trousers with splashes of mud, and was carrying a stick that was considerably thicker and more threatening than mine. He did not look friendly.

'What do you think you're doing here?' he shouted in German as he came up to me. He hardly glanced at the dog. '*Platz*,' he said, and it flopped down on to its stomach.

'I'm –' The words wouldn't come out; I could almost *feel* my brain short-circuiting.

'This is private land,' he snapped, not waiting for me to choke out another word. 'Didn't you see the fence?'

'No,' I said.

He pushed past me, with a sour whiff of body odour, and paced a few steps down the track, the way that I had come. His entire posture was stiff with irritation.

'Look here.'

I followed him reluctantly. There was indeed a kind of fence made of what looked like chicken wire, but where it crossed the path it had been pulled down and trodden deeply into the mud, so that I had not really noticed it when I picked my way along the path.

'I'm sorry –' I started to say in a wavering voice, but got no further before he interrupted me.

'What were you doing on this track?'

Finally the roughness of his tone forced me to collect myself. 'I was trying to find Michel,' I managed to say, and then realized how vague and unconvincing that must sound. 'He lives at the farm.'

'Michel Reinartz?'

'I don't know. I suppose so. He lives on a farm, somewhere in these woods, or near the woods, I think.'

'Hmm.' The man's gaze upon me was distinctly hostile. 'And if I tell you that *I* am Michel Reinartz? What do you say to that?'

'I . . .' I was not sure what to say. I stared at him in silence for a moment before light dawned. I noticed that his eyes were the colour of mud. 'Have you got a son?'

He looked at me for a moment, then he nodded grudgingly. 'Two.'

'Is one of them called Michel too?'

He nodded.

'Then I've met him. We're the people living in the Kreuzburg.'

He made a grunt which might have been acknowledgement or might have been disapproval.

'He said you might be able to give me a lift in the morning – to school, I mean.'

'Did he? That's up to him. I don't drive him.'

I groaned inwardly; this was even worse. It looked as though the offer of a lift came from Michel himself, in which case I was looking at twenty minutes shut up in the car with him every morning, not to mention the assumptions my new classmates would make if they saw us arriving together.

'Look, I'm really sorry I came this way. I really didn't know it was private. I'll go back the way I came.'

'No,' he said tersely. 'You come to the farm with me and talk to Michel yourself. He can take you back afterwards.'

With that he whistled for the dog, which leapt up and bounded to his side, then he turned away from me and began trudging back the way he had come. After a moment's hesitation I followed him, with one last uncomfortable glance towards the trodden-down fence.

For a little while we walked on in silence. Michel's father was much better dressed for the muddy conditions than I was. He had on stout boots with thick soles which gripped the ground, whereas my shoes were constantly slipping in the mud. I had to struggle to keep up with him, but he did not bother to slow down for me.

'I won't come into your part of the forest again,' I said.

There was no reply.

'The other parts are all right for walking, though, aren't they?' I continued, feeling slightly foolish at the one-sided conversation. 'I mean, they don't belong to anyone else, do they? There's no reason not to go there?'

At this he turned his head and gave me a look of naked contempt. 'Nobody can stop you walking in the public parts of the wood. They belong to the town. But if you have any sense, you'll stay in the castle.' He muttered something else under his breath which I did not catch, but I understood the sense of it: *Bloody townies*.

'Aren't the woods safe?' I persisted. 'Are there – animals?'

Herr Reinartz gave a short savage laugh like a bark. 'Of course there are animals.' He stopped and grimaced at me, baring his teeth. 'Badgers, foxes. Some of them have got the –' He named a word I did not recognize for a moment: *Tollwut*. Then I realized where I had seen it before: on the posters at the port when we had landed. Rabies. He was talking about rabies.

'There are animals with *rabies* in these woods?'

He grinned at the alarm on my face. Really, I did not like Michel Reinartz Senior one bit. 'Thousands of them,' he informed me. 'You get bitten, you'll need a lift to the hospital, not the bloody school.'

I eyed the dog nervously. 'Is he – I mean, has he had the . . .'

'The jab? What do *you* think?' Herr Reinartz stumped on ahead of me without waiting for a reply.

A few metres further on the path came out on to a wider track which bore the ruts of wheels. Up ahead I could see a screen of trees, behind which I could make out a cluster of grey rooftops. Evidently this was the farm. We skirted around the side of it and came to a section of whitewashed wall with a large wooden gate set into it, big enough for a tractor to pass through. Herr Reinartz opened a smaller door which was set into the gate and indicated that I should go inside. Then he walked off, whistling for his monstrous dog, without bothering to say goodbye.

I stepped inside and found myself in a yard surrounded by the farm buildings. There was a good deal of junk piled up on every side – sacks stuffed with what might have been animal feed, splitting at the seams; unidentifiable pieces of agricultural machinery, with horrific-looking spikes and blades sticking out at all angles; piles of logs and planks. I was debating where I might find Michel when a movement caught my eye, somewhere high up and to my right. I looked up, just in time to see a window closing, right underneath the eaves. With the light on the glass it was impossible to see who was inside. The next moment a door opened on the ground floor and Michel came out. Perhaps it was the door opening outwards, or the fact that Michel was dressed in a dark sweatshirt and jeans, but I was suddenly irresistibly reminded of the moment when I had first seen the Catholic priest, stepping out of the castle door.

When Michel saw me his face lit up. 'Lin!' Judging by the indecent haste with which he came hurrying over, he must have thought I was here to declare my undying love for him. A momentary image of the priest's stern face flickered across my mind. It was hard not to be irritable with Michel; there was something so pathetic about the way he looked at me.

'Hi,' I said non-committally. I couldn't help glancing up at the closed window, but there was nothing to see. 'I just came over to talk to you about the lift to school,' I added in German. 'Tuesday says it would be better if I went with you.'

'Great,' said Michel.

The fact that I had more or less told him that I had only come because Tuesday had made me do it passed him by completely.

'Do you want to come in?'

'No thanks,' I said hastily. 'I have to get back to the castle.' I paused, weighing up the options: walk through the rabies-infested forest on my own, or ask Michel to take me back. Common sense won, though I was afraid I would regret it later. 'Would you mind taking me back there? I met your dad in the woods and he says it's dangerous.'

'Dangerous?' Michel looked puzzled.

'Because of rabies,' I explained.

'Rabies?' he repeated.

I resisted the urge to shake him and tell him to stop repeating everything I said.

'He told me there are thousands of animals in there with it, foxes and badgers and stuff.'

'That's *Quatsch*,' said Michel. 'There's no rabies in this area at all. Maybe you misunderstood him.'

'I didn't misunderstand him,' I said rather coldly. 'But if there isn't any rabies I can walk back myself.'

Michel realized his mistake. 'No, don't do that. Look, I'll come with you anyway.'

I turned and he fell into step beside me. For once it was reassuring to have him there; he was half a head taller than me and broad-shouldered.

'I bet you came round the long way,' he was saying. 'I'll show you a short cut, then you can come over any time you like.'

'Hmm,' I said.

'Don't listen to Dad. I expect he was just trying to put you off walking around in the woods.'

'What for? He said they mostly belong to the town. And if there aren't any rabid animals I don't see why I can't go for walks.'

'Well . . .' Michel began reluctantly. 'It's not really – well, people don't really like anyone going through the woods here. It's not exactly private, that's true, but it's not really a tourist place, you know. People who want to go hiking normally go over to Bad Münstereifel.'

'Well, I live *here*,' I pointed out. 'It's not exactly convenient, going over to Bad whatever-it-is. Anyway, what's the problem with the woods? Have the local villagers got an illegal schnapps factory in there or something?'

Michel wasn't listening. He was staring absently at the sky, strands of dark hair flopping over his eyes. Suddenly he said, 'Have you got – you know, a boyfriend?'

'Yes,' I said immediately. 'In England.'

'Oh.'

He looked so disappointed that I almost felt sorry for him. It wasn't until much later that afternoon, after he had dropped me at the castle with a promise to call for me on the first day of school, that I realized he had never answered my question about the woods and what they had to hide.

CHAPTER FIFTEEN

Three days later the autumn term began. Michel was supposed to be calling for me at seven thirty. When I came downstairs, my father was already sitting at the pine table, surrounded by stacks of books and maps. He barely looked up, simply making a vague gesture of greeting in my general direction, and I knew better than to speak to him. When my father had the bit between his teeth he would work all day and half the night, barely stopping to eat, snapping at anyone who interrupted him. Since Herr Krause's visit he had been working like a demon, determined to prove the older man wrong, although judging by his uncertain temper he was making very slow progress.

Tuesday was still in bed. I had long since given up any hope that she would be bustling around the kitchen making bacon and eggs or packing me a lunchbox. In fact, she appeared to have finished off all the ham I had been intending to use to make sandwiches; there was a plate with the remains on it at the other end of the table. I searched the room until I found her handbag, a hideous creation in shiny emerald-green leather, which was lurking under a chair like an enormous tropical frog, its mouth gaping open. I shot a swift look at my father; he was deeply engrossed in a dusty-looking volume, feverishly jotting down notes. I fished Tuesday's purse out of the bag. There were four twenty-euro notes and one ten-euro note in it, plus assorted change. After some debate I took one of the twenties, reasoning that she would be more likely to miss the single ten. As I was sliding the purse back into the bag I heard the honk of a car horn and sighed.

'*Morgen*, Michel,' I said as I slid into the passenger seat of his car, a little red Volkswagen that had seen considerably better times. I did my best to keep my voice as neutral as possible, steering a hazardous course between friendly-enough-to-give-him-the-wrong-idea and downright rude.

The inside of the car was scrupulously tidy, in contrast to the scruffy-looking exterior. I noticed there was a smear on the dashboard as though someone had made an inept attempt at wiping it down. Balancing my bag on my lap, I pulled the door shut.

'*Morgen*.' Michel gave me a wide smile.

I noticed that he was looking considerably smarter than I had seen him look before; I sincerely hoped it was for the school's benefit. He had on a crisply ironed blue shirt and jeans, and he had washed his hair; now it fell across his forehead like a dark glossy wing. I even thought I could detect a subtle hint of aftershave. I found myself wishing that I had dressed down myself, rather than pinching the best of Tuesday's wardrobe for my first day at the new school. As it was, I had the uncomfortable feeling that we looked as though we were going out on a date.

'Well, are you going to drive, then?' I asked him in German as the moment stretched out. I could have sworn that he made a tiny jump, as though he really had forgotten what he was supposed to be doing.

As the car moved off down the track Michel said, 'How did you learn such good German?'

'At school,' I said. 'And last summer I went to stay with a family near Trier. My uncle Karl organized it – he's German.'

Michel digested this. 'Your family is partly German? So doesn't everyone speak German?'

'No.' I smiled inwardly at the thought; the nearest Tuesday got to speaking a foreign language was asking for a latte macchiato. 'Karl's not really my *uncle*,' I explained. 'He's married to Tuesday's cousin. He comes from Koblenz but he always speaks English with us. I mean, he has to. Tuesday can't speak German.'

'But your father – he speaks German?'

'Well, yes, but he's not all that fluent. He can read it really well and he knows all the words for bits of church windows and stuff, but he's never had to speak it much.'

'Hmm.' Michel made a sound of vague satisfaction. 'He won't get very far with his researches, then.'

I felt a stab of irritation. 'I told you, he can read it perfectly well.'

'Well, that's good, but he won't find anything out from reading books,' said Michel. 'If he talked to people who live here . . .' He shook his head. 'But if he can't speak German . . .'

'Someone came over a few days ago and offered to help,' I said, watching Michel carefully to see whether he would react. 'He said his name was Hermann-Joseph Krause, though how anyone can go around with a name like that –'

'Father Krause?' Michel rolled his eyes. 'Father Krause came to see you? *Mensch*.'

'*Father* Krause? You mean he's a priest?' I was puzzled. 'He wasn't wearing a priest's collar or anything.'

Michel snorted. 'No, he wouldn't. He's not a priest any more. He *used* to be one. What did he tell your father?'

'He said there used to be a letter in the archive at Trier proving that the Allerheiligen glass was destroyed. He said it doesn't exist any more. There's nothing to find.'

Michel risked a glance at me before looking back at the road ahead. 'Where did you say this letter was?'

'Well, it isn't *anywhere* now. He said it got burned or something in the war.'

'Hmm.'

'What?' I said crossly.

There was a pause during which Michel was evidently carrying on some internal debate. Eventually he said, 'Why does your father want to find the glass anyway? What's he going to *do* with it?'

I sighed. I didn't want to have to tell Michel the whole sorry story, that my father had failed to get the professorship he wanted and that this was his last chance. If he failed at this too he would be stuck in the same job forever – assuming he managed to hold on to it once Goodwin Lyle had taken over the department. I wondered where we would go if he did lose his job. I tried to imagine us living on the jewellery-making business Tuesday had been toying with when we lived in England. We would certainly starve.

Michel was looking at me again, evidently waiting for my reply.

'I suppose if he found it he'd be famous,' I said. 'I mean, he says it's worth hundreds of thousands of pounds, and it's supposed to be the best thing this Gerhard person ever made.'

'He wants to make money out of it?' said Michel.

I was struck by the tone of his voice – he sounded suddenly angry. I sneaked a glance at him. His brows were furrowed, although he was still apparently concentrating on the road ahead.

'He can't sell them, you know,' he told me. 'They don't belong to him. How can he make money out of them if they aren't his?'

'Herr – I mean Father – Krause says they don't exist at all,' I pointed out.

'Father Krause is a –' Michel checked himself.

I stared at him. 'So you think he wasn't telling us the truth? You think he was making it up, about the letter in Trier?'

'I don't think anything,' said Michel sullenly. 'I'm just saying it's a waste of time talking to him.'

We had come to a T-junction. Michel stopped the car at the line and glanced at me, his brown eyes clouded with irritation.

'If you're looking for a hundred thousand pounds, you won't find it.' He didn't say what he meant by *it* – the money or the glass.

CHAPTER SIXTEEN

Michel hardly said another word to me for the rest of the drive to the school. I bit my lip and looked out of the window at the changing vista of trees giving way to country roads and eventually the streets of Nordkirchen, a town with all the rustic old-world charm of Slough or Watford. I was irritated with Michel, not just for saying that my father would never find what he was looking for, but also because he was annoyed with me, quite unfairly. After all, I had not wanted to come to Germany in the first place; I would much rather have been at home in England, where I had friends and plans.

When we got to the school I was expecting Michel to put as much space between me and him as he possibly could. He had been so taciturn in the car that I guessed he was regretting his offer to drive me. To my surprise, however, once he had parked the little Volkswagen in a street near the school he made a point of walking with me into the school.

'It's OK,' I said to him in German. 'You don't have to look after me. I can find my way around.'

Michel shrugged and then shot me a sideways grin which I did my best to ignore. I had no idea which of the other students who were walking into school with us were my future classmates, but I had a horrible feeling that people were already jumping to their own conclusions. There was something just a bit too nonchalant about the way Michel greeted some of the others; I began to feel like one of the barbarian princesses whom Roman generals used to display in their triumphal parades. It was exasperating. I was not his property, and I did not like the way that people were looking me up and down.

My sister Polly had naturally fair hair – it had not been artfully spun into gold by an expensive hairdresser like Tuesday's. But I take after my father; I am jet to Polly's amber. My hair and eyes are dark, and I have also inherited my father's power of pleasing, which is not the gift you might think it is. At that moment I wished I had been mousy and nondescript. Also, looking at the scruffy jeans and scuffed shoes that everyone else seemed to be wearing, I began to suspect that I was horribly overdressed.

Once inside the building, I scanned the walls in vain for a notice-board which might tell me where I should be going. What seemed like hundreds of students were crossing the large foyer in all directions, some striding purposefully, others lingering to turn off mobile phones or chat with each other. The general effect was similar to that of a busy railway terminus at rush hour. I found myself hesitating to accost anyone to ask them how to find my class. I needn't have worried, though; Michel was at my elbow again.

'You're in Frau Schäfer's class, right?'

'Mmm-hmm.' I nodded.

'Come on, I'll take you up there.'

Reluctantly I followed him across the foyer and we began to climb the main staircase. Michel was saying something to me about Frau Schäfer, and I was looking at the logo on the faded T-shirt of a boy in front of me and wondering who on earth Rammstein were, when something made me turn round and look back towards the ground floor.

Instantly my gaze picked out a tall figure entering the foyer, a figure I recognized. I couldn't help myself; I stopped short and touched Michel's arm, feeling my face tingle and praying that I was not blushing.

'Who's that?' I asked, pointing.

Michel's gaze followed the direction of my finger. 'Him? That's Father Engels.'

I watched as the Catholic priest we had met outside the castle in Niederburgheim strode diagonally across the foyer and opened a door on the far side. He had on a black suit instead of the old-fashioned soutane he had been wearing on the day of the funeral party, and he still looked impossibly handsome. I could not tear my gaze away until he had entered the room and closed the door behind him.

Stop it, I told myself. *You can't possibly have a crush on a priest.*

'What's he doing in the school?' I asked Michel, making a titanic effort to keep my tone casual.

'He teaches *Reli*,' said Michel without interest.

'He does?'

'Well, he teaches the Catholic kids. Look, are you coming or not? The bell's going to ring.'

Reluctantly I followed Michel to the top of the stairs. I couldn't resist one more glance behind me, but there was no sign of Father Engels. Still, it was a thrilling and slightly delirious thought that we were sharing the same building. I might run into him every week – perhaps every day. He might even speak to me – if he recognized me as the English professor's daughter. The thought of standing there listening to his questions about my father's research while I bathed in the glory of those wonderful good looks made me feel quite light-headed.

It was only later that this brief sighting seemed to have been an omen – the single magpie that signifies sorrows to come.

CHAPTER SEVENTEEN

How do you dress for your own execution? was a question I might have asked myself that morning as I walked into Frau Schäfer's classroom and found myself facing the twenty-five strangers who were to be my new classmates. The answer was, *wrongly*. I knew it the moment I entered the room. I heard the buzz of voices change pitch and volume as they all looked up and checked out the newcomer. If I had known where to sit I would have scuttled to my place, but from where I stood I couldn't see a single free seat. Instead I stood there by the door, uncomfortably shifting the weight of my school bag from my shoulder to my hip, and thinking that I was having the most monstrous case of déjà vu ever. I knew this feeling; this was the one you got when you dreamt you were walking down the high street of your hometown stark naked.

I had thought that I would be creating a fabulously cool first impression when I had gone through Tuesday's things the day before and picked out an outfit which oozed bohemian chic – the designer jeans and jacket, the hippyish top and the killer boots. But what would have been enviable back home in a university town was about as inconspicuous here as a belly-dancer at a chess tournament. Everyone else

93

was dressed down, from the two gum-chewing blonde girls in the front row to the enormously fat boy with spectacles at the back, whose sweatshirt had the dimensions of a small marquee. They were all looking at me, and I could almost *feel* the gaze of twenty-five pairs of eyes moving up and down my outfit. I made a mental note that if I got through the day without actually dying of embarrassment, and if I had to come back here again tomorrow, I would wear something less conspicuous, like a chador perhaps.

'*Guten Morgen*, class,' said a severe voice behind me, and I heard the door close. Clearly this was Frau Schäfer. Hardly anyone bothered to even mutter a greeting in return; they were all too busy examining the strange new creature who had landed among them.

I turned and found myself eye to eye with a stern-looking woman of about fifty, with a helmet of black hair and heavy features which were not enhanced by thick-framed glasses and a strident shade of red-brown lipstick.

'Frau Schäfer? I'm Lin Fox,' I said.

'Lin?' She shot me a disapproving look and began to open the register she had been holding to her not inconsiderable bosom. She ran a finger down the column inside. 'Do you mean –' she began, but I cut her off before she could say it. My problems were bad enough without *that*.

'It's Lin,' I said hastily. 'Just Lin. That –' I fumbled for words. 'That's a formal name. Nobody uses it.'

Frau Schäfer gave me a distrustful look and glanced back at the register, but in the end she decided to let it drop; perhaps she was not confident of the pronunciation. She scanned the room with a gorgon look which petrified all conversation, and eventually fixed her gaze on a spot towards the back. 'There's a place free over there, next to Johanna.'

I followed her gaze and saw a tall red-headed girl looking at me with the kind of trepidation you might have expected to see on the face of an Aztec required to sit down with a Spaniard. I made a move to go to my place and get out of the combined glare of twenty-five pairs of eyes, but Frau Schäfer grasped me by the shoulder.

'Not yet, Lin.' She faced the class. 'This is Lin Fox from England. She's joining the class for a year.' There was an interested buzz of conversation at this. 'Lin, would you like to introduce yourself?'

It did not seem possible to say what I would like to have said, which was *Absolutely not*, so with an inward sigh I put my bag down on the floor and prepared to do my best.

'Hi, I'm Lin . . .' *Stupid, they know that already.* 'I've come to Germany because my dad has to do some . . .' Under the gaze of so many eyes I found myself floundering; I couldn't think of the German word for *research*. In the end I had to content myself with saying, 'He has to do some work here. He's a . . . he works at a university in England.' I glanced heavenwards as if for inspiration, but I couldn't think of anything else to say at all.

'That's interesting,' said Frau Schäfer when it became obvious that I was not going to proffer any more information. 'And what is your father working on?' Evidently she was from out of town; everybody else we had met since we arrived seemed to know the answer to this question already.

'He's interested in the stained glass from the Allerheiligen Abbey.'

I saw something pass among the other students as I said

it, an indefinable reaction, less obvious than a glance exchanged or a whispered phrase – something like a ripple spreading subtly through the class. I did not think for a minute that this meant they were all gripped with a mania for medieval art. I was not sure, but I had the impression that what they were expressing was recognition, as though they had suddenly put a face to a very ugly rumour. I was relieved when Frau Schäfer gave me up as a bad job and let me slink to my seat.

The red-headed girl called Johanna gave me a friendly enough look, but I noticed that she moved away slightly as I sat down in the space next to her. I gave her a smile that felt as unnatural as a mask and then busied myself hauling books out of my bag. As well as embarrassment I felt annoyance. Was there so little to do here that our arrival was such a big event?

Who cares? I thought, as I put my books down on the desktop with a slap. *Let them talk about me, see if I care.* I looked up defiantly, daring anyone to stare at me, and saw a couple of heads hastily turn back to face the front. *So what if the whole of Baumgarten and all of Nordkirchen knows why we're here? What harm can it do?*

On that I was wrong, however. It could do a great deal of harm – I just didn't know it yet.

CHAPTER EIGHTEEN

That first day at school seemed interminably long, though the school day ended earlier than it did at my school in England. I could understand most of what was said, but it was tiring; at the end of the day's lessons I felt as I might have done if I had spent the day watching foreign art films back to back. I could not really be bothered to talk to Michel as we drove back towards the Kreuzburg. Instead I slumped low in the passenger seat and stared out of the window at the scruffy streets of Nordkirchen unravelling past us. It was strange, living in a place where as yet I knew only a handful of people. The mind plays tricks; every so often I would see someone on the street, a boy of my own age with fair hair going into a shop, or a gangly-looking girl dragging an unwilling dog along the pavement, and for a moment I would think, *I know you*. I would think I recognized someone from my hometown, a friend or classmate or neighbour. Then he or she would turn and I would see that it was someone else completely – a stranger, with an unfamiliar face, with just a fleeting resemblance to someone from home. How could it be otherwise? Still, the mind tries to make patterns, to pick up the familiar threads of a life woven in another place and time.

I was pondering this as the streets melted into countryside

and we passed the yellow sign which told us we were entering Baumgarten. All of a sudden Michel braked so sharply that I was thrown forward, and felt the seat belt lock painfully across my shoulder.

'*Scheisse.*'

We were about three centimetres from the back bumper of the car in front of us, a smart red Audi whose owner would not have been thrilled to have a tonne of tatty Volkswagen rammed into its gleaming boot. Judging by the scream of tyres, followed by the irritable bleat of a horn, the driver behind us had had a near miss too.

'Are you OK?' said Michel, but he didn't listen to my reply. He was peering out of the windscreen with his brows drawn together in a frown.

I saw him reach up and brush his dark hair out of his eyes, squinting at the road ahead.

'What's she . . .' He sounded distracted.

'Michel?'

He wasn't listening. Evidently something was happening up ahead, but from where I was sitting I couldn't see anything at all, just the back of the Audi, vertiginously close. There was another blare of horns and then someone swung out into the middle of the road to try to pass us. The Audi was moving again, nudging forward, the driver evidently piqued at being overtaken.

'*Michel?*'

I was starting to feel annoyed at the way he was ignoring me. He put the car into gear again and it slid slowly forward, but instead of following the Audi he suddenly pulled on to the grass verge at the side of the road. There was an agonizing creak as he yanked on the handbrake.

'Why are we stopping?' I demanded.

I couldn't hear any sirens and there were no blue lights flashing. All I could see were cars nosing at spaces in the narrow road like fish clustering around bait.

'It's Frau Roggendorf.' Michel unclipped his seat belt.

'Who?'

'Frau Roggendorf. She used to run the bakery in Baumgarten.'

'Well, what's she doing?'

He wasn't listening to me. He already had the car door open and was climbing out. There was nothing else to do, so I undid my seat belt and got out too. It was a warm day and with so many cars idling in this small section of road the air was thick and poisonous with petrol fumes. Michel was already threading his way purposefully between the cars. Up ahead I could hear something. It sounded like a woman yelling. No, she was not yelling; she was *screaming*. I wondered if this was Frau Roggendorf.

Now people were winding their windows down and adding their loudly delivered advice to her shrieks. More horns sounded. As far as I could tell, though, Michel was the only one who had got out to see what the matter was. Everyone else just wanted the blockage removed so that they could drive on.

When I caught up with Michel he was pulling someone to the side of the road. It was a woman of about seventy, shorter than I was and with an impressively solid build firmly upholstered in blue and brown floral cotton. She had a quantity of wispy grey hair which had been caught up in a tight little bun but was now escaping in big tufts, so that she had rather the appearance of a large dandelion clock. I had no clear impression of her face other than a gaping maw from which a stream of hysterical screeches spewed forth.

A car accelerated past me, a little too close for comfort and I hopped on to the pavement. I could see the dirty looks we were getting from the drivers as they passed us; perhaps they assumed we were relatives of Frau Roggendorf's – or her keepers, I thought nervously, looking at the wild eyes and distorted features of the old lady.

'What's the matter?' I asked Michel.

He shook his head. He had taken her arm to steer her out of the road, and now he was holding on to stop her stepping back out into it. He looked like a man trying to drag an ox to the slaughter; clearly Frau Roggendorf was desperate to get away. The old lady's shrieks rose to a crescendo and then suddenly, shockingly, she burst into tears. The fight seemed to have gone out of her. She allowed Michel to guide her away from the edge of the road. There was a row of large chunks of stone on the grass to stop drivers from parking on it. Michel led the old woman to one of them and helped her sit down. He looked nonplussed. The traffic was clearing and now I could see his little Volkswagen sitting on the verge at the other side of the road, waiting for us.

'Frau Roggendorf?' said Michel loudly. 'What happened?'

There was no coherent reply. Michel and I looked at each other helplessly. Clearly she could not be left alone, but we were right on the edge of the town; there was no other person in sight and not even a house nearby. I looked both ways up and down the road but we were quite alone. We were standing close to a stone wall which ran for a considerable distance in either direction; it was high enough that I could not see over it, but I thought I could make out a gate further along.

If there were houses on the other side we might ask someone for help.

'Michel?' I said. 'What's in there?'

He turned to me. 'The cemetery.'

'The cemetery?'

I looked at Frau Roggendorf, hunched on the chunk of stone with tears streaming down her papery old cheeks. In spite of the warmth and brightness of the day I felt a sudden chill. It struck me that there was something unnatural about seeing an old woman like that without a handbag or any of the other paraphernalia old ladies like to take about with them – fold-up umbrellas and embroidered handkerchiefs and peeling tubes of cough sweets. Of course, she might be one of those poor old souls who wander about towns seeing the streets through some overlay of the past invisible to everyone else, and talking to the long dead; but I thought it more likely that something had upset her, and she had dropped everything she was carrying in her effort to get away. I looked up at the wall.

'Michel? Will you stay with her if I go and look around?'

'What for? We should call someone.'

I shrugged, not keen to tell him that I wanted to reassure myself there was nothing alarming on the other side of the wall.

'There might be someone who could help.'

I set off at a quick pace in the direction of the gate. As I passed Frau Roggendorf I saw her, out of the corner of my eye, silently turning her head to watch me go.

The gate was open. I wandered through a wrought-iron archway and found myself in the cemetery. It was a large one, and old. Some of the gravestones had a thick rime of lichen growing on them. Most of them were beautifully kept, though, and gazing over the ranks of knee-high granite and marble slabs was unnervingly like looking at a model village. There seemed to be nothing to alarm anyone. I could not see any other visitors; the gravelled paths, laid out with geometric precision, were all clear. I began to walk along one of them, reading the names of Baumgarten families who had laid generations of their dead to rest here: *Kolvenbach, Flamersheim, Ohlert.*

It had been very dry over the past few weeks and most of the flowers left out on the graves were dead or wilting. Those which had been recently left there stood out as bright splashes of colour against the greys and rusty browns of the tombstones. It was perhaps for that reason that I was able to pick out the grave of Hans-Pieter Roggendorf, the late lamented husband of the very Frau Roggendorf who even at this moment was rocking and sobbing on a stone outside the cemetery. I saw it because of the brightly coloured chrysanthemums which were scattered haphazardly all over the shiny marble slab and the arid earth around it, strident spots of glowing yellow, orange and crimson against the shades of brown. As I walked up the dusty path towards the grave I could see that it was among the older plots, and indeed when I was close enough to read the dates on the headstone I found that Herr Roggendorf had passed away in 1989. It was hard to imagine that after all this time Frau Roggendorf was still so traumatized by his death that she was moved to shower his grave with flowers.

That was not all she had showered his grave with, I noticed. A large and battered black leather handbag was lying on its side like a deflated lizard, its contents spilling out over the ground. I was not surprised to see the half-consumed tube of antacids, the ubiquitous packet of paper tissues which most German ladies seem to carry around as a talisman against the dark forces of the cold virus, or the old-maidish pink plastic comb. What were more surprising were the little gold watch, the seed-pearl necklace and the brooches. Evidently Frau Roggendorf carried her valuables about with her to prevent burglars getting their hands on them. Now it looked as though she had decorated her husband's tomb in true pharaonic style, with all the riches she possessed.

I stood by the grave, looking down at these assorted offerings and wondering what on earth could have possessed her to run shrieking from the graveside, as she clearly had. Scuffing my feet carelessly in the dust, I looked around me, trying to see what Frau Roggendorf had seen.

I almost jumped out of my skin. There was someone peering at me over the top of a gravestone, not three metres away. The first searing fizz of shock was instantly replaced with fury. No wonder the old woman had nearly had a heart attack. '*Du Arschloch* –' I started to say – at least, I drew in breath to shout at him, but the next second the words died on my lips, and all that came out was a long hiss of breath like the escape of steam from a boiler.

Whoever it was whose head I could see, the chin resting almost casually on top of the gravestone, was not looking at me at all, not looking at anything in fact. Nor was he – or she, it was impossible to say – likely to be offended at my trying to call him an *Arschloch*. In fact, he was grinning at me, but he was not grinning with amusement. He was grinning because he had no lips; they had long since pulled back from the rows of yellowing teeth and rotted away.

Frau Roggendorf was a screamer, but I was not. I could barely force out a whimper. The world seemed to have turned hot and flat and silent as I stared at the thing, and it stared back at me with empty eye sockets. My feet had taken on a life of their own; I heard the susurration of my boots moving across the dusty earth as I unwillingly rounded the end of the grave and gazed at the body in its entirety.

It was frozen in the act of climbing out of a grave – at least, that was what my eyes told me, though in some distant corner of my horrified brain some shred of detached logic was assuring me that that was impossible. A dead man doesn't splinter his tombstone into two; he doesn't haul himself painfully up towards the light and then collapse, his skull coming to rest on a headstone, the pathetic brown sticks of his limbs sprawled out as though trying to get some last futile purchase on the earth.

It can't be, whispered some disbelieving voice at the back of my mind, though my eyes were telling me that it *was*. I began to think that I *should* scream, that I should yell my head off so that Michel would come and drag me away, and I wouldn't have to look at this thing any more, this abomination which had crawled back up to the daylight with its message of grim mortality. I opened my mouth, but all that came out was a sound like the whine of a frightened animal.

In the end the only thing which spurred me into action was the knowledge that if I stood there any longer on legs which were trembling beneath me I might actually fall over. The prospect of tumbling into that open grave, of actually falling down among those tattered bones, was so terrible that I forced myself to step back, and once I had taken one step the next was easier. I backed away, and then I turned, and then finally I was *running* back down the dusty path between the gravestones.

The gate seemed much further away than it had before and I was horribly aware that there was no one else in the cemetery. *Nobody alive*, I thought dismally, scanning the ranks of polished headstones. Impossible now not to think what they stood for – that each of them was a sentinel placed over a thing like the one I had seen grinning at Herr Roggendorf's grave. The dead were all around me, legions of them. The blood roared in my ears and my throat seemed to constrict as I staggered the last few metres to the gate.

Michel was standing next to Frau Roggendorf, who was still hunched on the block of stone, her face ashen and her wrinkled old lips working soundlessly. He looked up as I came stumbling out of the cemetery and I saw his face change.

'Lin? What's happened?'

I almost fell into his arms, heedless of what he might think.

'There's a –' I couldn't think of a single German word to begin to express what I had just seen. 'There's a dead man,' I choked out eventually in English.

Michel looked down at me as though I had gone completely mad, glanced at the cemetery wall and then back at me again. *Of course there's a dead man in there*, said his expression. *It's a cemetery – what did you expect?*

'He's out – he – someone opened the grave.'

'*What?*' Now he looked as though he could not believe his ears.

'The grave is open.' I let go of Michel; a sour taste was filling my mouth and I thought I might be sick. 'Don't go,' I begged him, seeing that he was about to take a look for himself. If he left me here I thought I might run amok as Frau

Roggendorf had, throwing herself into the road in an attempt to get someone to stop.

Michel put his hands on my shoulders and squeezed gently. 'I have to look. I'll be back in two minutes. One,' he added, looking at my stricken face.

As he walked quickly away I sank down on to the dusty grass at the side of the road. I didn't want to catch Frau Roggendorf's eye. I was having enough trouble holding myself together; I didn't think I could bear to see the shocked expression on her wrinkled face again.

Michel was back very quickly. He no longer looked sceptical. Now he looked a little pale and sick, like someone who has nosed at a bad car accident and wished they hadn't. He did not try to touch me or comfort me. He was holding himself oddly, stiffly, as though we were both soaked in something disgusting and he was just keeping the bile down until he could scrub himself clean.

'We have to phone the police,' he said.

He spoke in English but his German accent was as strong as I had ever heard it at that moment. Suddenly he seemed an alien thing to me, part of this freakish place where the dead lurked around every corner, lying under apple trees like some strange and loathsome windfall, or bursting obscenely out of their resting places. I put my arms around my knees and hugged myself. I did not want Michel to touch me. I said nothing but watched through slitted eyes as he walked back to the Volkswagen to fetch his phone. He stood leaning against the car for several minutes, talking into it, sometimes pausing to listen and occasionally running a hand through his dark hair so that it stood up in untidy spikes. Eventually he put the phone into his pocket and walked back towards me.

'The police are coming,' he said.

I said nothing. Michel hunkered down beside me, not seeming to notice the way that I edged back away from him.

'They said not to touch anything.'

I could have snorted at that if the idea had not been so disgusting. Nothing could have induced me to go back into the cemetery and touch that brown and hideous thing. I put my head down on my knees and squeezed my eyes tight shut.

'Lin? You didn't touch anything, did you?'

'No,' I told him in a muffled voice.

'Are you sure? You didn't knock anything over?'

'*No*,' I said more forcefully. Why wouldn't he leave me alone? I put my head up and glared at him. 'I didn't touch anything, I didn't knock anything over, right?'

Michel didn't say anything. I looked at him for a moment and then I said, 'Why do you want to know?'

'Because,' said Michel slowly, 'there's glass on the ground. You know, by that grave. Broken glass.'

CHAPTER NINETEEN

The police came, and an ambulance came too. I sat on the grass and watched the ambulance slowly mount the verge, the blue lights revolving slowly. Idly I wondered why they had bothered with an ambulance – the thing in the graveyard was well beyond the reach of medical attention. But the ambulance was for Frau Roggendorf and me.

There were two policemen, a tall meaty-looking one and a smaller, skinnier one with an extravagant moustache bisecting his angular face, both of them dressed in bomber jackets and peaked caps and with guns on their hips. With a certain sense of déjà vu I watched them saunter nonchalantly into the cemetery and then emerge a few minutes later looking distinctly green in the face.

After that everything seemed to happen very quickly. The paramedics examined me and discovered that I was uninjured, but Frau Roggendorf was a very different matter. She was well over seventy and she had had a shock so sudden and severe that it was a miracle her old heart had not stopped dead like an overheated motor blowing a gasket. As it was, she was complaining of chest pains and shortness of breath, and the ambulance men were desperate to get her to hospital before she had the opportunity to follow the late lamented Hans-Pieter into eternity.

It was fortunate for us that Frau Roggendorf survived the shock of seeing that grisly head leering at her liplessly over the top of a gravestone. When the doctors had finished with her and allowed the police to speak to her, she was able to confirm that we had arrived *after* she had seen the ghastly thing propped against the headstone and had staggered out into the road to try to flag down a passing car. We had not been out of school for more than fifteen minutes when we had seen her, and she had been there for most of that time, first inside the cemetery and then outside in the road. She had first seen us when we stopped the car and Michel went to help her. If she had not been able to tell the police this, they would undoubtedly have drawn their own conclusions from the desecrated grave and the presence of two teenagers.

None of the other drivers who had edged their vehicles past the scene in the road came forward. In the days that followed, everyone that Michel or I met seemed to know someone who had been passing the cemetery that day – a cousin's gentleman friend, or a neighbour's sister, or the delivery man's aunt by marriage. Oddly, however, when you tried to pin anyone down to exactly who had been there, the answers were uniformly vague. Not one of those public-spirited disseminators of information ever spoke to the police. For official purposes, the road to Baumgarten had seemingly been as deserted as the surface of the moon that afternoon.

The rest of the day, spent mostly at the police station in Baumgarten, was a blur of conversations with the police, sometimes in German and sometimes in English. The skinny one with the moustache spoke relatively good English, which was a relief because most of my German seemed to have evaporated with the shock of what I had seen. Besides, there was nothing in the lessons I had had or the comfortable summer I had spent last year in the Müllers' homely farmhouse which could possibly have prepared me to describe what I had seen.

Eventually my father appeared to take me home. Someone had had to be dispatched to the Kreuzburg to fetch him away from his work, since it was impossible to get a mobile signal there and there was no landline. The police had finished with Michel too; I felt that they let us go with a slight feeling of regret, but it was perfectly plain that we were not the ones who had broken the gravestone and dug up that grotesque and tattered thing.

Outside the police station the air was still warm although it was almost evening. My father kept up a stream of cheerful-sounding chat as he led me over to the car and unlocked the door. I suspect that he thought this was the best way to cover the awkwardness of the moment. He had no real idea what to say to a seventeen-year-old who had just seen the cinema trailer for Judgement Day. He told me an anecdote I had heard before, about an archaeological dig where a lead-lined medieval coffin had been left in the sun during the lunch break and had exploded, showering the site with liquefied remains. He debated aloud my chances of making it into the local paper, an idea which seemed to please rather than mortify him; for my father, any event which occurred was nothing without an audience. He also made a remark which I knew was an attempt to jolly me along, to the effect that I could hardly be let out of the house without stumbling over corpses.

When he made this particular remark, we were still on the steps of the police station, with Michel at my shoulder, and I felt rather than saw him react to my father's words. He said nothing, and his goodbye, as he went off to fetch his own car, was perfunctory. All the same, I knew he had understood the significance of the word *corpses*. Not *a* corpse, but *corpses* plural.

Michel would be picking me up again at seven thirty the following morning. With a heavy heart I got into the car and pulled the seat belt across myself. I hoped he would have forgotten about the remark by tomorrow, but somehow I knew that he wouldn't. That wasn't the way things worked around here. Tomorrow morning I was going to have some explaining to do.

CHAPTER TWENTY

By the time my father and I arrived back at the Kreuzburg, the afternoon was blurring into evening and the castle ruins were golden in the late sunshine. I ran into the house and found the rest of the family clustered at one end of the pine table in the living room. The other was occupied by a mound of books and my father's notes, which were fanned out on the tabletop and fenced in by a cluster of coffee cups.

Ru was sitting in his high chair, or rather he was slumped sideways in it, clearly almost too sleepy to eat, while Polly tried to tempt him with spoonfuls of mush. It was immediately apparent that Tuesday had abdicated from the task of feeding Ru on the grounds of severe mental trauma; she was sitting bolt upright on one of the uncomfortable wooden chairs, with a handkerchief balled in her left hand and a little bottle of Bach Flower Remedy within reach of the right. She had a slightly fevered look which made me wonder whether she was about to seize the bottle and try to drink the contents. I recognized the expression on her face as her Earth Mother in Crisis look. I sighed inwardly. I had had enough to deal with that afternoon without having to cope with a full-scale scene as well.

In the event, Earth Mother in Crisis was instantly replaced with Outraged Fashionista, as Tuesday took in what I was wearing. She was on her feet immediately.

'Lin! That's *my* jacket! *And* my jeans – and is that my Ghost top you're wearing?' She took a step closer. 'It *is*.'

'Tuesday,' said my father, appearing at my shoulder. There was a mild warning tone in his voice. 'Later. Lin's had a shock.'

There was a minuscule pause as Earth Mother in Crisis struggled to reassert herself. Eventually Tuesday said, 'You're right, Oliver.' She came tip-tapping over the flagstone floor towards me and actually put an arm around my shoulders. 'Are you all right, sweetheart? It must have been *horrible*.' She stroked the shoulder of the jacket I was wearing. 'I would have just *died* if I'd seen something like that.' I could feel her fiddling with the collar of the jacket, caressing it as though it was a small animal, and it was all I could do not to shake her off with irritation.

'I'm OK.'

This was not strictly true. I thought I would never be able to sleep with the lights off again, and as for ever crossing another graveyard . . .

Still Tuesday didn't leave me alone. She was peering anxiously at my – her – clothes with an expression of what seemed to be perfectly genuine concern.

'You didn't touch the – the thing you saw, did you?' she said. 'I mean, you didn't get any of it – *on* yourself, did you?'

Now I really was annoyed. I shook her off like a dog shaking off a biting insect. 'No. I didn't get any bits of – of *corpse* on your top.' I shuddered at the thought. 'And of course I didn't touch it. Are you crazy?'

Tuesday put her hands up in a gesture of wounded motherhood, but thankfully she did not try to hug me again.

'I'm going to take Ru upstairs,' said Polly into the silence which followed.

Polly hated arguments, and if she could not smooth one over she would always prefer to put as much space between her and the row as she possibly could. Sometimes I wondered how we could possibly be sisters, when I seemed to be permanently fizzing with indignation. Lin Fox, the human bath bomb – just add hot water and stand well back.

'I'll come with you,' I said hastily.

Logic said that there could not possibly be any lingering smell of decay hanging about my clothes – I would have died rather than touch that brown and loathsome thing – but all the same I felt dirty, as though simply being near it had somehow contaminated me. I could not wait to change into something else. I wondered whether Tuesday would really want her clothes back. I had no intention of ever touching them again.

I went upstairs into the chilly but well-equipped bathroom and spent ten minutes under the shower. Then I put Tuesday's clothes into the hamper and pulled on a pair of jeans and a T-shirt. After a moment's consideration I put on a hooded sweatshirt too; I was shivering, and it wasn't just from the cold bathroom.

I sat on my bed in the room I shared with Polly. I could not stop myself rubbing my hands together. I felt restless and rather sick. I did not think I could face any dinner, though judging by the state of the table when my father and I had come home, the rest of the family had already eaten. It would probably not occur to Tuesday to worry about whether I had had anything.

'Lin?' Polly appeared in the doorway. 'Ru's asleep.'

I looked at her. 'Why do you do all that stuff, Polly? Tuesday ought to put him to bed.' My heart wasn't in it, though, and when Polly didn't reply I didn't push it.

Polly came and sat on the other bed. She looked tired, almost a little grey, but I noticed the fact without curiosity. My mind kept skipping back to that scene in the cemetery, like a worn recording with a jump in it. I had been standing there, with the afternoon sun hot on the side of my neck, and I had been looking at the flowers which were strewn over Herr Roggendorf's grave like vivid splotches of paint, and I had looked up and seen –

'. . . OK?'

'What?' I said stupidly.

'Are you OK?' Polly repeated patiently.

She was huddled inside an enormous knitted jumper which was too warm even for the evening. Dimly I wondered whether the chill which seemed to have crept into my bones was leaching itself into Polly too.

I gave her a smile which sagged limply across my face; even I could tell what a failure it was.

'I'm fine.'

'Do you want to – you know, talk about it?'

This was a generous offer from Polly, who recoiled from unpleasantness of any kind, who hated to face such things the way other people would hate to touch the warty back of a toad or a tumour. Polly's ideal world was one in which all nastiness had been covered over, like a snow plough smoothing out a ski run, shunting all the untidiness away and tamping it down until nothing remained but a smooth surface, absolutely clean and pure white and glistening.

'Not really,' I said.

It didn't occur to me to ask *her* how she was, why she looked so tired, why she was swaddled up in a heavy pullover on a warm early-autumn evening. I was still too preoccupied with what I had seen earlier; I was thinking about that moment when I had realized that the person peeping at me over the tombstone was not a live person at all. And I was thinking about what Michel had said, about there being broken glass on the ground. Was he telling the truth? I had not noticed the glass – if it was really there – and nothing would have induced me to go back and look.

I remembered how Michel had seemed so alien when he had come out of the cemetery and spoken to me with his heavily accented English. I had tried to keep my distance from the start, but that moment had opened a gulf between us. If he had been lying about the glass, he was part of the monstrous thing that was already taking shape in some dark corner of my mind. And even if he were not, if he were simply reporting the truth, that once again a body had been found with glittering shards of glass littered all about it – what then?

I couldn't help it. My mind kept jumping back to that long-ago day in my father's study at home, when I had been so terrified by the woodcut of Bonschariant climbing out of the window. It was ridiculous – it was impossible – clearly if there were any connection between the deaths and my father's hunt for the Allerheiligen glass it was because someone *wanted* us to make that connection. Human hands had strewn the broken glass around, like the dragon's teeth of legend, which once sown would grow into warriors – only these warriors were Rumour and Fear.

That was what I told myself, and yet dark imaginings gnawed at the edges of my rational mind. Long after Polly had gone downstairs I stayed on my bed, hugging my knees and gazing into the sunlight which streamed through the bedroom window. The sun was low in the sky and its rays seemed to blaze through the panes, gilding every reflective surface in the room – the oval mirror standing on top of a chest of drawers and the glazed pictures on every wall.

So much glass, I thought. It was everywhere. It's not something I had ever thought about before; I had just taken it for granted, though a thousand years ago it would have been a rarity. Even five hundred years ago, when Gerhard Remsich had designed his masterpiece for the cloister of the Allerheiligen Abbey, glass was a rare and costly thing. Small wonder that legends had sprung up about it among the poor, for whom it represented a glimpse of magic in their drab lives. For those who had seen the lives of the saints and the miracles of God portrayed in brilliant and glowing colours, it was a short step to imagining that something more than human might step right *out* of the glass and into their own reality. Could they have imagined that centuries later there would be glass *everywhere*? That every home, every shop, every school would be glazed with it, not just the houses of the rich?

It was a strangely chilling thought. Logically, I knew that there could be no such creature as Bonschariant, yet I couldn't help thinking that if there were, he would have an infinite number of passages into our world.

CHAPTER TWENTY-ONE

The next day Michel picked me up again at the same time. I was waiting for him outside the green gate. Tuesday had evidently heard the honk of the horn the morning before. 'I hope he's not going to do that *every* morning,' she had said severely, as though there were a dying person in the house whose comfort required that straw be laid outside and the hooves of passing horses be muffled. It was not Tuesday's comfort I was thinking of, though. I felt the need to be prepared for Michel's inevitable curiosity about my father's comment of the day before. I thought that if I got in first with a question of my own I might be able to head him off altogether, at least until we got to school and I could escape.

I opened the car door with brisk smartness and slid into the passenger seat. '*Morgen*,' I said in a determinedly cheerful voice.

'*Morgen*.'

My heart sank; Michel seemed in no hurry to drive off. He had turned in his seat and was studying me with those mud-coloured eyes as though he were somehow assessing me. I had a horrible feeling that that was exactly what he was doing. I dumped my bag on the floor at my feet and ducked my head for a moment, as though I was checking I had everything with me; anything rather than sit there staring into Michel's eyes.

'Shouldn't we get going?' I said in German.

After a second's pause, during which I still had the uncomfortable feeling that I was being appraised, Michel put the car into gear and we moved off.

'Your father –' began Michel, but I was determined not to let him get the question out.

'Your brother,' I cut in smartly, 'does he go to the same school as we do?'

'No.'

'I just wondered, because your dad –' I glanced at Michel and faltered. He was clearly nonplussed at my sudden fictitious interest in his brother. 'Your dad said he didn't drive you – but he didn't say what your brother does.'

Michel didn't say anything for a moment and I had the impression that he was trying to decide how to reply.

'Has he got his own car too?' I asked eventually, when it became apparent that I was not going to get an answer.

'Jörg's finished school,' said Michel shortly.

'Oh.' I was checked for a moment, but I dared not let the silence stretch out in case Michel reverted to the subject of my father's remark. 'Is he away studying or does he still live here?'

A memory flashed across my mind; seeing an upstairs window at the farm suddenly closed by unseen hands.

'He's not studying.' Michel didn't say what his brother did instead.

I began to feel vaguely irritated at his reluctance to speak. I wasn't really interested in Jörg; I had only asked in an attempt to steer the conversation away from my habit of stumbling over corpses. Now, however, I had the distinct feeling that Michel was keeping something from me and out of sheer pique I persisted.

'Well, what does he do, then?'

A tightening of Michel's jawline showed that he was irritated too.

'He just helps Dad,' he said in an uncompromising, ask-me-no-more tone.

With what? I wondered. Did the two of them patrol the woods night and day, accompanied by that monster of a dog?

'But, Lin . . .'

I could see the question coming. I cast around for some other topic to thrust like a stick into the spokes of the conversation, but it was no use.

'Your dad – when we were outside the police station yesterday, he said something about corpses. Not one corpse, but *corpses*.'

'Did he?'

Michel took his eyes off the track ahead for long enough to give me a very pointed look.

'What did he mean?'

'He was just . . .' I searched vainly for the German expression for *figure of speech*, and finally gave up. 'It was just a silly joke. It doesn't mean anything.'

'Then why –'

'Look,' I said irritably, 'it didn't mean anything, OK?'

I had inadvertently raised my voice. I saw Michel's eyebrows go up and regretted it; this was hardly going to smooth the topic over.

'I'm sorry,' I said hastily. 'It's just – I'm still upset about yesterday. I don't really want to talk about it.'

'Sorry,' said Michel, so promptly and with such a contrite look that I almost felt guilty.

I squashed the feeling. I still didn't know whether he had been telling me the truth about what he had seen in the cemetery. I suspected that a struggle was taking place here, only half-seen and half-understood – a struggle between my father, with Herr Mahlberg's shade at his shoulder, desperate to lay hands on the lost glass, and a person or persons unseen who were determined that he shouldn't. Michel might look at me with the yearning expression of a dieter at a patisserie window, but that didn't mean he was on my side.

Chapter Twenty-two

If I had hoped that dressing down for my second day at school would allow me to slip under the radar of class attention, I was doomed to disappointment. Evidently the tale of the grisly discovery in the Baumgarten town cemetery had spread with the deadly swiftness of an airborne disease. As Michel and I walked across the foyer of the school I was already aware of heads turning in our direction and a few elbows working like pistons as their owners alerted their friends to our presence. I tried not to look their way, but I couldn't resist scanning the foyer briefly for a glimpse of Father Engels.

He was nowhere to be seen. Perhaps he was only ever at the school on certain days of the week. Perhaps he would be in later, or tomorrow. For a few moments I allowed myself to drift off into an interesting reverie in which, despite my parents' religion being registered as 'none' on all the official forms, I somehow ended up in the Catholic religion class and was able to sit in the front row, where Father Engels would notice me (in spite of the nondescript clothes I had on today) and be strangely struck by my appearance (although he dared not show it). The interminable monologues my father used to deliver over the dinner table about various staggeringly uninteresting medieval saints would finally come in handy, as Father Engels would ask the class which order St Bernard of Clairvaux had belonged to, and I would be the only one to reply correctly that it was the Cistercians. And then Father Engels would turn to me and say . . .

'Is it true, then?' said a loud voice in German.

The owner of the voice was barring our way. Jerked gracelessly out of my pleasing daydream, I found myself looking at a boy of mountainous proportions, a solid mass of adipose stuffed into sagging jeans and a distinctly grubby sweatshirt with BAP stencilled on the front of it. Porcine eyes stared down at me over the bulging slabs of his cheeks.

'Is what true, Hendrich?' said Michel. His voice sounded terse and somehow rougher than before; I guessed he was sliding into *Platt*, the local dialect.

'What you and *she* –' he nodded at me – 'found in the cemetery.'

'And what was that?' asked Michel calmly.

'Don't be stupid, Reinartz. So?'

'So what?'

'So is it true?'

'Yes, it's true,' said Michel. He looked the boy in the eyes. 'Now can you get out of my way?'

'You,' said Hendrich to me, giving up on Michel. He leaned over me and I caught a whiff of whatever sugary thing he had stuffed himself with for breakfast, a waffle or a doughnut. 'You speak German?'

'Of course she does,' interjected Michel.

He grabbed me by the arm and began to manoeuvre me past the boy. I shook my dark hair out of my eyes and gave Hendrich a good glare but I didn't say anything. Let him think I couldn't speak German, if he would only leave me alone.

In the classroom it was no better. I tried to slide around the door frame and into the room without being noticed, but I was wasting my time. The bell rang and Frau Schäfer bustled into the room before anyone could come and ask me about what had happened the day before, but about ten minutes into the first lesson, when I was struggling to work out what part of German grammar the *Prädikat* was, I felt a dig in my ribs. The next second a small piece of paper, carefully folded, was slipped on to the open pages of my book. I looked up and caught the eye of Johanna, the red-haired girl who sat next to me. She looked away, ostentatiously facing the front. I looked down at the piece of paper and then I very carefully unfolded it and read the message scrawled on it in German with pink fineliner.

Is it true?

I folded the piece of paper back into a tiny square and slid it into my pocket, doing my best to ignore the surreptitious dig Johanna gave me with her elbow. At the front of the class, Frau Schäfer was holding forth about Schiller's *Don Carlos* with the dogged look of Polly trying to feed spinach to a recalcitrant Ru. I did my best to maintain an expression of earnest interest, but my mind was elsewhere, skittering all over the events of the past twenty-four hours like the fingers of a climber trying to find a purchase on an impossible rock face.

That I was once again the unwilling centre of attention was clear. I marvelled at the speed with which the tale of yesterday's horror had spread, and wondered how it had got out so quickly. *Perhaps it didn't get out*, said a niggling voice at the back of my brain as I let my gaze wander over my fellow pupils, over the rows of studiously bent backs. *Perhaps they were expecting it. Perhaps they* knew *it would happen.*

The thought chilled me. Did everyone except me know what was going on? I sneaked a glance at Johanna, whose face was resolutely turned towards the front of the class, so that all I could see was her profile, the straight nose and slight overbite, the sprinkling of freckles on her cheekbones. Was she trying to be friendly, with her little scrawled note, or was she fishing, to see whether I had got the message, whatever that message was – *go home, stop looking for the glass, stop now or it'll be the worse for you*?

The boy two rows in front who kept turning round to look back towards my desk, was he a friend or would-be friend of Johanna's? Was the smirk for me or for her? And the two blonde girls sitting together near the window, what were they whispering to each other? I very much doubted that they were discussing Schiller's contribution to Weimar Classicism.

I bit my lip, wondering whether I should try to brush off the inevitable questions as Michel had brushed off the objectionable Hendrich; on the other hand, I reflected, it might be an opportunity to ask some questions of my own.

When the bell rang, Johanna got to her feet without looking at me and began to stuff books into her bag. I guessed that she was slightly offended that I had not replied to her note.

'Johanna?' I said, conscious of the pairs of ears twitching on every side. I felt in my pocket for the folded piece of paper. 'This . . . did you mean what happened in the cemetery yesterday?'

I had kept my voice down as much as I could, but all the same I saw a boy at the next desk pause in the action of packing his bag; when he resumed it was much more slowly. Clearly he was not keen to get away if there was the prospect of some revelation in view.

Johanna nodded. 'Is it true, then? That there was a dead guy? Did you *see* it?'

'Mmm-hmm.'

'Was it – I mean, was he – was it *yucky*?'

I felt a retort rising to my lips at that: *No, he looked as though he'd just fallen asleep. His relatives would've been touched.*

'Not so bad,' I said. 'More of a skeleton than anything.'

'Wow. Did you scream? I would've.'

'Like a pig.'

'*Really?*'

Now I regretted saying it. By lunchtime the whole school would think that that weird new English girl had not only seen the body in the cemetery, but she had screamed so loudly that she could be heard in Nordkirchen. I pushed on anyway. I had to know whether Michel had been lying about the glass or not, and I couldn't think of anyone else I could ask. It meant taking a risk – I was still not sure whether the note Johanna had passed me was an overture of friendship or a sly taunt – but it had to be a thousand times better than asking someone like Hendrich.

'Look, Johanna – this is a bit strange, but . . . in the cemetery, Michel said there was glass all round the body.'

Johanna had been sliding the last of her belongings into her bag as we spoke. Abruptly she froze and turned a wide-eyed face to me.

'What?' I said instantly.

'You *are* joking, aren't you?'

'No, I'm serious.'

'*Scheisse.*' I watched her shiver, hugging herself.

I put out a hand and touched her shoulder. 'Johanna, what *is* it?'

She eyed me warily. 'It's – there are these stories. You wouldn't understand.'

She picked up a handful of pens and slipped them into her bag. In another moment she would be gone and I would have lost the opportunity to question her.

'About Bonschariant? The Glass Demon?' I gave her a straight look, which she did her best to avoid. 'Look, I know about that. My dad's studying the Allerheiligen glass, remember? But that's just an old story. There are no such things as –'

'Maybe not,' said Johanna. She sounded almost angry. 'And there are no such things as ghosts either, right? But you still wouldn't want to spend the night in a cemetery, would you?'

I didn't think I would *ever* want to enter one again, even in daylight, I reflected, trying unsuccessfully to push away the images which presented themselves whenever I remembered that terrible moment by Herr Roggendorf's grave. Johanna must have taken my momentary silence as an admission of guilt.

'You made it up, didn't you?' she snapped.

I shook my head. 'No, honestly.'

'And you saw this glass with your own eyes?'

'Well, no, I didn't. Michel saw it.'

'Michel Reinartz?'

I nodded. 'I was so shocked I didn't notice it. Michel told me it was there.'

With an air of brisk finality Johanna picked up her bag and swung it on to her shoulder. 'Don't believe anything he tells you,' she said. She gave a quick glance about her, as if to see who was listening in to our conversation. The boy who had been eavesdropping caught her eye and hastily moved away. Johanna looked back at me and there was a hard expression in her pale eyes. 'You can't trust a word he says, that Michel Reinartz.' The corners of her mouth puckered. 'I'd stay right away from him if I were you . . . him and that brother of his.'

'What's wrong with his brother?' I asked.

Johanna made a face, as though she had bitten into something rotten. 'What's right?' she said.

CHAPTER TWENTY-THREE

It was a week later, and autumn was very definitely in the air, when I came home from school just in time to hear my father say, 'She was found dead right there, in front of the glass, and she was only sixteen.'

'Who was found dead?' I said, stopping in my tracks with my bag halfway off my shoulder.

'Oh, it's some disgusting story of Oliver's about those stained-glass windows,' said Tuesday. She was painting her fingernails an alarming shade of turquoise. Now she spread out her fingers to show me.

'Horrible. You look cyanotic,' I said.

Tuesday gave me an evil look. 'You're as bad as he is. Such revolting ideas.' She picked up the brush and began to attack the other hand.

'Dad? Who was found dead?' I asked again, ignoring her.

'The abbot's niece,' said my father. He was holding a small hardback book in a faded green binding; now he flourished it at me and I was able to see the Gothic print stamped on the spine in gold, although it was impossible to read what it said from where I stood. 'This is a fascinating book,' he added. 'You should read it.'

I didn't take the bait. One glimpse of the Gothic title had convinced me that trying to read even a single page in that typeface would be like picking your way through a thicket of thorn bushes. Even if you got to the other side you would wish you hadn't tried it.

'What happened to the abbot's niece?' I said.

'Someone cut her throat,' said my father. He saw Tuesday making a face and grinned wolfishly. 'With a piece of glass,' he added for good measure.

'When?' I demanded bluntly.

'Cool it. About four hundred and fifty years ago.'

I dropped my bag on to the floor. 'So we don't need to call the police, then?'

My father ignored this piece of sarcasm. 'This is a fantastic story. Did you know that there has been a whole string of deaths connected to the Allerheiligen glass?'

He sounded thrilled. I supposed that he was already envisaging a new and glossy book which would be even more successful than the last one; it would be just as racy, only this time instead of SEX in the title it would have DEATH.

I went over to the table and cast a doubtful eye over the remains of the lunch. 'So who killed the abbot's niece?' I asked, picking out a cherry tomato from the limp remains of a salad still huddled in the bottom of the plastic carton it had been sold in. 'And what was she doing in front of the stained glass anyway?'

'That's the point,' said my father. 'Nobody knows. She probably wasn't his niece either – that was a euphemism. But according to the story she was only sixteen and very beautiful. They say she was so lovely that the master craftsman Gerhard Remsich used her as the model for one of his windows, the one showing the Queen of Heaven. Some say he was in love with her himself.'

I bit into the tomato; it was unpleasantly soft.

'She died the night before Gerhard Remsich was supposed to show the completed glass to the abbot of Allerheiligen. It had taken much longer to create than expected – there were all sorts of difficulties. The window showing the Ascension of Christ into heaven was mysteriously smashed. One of Remsich's apprentices died after apparently ingesting silver nitrate, a poisonous substance used in the making of yellow glass. And there were all sorts of complaints from the work-men – that tools were going missing and that someone was trying to hinder the work.'

My father was warming to his theme, imagining no doubt the laudatory reviews of the book as yet unborn. Tuesday was absorbed in applying a second coat of brilliant turquoise to her nails and probably hadn't taken in a single word. It seemed that I was the only one to be chilled by what he was saying. *A whole string of deaths*. And the hindrances which the workmen had experienced – was I the only one who could see history repeating itself in the way that my father was being frustrated in his search for the glass? With an effort I made myself concentrate on what he was saying.

'Remsich was to show the completed series of windows to Abbot Thomas after terce, the morning prayers. But an hour before the prayers had even begun, a servant came running from the cloister, screaming, "Murder." When the monks investigated, they found the body of the girl lying in a pool of blood, in front of a window showing Job being mocked by his wife. Her throat had been cut from ear to ear.'

I shuddered. 'That's horrible.'

'Yes, isn't it?' said my father, with satisfaction. 'The monks of that order wore white habits and they say that fully two inches of the hems of their robes were red from the blood on the flagstones. They never found the murder weapon. There was a rumour that the killer cut the girl's throat with a piece of glass and disposed of it in the glassmaker's furnace. The abbot, however, said that it was the work of the Devil and wrote to his brother abbot at Steinfeld for advice.'

'And what did the abbot of Steinfeld say?' I asked.

'He said that Abbot Thomas should tear down the stained-glass windows and have every one of them smashed,' said my father. He smiled slyly. 'But I think the fact that the Aller-heiligen windows were rumoured to be even more fabulous than the Steinfeld ones may have had something to do with it.'

I picked up another tomato but it was as pulpy as the first. I put it down again.

'Where did you get the book?' I asked.

'Herr Krause,' said my father. 'He came over again this morning – to see how I was getting on.' His voice was dry; I could imagine how Herr Krause's fussy offers of help and thinly disguised inquisitiveness had been received. 'He still says the glass was destroyed. I think he was put out that I didn't take his word for it.' My father flourished a piece of paper. 'In fact, when he turned up I was writing to Herr Mahlberg's executors to ask whether I can have access to his papers.' The corners of his mouth turned up ironically. 'Herr Krause was quite put out.'

I could well imagine it; my father never spared anyone else's sensibilities when it came to academic arguments.

'Anyway,' continued my father, 'he brought all these.' He

patted a stack of books which were piled up on one of the dining chairs.

I thought they looked unappetizingly dusty, and if they were all in that terrible Gothic typeface it would take my father years to read them all. A thought struck me.

'How did you find that story – the one about the abbot's niece?'

'Herr Krause.'

'That was –' I struggled to think what to say – 'nice of him.'

I wondered if Herr Krause was expecting his name to appear on the cover of the new book, as joint author, or even in the acknowledgements. I suspected he did; he was altogether a different type of creature from my father – a benign and placid sheep with no conception of the desires and impulses of the wolf. Very likely he expected his share of the fame and fortune to come, not realizing that when my father feasted not the slightest scrap was permitted to fall from the table.

'Hmm,' said my father, without much interest in Herr Krause's benevolence. He put the book down on the table. 'It's a great story,' he added. He sounded cheerful – the abbot's niece's misfortune was his gain.

'The slaughter of the innocent,' I suggested.

My father glanced at me. 'That's just what Herr Krause said.'

CHAPTER TWENTY-FOUR

After the exchange with my father I went outside; I was very alert to the danger of being roped into helping to read the stack of mouldy-looking books thoughtfully supplied by Herr Krause.

I wandered back to the green gate and looked out, in time to see Polly emerge from the forest. She was pushing Ru's buggy; Ru was asleep in it, slumped over to one side and with his mouth firmly corked with one thumb. I went over to meet her. She was pallid and her fair hair was sticking to the side of her face.

'Hi, Polls. Why have you got that jumper on? You must be boiling.'

'I wasn't when I went out.' She didn't seem inclined to discuss it.

I looked past her, at the green darkness of the forest. Under the canopy of trees something shifted in the mosaic of light and dark: a bird fluttering through the undergrowth, perhaps, or the wind moving the branches so that the pattern of sunlight and shade moved kaleidoscopically.

'Where did you go?' I asked her, conscious that I was beginning to sound like an interrogator.

There was nothing concretely *sinister* to see out there in

the forest and yet I felt obscurely uncomfortable at the thought of my sister walking through it alone, pushing Ru in his buggy over the rutted track. It would not be easy to move quickly pushing a child in a buggy, if something happened to alarm you.

'Just up the track a bit.' Polly shrugged. 'That guy, whatever his name is, the one who came once before and told Dad the glass had been destroyed –'

'Herr Krause,' I supplied.

'Yes, him. He turned up again and Ru wouldn't stop howling, so Tuesday told me to take him outside for a bit.'

I looked up the track in the direction she had come from. Perhaps a hundred metres from where we stood, a rabbit suddenly broke cover, dashed across the track and disappeared into the undergrowth, its tail a brief white flash.

'Polly . . .' I looked back at her. 'Don't you think . . .' My voice trailed off.

I had been about to ask her whether she didn't think the woods were a little creepy, but I was aware how lame that sounded. I could hardly tell my sister not to stroll in the woods simply because the thought of it made the hair on the back of my neck stand up. Perhaps that feeling I sometimes had, of being watched by unseen eyes, was simply overactive imagination on my part.

'I don't think you should go too far into the woods,' I said eventually. 'You know the time I walked to Michel's and I met his dad? That dog is vicious, and he doesn't have it on a lead.'

'I didn't go that far.'

Polly sounded uninterested. She was bending over Ru, brushing an insect off his trouser leg.

'Polly?'

This time she looked up, perhaps hearing the tension in my voice. Her grey eyes seemed very pale in the autumn sunshine, and for the first time I noticed that she had grown thinner. I could see cheekbones emerging from the form of her face, as if a completely new Polly were appearing, as though the clay from which she was made were being reshaped. I wondered whether the move to Germany had troubled her more than I thought; just because she had an escape route planned didn't mean that the upheaval hadn't affected her. It was hard to tell with Polly. Such things seemed to disappear to some hidden place inside her, like stones dropping into the dark depths of a well.

I suppose I had been studying her face for longer than I thought, because when she spoke she sounded faintly impatient.

'Lin? What?'

Polly was staring at me with her eyebrows raised. Hastily I reverted to the original subject.

'Look, there's something going on, I'm sure of it. That's why I don't think you should go into the woods alone. I'm not sure it's safe.'

'Because of the dog? Honestly, Lin, I didn't go that far.'

'No, not because of the dog. Well, not *just* because of it.' I ran my hands through my hair. 'The day the tree caught fire – I don't think it was an accident. Remember there was all that broken glass lying in the ashes?'

Polly didn't react; a closed look was coming over her face, a look I recognized. Something unpleasant was rearing its head and Polly would rather not have known. I persisted anyway.

'That thing I saw in the cemetery – there was broken glass there too. Michel saw it. And there was glass on the ground when we found that man in the orchard.' I didn't say *that dead man*; I was afraid Polly would shut me out completely if I said that. 'And when we found out about Herr Mahlberg, the guy who wrote to Dad about the glass, Frau Kessel – that was the old bag in the post office, the one who told us – she said they found glass all over the floor in his bathroom too.'

'So?'

Polly began to fuss over Ru, checking the straps on the buggy, smoothing a strand of sweaty hair from his forehead, making a show of being too busy to listen. I guessed that she was hoping I would give up, that I would simply conclude that whatever person from the Baumgarten town council was responsible for collecting glass for recycling was pathologically clumsy.

'So there must be a connection. I think someone's trying to threaten us.'

'But we didn't even know that man in the orchard,' said Polly. She sounded almost sulky.

'I know. But don't you think it's strange, the glass being there?'

'Maybe. But I don't know what you want *me* to do about it.'

'Help me. We could try to find out who the old man was. We could try to find Frau Kessel again – she said she lives in Münstereifel, wherever that is. Maybe she knows more about what happened to Herr Mahlberg.'

Certainly it seemed a good bet that if anyone knew what was going on it would be her; I had recognized that quality in her the moment she had asked us whether we were the

English professor and his daughter. I suspected that living next door to Frau Kessel would be like living next door to the FBI.

'But I can't speak German,' Polly objected.

'You could come with me anyway. You might see something I missed. And, Polly, I don't think I could go back to that cemetery on my own.' I gazed at her beseechingly. 'Please, Polls.'

'I don't know . . .'

'We can't just ignore all this stuff. People are dead. Supposing someone tries to – to do something to one of us next?'

I realized my mistake when I saw Polly's expression. We had veered over an invisible line into hostile territory. Polly's reaction was to shut it out, like a person walking through some terrible scene of carnage, looking neither left nor right because they know that if they do it will turn their brain.

'I'm sorry, Lin.' Polly hesitated; she hated to say no, even over something like this. 'There must be some other reason for those things. It can't have anything to do with us.'

I won't let it have anything to do with us, said her tone. A small furrow had appeared between her brows.

'Polly –'

'Anyway, in a few weeks I'm going to be going to Italy, remember?' She grasped the handles of the buggy and began to move Ru slowly back and forth, as though lulling him, although Ru was so fast asleep I doubted whether he would have woken up even if there had been an earthquake. 'Look – I have to get Ru inside.'

This was a blatant excuse; Ru didn't care whether he slept out here, inside the castle or on the wing of a biplane. I chewed my lip, trying not to let the frustration show on my face.

Before I could think of another tack, Polly said, 'We'll stay out of the woods if you're that bothered about it. It's useless trying to take the buggy in there anyway.' She looked at me. 'And if you really think it's *that* important, I'll stick to the main track when I'm running, OK?'

'Polly, can't we even –'

I gave up. She was already pushing the buggy forward, aiming for the green gate. I turned to watch her go in, a hard fist of resentment tightening in my chest. If I couldn't rely on Polly, then whom could I ask for help?

The buggy's front wheel caught against a stone and I saw Polly struggle with it. She looked a little pink in the face, and warmer than ever; why was she still wearing that stupid jumper? The sight of it simply made me feel more irritable. I wanted to shake her. I wanted her to march into the house and tell Tuesday to take Ru out herself next time, and while she was at it, to give him his bath and feed him too, instead of palming it all off on her. I wanted her to tell Tuesday to stuff her friends in Italy and stuff the history of art – she was going to bum around Asia for a year, or go and count gorillas in Africa. Most of all I wanted her to get angry, and make a scene, and not bury her head in the sand any more. *I* would have done it. I knew *she* wouldn't do it, and it exasperated me. I loved her for it, but sometimes I felt like screaming at her too. So I watched her go with the poisonous taste of resentment in my throat and I didn't think any more about that jumper, other than that it was typical Polly that she wouldn't even think of her own comfort.

CHAPTER TWENTY-FIVE

Two days later Michel failed to turn up in the morning. I stood outside the green gate with my bag, shivering a little in the fresh autumn air, and watching pale tendrils of mist seeping through the trees. Normally Michel was punctual; sometimes he was even waiting for me. Today there was no sign of him when I came out of the house, and after I had been waiting for a few minutes I realized that he was actually late. I looked at my watch; it was twenty-five to eight. If he did not turn up soon we would both miss the start of school. I listened, but there was no sound of an approaching car. All I could hear was birdsong and once, briefly, a harsh cry which might have been the bark of a fox.

At twenty to eight I went back into the house and with some trepidation roused my father. Neither he nor Tuesday was an early riser and it was difficult to make him understand that we needed to leave now, urgently. He seemed to take an age to get dressed and when he came downstairs he was muttering about coffee.

'Dad, we have to *go*.'

I watched him stumbling about like a sleepwalker. Clearly I was going to be very late. For a brief moment I considered writing a note to the school excusing myself for the day and signing it in Tuesday's hand, but then I realized there was no one to take it to school for me. The prospect of making myself conspicuous in the classroom again made me frantic. I cursed Michel inwardly. What was he playing at?

In the event I reached the school half an hour late and had to endure Frau Schäfer's grim reminders that lessons began at eight sharp. It was not until I was finally sitting in my seat next to Johanna, who was pointedly engrossed in her work, that I realized I had not made any arrangement for my father to pick me up after school.

During the morning break I scoured the foyer and the crowd around the vending machine for Michel but could not spot him anywhere. Eventually a familiar corpulent figure broke away from the others and lumbered over to me; it was Hendrich. I didn't need to smell that caries-laden breath to know that he had been gorging himself on something with chocolate in it; it was smeared on the sleeve of his grubby sweatshirt.

'You looking for Michel Reinartz?'

I looked at him silently. Naturally he took this to mean that I could not understand what he was saying. He repeated the question, this time more loudly.

'Mmm-hmm,' I said, trying to sound as non-committal as possible. The prospect that Hendrich might think I was *missing* Michel, or, worse, that he would drop this surmise into the current of gossip which ran through the school, like a hippo releasing a turd into a fast-flowing river, was too grisly to contemplate. I did my best to look as though I was completely indifferent to Michel's whereabouts.

'He didn't come to school today,' Hendrich informed me, observing me slyly for signs of disappointment.

'Really?' I said, and turned my back on him.

Michel still could've called me, I thought irritably, and then realized that he couldn't; there was no signal in the forest. I supposed he was sick. At any rate, it seemed he wasn't deliberately avoiding me.

I asked around before lessons restarted. Nobody was prepared to take me right back to the castle, but I found someone who was willing to drop me off at the village of Traubenheim, which lay on the other side of the woods. From there I would have to walk.

It was cool that morning, but later when my lift dropped me off at Traubenheim it was quite warm. After I had been walking for ten minutes I had to take my jacket off and carry it over my arm. The leaves of the beech trees which intermingled with the pines had not yet turned golden and the sunlight glowed green through them. My geography of the forest was still imperfect but I knew that the track from Traubenheim ran nowhere near the Reinartzes' land, where that monstrous dog roamed like a Minotaur lurking in a maze. This part of the forest seemed unthreatening.

My spirits lifted. I kicked up dust with the toes of my boots and felt the breeze lifting the ends of my hair, and smiled in spite of myself, enjoying a moment of absurd happiness. Annoyance and anxiety melted away; it was impossible not to feel good, any more than a plant can help itself growing towards the light. When I finally came out from the forest and strolled towards the castle gate, I was actually singing under my breath.

I was just stepping into the courtyard when I heard it: far off in the woods, a long drawn-out howl. If I hadn't known better I might have thought it was a wolf. But there were no more wolves in Germany – were there? I listened but the sound had died away, replaced with a silence that was somehow ominous.

The next moment the sound from the woods was forgotten. Polly was standing outside the house, close to the open front door, with her back to the wall. Her knees were sagging under her as though she would have collapsed without its support. Her face was ashen.

'*Polly?*'

She looked at me but said nothing.

'What's the matter? What's happened?'

'Did you see him?' she said in a choked voice. She was trembling.

'Who?'

She just shook her head helplessly. Her hands moved to her stomach; I guessed she was feeling sick.

'Where's Dad?'

Polly didn't even try to answer this time; she just pointed at the door. I swung my bag off my shoulder and hurried inside.

The scene which met my eyes was like some horrible parody: Dutch Interior with Sacrifice. The table had clearly been laid for lunch. There were three plates still on it, with the remains of food on them, and a fourth on the floor in pieces. A large piece of ham had been set out on a blue-and-white platter beside my father's place; there was a carving knife next to it on the table, but the fork still stuck out of the ham's back, as though it were a bull lanced by a picador. Next to the ham was a plastic tub of salad. There was a half-full bottle of Dornfelder and two wine glasses, one of them smeared with lipstick. I saw all these things but did not really notice them. I was looking at the thing in the centre of the table, the thing which had clearly landed there with some force, because one of the wine glasses was on its side, the dregs of the red wine forming a dark pool on the table and mixing with some other, more sinister-looking stains.

For a moment I could not work out what it was, the wedge-shaped thing sitting in the middle of the table, its surface marbled black and red, a single fly buzzing about it. I could see a horn, curling in a ridged spiral like an ammonite. There was a protuberance with a dull sheen to it which I queasily recognized as an eye.

It was the head of a ram. As I gazed at it, a second fly droned in through the open doorway and landed on the animal's nose. I saw it crawl into the nostril and disappear.

There was a smothered exclamation from the corner of the room. I jumped; I had thought I was alone. Now I saw that my father was standing there, with his back to the wall. He had one arm across his body, as though defending himself, and his other hand to his face. He looked as sick as Polly had. I scanned the room and realized that Tuesday was there too. She was curled into one of the battered armchairs, her feet tucked under her as if she were a little child. Ru was in her arms; she was holding him tightly to her, his little face buried in her neck.

It was some time before I could get enough sense out of any of them to understand what had happened. A scruffily dressed man – 'a lunatic,' said my father – had stormed into the house, and flung the ram's head, mangled and bloody, on to the dinner table. And then he had told my father and Tuesday that he would kill us all if we didn't get out.

CHAPTER TWENTY-SIX

'He really said he'd *kill* us?' I asked Tuesday for the fifth time.

It was half an hour since I had arrived home, but I was still having difficulty taking it all in. I was numb with shock. This was something different from mysterious fires which might or might not have been started deliberately, or unknown Germans whose deaths – though tragic – might have been accidental. Those things bore as much resemblance to what had just happened as a horror film does to newsreel footage of a disaster. This was *real*.

My father had finally roused himself from his shocked inertia and driven into Baumgarten to summon the police. The rest of us were huddled in the kitchen. Even if we could have borne to touch the bloodied head of the ram, we suspected it ought to stay where it was until the police came. All the same, none of us wanted to stay in the living room, where the blank gaze of those filmy eyes seemed to follow you around and the air was thick with the buzzing of flies.

'Well, it's *obvious* that was what he was saying,' said Tuesday. She had given Ru up to Polly and was clutching a mug of hot sweet tea as though it were some life-preserving elixir.

'He was yelling the place down. He sounded absolutely insane.'

'Are you *sure*?' It was almost too much for me to take in.

'Of course I'm sure.' Tuesday glared at me, her feelings finding vent in the familiar groove of irritation at my behaviour. She made a sweeping gesture which caused the bracelets on her skinny arm to clank together. 'He was *rabid*. Ask Polly.'

I glanced at Polly, but her face was turned away from me. She was hugging Ru as though both their lives depended on it, her face pressed close to his neck. She seemed to be murmuring something to him in a low voice, over and over again, comforting him. Somehow this made me uncomfortable. She must have been just as shocked as Tuesday, but she was not talking; she had retreated to a place within herself. As soon as I could get her away from Tuesday I would have to try to speak to her. For now, I needed to get to the bottom of what had happened.

'What exactly did he say?' I persisted. 'Did he –'

'I don't know,' snapped Tuesday irritably, cutting me off. 'He was shouting in German, of course. But it was obvious what he *meant*. He was completely *mad*.'

'But –'

'And don't tell me he wasn't,' continued Tuesday. 'He threw an animal's *head* on the table, for God's sake.' Her hands were shaking; tea slopped unnoticed on to the floor.

I sighed. It was difficult enough to get any useful information out of Tuesday at the best of times, and I could see that very soon she would have worked herself up into such a state of indignation that it would be impossible. I tried again.

'It must have been horrible for you,' I said sympathetically.

This tack generally worked well on Tuesday, who loved to talk about her feelings, and this occasion was no exception. It took another half-hour and several more cups of heavily sweetened tea before I had the whole story, but eventually I had pieced it all together.

The family were having a late lunch when it happened. My father was carving himself a slice of ham; Tuesday was sipping the Dornfelder; Polly as usual was supervising Ru. They were discussing a plan of my father's, to visit the offices of the archdiocese in Köln, which Tuesday thought she might combine with a shopping trip. They had been surprised to hear the courtyard gate bang and the next moment they had all heard someone crossing the courtyard with a quick, angry tread.

My father had put down the carving knife and turned to Tuesday to say something when the front door was flung open and a man had barged into the room, wild-eyed and red-faced, shouting something in furious German. He was followed by a younger man – Tuesday said he was about twenty, and 'he looked just as mad as the other one, only he wasn't shouting' – and an animal which Tuesday described as 'a wolf'.

Michel Reinartz Senior, I thought. It had to be him. The younger man might have been Michel's older brother.

Michel's father – if it *was* him – had strode right up to the table, until he was almost nose to nose with my father, and within a metre of Tuesday, who had recoiled from his unkempt appearance and the rank smell of body odour which roiled off him. A torrent of heavily accented German crashed over both of them with the battering force of a hurricane. My father, too stunned to know how to react, had put up a hand, as though trying to calm the man down, and the man had raised his own fist, aggressively, and they had seen for the first time what he was grasping in it: the severed head of the ram. He was holding it by one of the horns and flourishing it as though he meant to strike my father with it. Then suddenly he had hurled it down with all his force on to the centre of the table, where it had landed with a meaty thump, spilling wine and splashing unspeakable fluids on to the wooden surface.

By this time Ru had been screaming with fright, Polly was backed up against the sideboard, and the dog was snarling and rearing up, the whites of its eyes showing. Tuesday had uttered one short shriek when the man wheeled around and fixed her with a glare which silenced her in an instant.

'It was as though he was *angry* with me,' she said. 'So angry that he could have killed me.' Her voice shook.

He had raised his right hand and Tuesday clearly saw that the fingers were stained with congealed blood. He pointed at her, his filthy forefinger a few centimetres from her nose, and then he turned back to my father and thrust the finger towards him, stabbing the air as though he wanted to run my father through. His chest was heaving with exertion. He had paused for an instant, fixing the pair of them like a hellfire preacher with two sinners in his sights, and then he had spat out one sentence which was unmistakably a threat.

The next minute he was striding back out the way he had come, the dog at his heels. The younger man had lingered long enough to spit on the floor, then he had lumbered after them. During the entire time he had been in the house he had not uttered a word.

For a moment there had been a stunned silence. Then

Tuesday had flung herself at Ru and gathered him into her arms while bursting into a fit of hysterics which had probably frightened him as much as the violent intrusion. My father had sagged against the wall. Neither of them had thought to reassure Polly, who had stumbled out of the house as though the atmosphere inside was full of poison gas.

Tuesday could not repeat to me any of the German words used, nor could she say how long it had been between the men leaving and my arriving home. I judged it could not have been long, since no one had had time to gather their wits and go for help until after I got home, nor had I seen any sign of the men when I arrived. All the same, I remembered the distant howl in the forest and could not help shivering. If I had been a few minutes earlier, if someone had given me a lift back to the castle instead of letting me walk from Traubenheim, I might have run straight into them, all on my own.

CHAPTER TWENTY-SEVEN

My father returned from Baumgarten with a green-and-white police car in tow. The two cops inside looked bored and sceptical. One of them was the skinny one with the moustache whom I had seen at the cemetery; I thought his name was Esch. The other was a woman I had never seen before, whom he introduced as Polizeikommissarin Axer. She was taller than the officer with the moustache and perhaps ten kilograms heavier than he was; her uniform strained at the seams. She had bleached blonde hair which was too short for her heavy features and her face was bare of make-up. I could see her and Tuesday eyeing each other like members of inimical species.

When she saw the ram's head lying upside down on the dinner table, with a bloody stub of bone pointing at the ceiling, she gave a short grunt which might have been amusement or even approval. Herr Esch just looked at it as though it were nothing unusual at all, as though here in the Eifel it was perfectly normal for neighbours to drop in on each other at mealtimes and fling offal on to the table.

'*Schwarzköpfiges Fleischschaf,*' he said.

'What did he say? Does he know who it was?' whispered Tuesday to me.

'No,' I said shortly. 'He says it's a black-headed sheep.'

Herr Esch cleared his throat. 'May we sit down?' he asked in English.

'Do,' said Tuesday in a faint voice. She edged away from the dinner table; clearly she had no intention of sitting there herself.

Frau Axer was already opening a laptop on the corner furthest from the ram's head. Herr Esch pulled out a dining chair and settled himself on it. The head was within an arm's reach of him but he seemed unbothered.

He glanced around at us. 'Sit, please.'

I think we all had high hopes of that interview. All of us thought that it would lead to instant action, that the two men who had stormed into the house would be found and arrested for trespassing. My father, who had recovered his spirits slightly, was inclined to stand on his dignity as an academic. When Herr Esch called him *Herr Professor* he didn't correct him. He forthrightly expressed his opinion that the intrusion was an attempt to frighten him off his search for the Allerheiligen glass. Listening to him talking about pushing back the frontiers of knowledge, I felt rather disgusted; it sounded as though he were quoting from the book as yet unwritten. I could imagine him working the story up into a dramatic confrontation between himself and pitch-fork-bearing peasants in bloodstained lederhosen, a Gordon of Khartoum moment translated to the Eifel.

Tuesday, on the other hand, clung to the view that the two men were 'mad' and that they should be hauled away to a secure institution without further delay. She kept coming back to this viewpoint with the wearying regularity of a beast of burden which no longer knows how to plod anywhere except around the old familiar track.

Polly said very little, merely adding a quiet 'yes' or 'no' when asked to confirm something Tuesday or our father had said. I sat by her, holding her hand, which was as cold as marble. I had tried to put an arm round her, but she had instantly stiffened. I felt that she would have liked to disappear into the woolly jumper she was swaddled in.

As for me, I felt a certain sense of relief. The hostilities were out in the open at last. This was something concrete which the police could deal with. The charred bush, the broken glass scattered outside our door, these were things which might or might not have a meaning; sometimes I doubted their significance myself. But now the police would have to take action.

As I contributed what little I could to the story, I was conscious that this was the end between Michel and me. We were making a complaint about his father and brother. I imagined him glaring at me across a courtroom, his face blank with hate.

There was also the question of whether Michel had known what they were about to do. Perhaps that was the reason he had failed to turn up at school that morning; he wanted to place as much distance as he could between us. I thought of the time when he had asked me why my father wanted to find the Allerheiligen glass so badly, how he had seemed to be suppressing anger at my replies. Had he been fishing for information? The more I thought about it, the more likely it seemed. I should have listened to Johanna's words of warning. I began to feel the slow burn of anger. It would serve them all right, those Reinartzes, if the police arrested every single one of them, including Michel. Perhaps they would even impound that brute of a dog.

All of us waited for Herr Esch to say what he was going to do.

'Well,' he said at last, looking at my father very gravely, 'we will talk to them.'

There was a long silence.

'Talk to them?' said my father slowly. 'Aren't you going to arrest them?'

'It's difficult,' said Herr Esch.

'But you know who they are!' exploded my father.

'Your daughter says she knows who they are,' said Herr Esch, nodding at me. 'But you and your wife said that you had never seen either of them before, and your daughter wasn't in the house when they came.'

'We could identify them if we saw them again,' said my father. He scowled, his good looks suddenly saturnine. 'Damn it,' he said. 'They *threatened* us.'

'Yes,' said Herr Esch calmly. 'But what exactly did they threaten you with?'

'Well . . .' My father suddenly realized what Herr Esch was trying to say. 'I can't tell you the exact words,' he snapped. 'The man was raving like a lunatic. He wasn't coherent half the time.' He raked a hand through his hair. 'He could have been talking *Platt*. I can't repeat it word for word.' He glared at Herr Esch. 'It was obviously a threat from his tone.'

'*Herr Professor* –' began Herr Esch in a regretful voice, but my father didn't let him finish.

'Look.' He was on his feet now, his tone tight with suppressed fury. He thrust out an arm, pointing at the ram's head, which still lay upside down in the middle of the table. It was alive with flies now; when he swung his arm around half a dozen of them lifted into the air, droning, and then resettled on the raw meat of the neck. 'Look at that. Just look. You can't tell me that isn't a threat.' He was breathing heavily; I could see that he was working himself up into a rage. 'What other possible reason could there be for someone marching in here – into our *private* house – while we were eating and throwing *that* into the middle of the table? What other reason? Tell me that. Or is that normal round here? Maybe he thought we were having a pot-luck dinner or something?'

I saw Herr Esch's mouth set into a hard line at this piece of sarcasm. '*Herr Professor*,' he said coldly, 'this is not normal behaviour here. We will have to speak to Herr Reinartz and try to establish whether it was him and his son who came here, and with what purpose. Please –' he added, seeing that my father was about to interrupt again – 'be assured that we will do this. We will even investigate whether there is any evidence of cruelty against this – unfortunate animal.' His eyes moved to the ram's head. 'We will keep you informed.'

'That's it?' said my father. 'You'll keep us informed? There are madmen running about here – who knows what they'll try next time? And you're keeping us *informed*?' He shook his head in disbelief. 'We could be in danger. What are we supposed to do?'

Herr Esch looked him in the eye. At the other end of the table we heard Frau Axer shut the laptop with a faint *snap*.

'You could always leave,' said Herr Esch.

CHAPTER TWENTY-EIGHT

It never even entered my head to think that Michel would pick me up the following morning, now that the Reinartzes had come out and declared themselves our enemies. His absence the previous day told its own story.

Reluctantly my father agreed to drive me again. Both of us recognized the impossibility of Tuesday getting up early enough to do it; even so, I reflected, as I stood in the living room with my bag on my shoulder, impatiently tapping my foot and waiting for my father to come down, I was clearly in for a lot of 'late' marks. As I gazed up the stairs, willing my father to appear, I saw him cross the landing towards the bathroom. My heart sank. He was as fussy as an old-time film star about his appearance in public. If he was going to make himself look perfect every morning before we set off, I was going to miss the first lesson altogether every single day.

As the bathroom door closed I heard a faint sound from outside. I looked at my watch, then glanced at the front door. Surely not . . .

The next second a car horn sounded, once and then twice. Michel. He *had* come after all. It only took a split second for me to decide what to do. Michel was half a head taller than me and like his father he was lean but powerful-looking. None of this daunted me. I was burning with the cold fire of righteous anger: in my mind's eye I saw myself yanking open the car door and giving him a titanic slap across the face. A tangle of savage thoughts fought for supremacy in my brain. Michel had certainly known what his father was going to do – otherwise why had he avoided me the day it happened? But if the Reinartzes wanted us out, why had Michel even offered to drive me to school in the first place? It could only be that he wanted to pick my brains, hence the questions about my father's work. I had no idea what interest the Reinartzes had in stopping my father from searching for the glass, but I knew one thing: Michel had betrayed me. He must be stupid if he thought I was going to get into his car and just drive off with him as though nothing had happened. Or maybe he had come to gloat.

I dropped my school bag on the floor and went out of the front door without it, stalking swiftly across the courtyard on feet made hasty by anger. The green gate was open and I could see a glimpse of red bodywork on the other side. I thought that I would like to kick the side door of that tatty car in as well.

As I came out through the gate the horn was sounding for the third time. Somehow this simply made me angrier. Did he still think he could summon me like that? I balled my hand into a fist and banged it down hard on the roof of the Volkswagen as I rounded the back of it, hurting myself more than the car. Then I curled my fingers around the door handle and ripped the car door open.

'Lin?'

I could swear Michel jumped; he had not noticed me

coming out of the gate and going round the back of the car. He turned to me and I saw why.

He had the worst black eye I had ever seen. It had swollen up so much that the eye was almost closed, and the whole area was a terrible mass of deep purplish bruising, puffy and discoloured like some sickly overripe fruit. On his upper lip was a bloody cut that had barely scabbed over. He looked as though he had been in a car crash.

'Oh, my God.'

The force of my anger was instantly derailed, as though it had suddenly run out of track and I was plummeting into thin air. I took a step back. I couldn't help myself; he looked so terrible. I must have appeared totally aghast, because incredibly Michel tried to smile at me. The effect was horribly lopsided; the bruised side of his face was so swollen that it was almost immobile.

'Oh, my . . .' I could not stop myself gaping at him. 'What happened?'

'My dad,' said Michel grimly.

'*What?*' I was so shocked that I could hardly take it in. 'What did he . . . I mean why . . .' I shook myself. 'Look, can you wait a minute while I get my bag?'

I didn't wait for him to reply. I dashed back to the house and picked up my school bag. I had been formulating an explanation for my father in my head, but I needn't have worried. He was still upstairs in the bathroom. I rummaged quickly in my bag and found a sheet of paper and a marker. I wrote, *Don't need a lift, gone with Michel. Love, Lin* in big black letters and left it on the table where my father would see it when he came down. Then I slipped back out of the house as quietly as I could, closing the door carefully behind me. If he heard me go and came after me, I'd never get away.

As I slid into the passenger seat of the Volkswagen, Michel was already gunning the engine.

'We're going to be late,' he said.

I stared at him disbelievingly. 'So what?' I searched for words. 'Michel, did your dad *really* do that to you?'

Michel didn't reply. His gaze was fixed on the road ahead. He reached down to change into second gear and I glanced at his hand; the knuckles were scabbed over.

'Michel.' I reached out and put a hand on his arm. 'Michel, talk to me.'

Still he said nothing, but once we were far enough along the track that the castle had disappeared behind the trees, Michel slowed the car to a halt and switched off the ignition.

'Look, Lin . . .'

I could see that he was going to try to fob me off.

'Michel, your dad can't do that. You should go to the police or something.'

Even as I said this, I knew he wouldn't. And what if he did? Supposing they said the same to him as they had to us – that they'd 'talk' to Michel Reinartz Senior? We both knew that would be about as effective as trying to negotiate with Godzilla – and after they had gone, Michel would be there at home again, with that ruffian of a father and the mysterious and inarticulate brother I had yet to meet, the pair of them ready to solve the problem with their fists.

Michel gave a heavy sigh. 'He won't do it again. I gave him a couple back. I'm not a kid any more.'

'But . . .' I looked at that terrible face again. 'Why did he do it?'

An unpleasant suspicion welled up in my mind. I hesitated to put it into words – if I was wrong, it would sound as though I was horribly self-centred, thinking everything revolved around me. All the same, I realized, I had to ask.

'Was it about me?'

Reluctantly he nodded. 'He told me to stop picking you up.' He sighed. 'In fact, he told me to stop seeing you altogether.' He looked at me, his good eye hard and defiant. 'I told him to fuck himself.'

'Shit, Michel.' I leaned my head against the cool glass of the car window and shut my eyes. 'And he beat you up for that?'

'He tried.'

He did a pretty good job, I thought to myself.

'You really should tell someone,' I said aloud.

'Maybe.' I could tell from his tone that he wouldn't. Michel reached for the ignition keys and started the engine up again. 'Look, we should get going.'

'Michel, he can't go round doing stuff like that to people.'

'He doesn't *go round* doing it to *people*.'

'Well, he shouldn't do it to you.'

'He lost his temper.'

'That doesn't justify it,' I said hotly.

'You don't understand. He gets angry sometimes but not like this. I've never seen him like this. He just went mad. And afterwards . . .' He shook his head. 'He started crying. It was weird.'

'It's no use him being sorry afterwards,' I said angrily.

'I don't think it was that. All this stuff came out about my mother.'

'Your *mother*?'

I stared at him. I had never heard him mention his mother before, but I had drawn my own conclusions about that after meeting his rude and unkempt father. If I had been her, I wouldn't have stuck around either.

'He's got this sort of idea that when she died . . .' His voice trailed off.

She died? I thought. In spite of the matter-of-fact way Michel referred to it, I felt cold. *Don't be stupid,* I scolded myself. *She probably got sick . . . maybe she had cancer or something. You don't have to see murder everywhere.* All the same, I wouldn't have cared to live out there at that run-down farmhouse in the dank shadow of the forest, with its over-crowded courtyard a graveyard for rusting machinery.

'When she died . . .' I prompted softly.

'That it had something to do with the Allerheiligen glass.'

There was a long silence as I absorbed this.

'Let's not go to school,' I said suddenly. I glanced at Michel. 'Let's go somewhere. I don't know, a cafe or something.'

'Lin . . .'

'Don't say no,' I said as forcefully as I could.

Reluctantly Michel reached for the car keys.

'Do you know somewhere?' I asked.

He nodded. 'There's an *Imbiss* in Traubenheim.' He shot a glance at me. 'But, Lin . . .'

'Yes?'

'Why do you want to go there?'

'Because,' I said grimly, 'we're going to find ourselves a corner, where there's nobody else around, and nobody can hear what we're saying, and then you're going to tell me what the hell's going on.'

CHAPTER TWENTY-NINE

The *Imbiss* in Traubenheim turned out to be a little snack bar that was about three times as long as it was wide; it looked as though it had been shoehorned into the space between the two half-timbered houses which stood either side of it. There was a large board outside, with a green and gold Bitburger beer logo on it, and a list of dishes containing a terrifying amount of fat and protein. Early though it was, the smell of frying was heavy on the air, irresistibly delicious but fatally unhealthy, like the scent of a Venus fly trap. I glanced into the glass cabinet at the front of the bar as we went in. The sausages lined up inside were enormous and glistening with grease. I wondered who would possibly attempt to eat one.

We bought two Cokes from the dour-looking man lurking behind the glass cabinet and went to a table right at the very back of the bar, where there was no danger of being overheard.

'Right,' I said firmly. 'Talk to me.'

'Lin . . .' Michel spread his hands out helplessly.

I did my best to look him in the eyes, though the sight of that battered face made me wince.

'Michel, don't even *think* about lying to me. Tell me what's going on. Why did your father beat you up?'

There was a long silence. Then Michel sighed. 'I told you. He said I wasn't to see you any more – not to give you lifts to school and to stay away from the castle.'

'Why?'

'Because . . .' Michel hesitated. 'I think he was scared.'

'*Scared?*'

From what my parents had told me about the scene the previous day, it didn't sound as though Michel's father was scared at all; it sounded as though he had been the one doing the intimidating.

'Michel,' I said. 'You know what he did yesterday? To my family?'

Michel said nothing, but he glanced away, his expression unreadable. He might have been ashamed, or angry, or simply confused.

I put my hand out and touched him lightly on the wrist. 'I think you should stop giving me lifts to school. Dad can do it, or I'll walk down and get the bus.'

'No,' said Michel stubbornly.

'Michel, I don't want to be responsible if your dad does something again. I don't know what he thinks I've done but . . . maybe it's better if you don't drive me any more.'

'I said *no*.' Michel's head came up and there was a flash of real anger in his eyes. 'He's not telling me what to do.'

'But . . .' I saw the dour-looking man at the other end of the room turn his head and realized that I had raised my voice. With an effort I lowered it until it was just above a whisper. 'But, Michel . . . it's not worth it.'

Michel looked at me, and in spite of the black eye his gaze was so frank that I looked away. Neither of us said anything as I sipped my Coke and studied the floral pattern on the plastic tablecloth as though it was the most fascinating work of art I had ever seen. My face felt warm; I had a horrible feeling I was blushing.

'Michel,' I said eventually, when I had begun to feel that the lengthening silence was worse than any possible gaffe I could make by speaking, 'what *did* happen to your mother? What did your dad mean about the Allerheiligen glass having something to do with it?'

'I don't know,' said Michel. 'It doesn't make any sense. She died of an aneurysm. There was nothing strange about it. She just . . . died. She was in Kaufhof in Nordkirchen when it happened, looking for clothes for me and Jörg, and she just collapsed. They took her to hospital but she was already dead. There was nothing anyone could do.'

I sat in silence for a few moments, digesting this. Awful scenes arose in my imagination, of a woman of about thirty, with Michel's dark brown hair and puppy-dog eyes, standing among the racks of children's clothes, selecting something – a little T-shirt in blue, perhaps – and then crumpling without a sound, like a character gunned down in a silent movie. The same woman, sprawled on the floor with the contents of a rack of tiny clothes which she had pulled down with her, the blue T-shirt still clutched in one lifeless hand. Another shopper standing there with her hand to her mouth, staring. The shop staff coming running – a gangly assistant with a name badge pinned to the front of his shirt leaning over the fallen woman, his eyes round with panic . . .

'That's terrible,' I said finally and inadequately.

Michel sighed. 'I was little when it happened. I can't really remember her.'

'It doesn't make sense, though,' I said. 'I mean, someone

dying in the middle of a shop in a town centre . . . how can that have anything to do with the Allerheiligen glass?'

'My dad thinks it did.' Michel looked away, down the length of the bar, to where the dour-faced man was still lurking behind the counter, rubbing at the surface with a cloth. There was an appraising look on Michel's face and I guessed that he was wondering whether the man was within earshot. He turned back to me. 'He said my mother didn't believe all the stuff about the glass being unlucky. She used to say that it ought to be in a museum, where everyone could see it, not hidden away . . .' Michel paused and I had the sense that he was coming to a decision. 'She said it was beautiful.'

There was a silence.

'You make it sound as though she'd seen it,' I said slowly.

Michel looked at me. 'Oh yes,' he said. 'She'd seen it.'

CHAPTER THIRTY

There are a few times in life when you hear something or experience something so unexpected that for a moment you don't know how to react. Reality seems to be unravelling as though it were a piece of knitting and someone had taken the end of the wool and pulled until the stitches slipped, one after another, dissolution running back and forth across the work, faster and faster . . .

I sat opposite Michel at the dowdy little table with its plastic cloth and tatty beer mats, and stared at him with my mouth open, until I finally realized what I was doing and shut it.

'She'd *seen* it?' I managed to say.

'Keep your voice down.' Michel tilted his head in the direction of the door. 'Yes.'

'So it's here? Somewhere around here?'

He nodded.

Herr Mahlberg was right. I sat back in my chair and rubbed my face with my hands, as though there were some comfort in the familiar contours of my own features. A thought occurred to me. 'Have *you* seen it?'

'Yes.'

I looked at Michel, at the faded blue cotton shirt he was

wearing, at the dark hair which fell over his forehead, the clear gaze of his good eye, and the crusted scabs on his knuckles, and wondered if I had ever really *seen* him before. Was it really possible that while I had been knocking fruitlessly on the door of Herr Mahlberg's deserted house, and my father had been ploughing through books, writing letters, planning trips to Köln, Michel had known all along where the glass was, and had not only known but actually *seen* it?

'You're joking,' I said.

'No,' he replied shortly, and I could see that he really wasn't.

First I was stunned and then gradually I began to feel indignant. I leaned forward across the floral tablecloth.

'Why didn't you tell me?' I hissed, making a titanic effort not to shout.

Michel leaned towards me. Now our heads were almost touching and he looked almost as nettled as I did.

'And if I had? Your dad was going to try to make his fortune out of it, remember?' He glared at me. 'Anyway, I wasn't supposed to know about it myself.' Unconsciously he rubbed the scabbed knuckles of his right hand with his left. 'My dad'll go mad if he knows I've told one of you.'

His words fell like a shadow across me. *One of you.* He thought of us, my family, as outsiders from whom the truth must be hidden at all costs. I was stung that he saw me merely as one of them.

'Well, why did you tell me, then?' I retorted resentfully.

'You really want to know?' snapped Michel back. 'Because I'm sick of this – secrets and threats and this other crap. My dad thinks he knows something about my mother's death and he doesn't tell me until now . . . and when he does, it's

some rubbish about bad luck and curses. And anyway he . . .'
Michel scowled and looked away, leaving the sentence unfin-
ished.

He beat you up, I thought. That was why he was telling
me. It was revenge. With a sudden thrill that was close to
fear, I realized that this was my one chance. The iron will
which had made Michel hide the truth from me was suddenly
pliant, made molten in the searing furnace of his anger. If I
didn't get him to tell me now, it would be never.

'Where is it?' I demanded.

'It's here. Baumgarten, I mean.'

'Where?'

'In a church.'

Michel's expression suddenly changed and I heard the
reluctance in his tone. He was already thinking that he had
said too much, but it was too late. I had to know the rest – I
had to know where the glass was. At that moment I came
close to understanding how my father felt about it – the
rapacious, feverish need to know which seemed to consume
him, to ride on his back like the monstrous Old Man of the
Sea.

'How can it be in a church?' I said sharply. 'Everyone
would know where it was.'

'Not this church. Nobody goes there.'

'Well, where is it?' I said, resisting the temptation to seize
him by the collar of his shirt and shake him.

Michel looked down at his hands. 'I'm not sure I should
tell you.'

'What?' I almost screamed, and out of the corner of my
eye I saw the dour-looking man turning to stare at us again.
I balled my hands into fists in my lap, afraid that I would

actually hit Michel in my frustration. 'You can't tell me it exists and then not tell me where it is!' I hissed.

'Lin – you do realize it might not be safe?'

'What do you mean, it might not be safe? Is the church falling down?' Another thought occurred to me. 'You don't believe all that stuff about Bonschariant, do you? Michel, it's just a legend.'

'I know that.' Michel sounded offended. 'It's just . . . stuff happens. Look, there was this guy who was interested in local history – he'd never seen the glass but he was interested in it. He came over once and talked to Dad, but Dad almost threw him out of the house.'

'What did he do then?' I asked.

'Do? He didn't do anything. He's dead.'

'Dead?' I gaped at Michel. 'What was his name? It wasn't Mahlberg, was it?'

'Yes, it was.' Michel looked at me with new interest. 'Look, that's not all. This guy Mahlberg, he mentioned old Werner . . .'

I rubbed my face with my hands. I was beginning to feel bewildered trying to follow all of this.

'Werner?' I said faintly.

'Yes, Dad's uncle. He spent all his evenings in the *Kneipe* in Baumgarten, telling stories of the olden days to anyone who would listen. He knew everything there was to know about Baumgarten,' said Michel, with a certain note of respect for this intellectual miracle in his voice. 'I think he told Herr Mahlberg something. Maybe he just told him to talk to Dad, I don't know. But the thing is, that was right before Werner died.'

I looked at Michel, searching his face for any sign that he

was making this up, trying to frighten me. He looked deadly serious.

'What did he die of?' I asked.

'That's just it. Nobody really knows. He had this bit of land over near Niederburgheim – he had a lot of fruit trees there. He was pretty old, Werner, but still did most of the work himself. They think maybe he had an accident and fell out of one of the apple trees, but they're not sure.'

I did my best not to let Michel see the shock on my face, but I was terribly afraid that I had paled.

'Why aren't they sure?' I managed to say through lips that felt numb.

'Well, he had this massive thump on the head. His skull was shattered. It looked more like someone had hit him over the head with something. That's what Dad said anyway. He had to identify him.'

'Was it your dad who found him?'

Couldn't Michel see that something was wrong? My voice sounded strange to my own ears, the voice of a hostage with a gun to her head, telling the negotiators that everything was fine, yes, everything was just fine.

'No, it was some guy from Niederburgheim,' said Michel. 'He used to help Werner sometimes, and he'd gone to the orchard to tell him he couldn't work that afternoon. I heard him telling Dad about it.'

I was barely listening to Michel. I was thinking, *He has a name. The man in the orchard has a name.*

'Are you OK?' asked Michel suddenly.

'Of course I am. Why shouldn't I be?' I said quickly. 'Look, it's terrible what happened to your dad's uncle, but I didn't know him or anything.' I felt a hot little stab of guilt at that, but before Michel could notice anything I pressed on with, 'Anyway, maybe he just fell out of the tree, like you said. Maybe it was just an accident.'

'And maybe it wasn't,' Michel pointed out stubbornly. 'Maybe it was because he knew where the glass was.' He sighed. 'Maybe it's nothing. I mean, Dad's OK.'

I didn't say anything. It was hard to imagine anyone making an attack on Michel Reinartz Senior as he strode around the woods armed with a shotgun and accompanied by his deranged dog. I recalled him marching me back to the trodden-down fence and warning me off his part of the forest with tales of rabid animals. Rabid animals which Michel claimed did not exist . . .

'Michel,' I said suddenly, 'the church is in the forest, isn't it?'

Michel said nothing, but he could not conceal the reaction which flickered across his face.

'I'm right, aren't I?' I said.

'Lin, I'm still not sure I should show you,' he said.

'Look,' I replied firmly, 'if you don't show me I'm going to go exploring myself.'

'I don't think that's a good idea,' said Michel.

'Then show me.'

'I don't know,' said Michel, shaking his head. 'I'll have to think about it. And you can't tell your father. No way.' He looked at me fiercely, his good eye glowering. 'You don't know what you might be getting yourselves into.'

'If the glass is really there, you can't keep it hidden forever,' I pointed out.

'Why not? It's been hidden for two hundred years.'

'OK,' I said reluctantly. 'I promise I won't tell my dad.' *Yet*, I added silently. 'All right?'

Michel nodded, although he still looked uneasy.

'So can we go and see the glass?'

'Not now.'

'Then when?'

Michel looked at me for a long moment. I suppose he concluded that I was not going to give up, because eventually he said, 'Look, Dad sometimes goes down to Prüm to buy stuff for the farm, and Jörg goes with him. They're out most of the day. Next time he goes, I'll take you.'

CHAPTER THIRTY-ONE

When we came out of the *Imbiss* it was nine o'clock – well and truly too late for the start of the school day, but so early that my reappearance at the castle would have caused a hailstorm of questions. I imagined my father would already have a few words to say about having got up at the crack of dawn for nothing, and if either he or Tuesday caught a glimpse of Michel's black eye there would be no end of fuss. Since the only other option was to spend the morning kicking our heels in Baumgarten, where any number of public-spirited local citizens would be only too ready to take an interest in two truants, one of them with a black eye, we decided to cut our losses and go to school.

I arrived halfway through a double German lesson, where I delivered my excuses with an air of conviction that would have delighted even Schiller's heart, had the playwright been present to hear me tell Frau Schäfer that Michel's car had had a blowout on the road to Nordkirchen. All the same, I found myself wishing I had used another excuse; when I sat down next to Johanna she gave me the sort of look that would blister paint and then turned pointedly away.

'*Morgen*,' I said anyway, but I could feel the waves of resentment through the curtain of flame-red hair she presented to me. If she was hoping to get to me, she was wasting her time. As soon as I had hauled out my files and pens, she was forgotten, as was Schiller's *Don Carlos*.

It was just as well that Frau Schäfer did not call on me during that lesson. I doubt I would even have heard her. My body was in its seat, with its head up and an expression of perky interest on its face, but my mind was roaming the forest around the Kreuzburg, pursuing every path I had ever taken beneath the lowering cover of the trees, searching for any memory of a landmark or side path which might direct me to the hidden church. The thought of it was almost overwhelming. More than once I asked myself if Michel was really telling the truth, though I knew he was – I had read it in the savage tone of his voice and the curl of his clenched fists. He had paid his father back in the best way he knew, by telling me, the outsider, where the glass was.

The thought of it was at once fabulous and terrifying. Death surrounded that glass, and had done so for its entire history, since the day when the servant had run from the newly glazed cloister screaming *Murder!* and the horrified monks had clustered around the bloody body of the girl. The abbot had claimed to believe that it was the work of the Devil. *I* thought that there was no need for the Devil to perform such work when there were human hands ready and willing.

I turned my own hands over, studying them – the familiar lines, the ones which were supposed to map out your life, your loves and your death; the nail of the right index finger, which was torn down to the quick; the little scar on my left knuckle from a long-healed graze. What kind of work would I be undertaking if I went with Michel to the forest and saw the lost Allerheiligen glass with my own eyes – would it be for good or evil? I knew that a decision lay ahead of me, like an ominous mark on a map of a path as yet untrodden. The glass was not just a hidden treasure, the masterwork of a dead genius; it was not just an unimaginable amount of money, a million or more. For me personally it was dynamite. I could choose to show it to my father. If I did so, I would fulfil his wildest dreams of recognition, fame and fortune. I might also bring down on both our heads the wrath of whoever was trying to keep the glass hidden, a wrath which had already found murderous expression. Or I could say nothing, keep my promise to Michel, and carry the knowledge within me like an ungerminated seed, watching as our lives flowed onwards, knowing that I had had the power to change everything and had not used it.

At the end of the lesson I didn't bother to wait and see whether Johanna had snapped out of her bad mood; I was halfway down the corridor while she was still packing up her things. I had so much energy fizzing through me that I felt I would burst if I didn't let off some steam, though there was little I could do about it. During breaks most people stood outside the building in little huddles, some of them smoking, although this was supposed to be forbidden on school premises. If I roamed about I would simply stand out like a macaque accidentally introduced to a colony of sloths. Instead I slumped against a wall, fidgeting.

I was looking at my watch for the third time, thinking that if Michel was coming down for the break he was taking his time about it, when Father Engels walked past. As usual he was dressed all in black, and his handsome features were composed in a neutral expression. He looked like a beautiful statue come to life.

I gazed at him with a feeling akin to guilt, my heart thumping so wildly that I really thought some of the others might hear it. My cheeks were burning. *This is what love feels like*, I thought. I was going to be a scientist one day; I was supposed to be objective about things. Love, I had read somewhere, was the product of chemicals in the brain, not the work of a fat little cherub with wings wielding a bow and arrow. But whoever had written that was wrong. If Cupid existed, he hadn't just shot me down; he was standing there with his foot in the middle of my back, having a trophy photograph taken.

I watched Father Engels walk up to the main doors and pull one of them open. If I carried on staring like this, people would notice. I knew this and yet there was nowhere else to look. An image was forming in my head, an image so bold that it almost took my breath away. I saw myself approaching Father Engels, carrying my new secret with me like a precious gift. I saw him listening to me as I explained myself, the gaze of those dark eyes on my face, those perfect brows drawn together in concentration.

'Lin?'

I realized that Father Engels had passed through the door and gone. Even though I turned to face the speaker, I could not stop my glance slipping momentarily back towards the doorway.

'Michel,' I said. I wondered how long he had been there, whether he had noticed me gazing after Father Engels. I summoned up a smile. 'I didn't notice you standing there.'

CHAPTER THIRTY-TWO

When I let myself into the house, I was fully expecting my father to complain about my having hauled him out of bed for nothing that morning. In the event, I needn't have worried: neither he nor Tuesday even looked up when I came in. They were poring over a large number of hardback books which were spread out on the pine table; the remains of lunch – some bread and ham – had been displaced on to a chair. Ru was lying on his back on the overstuffed sofa, fast asleep. There was no sign of Polly.

'I don't know how you can look at these disgusting things, Oliver,' Tuesday was saying.

'They're not disgusting,' said my father equably. 'You're looking at them through modern eyes.'

'Well, I don't know what you'd call this one,' said Tuesday. 'Boiling someone alive.'

My father glanced at the page. 'That's St John the Evangelist. Actually, he died of old age. That's just a torture scene.'

'*Just?* See what I mean? It's disgusting,' said Tuesday, closing the book with a thump. She looked around and saw me. 'Lin, there you are.' She didn't bother with the conventional greetings, but went straight for the attack. 'Did you go with that Reinartz boy this morning?'

I shrugged. 'He came to pick me up.'

'Lin, after what happened, I really don't think it's such a good idea —' Tuesday began.

To my relief my father interrupted her.

'Come and look at this, Lin.' He opened the book that Tuesday had slammed shut. 'Your mother thinks it's disgusting.'

I didn't bother to contradict him about Tuesday being my mother; my father didn't want to understand. In fact it always made him furious when I argued about it. I went over to the table, glad to draw attention away from myself and where I had or hadn't been.

'What is it?'

My father flipped the book over to show me the cover.

'*The Woodcuts of Albrecht Dürer*,' I read.

I shrugged; it didn't mean anything to me, though this was nothing unusual. My father was always enthusing over strange bits of medieval art. At home in England we had a copy of a painting showing St Bartholomew holding his flayed skin. My father had wanted to hang it in the dining room, but Tuesday insisted he relegate it to his study; she said it would put her off her dinner.

'Look at the angel with the key throwing the dragon into the abyss,' said my father.

I stared at the illustration. In the foreground a winged figure carrying a great key was lowering a grotesque horned figure loaded with chains into a hole in the ground. Two other figures stood watching this scene from a hilltop, and beyond them there was what appeared to be a fortified town in the medieval German style, with the defensive walls disappearing into a thick forest behind it.

'Wouldn't this make a fantastic frontispiece for a book about the Allerheiligen glass?' my father was saying enthusiastically. 'This fellow with the horns would make a fine Bonschariant, don't you think? And with the German town in the background – it's perfect.'

He ran a finger along a text at the bottom of the page and read aloud: '*And he laid hold on the dragon, that old serpent, which is the Devil, Satan, and bound him a thousand years. And cast him into the bottomless pit, and shut him up, and set a seal upon him, that he should deceive the nations no more, till the thousand years should be fulfilled; and after that he must be loosed a little season.*'

'He must be loosed?' I repeated with a shiver, eyeing the scaly body of the demon. I imagined him wearing away a thousand years in the darkness and then creeping up towards the light again, eager for revenge. Could evil never be destroyed, only postponed?

'You're not becoming squeamish like your mother, are you?' asked my father.

I stifled the retort which rose to my lips. I shook my head and turned the page.

'Ah,' said my father, as though I had revealed a particularly pleasant view, 'the Four Horsemen of the Apocalypse. Stunning, isn't it?'

Stunning was not the word I would have chosen. A heap of lamenting human figures was being trodden down by four figures on horseback, brandishing weapons. At the very bottom of the picture someone seemed to be descending headfirst into the fiery mouth of a monster. But it was not the despairing human figures which caught my attention – it was the four mounted figures, and one in particular. Three of the horsemen were sturdy-looking warriors, but the fourth was terribly, dismally thin, the bones and sinews of his emaciated body showing through the skin, his attenuated limbs appearing unnaturally long, his fleshless hands like talons. The sight of it chilled me, as though a wind from some far-distant place, some desolate land of desert and night, had touched me.

'Well,' said my father heartily, 'can you tell me which of these gentlemen is which?'

I laid my index finger on the skeletal figure, although I could hardly bear to touch it.

'This must be Famine,' I said.

'Oh no,' said my father. 'This is Famine.' He pointed to one of the other horsemen, who was carrying a pair of scales. 'This one –' he pointed again to the thin figure – 'this one is *Death*.'

CHAPTER THIRTY-THREE

For nearly a fortnight very little happened. Michel picked me up every morning and, as the days passed, the swelling around his eye subsided, the deep purple of the bruises fading to yellow. Still there was no opportunity to go and see the glass. Michel's father spent every day at the farm, accompanied by Michel's simian brother, Jörg. Frustrated, I sat in lessons next to the uncommunicative Johanna, half-listening to Frau Schäfer and dreaming of unlikely scenarios in which I found myself alone with Father Engels, who would be strangely impressed by me and have to remind himself of his vows. Sometimes I fantasized about sneaking to the farm at midnight and stealing the supplies of whatever it was Michel Reinartz Senior bought in Prüm, so that he would have to go there for the day. I knew this was impossible – even if I passed safely between the Scylla and Charybdis of Jörg and the dog, any attempt to tamper with the farm would arouse his suspicions for sure.

All the same, I chafed under the burden of passing days, occasionally tempted to spill the load at my father's feet. I watched him setting off for Köln and for the Eifel Club library in Mayen. I saw him bringing home books and pamphlets and papers to add to the ever-increasing piles in the living room; or gazing intently at the glowing screen of his laptop as he composed yet another letter, asking for access to archives, copies of documents, interviews, recommendations, anything. I was sorely tempted to tell him what I knew – but then, what did I know? Michel claimed to have seen the Allerheiligen glass, but until I had seen it with my own eyes I had nothing but hearsay. Worse, if I told my father, Michel would probably refuse to take me to the glass at all. Even if my father knew for certain that it existed, the information would do him no good at all as long as its location remained a secret. It would be no use applying to anyone else in Baumgarten – that was clear. So I waited, and then something happened which almost blasted the Allerheiligen glass out of my mind forever.

It was a Wednesday afternoon, cool but sunny. Michel had dropped me off after school and driven away. Autumn was turning the leaves to orange fire. I kicked my way through a drift of them before I opened the green gate and stepped into the courtyard. I was not expecting anyone to be at home; my father had been planning to drive to Koblenz that day to talk to a superannuated Catholic priest who had had a parish close to the site of the vanished Allerheiligen Abbey and had an interest in the glass. Tuesday had intended to go with him, and I had assumed that Polly and Ru would go too.

Surprisingly, the front door was unlocked. The car was gone, so my father must have left as planned. I knew better than to think that Tuesday would have stayed behind, with nothing to look at but the forest: in her eyes, trees were only of any use when pulped, processed, printed and bound into the pages of *Vogue*. I guessed that Polly must be home. I went inside, dumped my bag on the table and took the stairs two at a time.

'Polly?' I burst into the bedroom, almost falling over Polly's training shoes, which were lying discarded in the middle of the floor. I looked around me and froze.

'*Polly?*'

Polly looked over her shoulder at me. Her face was agonized. She was struggling to get into her clothes as quickly as possible, but before she managed to pull the enormous sweatshirt over her head I had a plain view of her curved back, of the spine and ribs clearly showing under the pale skin. There was a dizzying moment when I thought, *I've seen this before*, followed by a searing sense of guilt which seemed to detonate inside me with the blinding force of a grenade. Was it possible that I had seen this before and not noticed it – that I had seen it and done nothing? Then the storm which seemed to be boiling in my brain cast up one clear image, of my father bending over a large hardback book, his forefinger on a woodcut illustration. That was where I had seen this dreadfully emaciated form before. *This one is Death*, my father had said. The realization loosened my tongue.

'My God, Polly –' I began.

'Get out!' she snapped at me, her face distorted with anger. 'Get out!'

'But I –'

'I want to dress in peace. Just get out, will you?' she flung back at me. 'Go!'

'But, Polly – what's happened to you? You're so *thin*.' I could hear my own voice wavering.

'Shut up.' Polly yanked the sweatshirt down over her hips

and turned to face me. 'It's none of your business. And don't even *think* of telling *her*.'

I didn't have to ask whom she meant. 'But –' I began again, and then stopped. I was out of my depth. Polly just stood and glared at me, hands on hips, waiting for me to leave the room. I saw her running kit lying on the bed and realized that she must have been jogging in the woods. Now it made sense, Polly getting up so early in the morning to go out. She didn't want anyone to see her getting in and out of her sports kit.

I looked at her helplessly. The shock of seeing how terribly thin she had become was still pulsing through me, but at the same time some tiny, selfish corner of my mind was wishing that I hadn't rushed up the stairs so quickly, hadn't barged into the room before she had the time to cover herself up, hadn't seen the truth. It was all too much: first the man in the orchard, then the horror in the cemetery and now this. I had the feeling that my sanity was suspended on wires and one by one they were snapping under the load.

What was I supposed to do? If I ignored Polly's plea and told Tuesday, Polly would never forgive me and it probably wouldn't do any good anyway. Tuesday, who was naturally skinny and could have munched on lard sandwiches all day every day without putting on a gram, would have no conception of how Polly felt. My instinctive reaction was to go to my father. When I was a little girl he had seemed so strong and handsome and clever, like the hero in a fairy tale who alone has the power to make everything right. But as I stood there, staring at my sister and feeling as though the shreds of my life were hanging off me like rags, I felt the creeping coldness of doubt coming over me. I thought of my father smashing the glass horse in the hallway in our house in England; I thought of him bent over stacks of dusty books at midnight, flipping pages with one hand and scribbling furiously with the other. He was a driven man; if I presented him with this problem he would go at it with his usual directness, like Alexander the Great hacking through the Gordian knot with his sword. Polly would close up like a sea anemone, withdrawing to some place inside herself where none of us could reach her. I knew too that she would think I had betrayed her. It had always been me and Polly, Polly and me, whenever there was a family row or Tuesday became too unbearable. It had been me and Polly all those years ago, when we had been motherless and confused, clinging to each other for comfort. I knew that if that ended, I would be just as lost as she would.

My legs felt as though they were about to crumple beneath me. I sat down on my bed and put my head in my hands. Polly said nothing but when I looked up she was pulling on a body warmer. It was too warm for the day, which was mild, but now I understood why she was doing it. Layers provided an appearance of bulk.

'Polly –'

'Don't say it,' she snapped. She sounded close to tears. 'It's all right for you. You're the same as her. You even wear her clothes.'

Instinctively I looked down at myself, although in fact I had kept my hands off Tuesday's things since the day in the cemetery.

'Oh God,' I said uselessly. 'Look, can't we just –'

I stopped. I had been going to say, *Can't we just tell someone?* But who would we tell? If not Tuesday or Dad, who

184

else could I talk to? Frau Schäfer? Polly wasn't at school, so I wasn't sure Frau Schäfer or anyone else would – or could – do anything, even if I told them. Anyway, I was pretty sure that the first thing she would do if I *did* tell her would be to contact our father or Tuesday. I racked my brains. I had a vague feeling that there were people you could call in Britain, telephone lines set up to advise people about this sort of thing. But we weren't in Britain any more, I reminded myself. Nor, come to that, did we have access to a working telephone. I looked at my sister and I felt a kind of dull despair.

'Polly, what are you *doing*?' I asked her eventually.

Abruptly she sat down on her own bed opposite me. 'I'm not doing anything. I'm not – you know, making myself throw up or anything.'

I was not sure I believed this but I didn't say anything.

'I'm just doing lots of exercise and eating less. That's healthy, isn't it?' She looked at me defiantly.

'Polly, you're skin and bone,' I blurted out.

'I'm not,' she snapped. She looked down at herself and I wondered what she was seeing, whether in her mind the skinny limbs and jutting angles were encased in a soft layer of fat. 'What's your problem anyway? Are you jealous, now I'm finally getting the weight off?'

I couldn't even formulate a reply to *that*. I might just as well have envied a death's head its sharp cheekbones.

'Look,' said Polly eventually in a softer voice, 'I didn't really mean that. It's just – you don't know what it's like. You've always been the thin one.' She reached out and touched my hand. 'Can't you be pleased for me?'

'No, I can't,' I said stubbornly. I looked her in the eyes. 'You're starving yourself.'

'That's rubbish,' snapped Polly, withdrawing her hand. 'Everybody diets. Tuesday's always dieting.'

There was some truth in this. Periodically Tuesday would pat her non-existent stomach and announce that she was going to detox. But this was worlds away from what was happening to my sister, who seemed to be melting away like a wax taper burning down.

Perhaps Polly took my silence as agreement. At any rate she leaned forward with a conspiratorial air, as though about to impart a secret.

'Listen, Lin, you're not going to tell Tuesday or Dad, are you?' she said in a wheedling tone. 'Promise?'

This was too much. 'No, I'm not promising.'

'Lin, if you –'

'I didn't say I'd tell them either,' I said. 'I just need to think.'

I stood up. For a moment I waited for her to say something – anything. But she just sat there examining her hands in her lap. Her hair hung in lank strands over her face; I couldn't even see her expression.

In the end I left the room and went downstairs. Before I was even halfway down I heard the door close behind me and the click of the key turning in the lock. There was a silence and then a sudden *thump!* as though something had hit the closed door. I guessed Polly had thrown a shoe at it.

Down in the living room I couldn't think what to do with myself, and there was always the risk that my father and Tuesday would come home. I could imagine Tuesday taking one look at me and saying, 'What on earth's the matter with *you*?' She still hadn't cleared up yesterday's lunch either, so the living room had a slatternly look about it. There were even several flies buzzing about. I opened the front door and went out into the courtyard. I went and looked at the burnt remains of the tree. The sooty patch was still there, like some sinister lichen trying to scale the wall, although someone had swept up the shards of glass. I stared at the black patch and all of a sudden tears were pricking at my eyes. I couldn't make sense of it; after everything that had happened, I could feel myself about to cry my eyes out over a fire that had been put out quite safely. Nobody had been hurt. The house had not burned down. The landlord had not even appeared to berate us, which suggested that nobody had told him the evil news. I stared at the wall and tears trickled down my cheeks. My chest heaved and a great sob forced its way out.

Above me there was a sudden bang. I looked up. Evidently Polly had just slammed a window shut. I could hear a clatter as she struggled to force the handle into the locked position. Since I was clearly not welcome in the house, I stumbled over to the gate and stepped outside, with the vague idea that I would set off through the woods. I would howl out my misery to the trees and the ferns. I would walk until I had calmed down again – that way nobody would have to see me –

Oh *no*. 'Michel,' I said under my breath. His name was bitter in my mouth, the coppery taste of the bad penny which always turns up. The red Volkswagen was parked under a tree at the side of the track and he was standing next to it. I wondered whether he had driven off at all, or whether he had been here the whole time. Surely it was not possible that he could have heard me and Polly rowing? I remembered the window Polly had banged shut. *Had* he heard anything?

Michel raised his hand. 'Hi, Lin.'

'Hi.'

It came out as an angry squeak. I knew he would notice and I could feel my face growing hot. I hoped I was not blushing.

'What's the matter? Are you OK?'

Now he was coming towards me, and the expression of concern on his face made me want to scream. Why did he have to be here, when all I wanted was to be alone? The last shreds of my self-control broke.

'Oh – fuck off,' I snapped in English, turned on my heel and started to walk away as fast as I could without the indignity of breaking into a run. I could see a small path leading away into the forest – it was much too narrow for a car. *That should prevent him following me*, I thought.

It didn't. I had only got about ten metres into the woods when I could hear him panting right behind me. I guessed he had run after me. I wheeled around, very seriously tempted to slap him with the flat of my hand. With difficulty I restrained myself.

'Leave me alone, can't you? What's wrong with you?'

'I'm sorry.'

He really did look sorry, I had to give him that, but for some reason this simply infuriated me more.

'It's no use being bloody sorry. Just leave me alone!' I was almost shouting in his face, heedless of the fact that I was using English and most of it was probably going over his head. 'I mean, what are you going to do? You think you can help me?' My hands flailed the air, as though I would have liked to claw something. 'You can't do *anything* to help. Nobody can. You don't know what it's like. I don't even feel *safe* here! The house nearly burned down, I can't go for a walk without your dad's horrible mad dog trying to tear my throat out and now Polly's starving herself to death.' I glared at him, my chest heaving. 'You think you can sort all that out? Be my bloody guest!'

There was a long silence. I turned my back on Michel so that he would not see the tears running down my face. My view of the little path winding away between the trees blurred, so that it looked as though it was leading away into nowhere.

'Lin?' said Michel eventually in a low voice.

I shook my head, lips clamped tight shut. I didn't trust myself to turn round.

'Lin, I don't know what's wrong with your sister, but the house – you know, it's OK. That black stuff can be cleaned off.'

I wiped my eyes with my sleeve. Slowly I turned to face Michel, uncomfortably aware of my red eyes and puffy face. If anything could make him stop looking at me the way he always did, as though I were some particularly tempting delicacy he was dying to devour, it would probably be the sight of me at that moment. Somehow this did not make me feel any better. I supposed I should say sorry for making him the butt of my fury, but the truth was I wasn't sorry – I was still angry with him for witnessing it.

'Why are you here anyway?' I demanded in German. 'I thought you'd gone.'

'I had,' said Michel. He looked at me seriously. 'I came back. I came to tell you that my father's going to Prüm tomorrow.'

CHAPTER THIRTY-FOUR

The next day when I awoke Polly was already gone. I guessed that she had gone running again, though whether to work off more calories or to avoid talking to me I could not say. The morning at school dragged by. When I went downstairs at breaktime, Father Engels was standing in the foyer talking to a man I recognized as the headmaster. Involuntarily I slowed my pace. It was impossible not to look at Father Engels. He was so perfectly good-looking, with his dark eyes and sleek black hair. How I wished we were Catholic, so that I could sit in the front row of his *Reli* class and feast my eyes on him for a whole forty-five minutes each week.

'Hey, don't bother looking at *him*,' said a voice.

I turned around. One of the blonde girls from my class was coming down the stairs behind me. I couldn't remember her name.

'I wasn't looking at him,' I said hastily.

She stared at me, her expression not unfriendly but rather too knowing, shifting her piece of gum from one side to the other.

'Everyone has a crush on him,' she told me. 'But it's a waste of time. He's a drag.' She ducked past me and hurried down the rest of the stairs, leaving me standing open-mouthed.

After school Michel drove me back as usual. I badgered him to take me straight to the mysterious church in the woods – Tuesday and my father wouldn't even notice that I hadn't come home, I pointed out – but Michel was adamant; he was not taking me anywhere until he was sure his father had left. I spent the rest of the journey looking out of the window and imagining how much more interesting it would be if Father Engels were driving me around. I thought if I could just sit next to him in silence while we drove along the forest track, with the sun filtering down through the trees, that would be enough; it would be heaven. This pleasing idea sustained me through a late lunch with Tuesday and Ru (neither Polly nor my father was to be seen) and a very dull hour of schoolwork.

Michel turned up at three o'clock, much to Tuesday's disgust. 'I thought you could look after Ru this afternoon,' she complained. 'Can't you stay here?'

As far as I knew she had nothing particular to do. The thought of staying indoors for the rest of the afternoon with Ru when I was bursting to see the glass was too much; I said no.

'It's all right for you,' she grumbled as we were leaving. 'Gallivanting around with your boyfriend.'

I didn't bother to tell her that Michel was not my boyfriend, would never be my boyfriend in a million years, and nor did I tell her that we were not going gallivanting. I simply made my escape as quickly as I could and hoped that Ru, who was having his nap upstairs, would not wake up. Judging by the look on Tuesday's face, he would have a hard time of it if he did.

'Are we taking the car?' I asked Michel as we left the castle.

He shook his head. 'No, you can't take the car up there.' He sighed. 'I'm still not sure this is such a good idea. I shouldn't have said anything.'

'You're not backing out now,' I told him. 'Anyway, I *said* I wouldn't tell anyone.'

Michel looked at me for a moment without saying anything. Then he turned and headed towards the edge of the forest. I had to trot to keep pace with him and even then he turned round impatiently to see where I was.

'Come on. I want to get under the trees before someone sees us.'

It was sunny now, but it had rained that morning while we were at school and the ground was unpleasantly soft and muddy, sucking at our feet as we walked. Before long my shoes were caked in mud and the legs of my jeans were spattered with it. In places it was so wet that it was difficult to move quickly without slipping. Michel moved with a stealthy confidence that was hard to reconcile with his usual offhand behaviour. I did my best to keep up.

We followed the track I had taken the day I met Michel Reinartz Senior and his dog. As I struggled along in the mud, I could not help looking around me with a kind of wonder at the wet tree trunks and straggling undergrowth. It was staggering to think that I had already had my feet on the path which led to the church. I had wandered along this very track, blissfully ignorant of the secrets hidden deep within the forest. No wonder Michel's father had reacted with such hostility; he probably thought I was snooping on purpose.

We came to the St Hubertus shrine and once again took the right-hand path. It was narrower here and it was impossible to avoid brushing against the overhanging branches and bushes which lined the track; it was unpleasantly like running the gauntlet through a host of feebly clutching hands. Soon my jacket was wet.

'Yeuch,' I complained, trying to shake off the droplets of water spotting the sleeves like tiny crystals.

Michel gave no sign of having heard me; oblivious to raindrops and mud, he simply ploughed onwards. After a while we came to the trodden-down fence. It was still down, but clearly someone was in the process of mending it – a little bundle of stakes lay on the ground nearby, ready to prop the wire up again. I guessed that if we tried to return this way in a day or two the fence would be blocking the path. I stepped carefully over the crumpled wire.

For a while we followed the path towards the farm. I trudged on in my damp shoes, watching Michel's back as he strode along. It occurred to me that here in the woods, where he felt at home, he moved just the same way his father did, with a long stride and an air of self-assurance. This was not comforting. With a sudden stab of doubt I wondered whether he was stringing me along, paying me back for getting him into trouble with his father. Perhaps there was nothing in the forest at all and he was simply going to laugh his head off at me, the idiot he had taken in so easily.

Suddenly Michel looked round at me, caught my eye and then stepped sideways off the path. He beckoned to me. 'Come on.' There was no drainage ditch to negotiate here but the undergrowth lining the path was full of brambles and it took me a few moments to struggle my way through it. My jacket caught on something and there was an audible rip.

'*Mist*.' Michel came back and began to disentangle me from the branch.

There was a tiny scrap of fabric left clinging to it and he was very careful to pick it off and put it in his pocket. He was covering our tracks, I realized, and a thrill of excitement that was close to fear ran through me – he would not go to all this trouble if he was playing a practical joke on me.

'Is it far?' I asked, but he would not reply.

He set off again, weaving his way between the tree trunks and bushes, careful to keep to the drier patches of ground or those covered with fallen leaves, where we would not leave footprints.

We had been picking our way through the undergrowth for about five minutes when we suddenly stepped out on to a path again. It was hardly a path at all; more a rabbit's track. Michel indicated that we should go left along it. I looked to the right but in that direction it appeared to peter out altogether among the trees. I was starting to feel slightly disoriented; which way was the castle? The small patches of sky visible through the thick canopy of trees were a uniform grey. I could not even tell where the sun was. There was no way to work out where we were in relation to the Kreuzburg or even to the farm.

I had the uncomfortable feeling that we had strayed into hostile territory. With no houses, not even a path, to create a sense of scale, the trees seemed enormous. As we trudged on, I gazed up at the trunks of pines which seemed to stretch endlessly upwards, their crowns lost in the distant sky, and felt myself diminish. I felt as though I were a little child again, as though Michel and I were Hänsel and Gretel, wandering hopelessly along winding tracks which led inexorably to the witch's house. Were the woods always so still? All I could hear was the rustle of our footsteps, the sound tiny in the vast auditorium of the forest.

Once we passed an object carved in rough red stone, half-hidden by drooping branches. For one shocked moment I thought it was a gravestone and then I realized it was some sort of religious monument. There were figures carved into the front of it, but they were so eroded by the passage of years and the work of the elements that the figures had a strange leprous appearance. It was impossible to tell what the scene might have been. I could just make out a large nine in Roman numerals.

'It's a Calvary stone,' said Michel, seeing me hesitate in front of the object.

'A what? Why does it have nine on the front?'

'It was the ninth stone. There were probably twelve, but only one or two are left now. They showed the whole crucifixion story, you know, Jesus stumbling and St Veronika and all that stuff.' Michel laid a hand on the crumbling red stone.

'But what is it *for*?' I asked.

He shrugged. 'They lead to the church. You start with number one and when you get to twelve, well, there it is.' He spoke casually and I wondered at his nonchalance; to me there was something sinister about this single stone half-hidden in the undergrowth, like the last decaying tooth in a rotten jaw. How long had it been here and what had happened to the others?

Michel turned and started off down the path again. With one last look back at the red stone, I followed him. I was oblivious to my damp jacket and muddy shoes now. My whole body seemed to be seething with suppressed tension, as though I were not a single being at all but a swarm of insects, thrumming to the beat of blind instinct. I was afraid, for the atmosphere of the wood was undeniably hostile, but I was also excited almost to the point of jubilation. I trotted after Michel as fast as I could, almost falling over him in my eagerness to see what lay ahead. In fact when he suddenly stopped I ran into him and would have sprawled headlong into the mud if he had not grasped me by the arm.

'Where is it?' I panted, scanning the trees.

'There.'

He pointed. I stared in the direction he was pointing and for a few seconds I could not see anything at all. I felt an echo of the vertiginous feeling I had had before, that perhaps Michel was simply stringing me along, there was nothing at all in these woods . . .

Then finally I saw it. My first thought was, *No wonder no one has ever found it*. At first glance the little church was almost invisible. Closely surrounded by trees and bushes, it was hidden in shadow, but at that moment the sun came out and I was able to see it clearly. The front wall, which was all I could make out from where we stood, was obscured with some dark growth, moss or lichen, and almost blended into the surrounding vegetation. I could see the shape of a door, the wood blackened and spotted with damp, and a small window above it, opaque with filth. There was nothing to attract the eye; even the metal door handle was tarnished to a dull and dirty black. Anyone who came through this part of the woods might easily miss the church altogether. I imagined the forest animals passing it unheedingly, not smelling human beings but the more reassuring scents of damp wood and stone, wet leaves and moss.

A moment later I was running towards the church. I was already wrenching uselessly at the door handle when Michel came up beside me.

'Stop it,' he hissed in an urgent voice. 'You'll never open it like that and if you break the handle Dad will know someone's been here.'

'Well, open the door, then.'

With what seemed like agonizing slowness Michel knelt down at the side of the door and reached towards the bottom of the wall. I saw that there was a rough slot there, where probably there had originally been a brick or a ventilation grille. Michel put his hand right inside and drew something out. He showed it to me. It was a key, of a rather old-fashioned design, heavy and speckled with tarnish.

'Open the *door*.' I was almost beside myself.

Michel slid the key into the lock and with a little difficulty twisted it. There was a click as the lock drew back. He turned the door handle and pushed the door so that it swung open with a long arthritic groan from the hinges. I needed no further invitation. I pushed past him and stepped inside.

CHAPTER THIRTY-FIVE

'But it's dark! I can't see a thing!' I wailed.

The interior of the church was almost pitch-black. The only light came from the open door and all it revealed was a couple of square metres of floor covered with old-fashioned tiles decorated with a repeating design of diamonds and quatrefoils, and the dim shapes of wooden pews. I put out my hand and touched one of them but instantly drew my fingers away; the wood had an unpleasant encrusted feel, the residue of cobwebs, dust and the dry corpses of dead insects.

'Can't you put the light on?' I snapped.

'There isn't one,' said Michel's voice very close to me.

I felt his hand touch mine and instinctively pulled away, but too late. He took my hand in a very firm grasp and began to pull me down the aisle into the black heart of the church. I tried to drag my hand out of his.

'Let go of me! What are you doing?'

'I'm showing you,' said Michel calmly.

Abruptly he stopped. He let go of my hand, but before I could move he had grabbed me by the shoulders. For one moment I thought he was going to take advantage of the darkness to try to kiss me. Before I had time to react he had spun me round so I had my back to the door.

'Stay there. Shut your eyes and don't open them until I tell you to.'

'What for? Where are you going?'

I stared into the darkness and felt the first stirrings of panic. I envisioned Michel hurrying to the door, slamming it shut and turning the key, leaving me here in the darkness, fumbling my way to the doorway and thumping on it uselessly, screaming myself hoarse as he walked away, pocketing the key and secure in the knowledge that nobody else would pass this way for weeks . . .

'Just wait,' I pleaded.

'No. You stay here.'

He gave me a little shove and I stumbled forward. By the time I had recovered my balance and turned round he was out of the church. A second later my worst fears were realized and he closed the door behind him, shutting out the light.

'Michel?' My voice was rising but I made an effort to sound calm. If he thought he had really scared me it would only make matters worse. 'Michel, that's not funny. Let me out.'

Michel called something from the other side of the door, but it was impossible to make out what he said. It might have been, 'Wait,' but I wasn't sure. I stood still and listened, my heart thumping painfully in my chest. I willed myself to breathe deeply and suppress the rising feeling of panic, but the thick musty smell that I inhaled with every breath was a pungent reminder that I was trapped in a place virtually never visited by a living soul.

'*Michel?*'

As though in answer to my cry there was a sudden thunderous *crack!* and instantly a triangle of light appeared in the blackness, bright as a laser, as brilliant as a jewel and stained with the tints of gemstones – the flaming crimson of rubies, the glowing green of emeralds. For several seconds my brain failed to process what my eyes were seeing and then mingled wonder and relief flowed through me. I knew what Michel was doing. I stood perfectly still, a smile on my lips, and closed my eyes.

It must have taken him about ten minutes altogether to remove all the boards. Even with my eyes shut tight I could tell that the church was bathed in light where before it had been plunged into darkness. Orange spots hovered behind my eyelids. I longed to open my eyes but stuck to my resolve and kept them shut. At last I heard Michel's footsteps behind me. A hand touched my shoulder.

'Lin? You can open your eyes now.'

I didn't, though; not for a few seconds. I wanted to savour the moment before I saw the truth. So often the things we long for are a disappointment. I wanted to taste that moment of anticipation, the expectation of seeing something wonderful. And it was wonderful. I opened my eyes and found I was standing in a rainbow.

Only a handful of living people have ever seen the Allerheiligen glass and it is hard to describe something which so transcends the usual vocabulary of beauty. It was as though the eye of heaven had opened and its glory streamed out in every colour of the spectrum. Rich golden yellow mixed with vivid cobalt blue, with the scarlet of a cardinal's cape and the flaming orange of an autumn sunset. Figures of men, saints and angels strode and gestured in robes of dazzling coloured light. Among them moved strange creatures and beasts whose fur glowed with the radiant tints of butterfly wings.

I recognized some of the scenes. Here was the Garden of Eden, with an apple tree growing up through the centre of the picture, its leaves and curling branches forming a canopy at the top under which a paternal God extended His hand to Adam and Eve. Here was Moses, dressed in crimson and blue, gazing in wonder at the burning bush, while in the background sheep grazed in the shadow of a castle. I picked out the Fall of the Angels and Abraham preparing to sacrifice his son Isaac.

There were others which I did not recognize. 'Who's that?' I asked Michel, pointing at a scene depicting a figure submerged in a flowing river, the running waters a fabulously clear cornflower blue.

'It's Naaman bathing in the River Jordan,' said Michel.

I took a step nearer to study the picture more closely. 'How do you know that sort of thing?'

He shrugged. 'The name is in the picture – look.'

He was right. The name NAAMAN was picked out in Gothic lettering on a fluttering scroll above the figure's head.

'I looked it up on the Internet,' said Michel in an offhand voice, looking slightly embarrassed at the confession. 'I was interested in that stuff when I first saw the glass.'

I didn't ask him why he was no longer interested in it. It was incomprehensible that anyone could become used to such splendour, could become blasé about it. My father had said that Gerhard Remsich was a truly great artist. I thought that he was something greater than that. I also knew that no price tag anyone could put on the glass, whether eight hundred thousand pounds or a million pounds or ten million, could ever be meaningful. It was a priceless thing. I understood Michel's reluctance to let me tell my father where the glass was. The Allerheiligen glass was worth more than one man's career and one man's fortune. It was a masterpiece; it was a miracle. I gazed at it, lost in wonder.

'Look,' said Michel. He pointed at one of the windows. 'I think that's the one that started the legend about a demon haunting the glass.'

I looked at the panel he was indicating; it was the one showing the Fall of the Angels. The upper part of the window was crowded with a throng of white-robed winged figures wielding swords and spears, descending out of skies the colour of Ceylon sapphires. Below them were the rebel angels, grotesquely ugly horned and winged creatures whose skin was tinted the crimson of blood or the green of decay. They tumbled down through empty space towards a bleak landscape of rock and fire far below, twisting and turning as they fell, jaws bared to reveal rows of jagged teeth snarling uselessly at their pursuers. Only one had his face turned outwards, as though staring out of the window directly at the observer. The expression on the red-tinted face was sly and complacent, even challenging, and painted with such detail that I could understand the rumours that Remsich had taken his figures from the life.

'It's creepy,' I said.

'Yes,' said Michel, but he wasn't looking at the window. He had stepped close to me – a little *too* close, I was thinking – and then suddenly he had his arms around me and was kissing me.

I was so shocked that for several moments all rational thought seemed to have short-circuited itself and I did not react at all. I simply let him go on kissing me. Eventually I suppose Michel realized that to all intents and purposes he was kissing a dummy; he stopped what he was doing and let me go.

'I didn't – I mean, I'm sorry . . .' he mumbled, but he didn't look particularly sorry; he was eyeing me covertly to see how I was going to react.

'Michel . . .' I began, and stopped. What was I to say? *Think nothing of it?* I looked at the floor and then at the window again, where the falling demon seemed to be smirking at me. 'Michel,' I began again more resolutely, 'I don't think that's a good idea.' I was instantly aware how lame this sounded.

Michel had that look on his face, the look that meant I was going to hear something very unwise. 'Lin, it's finished between me and Johanna.'

I hardly had time to digest this remark. Before I could interrupt him he said, 'It's just that – I love –' He stopped abruptly, but the damage was already done. He might have been about to say, *It's just that I love sixteenth-century stained glass* or even, *It's just that I love pepperoni pizza*, but I doubted it. A scene of disastrous, train-wreck proportions was about to unfold. Underneath my alarm there was also a twinge of annoyance; I was pleased he had shown me the glass – all right, I was *thrilled* he'd shown it to me – it was *fabulous* – but that didn't change anything between us. Did he think I was going to say, *Great! Thanks, Michel. Now I'll be your girlfriend*?

I opened my mouth to deliver a watered-down version of this unpalatable sentiment, but then I noticed Michel's expression. He was staring past my shoulder with wide eyes and his mouth open. For a split second I thought that he had somehow read my mind and knew what I was about to say to him, but then I realized that he was not thinking about me at all. His expression was almost comically shocked. I waited for a moment and when I saw that he was not going to shut his mouth I said very cautiously, 'Michel?'

'*Shhhhh!*' His voice was low and urgent.

'What?' I said in a stage whisper.

Michel did not reply; he simply pointed. I half-turned and followed his gaze. He was staring at one of the windows, the one with the Garden of Eden scene in it. Clearly visible through the glass was a dark shape, a shadow as tall as a man, but grotesquely warped and crooked where it fell across the differing angles of the coloured panes.

A stifled squeak escaped my lips and without thinking I grabbed Michel's arm. We stood there in silence, not daring to move, and watched as the dark shadow shifted, writhing across the planes of the glass, and then moved to the side of the window. It vanished behind the wall and a moment later it reappeared with a horrid stealth behind the window showing Abraham and Isaac. *Bonschariant!* boomed my thoughts. In that moment I believed. I was really afraid that I might faint. I hung on to Michel's arm with such ferocity that it must have hurt him, but he was oblivious. I saw that he had gone a sick grey-white colour.

Was this what had happened to the abbot of Allerheiligen? I wondered. Had he seen the same dark shape moving through the windows, keeping pace with him as he passed along the cloister? Had the fear of what lay behind the glass been enough to stop his aged heart, or had the demon shown him its face? And had he had long enough to take it in, to realize the full horror of it, before Death had sealed his eyes forever?

'Michel!' I hissed under my breath.

He didn't react.

'*Michel!* Lock the door!'

For a moment I thought he hadn't heard, but then without a word he pulled away from me and slipped over to the door, treading as lightly as he could. It was still half-open, but he pulled it swiftly shut and jammed the key into the lock. He was struggling to turn it when I caught a sudden movement at the edge of my vision and realized that the misshapen shadow beyond the glass had vanished. There was a click as the key turned in the lock.

Michel came back to me, his face pale and serious. Silently he put his arms around me. I pushed my face into his shoulder as though to shut everything out, but still I was listening, listening with straining ears, and I knew he was too. I don't know how long we stayed like that; it could have been as little as five minutes but it felt much longer. There were no sounds from outside – no tapping on the glass, no footsteps. Michel was stroking my hair. At first he was just doing it mechanically, as though he were petting a dog, but after a while there seemed to be more purpose in it, so I pushed him off.

'Do you think it's gone?' I asked him in an urgent whisper.

We looked at each other.

'I don't know.'

'Have you ever seen him – I mean, it – before?'

Michel shook his head. 'I wouldn't hang around here if I had.'

'So you think it's . . .'

My voice trailed off. I didn't want to say it; it sounded too stupid and too frightening. *Bonschariant. The Glass*

Demon. I didn't want to believe it myself, but I had seen the grotesquely shaped shadow with my own eyes. It was too soon to start rationalizing it away. I shivered.

'I want to go back to the castle . . . but what if it's still out there?'

'I don't think it is . . .' began Michel.

'What if it is?' I asked, trying to keep the tremor out of my voice.

There was a silence.

'I'll go and look,' said Michel finally.

There was a brittle resolve in his voice. I knew he didn't want to go any more than I did. I stood and waited while he unlocked the door and went outside. A moment later I could hear him crunching through the undergrowth. While I waited for him to come back I tried to distract myself by looking around me.

If the windows were magnificent, the rest of the church was in a sad state. The pews – those which had not actually collapsed – were broken and filthy. The patterned tiles underfoot were cracked and missing altogether in places. There was a pulpy mass on the floor which might have been the waterlogged remains of a hymn book; it was difficult to tell. I touched it gingerly with my foot and it broke apart like the gills of a fungus. There was no pulpit and the altar – if there had been one – was gone too. In its place stood several wooden crates fastened with metal bands. I judged them to be perhaps a little over a metre and a half long, which made them just long enough to be . . .

'Coffins,' I said under my breath.

I eyed them for a moment, then swung round so that my back was turned to them. That was no better; now my imagination peopled the little church with pallid, red-eyed creatures, horribly thin in the arms and legs, clambering out to lurch across the broken floor towards me . . . With a shudder I went to the door and looked out.

'Michel?'

He appeared a second later around the corner of the church.

'There's nothing,' he said, trying a smile with limited success; I could see the strain on his face.

'Then can we go?'

'I have to put the boards back first,' he pointed out. 'Otherwise . . .'

He didn't need to finish. Otherwise Michel Reinartz Senior, when he next called to check the church was still secure, would know that someone had been there. I didn't like to think how he would react to the discovery.

'Do you want to wait in the church?'

'No,' I said hastily. 'I'll wait out here.'

I hugged myself and watched as Michel went to pick up the first board. A moment later he had disappeared round the side of the church and I heard a thumping sound as he pounded it back into place. Clearly the job was going to take some time; there were at least eight boards. I looked at the silent trees and bushes. Was it always this quiet in the forest? I could not hear a single bird singing, or the rustle of wind through the trees or the crack of a falling twig. Once again I had that feeling of being watched. I began to whistle through my teeth.

Hurry up, Michel.

I glanced around me. There was no movement anywhere. Far off in the woods I heard a faint cracking noise, which might have been a twig snapping or the creak of a branch. In the end I hauled my useless mobile phone out of my pocket. Predictably there was still no signal, but I could mark the minutes as they dragged by from the time and date display on the tiny screen. It took twenty-seven minutes for Michel to replace all the boards to his satisfaction; twenty-seven minutes which stretched out interminably.

In spite of the sunlight filtering through the trees I found myself shivering. I hardly dared to think of the twisted shape we had seen moving outside the windows; to think of it was to beg the question of whether it had really gone – whether it might come back. *Could* it come back? I wondered. Perhaps it could only be seen *through* the stained glass. When Michel boarded the windows up again, it was like placing a patch over an open eye, blinding it. A momentary image flashed across my mind: Bonschariant, freakishly two-dimensional, trapped within the glass, writhing and shrieking in frustration . . . With an effort I thrust the thought away from me. *It's not possible*, I told myself. *Whatever you saw, it can't be a demon.* I stared at the mobile in my hands, a little chunk of modern technology, loaded with fuzzy snaps of my friends back in England. *That's the real world*, I tried to tell myself. *There are no such things as demons*. But my teeth were chattering and I was afraid to turn my back on the church.

By the time Michel returned, wiping his green-streaked hands on the legs of his jeans, my imagination had almost driven me into a state of blind terror. Ironically, the one thing I did not think about was what someone else might have done with those twenty-seven minutes. It was quite enough time for someone to race through the woods to the castle; quite enough time for him – or it – to carry out their plan. As I stood there among the trees, trembling and hardly daring to look around me, it was not I who was in danger at all.

CHAPTER THIRTY-SIX

Michel and I hardly said a word during the walk back to the castle. It was an unspoken agreement that he would go with me; I could not have faced the trip through the silent forest on my own. When he took my hand I did not resist. The warmth was somehow reassuring. Michel looked preoccupied; I guessed he was worrying about the boarded-up windows, whether he had done a good enough job. If Michel Reinartz Senior noticed anything next time he went to check on the church, we were both for it.

If we had been talking – if I had been happily babbling to Michel about the wonder of having seen the lost Allerheiligen glass, as I should have been – we might not have heard anything at first. As it was, the cry was so faint that I was not sure what I had heard. It might have been the shriek of a startled bird rising up out of the undergrowth, or even the distant yelp of a fox. I broke my stride for a split second and then carried on, eyeing the ground as I went so that I could avoid the muddiest places.

Moments later the cry sounded again and this time there was no mistaking it: someone was screaming. I pulled up short, dragging Michel to a stop, and twisted my head this way and that, trying to fix the direction of the screams. It was always difficult to orient myself in the forest but whoever it was could not be far away. With a sickening lurch in my stomach I realized that the cries were coming from the castle. I wrenched my fingers from Michel's grasp and broke into a run, hurling myself across the last few metres of forest and out into the clearing in front of the castle. As I ran towards the green gate someone burst through it in a jumble of stumbling feet and wheeling arms. It was Polly.

She spotted me at once. 'The phone!' she screamed.

I looked at her stupidly, not understanding.

'Your *phone*!' she shrieked at me, her face contorted with fear and frustration. 'Give me your *phone*!'

'I –' I was stricken, not understanding what was going on but seeing clearly that something was dreadfully amiss. I fumbled in my pockets, trying to find the mobile phone's smooth pebble-like shape among the crumpled tissues and loose change. My fingers closed around it and I yanked it out of my pocket. 'It's here –' I began, but before I could finish Polly had grabbed it from me.

She began stabbing at the buttons with her forefinger, almost weeping with frustration.

'Polly –'

'Shit!' She pressed Cancel with her thumb and began jabbing the buttons again, so wildly that it was clear she would never succeed in entering the correct number.

'Polly –'

'Shit! Fuck! What's *wrong* with it?' She grasped the phone in her fist and I could see that for one moment she considered hurling it to the ground, where she could stamp it into the dirt. With an effort she restrained herself, but I could see that she was shaking with emotion. 'What's *wrong*? What's *wrong* with it?'

'Polly – it won't work here,' I said, putting a hand on her arm.

A cold feeling of dread washed over me. I had never seen Polly like this before, not even after the fire.

'Calm down –' I started.

Polly shook me off, glaring at me through dishevelled strands of sand-coloured hair.

'There's no signal here, remember?'

'Shit!' This time she let out a roar that was almost incoherent and the phone did hurtle to the ground. 'What are we going to do? Oh, God!'

She was weeping. I looked at Michel, who was standing a couple of metres away, staring at this scene with his mouth open. No hope of sensible assistance there, I judged. I reached out and grasped my sister by the shoulders.

'Polly! What's the matter? What's happened?'

'It's Ru,' she choked out at last, sending icy splinters of fear into my heart. 'It's Ru – it's – it's –'

'What do you mean, it's Ru? Is he hurt?'

She stared at me with eyes that were blank with shock. 'Someone –'

She didn't finish and I was terribly afraid that she had been going to say, *Someone's killed Ru.*

'Polly.' I spoke to her as sharply as I could, desperate to get her attention. 'Where are Dad and Tuesday?'

'They're in the house. Somebody's been there – in Ru's room – while we were downstairs.' She looked at me wildly. 'We were downstairs – we didn't know – and he was asleep.

He –' Her hands fastened in her fair hair, as though she would uproot clumps of it.

This time I actually shook her. 'Polly! Is Ru alive?' I was almost shouting. 'Just tell me! Is he alive?'

Slowly she nodded, and I let out a long breath. 'Who were you going to call? Police? Ambulance?'

'Po-police,' she stammered.

'Michel.' I turned to him, but he did not react. '*Michel!*' This time he responded to the harshness of my voice and looked at me with a dazed expression. 'You have to run back to the farm and call the police. Right *now*, Michel. And tell them to come to the castle, OK?'

He was staring at me so stupidly that I thought there was a real danger he might send them to the farm instead of the castle.

'Tell them –' I realized that I did not know exactly what he should tell them. 'Say there's been a break-in.' I glared at him. 'Michel – *go!*'

Michel finally stumbled off and I turned back to Polly.

'Where are they?'

Polly pointed back at the green gate. 'In the house. In Ru's room.'

I pushed past her and ran for the gate. If I thought about this for too long I would lose the nerve to do anything at all. I was across the courtyard in seconds, burst into the living room and raced for the stairs. As I hurled myself up them three at a time I could hear raised voices coming from above. My father's booming voice drowned Tuesday's higher, wavering tones, as though a Great Dane were trying to bark down a chihuahua.

Abruptly the voices broke off. Tuesday came out of Ru's

room at top speed, as though she had been propelled from behind. She was holding something in her arms, a white bundle which she pressed close to her body. Her gaze flickered past me but I might not have been there. Without a word she hurried into the room she and my father shared and a second later the door slammed shut.

I ran down the landing and into Ru's room. My father was standing there, by the cot Ru slept in. I hardly glanced at him. I was looking past him instead, and the shock of what I was seeing hit me like a sucker punch.

Sticking straight up from the tangled bedclothes was what appeared to be a great metal spear, fixed as firmly as if it had been planted there. It must have been fully two metres long and it was black and corroded with age. It had been thrust into the cot with such savage force that it had gone right through the mattress and the base. The blunt end rose up from the cot like a grotesque flagpole and I glimpsed the sharp end underneath, the tip almost touching the floor. I looked at that, and thought my legs might give way under me.

'Ru . . .' I whispered.

I stumbled over to my father on unsteady legs, like a seafarer trying to struggle up a pitching deck in a storm. My eyes would not leave the obscenity of that spear sticking straight up out of the centre of the cot, thrust there by hands whose brutal strength was born of rage or insanity. I found it hard to imagine how Ru could still be alive if that wicked sharpness had pierced his flesh. Still, I had to know.

'Tuesday took him,' said my father. 'He's –' He covered his mouth with the back of his hand. 'He's not hurt.'

'Dad?' My voice sounded strange in my own ears; every word was like spitting out a pebble. 'What *happened*?'

'I don't know.'

His voice was wretched, not a trace remaining of his normal bonhomie. The great Oliver Fox, would-be professor and media darling, had quite vanished. In his place was a shocked and frightened and somehow diminished man.

'How did that spear get in? Who –'

'I said I don't *know*.' My father's voice tightened, as though he was gratefully moving on to the familiar territory of irritation. He ran a shaking hand through his thick dark hair. 'Tuesday thinks she heard something.'

'Something?'

'A thump. We were downstairs – I didn't see anything. Tuesday thought maybe Ru had tried to climb out of the cot and had fallen on the floor. So she came up and . . .' His voice trailed off. 'How could this happen?' he said.

'Dad?' I went closer to him and touched his arm. 'Are you sure he's – I mean, is Ru really all right?'

'Tuesday took him,' said my father. I remembered the bundle she had been clutching to herself. 'I told her she should leave him where he was – the police –' He turned a haggard face to me. 'They ought to see how it was.'

I said nothing. Even when I was looking at my father, the black stripe of the spear was at the edge of my vision, as dark and ominous as the shadow of a gibbet. I could not blame Tuesday for snatching her infant son out of his bed; letting him lie there would be like leaving him naked on a butcher's block.

'He's really not hurt,' said my father in a distant voice. 'The spear didn't touch him. There was . . . there was about three inches between him and it. It didn't touch him at all.'

Three inches? I thought sickly. That was like saying you

had decided at the last minute not to take the flight which plunged flaming into the sea, or you had walked out of a building seconds before a gas explosion. You were unhurt, but you'd spend the next year surreptitiously feeling your own arms and legs, wondering whether you were really in one piece.

'Polly . . .' said my father. He sounded distracted.

I knew what he was thinking. 'It's OK. Michel's gone to call the police.'

My father didn't ask how Michel came to be involved; nor did he ask me where the two of us had been while Ru's attacker was creeping into the house. He looked at me as I was speaking, but his gaze seemed to drift past me like smoke.

I looked at Ru's cot, at the spear sticking up out of it, at the rumpled bedclothes. I had the most peculiar feeling when I did – not just shock, but a feeling of déjà vu. As though I had seen the scene somewhere before – or as though I had somehow expected it.

CHAPTER THIRTY-SEVEN

The police, when they arrived, turned out to be Herr Esch and Frau Axer. Herr Esch's flourishing moustache did little to conceal the expression of resigned disapproval on his lean face; Frau Axer simply looked bored. She manoeuvred her vast haunches on to one of the wooden chairs, which trembled alarmingly under her weight, and opened her laptop on the dining table. She listened without apparent emotion while my father explained that someone had broken into the house and attacked his son in his bed. Polly and I sat huddled together on the sofa, silently listening. Tuesday was still upstairs with Ru.

At first my father still sounded as though he were numb with shock. His description of how he had found Ru, of seeing the spear sticking up from the middle of the cot and thinking for one terrible moment that it had pierced his son's body, was halting and riddled with repetition. He stumbled through it like a man in a maze, taking wrong turns and going up blind alleys. Herr Esch listened, every so often repeating what my father had said, in a bland tone which somehow suggested incredulity.

After a while my father began to sense that the mood of the audience was subtly against him and then his voice became terse and finally irritable. When Herr Esch stopped him in mid-flow to ask what it was exactly that had been thrust through the bed, a pike, a javelin or a lance, my father lost his temper. He thumped the table with his fist, making the unwashed lunchtime plates jump on the wooden surface.

'What does it matter what it was? It's six feet long and someone tried to kill my son with it.'

'Is the child injured?' asked Herr Esch in that infuriatingly mild tone.

'No,' snapped my father.

'Has he been checked by a doctor?' Herr Esch must have known that he hadn't been; there was no ambulance.

'He's not hurt,' said my father defensively.

'Nevertheless,' said Herr Esch. He raised his eyebrows. The inference of parental neglect hung in the air between them like an ugly spectre. 'The child should see a doctor.'

'Of course,' said my father angrily.

'We can direct you to the hospital.'

'Thank you,' said my father, spitting out the words as though they had a foul taste in his mouth. He leaned forward across the table, his face flushed with anger. 'But before you start telling me my responsibility as a parent –'

I winced, seeing the expression on Herr Esch's face.

'– how about you carry out yours and arrest the person who did this, like you should have done the first time?'

'Herr Fox –' began Herr Esch.

I noticed that he had dropped the *Herr Professor*.

'We all know who it was,' interrupted my father.

Frau Axer looked up from her laptop and exchanged a glance with Herr Esch.

'Did you see the person you say broke into the house?' asked Herr Esch.

'No,' snapped my father. The silence which ensued was heavy with insinuation. 'It's obvious,' said my father eventually.

Herr Esch stared at him coolly. 'We should look at your son's room now,' he said, ignoring my father's accusation. He got to his feet and my father was obliged to stand up too.

They were upstairs for some minutes. When they came down again, Herr Esch was still wearing the same neutral expression. My father was close behind him, his face a mask of suppressed fury.

'It's not possible,' he was saying.

'We have to consider everything,' said Herr Esch calmly.

'It can't have been an accident,' said my father. His fists were clenching and unclenching, as though he would have dearly loved to take a swing at the policeman. 'How could it be?'

Herr Esch made a vague gesture encompassing the whole room. 'There are things on all these walls. It's possible for them to fall down.'

'You think we'd let our son sleep under a spear?' My father sounded as though he were on the brink of a cataclysmic eruption of temper.

'I cannot say,' said Herr Esch.

'Someone attacked my son,' said my father, making a visible effort to keep his temper under control. 'Are you going to do something about it, or do I have to –' he cast about him wildly – 'contact my embassy?'

There was a silence. I doubted that my father even knew where the nearest British embassy was, but Herr Esch got the message: he wasn't giving up. He studied my father for a few moments, his mouth a tight line. Then he looked at Frau Axer.

'Kripo,' said Frau Axer succinctly, shaking her head.

Herr Esch's mouth twisted, but his shoulders slumped in resignation.

'We will contact the Kriminalpolizei in Bonn,' he told my father.

'The Kriminalpolizei?' repeated my father belligerently, suspecting that he was being fobbed off.

'It is normal for the Kripo to handle cases of this type,' said Herr Esch stolidly. 'Assuming that there has been an attack, as you say.'

'*Assuming?*' For a moment I thought that my father might actually seize the policeman and shake him, but he managed to hold himself back, although I saw his fists clench.

'When will they come, these Kriminalpolizei?' he enquired in a voice that was taut with suppressed anger.

'As soon as possible.'

'And while we're waiting?' retorted my father. 'What about the lunatic who did this? How are you going to protect us?'

'Herr Fox,' said Herr Esch deliberately, 'in cases of this type, police protection is not normally recommended.'

'Cases of this type?' repeated my father incredulously. 'What do you mean, cases of this type?'

'Statistics show that in seventy per cent of murders or attempted murders of children, the perpetrator is related to the victim,' said Herr Esch.

Frau Axer looked up. 'Seventy point two per cent,' she said.

'The Jugendamt, the children's department, will want to visit you,' added Herr Esch.

Open-mouthed, my father looked from Frau Axer to Herr Esch. Then his face flushed and he said nothing more.

Herr Esch was on his feet. He nodded at Frau Axer, who was shutting down the laptop, and then glanced back at my father.

'Make sure the child sees a doctor as soon as possible,' he said.

CHAPTER THIRTY-EIGHT

It was not until very much later that evening that it came to me. None of us felt like going to bed, even though we were drunk with exhaustion. The police had closed Ru's room, but even if they hadn't, it was unthinkable that Ru should sleep there again. Tuesday had settled him on her own bed and was curled up next to him. Generally Tuesday acted as though she had not a maternal bone in her body, but even she knew how close we had come to losing him. She clung to him and wouldn't even let Polly take over. She made a pretence of reading a novel, but whenever any of us went into the room to see how she was, she was always staring into space or out of the window, her eyes blank and scared.

My father had gone out to call Uncle Karl, then he had gone around the entire house checking all the doors and windows. He had also checked the outbuilding, but if it held any secrets it was keeping them to itself. The stack of rusting pikes was still leaning against the wall and there were a few scuff marks on the dusty floor which might have indicated that someone had been inside the tumbledown building, or might mean nothing at all.

Now my father was sitting over a pile of books, one hand pressed to his brow and the other one clutching a pen which moved with lightning speed as he made notes. I think he had gone to work out of sheer habit, or perhaps to shut out thoughts of what might have happened, but now it had drawn him in and he had forgotten the rest of us completely.

Polly was huddled in an armchair, her ears plugged with an MP3 player. I thought I was the only one who had noticed that she had eaten nothing at dinner. I supposed that if anyone *had* noticed, they would have put it down to shock – only I knew better. From time to time I looked her way, but she never caught my eye. The question of what to do about Polly was like a constant nagging ache.

I had settled myself in a corner of the living room where I could rest my head on the wall, but every time I closed my eyes I kept reliving the terrible scene in the bedroom. The sleeping child, the spear piercing the mattress, the bunched bedlinen. I still had that vertiginous feeling of déjà vu.

Outside it had started to rain, a squally downpour which pattered spasmodically on the window like a handful of gravel thrown at the glass. I stared at the darkness outside and tried to empty my mind, to make space for the elusive memory to pop back into it, if it really *was* a memory and not some strange side-effect of shock I was experiencing. I let my eyes drift out of focus. *I was walking* . . . walking out of bright light and into darkness. A dark place – the ground hard beneath my feet, my footsteps echoing. Sudden light breaking into the blackness; shapes and colours etched on to the air. *The church in the wood.*

Frowning, I envisaged myself walking down the aisle of the church, gazing up at the brilliance of the windows. I counted them in my mind: four windows on each side. The Garden of Eden; the Fall of the Angels; Naaman washing in the River Jordan; Moses and the burning bush; Abraham and Isaac. What were the others? The Raising of Lazarus, that was one of them – it was pretty unmistakable, with Lazarus's friends turning away from the open grave with their hands clamped to their noses in disgust. Pentecost – that was another: tongues of vivid fire hanging over the heads of the assembled disciples. But what was the last scene? I thought the missing one, the one I could not remember, was in the furthermost window on the left-hand side.

Like a thunderclap it came to me. *The Slaughter of the Innocents.* A horrific scene in which the armour-clad soldiers of King Herod tore babies from their mothers' arms and spitted them on swords. To the right of the picture one of Herod's men, his bearded face grim under his helmet, was holding a child by its feet and taking a swing at it with a wickedly sharp blade. And to the left of the picture a second man stood with his sturdy legs apart, as though bracing himself, his hands gripping the long spear which pierced the swaddled child at his feet, running right through it and into the ground below.

Instinctively I rose from my seat, the chair legs scraping on the floor. *Tell someone*, was my first thought, and the second one, *But who?* Who was going to listen to me? They'd think I'd gone mad, raving about stained-glass windows and soldiers with spears. I sank back on to the chair. They'd be right – it *did* sound mad, not to mention the fact that it would mean telling people – other people – about the church in the wood. I didn't like to contemplate the fallout from *that*. Michel would be furious with me for betraying him, but that I could live with; I was more worried about what Michel Reinartz Senior would do.

I rested my elbows on my knees and put my head in my hands. What was the meaning of the attack on Ru? And why copy *that* window? There had to be so many other ways of trying to kill someone which did not involve anything as arcane as an antique spear. You could smother them. You could cut their throat, as Abraham was threatening to do to Isaac in another one of the windows. You could drown them . . .

I sat up straight with a dizzying intake of breath. *Drown them* . . . why hadn't I seen it before? The scene showing Naaman submerged in the River Jordan. Some might have depicted Naaman discreetly taking a dip, perhaps standing modestly waist-deep in the water and pouring cupfuls over himself. But Gerhard Remsich had shown Naaman completely submerged in the water, as if he were a Baptist undergoing full immersion. His reclining shape appeared through the cornflower blue of the flowing waters like the body of a drowned man frozen under ice. Much, I supposed, as Herr Mahlberg had looked when the bathroom door yielded to the knocking of the unfortunate cleaning lady and she had seen him lying there, his dead face glimpsed through the distorting medium of the water.

No. It was completely insane. Herr Mahlberg had had a drink too many and fallen asleep in the bath. There couldn't possibly be any connection to the scene in the glass. All the same, now that the germ of an idea had sprouted there seemed to be nothing I could do to stop it growing into a vast and baroque rhododendron of suspicion. There was the tree in the courtyard, the one which had caught fire so mysteriously and left the ghostly trace of its immolation as a sooty shadow on the wall of the house. *The Burning Bush.*

And there was the body I had seen in the cemetery in Baumgarten, poised in the act of climbing from its grave. *Lazarus*.

I got up again and began to roam the room like a zoo animal in a compound too small for it. The ideas swelling monstrously in my brain made me want to be outside in the open air, where I could feel space all around me, where I could scream at the top of my voice, where I could run and run until I had left my fears behind me. Energy seemed to fizz through my body, down to my fingertips. Again my mind's eye ran through the sequence of windows in the little church. I could see all the scenes on the right-hand side – the Fall of the Angels, Naaman in the River Jordan, the Slaughter of the Innocents, the Garden of Eden and in the centre of it an apple tree.

The last piece of the puzzle fell into place. Werner, lying under the apple tree, with that single apple a few centimetres from his outstretched hand. The mark of one single, fatal bite standing out white on the red skin of the fruit. All around him, the ground glittering with glass.

'Lin?' Polly had taken her earphones out and was peering at me uncertainly. 'What's wrong?'

I looked at her dully, like a person woken from a dream. I supposed I must have made some sound out loud, a gasp or cry. My father had looked up too, although he hardly seemed to notice that I was there; his gaze was distant, as though he were peering down the corridor of centuries to the time when Gerhard Remsich was still crafting his masterpiece.

'I'm – I just –'

My voice trailed off. What could I say? That there was a building out in the dark forest by the castle, a building that hardly anyone knew existed, and in it was an art treasure worth the best part of a million pounds? That I suspected it was haunted by something savage and unholy, which had long ago killed a beautiful young girl at the Allerheiligen Abbey and given the abbot a fatal heart attack? That some-one – or something – was stalking people here and now, taking the inspiration for these murderous attacks from the stained-glass windows it haunted?

One word was booming around my brain like the repeated strokes of a hammer, buzzing there like flies on carrion. Bons-chariant. *Bonschariant*. That was whom Michel and I had seen through the stained glass as we clung together in terror. That was who had circled the little church, passing behind each window like a dark shadow, yearning to show us the horror of his face. It could not be, it was impossible – and yet somehow it *was*.

We had cheated him, I realized now. We had locked the door and we hadn't looked. He had circled the church, unable to come in, unable to make us look at him through the glass. So he had left us there and in his rage he had flown back through the forest, to the castle and our house, and he had vented his wrath against me on my baby brother as he lay sleeping in his cot. Only by a miracle, only by a few centi-metres had he missed killing him.

'What's the matter?' said Polly as I sprinted into the kitchen.

I did not reply; I was too busy hunching over the sink, vomiting and vomiting until my gut ached and there was nothing else to bring up.

It was my fault, I thought. *My fault*.

CHAPTER THIRTY-NINE

In the early hours of the morning Uncle Karl arrived. My father was upstairs with Tuesday and Ru. Polly and I heard the faint purr of a car engine and then the sound of feet crunching across the courtyard. The knock, when it came, was thunderous. Polly and I were looking at each other, wondering what we should do, when a voice called, 'Oliver? It's Karl.'

I unlocked the door and opened it to find the tall angular form of Uncle Karl, looking like a 1940s private eye in a tan-coloured mackintosh with the collar turned up. Uncle Karl had a stern face, all square jaw and razor-sharp cheekbones, but he generally had a twinkle in his eyes which showed that his bark was considerably worse than his bite. Now, however, he looked severe. He wasted no time on the niceties.

'Lin, where is Oliver?'

'He's upstairs with Tuesday and Ru. I'll show you.'

I stared at him as he stepped inside, aware of an overwhelming sense of relief. Uncle Karl would sort everything out. He knew the area, he knew the system – best of all, he knew the language. He wouldn't be at a disadvantage, as I was, feeling that I was playing a complicated game in which

I was the only person who didn't know the rules. Uncle Karl would not have to struggle along, doing his best to find the right words in a tongue that was not his own; he could carve out great chunks of irony and insinuation from the living rock face of the language and use them to bludgeon the uncooperative and the malicious.

'Wait,' said Uncle Karl, when I began to move towards the stairs. He looked at me narrowly. 'Did you see what happened?'

'No. I was out – with a friend,' I said, not wanting to be too specific.

Under the crust of exhaustion and shock which was enveloping all my thoughts there still ran a hot current of guilt, like molten lava. If I had not been out – if Michel and I had not been poking around in the church . . . It was still too soon to tell anyone else about the stained-glass windows. I wanted time to think through the possible implications.

'Polly was there, though,' I said.

Polly was slumped on her chair as though half-asleep, but she shot me a glance that showed she was wide awake. 'I didn't see it *happen*.' She sounded defensive.

Uncle Karl looked from me to Polly and back to me again. I did not like the expression which flickered across his face and disappeared almost as quickly as it had appeared. I knew that look; it was suspicion. My feelings of relief at his arrival began to drain away. For the first time it struck me that we might all be in trouble – very serious trouble. Ru had been attacked in his own room – in his own bed – while nearly all of us were in the house. I was the only one who hadn't been there, and I had not accounted for my whereabouts when it happened.

229

Uncle Karl was looking at me completely normally now; he appeared concerned, but that other expression had gone. He had dismissed it from his mind; Tuesday was a relative of his – it was ridiculous even to think of suspecting any of us. All the same, the thought had streaked across his mind with lightning speed. It was a look I was to see on many other faces over the following days.

'Oliver said someone tried to stab Reuben with a –' Uncle Karl paused, searching for the correct English word.

'A spear,' I said. I was amazed how calm my voice sounded, as though it were some other girl altogether who was doing the talking. 'A *long* spear. About – as tall as me,' I added. 'The police said it might have fallen down . . .' I grimaced. 'There's stuff stuck up on the walls all over the house, but I don't think it came from Ru's room.'

Uncle Karl's eyebrows went up but I thought I detected a slight look of relief on his face at finding a possible explanation. He opened his mouth to say something and then both of us heard a voice we recognized. The words were inaudible but the complaining tone was unmistakable.

'Your mother is there,' said Uncle Karl, looking up towards the landing.

'She's not –' I started to say, but gave up.

It was pointless getting into *that* argument again, especially with Uncle Karl, who hadn't been around when Polly and I were tiny. All the same, I couldn't help feeling a small sad twinge of regret; the real mother, the mother I imagined for myself, would be a tower of strength in situations like this. She'd never desert us in our hour of need. We would all lean on her and she would support us.

Now Tuesday came marching down the stairs, sweeping

her mass of blonde hair off her face with one skinny hand, her dress a mass of wrinkles.

'I thought you were never coming,' were her first words to Uncle Karl.

He spread his hands in a placatory gesture. 'Marion is away. I had to find someone to take care of Johann.'

Of course. My father and Tuesday would not have thought of that; it would never even have entered their heads. We had an emergency – we needed Uncle Karl here *now* – that was all that mattered.

Tuesday was frowning, her face ugly with anxiety and frustration.

'The police were here,' she said in an accusatory tone. 'They said all sorts of horrible things. They implied *we* had something to do with it.'

'It happens, you know,' said Uncle Karl. 'There was a case last year, a woman in Koblenz who suffocated her two-year-old because he wouldn't stop crying.'

'But I –'

Tuesday was too horrified to continue. I could see her visibly crumbling under the idea that she herself might have anything to do with what had happened to Reuben.

Uncle Karl realized his mistake too. 'Look, I'm sure there is no problem.' He spoke soothingly, making it sound as though the police enquiries were nothing but a boring bit of bureaucracy. 'Where is Oliver? Maybe I should speak with him.'

'He's with Reuben,' said Tuesday. She gave a sob. 'I want to go home,' she said, sounding like a little girl. 'I just want to go home, right now, to England.'

Uncle Karl looked at her very seriously. 'I don't think you can.'

'Oh yes, we can,' said Tuesday, wiping her eyes with the back of her hand. Her voice broke. 'I don't care about Oliver's job, about the stupid stained glass. I don't want to stay in Germany one day longer.'

'I think you have to,' said Uncle Karl.

'Why?' demanded Tuesday mutinously, glaring at him. 'I don't *want* to stay here. It might not even be *safe*.'

'You don't have to stay in the castle if you are afraid,' said Uncle Karl. 'I can find you a hotel. But,' he added, seeing that she was about to protest, 'I think you have to stay in Germany. If Reuben was attacked, the police have to investigate it.'

I looked down at the floor, then out of the window. Anything to avoid watching the painful procedure of Uncle Karl trying to communicate the truth of the matter to Tuesday, without coming right out and saying that we *couldn't* leave in case we were the ones who had attacked my brother.

'Lin?'

Polly spoke my name in an undertone. Her eyes were wide, an expression of dumb beseeching in them. It was the first time in days that she had really looked at me, really caught my eye. I went and sat next to her.

'Dad'll get a hotel room, won't he? I don't want to stay here at the castle either.' She was shivering, I noticed.

'I don't know,' I said helplessly.

Polly gave a little snort, and for one crazy moment I thought she was laughing, until I realized that she was sobbing, her shoulders shaking. I put an arm round her; she was wearing a thick jumper and a jacket, but still I could feel how thin she was.

'He could have been killed,' she choked out.

I squeezed her shoulders more tightly.

'It's OK,' I said. I could not think of anything else to say.
'It's OK.'

CHAPTER FORTY

The next morning I didn't go to school. I had left a note for Michel tacked to the gate, telling him to go without me. I couldn't face speaking to anyone, but most of all I didn't want to desert Polly. It was useless leaving her to Tuesday; Tuesday had the fragile elegance of a butterfly, but when it came to sensitivity a rhinoceros sprang to mind.

I woke before the others, as the first rays of autumn sunlight were coming through the crack in the curtains. No one else was stirring; I guessed that they were all still sleeping. I should have been sleeping myself; I could feel fatigue eating away at every cell of my body like some malignant virus. Still I knew that even if I stayed in bed I would never get back to sleep. I had a feeling of immediate and unnatural wakefulness, as though I had had too much caffeine.

There was something I had to know, something which was pulling at my consciousness like a fishhook. The scene flashed through my head again: Tuesday hurrying from the bedroom with Ru in her arms; my father standing by the cot; the stark black line of the spear piercing the mattress. I thought about what I had seen in the orchard in Niederburgheim – the glass glittering on the earth all around the body – and about what Frau Kessel had said about Herr

Mahlberg drinking in the bath; everyone had assumed that because of the broken glass on the bathroom floor. I had a strong conviction that were I to go into Ru's room and approach the bed, were I to crouch on the floor and look underneath it, I would see the tip of the spear protruding from the bottom of the mattress, like a finger pointing at Hades, and underneath it a little pile of broken glass.

The compulsion to look grew stronger and stronger. I knew that the police had sealed Ru's bedroom; the door was locked and there was a notice pasted to it forbidding entry and threatening legal action to anyone who attempted it. Even if I had defied this threat, the sound of my forcing entry to the room – if I managed it – would wake the rest of the family for sure. That left one option.

I didn't bother dressing properly; the longer I was in the room, the greater the chance that Polly would wake up. I pulled on my dressing gown and crept out. There was a pair of shoes lying discarded by the door. I slipped my bare feet into them and let myself out as quietly as I could.

The front of the house had a rosy look to it in the early-morning sunlight, marred only by the black smudge of soot on the wall near the cremated remains of the tree. I swiftly turned the corner and gazed up towards Ru's window.

It was as I had hoped: the castle wall ran right up to the side of the house. It met the wall perhaps a metre and a half below the window. I let my gaze run back along the wall to a worn stone staircase. The stairs were crumbling and broken, and there was no handrail of any kind, but I was pretty sure I could climb them, and then it would be a very easy matter to run along the top of the wall and peep through the window into Ru's room. I could satisfy my curiosity once and for all.

There was no sense in wasting time; at any moment one of the others might wake up and come looking for me. I trod carefully over to the bottom of the stone steps and began to make my way cautiously up them. It took longer than I expected to get to the top; even a drop of two or three metres was intimidating and there was nothing much to hold on to.

Finally I set my foot on the top of the wall and instantly felt something crunch underneath my shoe. I waited until I had got myself right on to the wall and was no longer in imminent danger of falling off, and then I stood on one foot so that I could look at the sole of my shoe. I was not really surprised to find that there was a large shard of glass protruding from it. I felt a kind of cold satisfaction: the discovery merely confirmed what I had already suspected. I picked the piece of glass out with care and dropped it down the side of the wall. Then I glanced towards the house and Ru's window. In the warm dawn light the broken glass which lay scattered along the top of the wall glittered and flashed, as though someone had strewn a handful of diamonds there on the rough yellow stone.

Ru's window was only a few metres away and now I saw that it was open – not wide open, just a few centimetres. Not enough for us to have noticed in the heat of an emergency. I had only noticed it now because there was a little tail of white curtain sticking out under the window frame.

I stood there for perhaps two minutes, staring at the window. I no longer wanted to go over and peer through it; in fact the idea made me feel rather sick. Common sense still tried to reassert itself, telling me that there were no such things as monsters, ghosts or demons; that those who really thought such things influenced our daily lives were about on a par with people who had their pets' horoscopes read or believed that Elvis had been seen on the moon. And yet . . . I had seen that shape through the stained glass with my own eyes, had seen it moving slyly past the coloured panes, as though tempting me to look more closely. I had seen the broken glass which sparkled like ice crystals around the body of Werner. And I had seen the deadly pattern in the attacks – the re-creation of scenes devised in the tortured brain of a sixteenth-century genius inspired by demons. Here was the last piece of the puzzle, the last tile which completed the mosaic. Whoever or whatever had attacked Werner and Herr Mahlberg had also attacked my brother. *Bonschariant* – the Glass Demon.

'Lin?'

I jumped at the sound of my name and nearly overbalanced. Uncle Karl. He was calling me, probably from the courtyard in front of the house. Panicking, I stumbled back down the stone steps and away from the wall. No thought of laying the matter before Uncle Karl even entered my head; once I had got beyond the first sentence about haunted windows he would be thinking I had gone completely mad. I wasn't even sure myself that I hadn't.

I rounded the corner of the house and he was there on the doorstep, already dressed in a neat shirt and trousers with knife-edge creases. He turned at the sound of my footsteps and I saw his expression of recognition fade into one of concern.

'What's happened?' He came over to me, his brows furrowed. 'Where have you been?'

'Round there.' I made a vague gesture behind me. 'I –' I struggled for words. 'I was sick.'

'You were *sick*?'

If I had said this to Tuesday she would have made a face and stepped backwards to avoid possible contamination. Uncle Karl, however, clearly shared the time-honoured German preoccupation with health matters. I could see that with very little encouragement he would demand to see the sick in question.

'In the bushes,' I said hastily, hoping to head him off. This did not stop him from looking over my shoulder, so I added, 'I'm coming back in.'

'Of course.'

He was looking at me curiously. I hoped that it would not occur to him to ask why I had gone outside to throw up instead of using the bathroom. I hurried inside, leaving him standing on the doorstep, peering out into the courtyard with a bemused look on his face. I took the stairs two at a time.

When I went into the bedroom Polly opened her eyes, though she did not venture out from under the duvet which enveloped her like a protective cocoon.

She stared at me, then said, 'You look like you've seen a ghost.'

I sank down on the bed. 'I'm not sure I haven't.'

'What's the matter?'

I raked my hands through my hair. 'I don't think you'd believe me, even if I told you.'

I'd intended to speak lightly, as though I was joking, but even I could hear the grimness in my voice.

'Lin?'

I glanced at Polly. She was still staring at me.

'Are you OK?' she asked me, sitting up.

There was warmth in her voice and I had the sense of an

unseen barrier between us at last dissolving. Since the moment I had burst into the room and seen her without her sweatshirt on, we hadn't really talked. She had screamed for my phone when I had come out of the forest that same afternoon, she had wept on my shoulder over what had nearly happened to Ru, and we had had dozens of conversations since then, but we had never really *talked*.

'I don't know,' I said truthfully.

There was a long silence.

'I wish I wasn't going to Italy,' said Polly suddenly.

'I wish you weren't going too,' I said. 'But, Polls . . .'

You're better off leaving, I wanted to say. *It's too dangerous here*. My voice tailed off. I knew what I had seen, I knew what it meant, but I also knew how crazy it would sound to other people.

'What?' said Polly instantly.

'I – guess it's too late to change it now,' I finished awkwardly. I tried a smile, but it felt stiff and unnatural. 'You should go. It'll be great.'

'Hmm.' Polly's gaze drifted away from me, towards the pale square of the window. 'It just doesn't seem . . .'

Real? I wondered. That was probably because it had never been Polly's idea. It was not her dream; it was my father's and Tuesday's. I wondered how many years of art history she would wander through before realizing that.

'Polly?' I waited until she had turned her pale eyes back to me. 'If you don't want to go, then don't.' I saw her open her mouth to protest and hurried on. 'They'll make a fuss, but so what? It's your life. You could get a job for the rest of the year. You could get yourself sorted out . . .'

'You mean the eating?' Polly's gaze met mine and I was

relieved to see that there was no anger in her expression. She looked relaxed and calm. 'Lin, I wanted to tell you about that.' She smiled at me. 'Look, I had a problem, but I really feel much, much better now. Honestly, Lin.'

'Polls –'

'It was the stress of doing my A levels and then having to move. I really feel OK now. I want to eat, Lin.'

I looked at her doubtfully. It was the way she kept saying my name all the time – *Lin, Lin* – that made me suspicious. She sounded as though she was trying to persuade me.

'Don't look at me like that. I'm fine.'

'Polly, you're so *thin*.'

It wasn't just that. Her skin had a bluish tinge to it, as though she could never quite get warm enough, and her hair was dull and lifeless. She didn't *look* as though she was fine.

'I'm –' For a moment I thought she was going to lose her cool, but then she smiled reassuringly. 'Look, Lin, it's bound to take a while for me to – to look better. I was really stressed out. I know I wasn't eating enough, all right? But really, you don't need to worry about me. Once I get to Italy – all that pasta . . .'

And no one watching to see whether you eat it, I thought.

I studied my sister's face. She sounded so calm and reasonable that I doubted my own opinion. More than that, I *wanted* to believe her. I wanted her to be healthy; I wanted everything to be all right. It would be such a relief. I wouldn't have to have these endless internal discussions with myself: should I tell anyone about Polly, and if so whom, and how could I stop her from hating me for it?

You have your own problems anyway, said a selfish little voice inside me. *You have to decide what to do about the glass. You have to deal with it. If you try to tell anyone else the truth, they'll think you're absolutely insane. Polly says she's fine now. Maybe she really is fine.*

Maybe. That was the crux of it. I stared at my sister and still I couldn't make up my mind. When eventually she got out of bed, she was almost entirely covered up with a huge baggy T-shirt and leggings. I could see that her legs were painfully thin, but even if she were eating properly again, it would take time for her to put the weight back on . . .

In the end I decided to do what I had already been doing for so long, which was to wait and see. I would wait for a week or two, I decided, and if I could see that Polly was really eating and looking better, I would stop worrying about it. If she seemed just the same, or worse, then this time I really would tell someone.

At the time, the decision seemed perfectly reasonable.

CHAPTER FORTY-ONE

Later that morning Michel called at the castle to see how I was. My father and Uncle Karl had gone into the town together with the intention of speaking to the agent who had rented us the castle, to see whether we could extricate ourselves from the rental agreement. Polly and Ru had gone with them; Polly said she would rather push Ru in his buggy around Baumgarten for the entire day than stay at the castle. Of Tuesday there was no sign at all; at ten o'clock she was still in bed, doing her best to sleep through all the unpleasantness. It was left to me to open the door to Michel's rather diffident knock.

'I'm fine,' I lied as I stood on the doorstep in an ancient T-shirt and a pair of old jogging bottoms. I knew I looked horrible but I was past caring. 'Aren't you supposed to be at school?' I asked.

In truth I wished he had stayed at school; I knew it was ungrateful, since he had called the police for us, but I couldn't face talking to him or anyone else.

Michel shrugged. 'I said I had to go to the dentist.'

'Oh.'

'What happened? Is your little brother all right?'

I closed my eyes briefly, trying to shut out the brilliant morning sunshine. 'He's all right.' I really didn't want to talk about it, but I realized this wouldn't be enough. 'Someone got into the house. They tried to attack him but they missed, or . . . I don't know, maybe they missed on purpose. Maybe it was a warning. But he's OK.'

'They attacked him? What with?'

I sighed inwardly. There was a horrid inevitability about the reaction my reply would provoke.

'A spear.'

'A *spear*?'

I looked down at my bare toes curling over the edge of the doorstep. I supposed that I would be having this conversation a hundred times in the next few days. The thought of it made me weary.

'Somebody put a spear through the bed. Ru was in it, but it didn't touch him.'

How neat and succinct that sounded. It could no more summon up the horror of seeing that spear thrust through the mattress just centimetres from where my brother had lain than a trite epitaph on a gravestone can express the horror of losing a loved one. I did my best to tune out of Michel's exclamations of shock and sympathy.

'Michel, he's OK,' I said eventually.

'Do they know – I mean, the police, do they know what happened?' he asked. I noticed that he avoided asking whether the police knew who *did* it.

'I don't think so.'

Michel moved a little closer and lowered his voice conspiratorially. 'What do *you* think happened?'

I didn't reply to this. Instead I asked another question. 'Michel, what do you think we saw when we were in the church? The shape on the other side of the glass?'

Michel was silent.

'Supposing . . .' I lowered my voice to a whisper. 'Supposing it was him? *Bonschariant?*'

'That's crazy.'

He didn't have to tell me that. Twenty-four hours ago I would have said it was crazy too. Demons don't exist in the real world. But now the rule book had been torn up. The real world, the world of school and home and arguing with Tuesday and dreaming of being a scientist one day, all that was a bubble, a mirage. That reality was as thin as an eggshell, and outside it monsters prowled.

'You saw it,' I said. 'It was moving along behind the glass.'

'It could've been –'

'It could've been *who*? Your dad was away that day, remember? And we didn't see anyone else in the woods the whole time. Anyway, I thought nobody else knew about the church.'

'They don't,' said Michel unhappily. 'At least, there are rumours . . . you know. But nobody really *wants* to know.'

'So maybe it *was* him. The Glass Demon.'

Michel was shaking his head.

'Look, when we came out of the church, there was nobody there, was there? And when we got back to the castle and Polly came out . . . whatever happened in Ru's room, well, it had already *happened*.' I hugged myself, shivering. 'He went for Ru because he couldn't get at us. And glass – Michel, there was broken glass, like at the cemetery.'

Michel wasn't listening. 'Nobody would ever believe this, Lin. You can't tell the police a *demon* attacked your brother.'

'I'm not *going* to tell the police. I'm not stupid. I know

they wouldn't believe me.' I ran a hand through my hair. 'I don't know whether I believe it myself.'

'Then what's the point of even discussing it?' There was a tinge of exasperation, or perhaps anger, in Michel's voice. 'There's a reason why people round here don't want to know about that glass, you know. They're right. It's unlucky.'

'Michel.' I put my hands on my hips. 'It – he – came out of the woods and tried to kill my brother. And that time the house nearly burned down – that was him too.' My eyes scanned Michel's face. 'I can't just pretend nothing is happening. We've got to *do* something.'

'Like what?'

'Like finding a way to stop this.' My voice was beginning to rise and I saw Michel glancing around nervously to see whether anyone else was within earshot. With an effort I controlled myself. 'We have to do something before someone else is killed.'

Michel rubbed his face with his hands, as though trying to wake himself up. Then he looked at me. He was standing quite close, and now that his eyes were staring into mine I realized they were not mud-coloured at all, but a clear hazel.

'Look, Lin,' he said in a voice which was considerably firmer than his usual tones, 'the best thing we can do is forget about that church in the woods. I should never have taken you there. I shouldn't have gone myself in the first place either. We should forget about it.'

'But –'

'If there is any such person as –' he lowered his voice – 'Bonschariant, then he's trying to scare us off. We have to stay away from the church and we can't tell anyone else. Nobody. *Especially* not your father. If anyone else goes there,

God knows what will happen next time.' Michel shook his head. 'We keep this a secret, eventually your dad gives up and then maybe the attacks will stop.'

'*Maybe?*' I was incensed. 'I'm not sitting here hoping it's all going to go away. What if they *don't* stop?'

Now Michel looked alarmed. 'What are you going to do?'

'I don't know yet,' I had to admit. 'But I'm going to do *something*.' I paused. I had no idea what the German word for *exorcism* was; it was not a word I had ever had to use in my studies to date. Eventually I settled for, 'We could get a priest to come.'

'No,' said Michel emphatically. 'We're not telling anyone else.'

'*Michel!*' My voice was rising again. This time I found myself glancing round, but there was no sign of Tuesday stirring. 'We only have to tell the priest. We won't tell my father or – or anyone else.'

'You think it's not going to get out if you do that?' demanded Michel.

'Yes,' I told him. 'Aren't priests supposed to keep everything you tell them secret?'

'Only if it's in confession. But anyway, if he thinks we're crazy or we're trying to play a joke on him, he'll tell for sure.' Michel grasped my upper arm. 'Lin, please, *don't* tell anyone. It could make things a lot worse.'

I tried to pull away. 'How much worse can it be? My brother nearly died.' We glared at each other. Eventually I dropped my gaze. 'All right, if it's that much of a problem, we don't have to tell anyone.'

Michel let go of my arm with a sigh of relief.

'But,' I continued, 'we still have to do something about it.'

'Like what?'

'We go back to the church,' I told him. 'We go back, you and I, and we find a way of stopping this ourselves.'

'That's insane. No chance,' said Michel.

'In that case, I'm telling someone,' I said defiantly. 'I'm not just *forgetting* it.'

'All right, all right.' Michel sounded resentful. His hands hanging at his sides had curled into fists. 'Look, I have to go or I'll be late. I'll come back later, OK?'

I nodded.

'But in the meantime, you don't tell *anyone*, understand? Nobody. *Especially* not your dad,' he added.

'I won't,' I promised.

All the same, I was thoughtful as I watched Michel step through the green gate and heard the sound of his car's engine firing up. I had promised not to tell my father about the glass, but I still had to make up my mind about the other person I had considered telling.

CHAPTER FORTY-TWO

A couple of hours later we had a less amicable visit. Tuesday was still in bed when I heard the knocking. I ran my hands through my still-unbrushed hair and went to open the door.

There were two of them on the doorstep, a man and a woman. They were both in plain clothes but there was something indefinable about them which screamed *police*, even before the man showed me an ID. At the first glance I decided that the woman was the harder of the two. She was small and skinny, with rather lank-looking blonde hair and blue eyes like gas jets. The man was tall, broad-shouldered and heavily built; with just a few kilograms more he would actually be fat. He had a very full brown moustache and as I stared up at him I found myself thinking how terrible it would be to have to kiss him; I wondered if he had ever persuaded anyone to.

'Good morning,' said the man in English. Incongruously, he had a distinct American accent. 'We are looking for Dr Fox.'

'He's out,' I said.

This earned me a distinctly unfriendly look. 'Is Mrs Fox in the house?'

'She's . . . um, she's in bed. Sleeping.'

'I'm sorry.' He didn't look particularly sorry, nor did he offer to go away and come back later. He waited for a moment with an expression of long-suffering patience on his stolid features, then he said, 'May we come in?'

I stood back to let them both into the house. Once inside they had a rather oppressive effect on the room. He was so tall that he seemed to blot out the light from the window.

'I am Mr Schmitz and this is Mrs Ohlert,' drawled the policeman.

I wondered where he had learned English; on a foreign exchange with the States, for sure. It was unnerving listening to him – like watching a well-known actor who had been dubbed into a foreign language.

'I'm Lin Fox,' I said.

'The daughter of Dr Fox?'

'Ye-es . . .' I said reluctantly.

'We are from the Bonner Kriminalpolizei. We need to speak to your mother, please.'

'Tuesday's asleep,' I reminded them.

'Will you wake her up, please?'

I could imagine how delighted Tuesday was going to be about *that*, but I didn't say anything. I went upstairs and knocked on Tuesday's door. When there was no reply I went in and shook her shoulder.

'Tuesday!'

She had been lying with her face pressed into the pillow; now she turned her head and looked at me blearily.

'Go away.'

'Tuesday, the police are here.'

'Tell *them* to go away, then.'

'I –'

'I need to sleep. Can't you see that?' She thumped the pillow and put her head down on it again.

'I told them you were asleep. They said to wake you up.'

Tuesday gave a grunt of irritation but she did finally sit up. 'They can't do this! For God's sake! I've been up practically all night . . .'

She continued to grumble as she groped for her dressing gown and slippers. Her mane of fair hair was a tangled mess and she had dark rings under her eyes. I thought of the police waiting downstairs and for once I felt sorry for her. I went to her chest of drawers and found her hairbrush.

She slapped it away. 'I'm not tarting myself up for them.' She glared at me. 'If they haul me out of bed like this they can put up with me as I am.' All the same, she glanced in the mirror and gave a groan. 'I look *ill*. I hope they feel good about this, dragging me out of bed . . .'

There was more in this vein as she made her way downstairs. I followed her in silence.

The tall policeman was looking at one of my father's books, which lay open on the table. I recognized it as the collection of Dürer's woodcuts. That was all we needed, I thought. Let them take a look at all those pictures of skeletons on horses and horned demons and they would think we were all completely mad. The policeman looked up as we came down the stairs and he carefully closed the book.

'Mrs Fiona Fox?' he said.

At that Tuesday's face creased into a thunderous scowl. Above anything in the world she hated people to use her given name, which she considered far too pedestrian. The only reason it still appeared on official documents was that

Tuesday had never summoned up the energy to do anything about formally changing it. To her friends and acquaintances she was always Tuesday, and she would have died before she let any of them know her real name.

'I don't use that name,' she snapped.

At this a slight flicker of interest crossed the policeman's face. I suppose he thought Tuesday was admitting that she was living under an assumed name.

'Fox?' said the blonde policewoman.

I had not heard her speak before and her voice was very harsh, like the caw of a raven.

'No,' said Tuesday irritably. 'Fiona.' She made the name sound like a swear word. 'I don't use that name. Everyone calls me Tuesday.'

I could imagine how this piece of information would go down. Added to the pictures of monsters and tortured saints lying about our house, we went around naming ourselves after days of the week. I was thankful they had not asked me for *my* full name.

'Mrs Fox, may we ask you some questions?' That was the tall policeman again.

'Oh, if you must.' Tuesday's voice was deeply ungracious. She threw herself into a chair and raked through her hair with her hands.

'May we sit down also?' He had his hand on the back of one of the dining chairs.

Tuesday nodded wearily. She looked at me. 'Lin, would you make some coffee? I'm not going to stay awake otherwise.'

Reluctantly I went through into the kitchen, though I would much rather have stayed to hear what the police were going to ask her. I glanced back and saw the blonde police-woman opening a laptop. Then I had to concentrate on making the coffee. This was no easy task, since the filter machine was clogged with what looked like the droppings of some prehistoric creature, there was not a clean cup in the entire kitchen and nor was there any washing-up liquid with which to wash one. As I scrubbed and chipped uselessly at a mug with a plastic brush, I realized that I had better make some coffee for the police too, though they were risking poisoning themselves with anything which came out of *this* kitchen.

When I finally went back into the living room, the tall policeman was saying, 'Can you think of any reason why anyone would attack your son, Mrs Fox?'

Tuesday made a vague gesture which might have been confirmation or dismissal; it was hard to say. 'Reason? I don't know what reasons they might have.' She didn't say whom she meant by *they*. 'That man from the farm is completely off his head –'

'From the farm? Which farm?'

I set the tray with the coffee on it down on the table and then I leaned against the sideboard with my arms folded and listened dispiritedly as they went through the same familiar routine. Tuesday hurled out accusations in all directions and the policeman sifted through them with infinite patience, like a prospector panning for gold in a mountain of silt. I wondered if he would suggest anything more definite than 'talking' to Michel Reinartz Senior at the end of it. If not, the whole conversation was pointless.

Just listening made my head ache. I no longer knew where reality ended and imagination began. I knew what I had seen in the church, the warped and twisted shadow moving behind the coloured glass. In the face of such things the policeman's questions seemed irrelevant, an attempt to define dreams with mathematical formulae. I had almost switched off completely, staring dully out of the window, when something he did brought me back to myself with the brisk efficiency of a slap in the face.

'Do you recognize this man?' He was holding a photograph out to her. His expression was neutral, almost bored. I guessed that he did not expect her to recognize whatever he was showing her. 'His name is Werner Heckmann.'

It was fortunate for me that both officers were looking at Tuesday, watching her reaction, when he said the name, otherwise they would have seen me start as though someone had stuck a pin into me. The female officer must have seen a flicker of movement out of the corner of her eye, because she turned her cold blue gaze towards me for a moment. I did my best to look uninterested, jiggling my heel against the sideboard as though desperately bored. The blue gaze moved back to Tuesday, like a searchlight sweeping the room on a restless beat.

I couldn't see the photograph from where I stood. Tuesday was holding it with both hands, studying it. She looked at it for a long time. I began to feel the cold prickle of anxiety in the pit of my stomach. I thought she recognized him, or perhaps she was unsure. Did she remember where she had seen him? I would never forget any detail of that scene, not in a million years, but then I was not Tuesday. This was a woman who could remember the names of ten different Hermès handbags but forget her own PIN code. Supposing she remembered him, but not where she had seen him and in what circumstances? Would she be so stupid as to admit it?

Say no, I willed her silently. If she said yes, she would drop all of us in it to a catastrophic extent, but I couldn't think of anything I could do to prevent it. We could not tell the police that we had seen the dead man without admitting that we had been in the orchard that day, and that even if we had not been responsible for the murder, we had not reported it to anyone.

'I think . . .' began Tuesday. She hesitated, and I saw a change pass over her face. 'No,' she said finally, putting the photograph down on the table. She sat back and put her hands in her lap. 'I've never seen him before.'

The tall policeman said nothing; he simply nodded.

'*Sie weiss etwas, Dieter*,' said the blonde policewoman in a low voice.

I must have jumped, because the tall policeman glanced at me.

'*Sprichst du Deutsch?*' he asked me.

I nodded. '*Ein bisschen.*'

My instinct was not to admit that my German was fluent. If the police had any reason to think there was a connection between us and the death of Werner, anything which made it easier for us to become involved in local matters could only make things worse.

Silence fell.

'What did that man have to do with what happened to my son?' asked Tuesday.

I groaned inwardly. To my ears the nonchalance with which she asked the question was obviously fake. Worse, she had asked what he had to do with what happened, and not whether they thought this was the man who had attacked Ru, since she already knew that he was dead. It was easy to infer that she knew it.

'You're sure you don't recognize him?' said the tall policeman, but he didn't answer her question.

'Absolutely,' said Tuesday with enthusiasm.

They spent some time after that going through the events of the day Ru was attacked. As far as I could see, they weren't covering anything new. They asked me where I had been when the attack had taken place; I looked them in the eyes and told them I had gone over to Michel's. I was prepared to describe some fictitious piece of coursework which he had been helping me with, but they seemed satisfied with the explanation and didn't ask me any further questions.

The moment they were out of the house, Tuesday went back to bed. I started to ask her about the photograph, but she put up a hand, like a film star warding off paparazzi, and hurried back up the stairs.

I went and stood in the courtyard, looking through the gateway, and watched as the police got into their car. When they drove away, I went back into the house. I was glad Tuesday had gone upstairs; I needed time to think. I had understood what the blonde policewoman had said: *She knows something, Dieter.* But she was wrong; it was not Tuesday who knew something, it was me.

CHAPTER FORTY-THREE

We had one other visitor that day. Late in the afternoon Polly opened the door to Frau Pütz, a diminutive woman from the Jugendamt in Nordkirchen, whose forbidding face softened into a pleasant smile when she saw Ru. To the relief of all of us, she was clearly more concerned with the effects of shock on the family than anything else. All the same, this struck me as a little odd. Herr Esch had made a visit from the Jugendamt sound like a threat, as though my father and Tuesday were one step away from being prosecuted for child abuse. Watching Frau Pütz speaking to Ru in a crooning voice and patting Tuesday's hand reassuringly, I could only conclude that this had been bluster on Herr Esch's part. Frau Pütz was from Nordkirchen and she was here to do her job; Herr Esch was from Baumgarten and he wanted us gone.

On Saturday morning Uncle Karl went back to Koblenz. My father and Tuesday took Ru and went into Baumgarten to investigate the possibility of a hotel or apartment. Uncle Karl had had no success with the agent who had rented us the castle; we could disentangle ourselves if we wished, but only at a punitive cost.

Tuesday had had some difficulty in accepting this. She had not quite come out and said that she would scream and scream until someone found her somewhere else to live, but she might just as well have done. She plagued my father until he agreed to go and see if there was anything cheap enough that we could rent it even without getting rid of the castle.

Polly went out too, dressed in her running gear: she said she would run in the park in Baumgarten. I had looked at her uneasily, wondering whether she had been telling me the truth when she claimed she was OK now. At any rate I was glad she was avoiding the forest. I shuddered at the thought of my sister jogging along those lonely tracks, where anyone or anything might be lurking among the mist-veiled trees and where danger once seen would be impossible to outrun. The tangled undergrowth would trip you at every other step and the ground was treacherously slippery with mud.

I watched the others drive off with a feeling of oppressive sadness. I had sat at the scrubbed pine table at breakfast-time and watched Polly feeding Ru, while her own breakfast sat neglected in front of her. Ru was being difficult, refusing the spoon and kicking his little legs, but all the same I wondered if Polly's dedication to the task was a tactic to avoid eating. Tuesday was sipping black coffee with a don't-speak-to-me look on her face and my father was engrossed in a book about sixteenth-century methods of creating stained glass. I felt a stab of anger looking at him studying the densely printed pages. He was the one who had dragged us to this remote part of Germany, chasing another of his wild plans for instant fame and fortune, and it was still so important to him that he couldn't see what was happening right in front of him. I felt like snatching the book and throwing it on to the floor. Instead I sat and sipped my orange juice and wondered what on earth I was going to do.

After they had gone I started to go through some of the books scattered around the living room. I had no better idea of where to start looking for information about exorcizing demons. I opened a heavy book with the title 'Witch Trials in the Eifel' written in German on its shiny cover and had just found the word *Exorzismus* in the index at the back when there was a knock at the door.

Michel, I thought. Well, he could start looking through this book for me; he would be able to skim-read it far faster than I ever could. I went to the door.

To my surprise I found Herr Krause standing on the doorstep. He was dressed all in black and I remembered that the locals called him Father Krause. I couldn't resist looking down to see whether he was wearing those shoes again. He wasn't, but the ones he had on were just as bad. I looked up and found his blue eyes staring intently into mine.

'*Guten Morgen –*' I said, and stopped short; I had been about to call him *Pfarrer Krause*.

'Good morning,' he returned in English. 'Is your father at home?'

'He's gone to Baumgarten,' I said. I hesitated, unsure whether to invite him in.

'To Baumgarten?'

I thought his voice was just a little too innocent-sounding. Of course; everyone in Baumgarten knew what had been going on here. I imagined them all working away in their sitting rooms and front gardens and allotments, straightening up to watch the blue lights shooting past on their way to the castle. From my conversation with Frau Kessel it was quite clear that nothing could be concealed from anyone for very long.

'Mmm-hmm,' I said non-committally, determined to give away as little as possible.

'I hope that everything is in order?' said Herr Krause primly.

'Yes,' I said. 'There's . . . lots of order.'

'So,' said Herr Krause after a long pause, 'your father is not at home?'

I shook my head. 'He won't be back until this afternoon.'

'And Frau Fox?'

'In Baumgarten too.'

I wondered whether he would ask me about Polly next, but he didn't.

'That is a shame,' he said. 'I had something I wished to discuss with your father. About the Allerheiligen glass.' He reached into a pocket and drew out a little leather-bound notebook. He looked at me. 'May I come inside for a moment, *Fräulein*?'

I stood back to let him in.

'I shall write him a note,' he said, tearing a page from the notebook.

I watched him slip a pen out of the inside pocket of his unfashionable jacket and begin to write. I could not read what he had written; it was upside down. But I could tell that his handwriting was almost unnaturally neat and slightly old-fashioned. *A priest's hand*, I thought. My heart began to pound. If it had only been Father Engels standing there, so close that I could have reached out and touched his sleeve . . . And then I thought, *Why not ask Father Krause?*

I had no intention of telling him the whole story. I knew Michel would be furious if I told anyone I had *seen* the

Allerheiligen glass. Even if I tried to make Father Krause promise not to tell anyone, I did not think the promise would be worth anything. Gossip was the throbbing lifeblood of small towns, and anyway, this was too big a story to be suppressed: nearly a million pounds' worth of medieval art stashed away in the middle of a forest. Once the information got out, Michel would never speak to me again, and who knew what Michel Reinartz Senior would do? I thought of him striding along the forest track with that great slavering monster of a dog at his heels. He might blame Michel, and I didn't think he would be content with delivering a ticking-off.

I was not ready to risk any of that. Besides, I would never have chosen to confide in Father Krause, not when faced with the far more appealing alternative of pouring out my story to Father Engels and feeling the gaze of those beautiful dark eyes riveted upon me. But I could ask Father Krause for advice. He was an expert on the glass in his own way – fussy, obsessive and geeky perhaps, but still an expert. And he *had* been a priest.

'Herr Krause?' The words had left my lips before I even realized I had made my decision.

Herr Krause stopped writing and looked at me, his pudgy face solemn.

'The Allerheiligen glass . . . how can you be *sure* it was destroyed?'

'There was a letter from the last abbot, in the archive at Trier,' he said.

'But . . .' I hesitated. 'The letter doesn't exist any more.' I could feel my face growing warm and guessed that I was blushing. It sounded as though I were calling him a liar.

Herr Krause did not seem to notice. 'My uncle saw it, before the archive was damaged,' he said.

'Could –'

I stopped short. I had been going to ask whether his uncle could have been mistaken, but I decided this was actually rude. I thought for a moment and then tried another tack.

'People keep telling us my father shouldn't be looking for the glass anyway. They say it's unlucky and that nobody would tell us where it was, even if they knew.'

At this, a faint and rather grim smile lifted the corners of Herr Krause's mouth. 'That is unnecessary,' he said, 'since the glass no longer exists.'

'But if it *did*,' I persisted, 'I don't see why it would have to stay hidden. It ought to be in a museum or something.'

'Perhaps,' said Herr Krause. 'But you have to understand how people feel about it here. *If* your father were to discover it, do you think it would stay here, in the Eifel? No.' He shook his head. 'It would end up in a museum, maybe in Bonn, maybe in London like the windows from Steinfeld Abbey, or even in New York.'

'But wouldn't that be a *good* thing?' I asked. 'Then thousands of people would see it, wouldn't they?'

'But the glass would not be where it belongs, which is here,' he said. He glanced down at the note he had been writing. 'All this is theoretical,' he added sternly. He pronounced it *teoretical*. 'There is no Allerheiligen glass; there has been none for two hundred years.'

'I know,' I said mendaciously. 'But if there were, I still don't see why people would be so against it being found.'

'People here are superstitious,' said Herr Krause. He signed the note carefully. 'You have heard the story of Bonschari-ant?'

Now we were getting to the meat of it. I nodded enthusi-astically. 'My father told me. He said the glass is cursed. That the abbot who had it made saw Bonschariant looking at him from the other side of the window and he had a heart attack.'

'You know he was not the only one?' asked Herr Krause. 'There were other deaths. The glass had an evil name. People are still a little afraid of it now, you know. You can imagine the stories which were told about it hundreds of years ago, when people lived in fear of the Evil One.' He raised his eyebrows. 'If the French soldiers had not smashed every one of the windows, I think the local people would have done it themselves when the abbey closed down.'

Maybe that's why they were taken down and hidden, I thought.

'But . . .' I said slowly, 'couldn't the abbot have done something? Couldn't he have blessed the windows or – or –'

'Or exorcized them?' supplied Herr Krause.

His blue eyes had such an ironic look in them that I began to feel foolish for even raising the topic. I could not imagine asking him how one might go about such a thing. Miracu-lously, I didn't need to; the local historian inside of him got the upper hand and he brought up the subject himself.

'Don't forget, the last time there was an abbot of Aller-heiligen was two centuries ago. The abbot would have been more educated than the local people, but he still would have shared many of their superstitions. The thing which walked behind the glass was not a harmless little ghost, a nun who died of a broken heart. It was a demon, a monster from hell. If he stood in front of it with a Bible and a flask of holy water, and read the rite of exorcism, he would have taken his life in his hands. Or so he would have *believed*.' He shook his head. 'Far easier to smash the glass instead.'

'Father Krause?' The name was out of my mouth before I realized what I was saying, but he didn't react; I suppose he must have heard it a hundred times before. 'Can *anyone* do an exorcism?'

'Of course not.' He sounded indignant at the question. 'It must be a priest.'

'Why?'

'You would not ask someone to do brain surgery unless they were a qualified surgeon.'

'But that's different,' I said. 'If I tried to do brain surgery, someone might die.'

'It's not different at all,' said Herr Krause. 'If you tried to exorcize a demon, you might die too.'

I studied his face to see if he was teasing me, but his expression was perfectly serious. A cold stab of fear ran through me like an electric shock darting through my body. *He meant what he was saying*. Ever since that moment in the church when I had seen the dark shape moving behind the glass, a war had been going on inside my head, a war between my rational side and the evidence of my own eyes. For two days my own belief had been veering towards the fantastic, the acceptance of something which existed outside the material world, crazy though it sounded. Now I realized that I had been hoping that something would happen to pull me back from the brink of what was surely madness. Instead here was an adult – a geeky one, admittedly, but still an adult – talking about exorcism and demons as though they were real.

Herr Krause was looking at me too; we were staring at

each other like a pair of owls. I could see something dawning in his face, an unpleasant realization which spread across his mild features like a scum forming on soured milk. I quailed. I was not afraid of Herr Krause's displeasure; he seemed like the fussiest, most repressed person on the planet, and I suspected that his anger would back up on him like sewage in a blocked pipe, until he was just about fit to rupture himself. What worried me was the sure knowledge that the longest, most pedantic and tedious lecture of my life was about to be delivered, with the topic being the foolishness of young people meddling with things they did not understand.

He took a step towards me and I mentally braced myself. For a moment he said nothing.

His gaze roamed the room, as though searching for something. Perhaps he thought I had a Ouija board lying around among the piles of books and dirty cups cluttering every horizontal surface.

Into the silence the sound of knocking fell like thunder. Grateful for the distraction, I ran to open the door. Michel was standing on the doorstep. He looked apologetic, but I was delighted to see him.

'Fa– Herr Krause is here,' I said in the most neutral voice I could manage.

'Oh.' He shrugged and would have turned away.

'No – don't go.'

I almost pulled him into the house. I thought I could bear the brunt of whatever tirade was about to burst over my head like a tropical storm if I did not have to face it alone. Assuming, that was, that Herr Krause did not take Michel for another member of my coven.

But Herr Krause had evidently thought better of whatever it was he had been meaning to say. He was fussily brushing the arms of his dark jacket with his hands, as though literally shaking off the dust from our house. Then he reached over and picked up the sheet of paper on which he had been writing to my father. Very carefully he tore it into little pieces and then swept them up and stuffed them into one of his pockets.

'A letter is not necessary,' he told me. 'Please, tell your father I will call again.'

He made me a stiff little nod instead of saying goodbye, a gesture which would have been cutting if it had not been faintly ridiculous, and strode to the door. He did not acknowledge Michel at all. As the door closed behind him, I let out a great sigh.

'What's the matter?' asked Michel in German.

'Him.' I tilted my head towards the door. 'He's probably going to go and tell half of Baumgarten that I'm holding black masses out here.'

'Why does he think that?' asked Michel suspiciously.

'Because I asked him about . . . exorcism,' I said, pronouncing the word carefully.

'*Lin!*' For the first time since we had met, Michel actually looked furious with me. 'You didn't tell him about the glass, did you? Tell me you didn't.'

'OK, I didn't,' I said crossly. I sat down on one of the wooden dining chairs and folded my arms. I looked at him. 'I *didn't*, all right?'

'Well, why were you talking about exorcism with him, then? It's not exactly a normal thing to talk about, is it?'

'Look, if you don't believe me . . . OK, he came to tell my

dad something and I was asking him why everyone around here is so keen that the glass shouldn't be found. I didn't say anything about where it is. Do you think I'm stupid or something?' I glowered at him. 'He said people are superstitious and then we started talking about exorcizing the demon. That's all.'

'That's *enough*,' said Michel in a hard, sarcastic tone that I had not heard from him before.

'Michel –'

'Do you have any idea what my dad is going to do if he finds out we've been in that church?'

'But he won't . . .'

'How can you be so sure? Father Krause is bound to guess we know something about the glass. He's obsessed with all that history stuff. And if he finds out, he won't keep his beak shut. You shouldn't have talked to him.'

'Look, honestly, he doesn't suspect anything. He's the one who keeps saying the glass was destroyed, remember? He's mad with me because he thinks I'm playing about with black magic or something.' I raked my hands through my hair. 'He started looking around like he was expecting to see upside-down crosses on the walls or something.'

Michel was not mollified. He looked at me resentfully. 'Well, we can't do anything about it now.'

'I'm sorry.'

I looked at him, hoping for some sign of softening. He was still glaring at me sullenly, but I could not help taking in the freshly washed hair and neatly pressed shirt. He'd obviously made an effort with his appearance – *as though he were visiting his girlfriend*, I realized with dismay – but now I had totally ruined his mood.

'At least promise me you won't talk about anything to do with the glass with Father Krause again,' he said.

'I promise,' I said promptly.

I meant it too; there was no way I was ever going to raise the topic of exorcism with Herr Krause again. I had enough on my plate without him complaining to my father that I was dabbling in the black arts. I gave Michel what I hoped was a conciliatory smile and in spite of himself he smiled back. But all the time one thought was going round and round my brain: *I didn't promise not to tell Father Engels.*

CHAPTER FORTY-FOUR

The following Monday I went back to school. There was nothing else for it, unless I could produce a doctor's note, and I thought that was beyond my powers of forgery.

'We're late,' said Michel by way of greeting when he picked me up.

I looked at my watch. I didn't think we were any later than normal but I shrugged and slid into the passenger seat. After that we sat in silence while Michel drove. It was not a companionable, friendly silence; I had the distinct impression that he was still angry with me. I pretended not to notice and stared out of the window at the forest flashing past. Michel was driving rather fast this morning and whenever we went over a pothole or rut the car lurched nauseatingly. There was no sign of movement under the trees, no reappearance of the bulky shape I had seen there once before on our morning drive to school. Still the forest struck me as somehow menacing. I could not drive under the overarching trees with the sunlight filtering down between them without being reminded of the church in the woods. There was no beauty in those tall pines for me now. They seemed like a towering palisade hemming us in, separating us from the outside world; within their limits something unearthly roamed, something beyond our normal perception and utterly malign.

When we got to school Michel dropped me off at the gate and went to park without asking me to wait for him. I went inside, surreptitiously scanning the lobby for any sign of Father Engels's suave black-clad figure, but he was nowhere to be seen. As I was standing there, someone brushed past me, then turned to look into my face. It was the blonde girl who had spoken to me on the stairs once before. The look she had given me then was rather arch; now her expression was curious, as though she were examining me.

'*Morgen*,' I said.

'*Morgen*,' she returned after a second's pause.

She sounded very faintly surprised, as though she had not expected to be spoken to. Her gaze flickered up and down my body until she must have taken in every detail, from the boots on my feet to the silver clasp in my hair. Then she turned and walked off. I looked down at myself in confusion, wondering whether I had made some terrible mistake putting my outfit together that morning, or whether I had my breakfast all down my front. But there was nothing to see.

By lunchtime I *knew* it wasn't my clothes or food down my front. They were *all* doing it. Glancing at me furtively and looking away. Staring at me when they thought I wasn't looking. Half a dozen times I looked up from a piece of work I had just completed, to meet a pair of eyes which hastily turned their gaze elsewhere. The glances weren't unfriendly, they were curious. Very curious.

During breaktime one of the girls from my class came up to me and said, 'Hi, Lin, is your brother OK?'

'Fine, thanks,' I said warily.

'Oh.' She waited, but I did not offer any more information. 'Well, that's good,' she said, and beat a hasty retreat.

So that was what it was all about. Their faces weren't hostile, so I guessed they didn't think *I* had had anything to do with the attack on Ru. But there was a hungry interest in their eyes. *What is it like knowing that one of your family is a potential murderer?* said those looks. *Do you know who did it? Have you had to talk to the police? Are you scared it might be* you *next?*

When I looked up from the maths problem I had been working on to find Frau Schäfer staring at me in a speculative manner, I started to feel really uncomfortable and then annoyed. I wondered whether she would say something, or offer some advice or support. But she didn't. As soon as she realized I had seen her staring, she turned away. I watched her for a few moments as she fussed with the papers on her desk and flipped through the pages of a textbook, studiously avoiding meeting my eye. What would I have told her anyway, even if she had asked me if I needed help? There was nothing I could say that wouldn't sound completely insane.

You could still talk to Father Engels, though.

My conversation with Herr Krause had taught me something. Even though he was no longer a priest and even though he claimed that the story of Bonschariant was just something which the uneducated had believed in the past, he had still been deadly serious when he warned me of the dangers of trying to carry out an exorcism. He had spoken of demons as dangerous adversaries, not as fairy tales to frighten children and the terminally gullible. Father Engels was actually a priest; that meant he *must* take my story seriously.

The maths problem was forgotten, and Frau Schäfer did

not call on me for the rest of the lesson, even though she must have noticed that I was miles away. In my imagination I was already pouring out the whole story to Father Engels and basking in the radiance of those fabulously good looks, while he nodded sympathetically and perhaps – thrilling idea – laid a hand on mine to comfort me.

He's the right person to tell, I said to myself. *It's irrelevant that he's the best-looking man I've ever seen in my whole life. I'm telling him because he's the only person who can help. That's why. He's the only person.* Who was I trying to fool?

CHAPTER FORTY-FIVE

It was after lunch on that same day that my sister collapsed. Tuesday had – unusually – taken Ru out with her, so my father had cooked a late lunch for us when I got home from school. I think he was aiming at pasta with a tuna and vegetable sauce, but it was rather difficult to say. Even my father was rather discouraged when he took his first bite of overcooked and slimy pasta twists, and Polly ate nothing at all. I couldn't blame her; I ate hardly anything either. After the meal my father went into the kitchen to make coffee, though I could not imagine what effect strong black filter coffee would have on a stomach traumatized by the tuna sauce. I followed him into the kitchen and rummaged around in the cupboard until I found a tin of biscuits.

I was closing the cupboard door when I heard a noise in the living room. It was undramatic; there was no shriek, no sigh, no loud crash. Just a sound as though a stack of books had slipped over, spilling across the floor, or a heavy bolt of cloth had fallen down, unfurling as it went.

'Polly?'

I stood in the kitchen doorway and for a moment I could not see her anywhere. I thought that the living room was empty. She must have gone upstairs. Then out of the corner of my eye I saw something pale against the darker hues of the carpet. It was Polly's foot. She was lying on the floor on the other side of the dining table.

'Polly? *Dad!*'

I ran around to the other side of the table, the tin of biscuits still clutched in my hands. Polly was already trying to sit up. She looked grey at the lips and groggy. *She said she was better*, I thought. *How could I have believed her? How could I have been so stupid?*

'My God, Polly!'

My father came out of the kitchen, the jug of the coffee machine in his hand.

'Lin? Is everything all right?'

'Polly fell over. I think she fainted.'

'I'm fine,' said Polly feebly.

She reached up for the back of the nearest chair and began to try to struggle to her feet, using it as support.

'Just stay there for a minute,' I said, reaching out a hand to help her up. 'You need to –'

'I'm *fine*. Stop fussing.' Polly glared at me.

In truth, she did not look fine at all; she looked like some starving medieval ascetic carved in white marble. Even my father couldn't fail to see it now.

He came around the table, with the coffee jug still in his hand.

'Polly, you don't look well.'

'Dad . . .' Polly sounded irritated. 'I just felt a bit dizzy. It's nothing.'

He studied her for a moment. When the set line of his jaw began to relax I knew that he had made the decision to defer the whole thing to Tuesday. He was so transparent that he might as well have been one of the figures in the glass he was so desperate to find. I could see him thinking, *Polly's not well, Polly's a girl, that's Tuesday's department.* I looked from his weakening face to her resentful one, and I knew with a horrible sense of fatality that *I* was going to have to do something. I took a deep breath.

'Dad, it's not *nothing*. Polly's not eating enough. She –'

'Shut *up*, Lin!'

I shook my head. This time I was not shutting up, not for her or for anyone. 'She's hardly eating anything and she's running all the time. She's so thin – she looks like a skeleton –'

'I'm not listening to this! This is crap!' Polly sounded beside herself with fury.

'It's not crap,' I said. Before she could turn away I grabbed her arm. It was like grabbing the handle of a broom. It felt as though there was no flesh at all on her bones. I looked at my father beseechingly. 'She needs help. She's already made herself ill and she's going to starve herself to *death*.'

Death. The word dropped into the sudden silence that had fallen between us with the horrid finality of a funeral bell tolling.

'Maybe . . .' began my father at last, and stopped. He put down the jug and looked at us both helplessly. 'Maybe . . . when Tuesday gets back . . .'

I was so disappointed that I could have screamed. When I was little my father had always seemed so strong and clever, a hero. Now I looked at him and I could see a weak man who was going to turn his back on a difficult problem. It was all I could do not to pummel him with my fists.

'It's no use telling Tuesday,' I retaliated furiously. 'She's half the problem.' I could still hear her words echoing in my head: *Don't be a pig and eat all the tomatoes . . .*

Polly wrenched her arm out of my grasp. 'Shut up!' She looked at me with naked fury. 'Can't you keep your nose out, Lin? What's it got to do with you anyway? It's *my* body.'

'I'm your *sister*.'

'So – bloody – what?' shouted Polly, punctuating each word with a shove as though trying to push me away, out of the room, out of her life altogether.

I was so stunned that I simply stood there with my arms by my sides and let her shove me. I couldn't remember Polly *ever* losing her temper like this; it was as though some dark oubliette inside her had suddenly overflowed and vomited out its noisome contents.

'Polly . . . Lin . . .' began my father, but I don't think Polly even heard him. She was halfway to the stairs already. She stormed up them and a moment later we heard the bedroom door slam shut with a thunderous crash.

Suddenly I felt weak and shivery. I sat down on one of the dining chairs and put my head in my hands. *Well handled, Lin*, said a spiteful little voice in the back of my brain. *Bloody well handled.*

'Polly?' called my father uncertainly, but he did not attempt to go after her.

I looked up at him, shaking my hair out of my eyes, but any last little hope I might have been cherishing died at that moment. He was standing there looking after her, but still he did not move, and there was something hesitant in his posture, as though he were a young boy on the edge of a fight or a football match, wanting to join in but afraid to try. He saw me looking at him and grimaced.

'Dad?'

He sighed. 'Yes, Lin?'

'I'm not making it up. She's making herself ill. She hardly eats anything and she just runs and runs all the time, trying to work off food she hasn't even eaten. You haven't seen her without all the jumpers and stuff – she's like a skeleton.'

'Lin –' He spread out his hands helplessly. 'I don't know what to say.' He shook his head. 'I don't have any experience of things like this. Maybe your mother –'

'My *mother*?' My voice was rising. 'She's –'

'Lin, *no*,' snapped my father. 'We are not discussing *that* again.'

I glared at him. 'Say what you like. There's no point in telling *her*.'

My father controlled himself with an effort. 'Well, I'm not an expert. If what you say is true –'

'*If* it's true? Of course it's bloody true!'

'If it's true,' he went on, 'Polly needs professional help.'

I felt like screaming. 'It's no good just saying that. I *know* she needs help. But where are we going to get it, stuck out here in the middle of nowhere? Polly can't speak German – it's no use trying to see anyone here. We have to – we have to –' Suddenly I had got it. I made myself stop rushing on, hurling the words at my father like projectiles. Deliberately I lowered my voice. 'We have to go back to England.'

I heard the intake of breath as my father opened his mouth to say something. Then he changed his mind. He eyed me for a moment and then he swung around until he had his back to me and he was apparently gazing out the window, lost in thought.

'Dad?'

For a moment I thought he hadn't heard me.

'Dad?'

'We can't just go back to England,' he said in a low voice, without turning round.

'Why not?' I demanded.

Now he did turn round and face me. 'You know we can't go anywhere until the police inquiry has finished.'

'Well, we can go as soon as they've finished asking questions, can't we? Or we could tell them it's an emergency.' I glared at him. 'I mean, it *is* an emergency.'

'You don't know that,' said my father. 'You're not a psychologist.' He raked his dark hair with his fingers until it was standing up in all directions. 'I don't know . . .' he said in a curiously vague voice. 'To leave now . . . without anything . . .'

For one mad moment I seriously considered blurting it all out, telling him everything, saying, 'But it's all here, the Allerheiligen glass, it's right under our noses.' But hot on the heels of that first wild impulse came the realization that it would not solve anything at all. In fact it would probably make things worse. Finding the glass would not be the end of the story; it would not enable us to go home. My father would never relinquish the trophy so easily. He would want to stay here and supervise every aspect of its publication. He would want to be photographed and interviewed, and most of all he would want to be the first academic to make a full assessment of the windows.

I bit my lip.

'Dad? We have to do *something*.'

'I know. I . . .' He pinched the bridge of his nose with his fingers, suddenly looking tired. 'Look, I'll talk to Karl. Maybe he can recommend someone who can talk to Polly, someone who speaks English.'

The vague tone of his voice was not reassuring but at least he wasn't suggesting we let Tuesday handle the whole thing any more.

'Could you call him from Baumgarten?' I suggested.

'Yes,' he said, sounding a little dazed. 'Yes, of course.' He looked around him, as though searching for something. 'I think I need that coffee,' he told me, with a weak smile.

His fingers were already curling around the handle of the coffee jug; I could see that I only had a nanosecond of his attention left. I stepped a little closer and fixed him with what I hoped was a gaze of laser-like intensity.

'Dad, will you just promise me one thing?'

'And what is that?'

'That you won't leave Polly alone here – not ever.'

'Lin, she's almost an adult.'

'I know. But will you just promise anyway?'

He glanced down at the coffee jug. 'All right, I promise.'

I folded my arms and watched him as he disappeared into the kitchen. I had extracted the promise, but it didn't make me feel any better. *If he breaks his promise I'll never forgive him*, I thought, and I could feel the anger already like a foul taste in my mouth, as though he had already broken it. That was all I thought about it at the time – how furious I would be if he broke his word. I never imagined what the other consequences would be.

CHAPTER FORTY-SIX

The next day, I decided, was to be the day when I spoke to
Father Engels. I said nothing of this to Michel, of course, but
he noticed that something was up anyway. When I got into
the car he looked me up and down and gave a little whistle
through his teeth.

'You think it's too much? For school, I mean?'

'No.' Even after he had started the engine, he kept giving
me covert little glances. 'You look good.'

As the car pulled away from the castle I flipped down the
passenger sun shield and eyed myself in the little mirror.

'Is something special happening today?' asked Michel,
negotiating his way around a large pothole.

'No,' I said as innocently as I could, rubbing surreptitiously at my eyeshadow. I should have known better than
to pinch Tuesday's Dior – she always went for much more
strident colours than I would ever have chosen for myself.
As I adjusted the mirror the reflection of the castle flashed
past my line of vision. Polly had still been asleep when I left
– or pretending to be. I hoped my father would remember
his promise.

After a short pause Michel said in a casual voice, 'The
police came to see me.'

That caught my attention. I flipped the sun shield back up and turned to face Michel. 'What did they ask you about?'

'You know. When your brother was attacked . . . what we were doing. Where we were.'

An unpleasant thought struck me. 'What did you say?'

'I said we went to McDonald's in Nordkirchen.'

'*Scheisse.*' I put my hand over my eyes. 'I told them we went over to your place.'

'What did you do that for?' asked Michel incredulously.

'What was I supposed to say?' I said hotly. 'I wasn't going to tell them where we'd really been, was I? Not since you made such a fuss about me talking to Father Krause,' I added. I hunched my shoulders angrily.

'They didn't know we'd been in the woods,' Michel pointed out. 'We could have been anywhere.'

'Well, why did you say we'd been at McDonald's?'

'Because I didn't want them poking around in the woods, checking our story.'

'As if. We weren't even at the castle when it happened. Why should they want to check our story?'

Michel shrugged. 'Look, I couldn't tell them we were at my house. Those police, the ones from Bonn, they might believe it, but the ones from round here, they all know what my dad's like.' He sighed.

'He wasn't there that day,' I pointed out.

'Yes, but supposing they decided to check with him anyway? He might get suspicious.'

I thought about this. 'Michel, if your dad is – well, I don't know, looking after the glass or something . . . won't he have to talk to you about it sooner or later?' I looked at him. 'I mean, when he gets too old, or when he dies, what's going to happen then?'

The answer flashed across my mind before Michel had had time to reply.

'Jörg,' I said instantly.

'No,' said Michel. He was shaking his head.

I took no notice; my imagination was streaking ahead. 'Maybe he's already told him,' I said. 'Maybe Jörg has already been there too.'

I remembered the dark shadow writhing along the mosaic of windowpanes and for a moment I wondered whether it could have been Michel's brother stalking us through the glass. I had never seen him, but the way Tuesday had described him he sounded like a gorilla. Was it possible? But no – Jörg had gone to Prüm that day with Michel Reinartz Senior, I remembered.

'He wouldn't tell Jörg,' said Michel firmly.

I eyed him doubtfully. 'Why –' I began, but he cut me off.

'Forget Jörg. It's got nothing to do with him. Look, we have to think what we're going to tell the police if they try to check up on us. We can't say we were at my house. You'll have to say that you forgot, that we were actually at McDonald's.'

'But your car was outside the castle the whole time,' I pointed out.

'*Verdammt.*'

We rode on in silence for another hundred metres, rattling and bumping over the uneven road surface.

'We're going to get into trouble, Michel,' I said finally.

He gritted his teeth. 'No, we're not.'

'Well, what are we going to tell them, then?'

'Maybe they won't ask.'

'And if they do?'

'If they do,' said Michel grimly, 'we'll tell them we went into the woods to –' his voice sank very low and he used a word I was not familiar with – '*knutschen.*'

'*Knutschen?* What does that mean?'

'It means – you know – to kiss . . .'

'To *kiss*?'

Michel was red to the tips of his ears. 'And stuff.'

'*And stuff?*'

By now I was clutching my school bag so tightly to my chest that if it had been a live thing I would have smothered it. 'I'm not telling them *that.*'

'Have you got a better suggestion?' demanded Michel.

'No, but . . .'

'But what?' He looked at me defiantly. 'You needn't look so shocked.'

I realized that my mouth was hanging open and shut it hastily. There was a silence.

'Maybe they won't ask,' I said.

CHAPTER FORTY-SEVEN

When we got to the school I gave Michel the slip and went up to the *Sekretariat*.

'I'd like to make an appointment with Father Engels.'

I tried to inject a serious tone into my voice, but as soon as the words were out I could feel my face tingling. I hoped I was not blushing too obviously.

The school secretary looked at me over the top of her glasses and said nothing at all.

'How do I . . .' I was floundering. 'How do I do that, please?'

'What's it about?' She was reaching under her desk for a thick file.

'Um . . . I want to ask him about something.'

'Counselling?' Scepticism dripped from her voice like poison.

'Sort of.'

'We have a school counsellor, Frau Müller,' she said, bringing the file down on to the desktop with a slap.

'It's . . . um . . . it's a religious problem.'

Now I was sure I was blushing; my skin felt as though it was burning. I could feel her gaze on me again.

She opened the file with a firm thump, licked her finger and began to leaf through the pages inside it at high speed.

'Fox, hmm?'

I nodded.

'Here's your registration form. It says *no religion*.'

'I know. I'm . . . thinking of converting.'

'Converting to Catholicism?'

Why did she have to make it sound as though I were converting to Satanism?

'Yes.'

There was a very long pause, during which the secretary managed to convey her doubts about my religious tendencies, my motivation and the general state of my mental health through the pursing of her lips and the strenuous knitting of her brow. Finally she said, 'He has an office on this floor, at the end of the corridor, the last on the right. You'll have to make the appointment yourself. I don't manage his diary. *Bitte schön*,' she added acidly to my retreating back, but I was halfway out of the room already.

I looked at my watch. The bell for the first lesson was going to ring in approximately one minute. If I went to see Father Engels now, I would definitely be late. On the other hand, I realized, watching last-minute arrivals dashing into their classrooms, there probably wouldn't be anyone else around to see me do it. I opted for a slow saunter down the corridor. When the bell had rung and there was a chorus of classroom doors slamming, I picked up speed and made a beeline for the last door on the right. My hand was actually on the door handle when a clear, cool voice behind me said, 'Are you looking for me?'

I jumped as though the door handle had been electrified. My school bag slipped from my shoulder and hit the floor, where it burst open, spilling folders and textbooks across the tiles. A pen rolled away until it came to rest against the door.

'Oh, God!' I tried to stamp on a fifty-cent piece which was rolling across the floor, but missed. Then I realized what I had said. 'I mean – I didn't mean . . .' I crouched on the floor and tried to gather up the books as quickly as I could. Father Engels didn't help me; he stood there as silent and immovable as a figure on a monument. 'I'm so sorry.'

Eventually I had gathered up everything except the fifty-cent piece, which had vanished, and had stuffed it all back into my bag. 'I'm sorry,' I said again.

'This is my office,' said Father Engels.

'I know,' I said. 'I was looking for . . . I mean, I wanted to make an appointment with you.'

'I don't believe you are one of my students.'

'No – I . . . I wanted to ask your advice about something.'

'Frau Müller –' he began, but I shook my head.

'It's a – a religious – problem.'

'What type of religious problem?'

'It's rather complicated,' I said.

'Hmm.' He reached into his pocket and took out a key. 'You'd better come in,' he said reluctantly. 'Don't you have a lesson now?' he asked, as he unlocked the door.

'Yes, but – it's quite urgent,' I said, cringing inside about how stupid that must sound. He probably thought . . . well, I didn't want to consider what he probably thought about me. *Everyone has a crush on him*, the girl from my class had said.

Father Engels's office was quite small and bare, as though he were trying to replicate a monastic cell. The chair he offered me was hard and upright, designed to prevent any visitor from becoming too comfortable. I settled myself under the tortured gaze of a crucified Christ that was the room's only adornment and looked at Father Engels across the vast polished wasteland of his desk. There was not a single sheet of paper, not so much as a propelling pencil on it. I noticed that Father Engels had left the door wide open, although whether that was for my benefit or his was not clear.

'So,' he said. 'You are the daughter of Professor Fox, are you not?'

I nodded, wondering whether I should point out that we had actually spoken before, outside the castle at Nieder-burgheim.

'And how is Professor Fox's research progressing?'

'Um . . . good,' I said.

'Really?' One sleek black eyebrow went up. There was a silence during which we both eyed each other. Then he seemed to make his mind up about something. Leaning forward, he said, 'So what is the religious problem you wanted to talk to me about?'

Faced with this straightforward question, what little confidence I had left seemed to shrivel up. Father Engels's good looks were almost terrifying; being so close to him was like bathing in the dazzling brightness of a conflagration. It was impossible to come right out and say, *Someone's terrorizing my family and it might – just might – be a demon.*

'My brother . . .' I started, and stopped. 'My brother Reuben,' I began again, 'he's only one – well, one and a half –'

'He's sick? You want me to pray for him?'

'No . . .' I shook my head. 'He isn't sick. Someone tried to – someone attacked him.'

'Someone? Do you know who?'

'No.' This time I looked at him boldly, daring him to let slip one flicker of suspicion, the kind I had seen sliding across Uncle Karl's face. 'Someone broke in.'

'I'm sorry,' said Father Engels, taking the safe option.

'The thing is, I don't think any of us is safe. I think my whole family is in danger –'

'Wait a moment.' Father Engels raised a hand as though warding me off. 'If you think your family is in some sort of danger, shouldn't you be talking to the police?'

'The police are already trying to find the person who attacked Ru.'

'Then why . . .'

I took a deep breath. 'Please don't think I'm crazy or anything. I'm not completely sure it was a *person* who attacked my brother. I mean, not a human being. I saw something – I can't explain it . . .' I could see him opening his mouth to speak so I rushed onwards. 'It wasn't just Ru, there was Herr Mahlberg, and this man Werner – he was a relative of Michel's – Michel Reinartz, I mean. Herr Mahlberg was supposed to talk to my father about the Allerheiligen glass, and Werner knew about it as well.'

A deep furrow was appearing in Father Engels's brow.

'I think they were killed to stop them telling my father where the glass is.'

'Killed?' Father Engels's voice was cold and incisive. He did not appear to be remotely shocked. 'By "Herr Mahlberg", do you mean Herr Heinrich Mahlberg – the local historian?'

'Yes.'

'Herr Mahlberg is supposed to have drowned in his bath, is he not?'

I had the uncomfortable feeling of being cross-examined by a prosecuting lawyer. 'Yes . . .'

'And you believe you have some information which suggests otherwise?'

'No,' I said. 'Not information, not exactly.'

I was beginning to feel dismayed. This was not going the way I had hoped it would. There was no warmth in Father Engels's voice, no sympathy in his glance. We might have been discussing a discrepancy in the parish accounts.

'And this Werner, what about him?'

'Well, he was supposed to have fallen out of an apple tree, but Michel's father said it looked like someone had hit him over the head.'

I could feel myself starting to stumble over my words. Everything sounded so stupid and unlikely when I tried to explain it. All the same, I was committed now. If I left without saying what I had come to say, I would look even sillier. I blundered on.

'And Michel said he – Werner – knew where the glass was.'

I stopped short, horrified. I had not meant to tell Father Engels about the existence of the glass, not yet, not until I was sure he would help me. For a split second I hoped he would not notice what I had said, but I saw a fleeting shadow cross his face, before he smoothed it over again.

'No one knows where the glass is,' he said.

I could not think of anything to say to this. I looked down at my hands.

'I still fail to see why you came to speak to *me* about this,' said Father Engels. 'Attempted murder is a police matter.'

I winced at the incredulous tone in which he pronounced

the words *attempted murder*, as though he were handling something too disgusting to be touched.

'*If* you know something, you should be talking to them.'

'They wouldn't believe me,' I said.

'Nevertheless –'

'It's not what *happened* that they wouldn't believe,' I said, cutting across his protestation. 'It's who did it.'

Father Engels opened his mouth to say something and then shut it again. He studied me for a moment. 'You said this was a religious problem. Are you telling me this because I am a priest? You think you can tell me something you wouldn't tell other people, because it's all under the seal of the confessional?' He shook his head. 'We're not in the confessional. I've not seen you in any of my classes so I imagine you're not even a Catholic, are you?'

I shook my head.

'Then if you have something incriminating to say, I suggest that you don't say it to me. There would be no reason for me not to pass it on – to the police, perhaps.'

'That's not the reason,' I said. I threw caution to the winds. 'Look, I think the person who attacked my brother and those other people did it because of the pictures in the glass.' I took a deep breath. 'The thing is, we saw him – behind the glass. I think it was Bonschariant.'

There was a silence, which I took as encouragement. There was still a chance I might persuade him to take me seriously.

'You know, Bonschariant, the Glass Demon. He's supposed to walk behind the glass and –'

'I know who Bonschariant is. I'm fully aware of all the local superstitions,' interrupted Father Engels.

'It's not a superstition. We've seen him.'

'Seen him?' Father Engels gave an incredulous laugh. 'That's impossible. You can't have seen him.'

'Why not? Father Krause thinks demons really exist. He said people could die trying to exorcize them.'

'Father Krause?' Father Engels's lip curled in contempt. 'Don't listen to him. If he's been filling your head with nonsense . . .'

'He didn't. I told you, we saw him. It.'

'Look . . .' Father Engels was beginning to sound weary. 'I don't know what you think you saw or what you think you know, but it wasn't the Glass Demon. If I recall the story correctly, Bonschariant was supposed to appear behind the stained-glass windows of Allerheiligen. No one has seen those windows for over two hundred years. They were probably smashed to bits long ago. I think someone has been playing tricks on you, young lady.' He paused. 'Or else you are trying to play tricks on me. I hope that is not the case. Now, if you don't mind . . .'

'I know what I saw,' I said stubbornly. Now that Father Engels was so clearly angry with me I found I was no longer intimidated. I found the courage to look into that beautiful face and to hold the gaze of those dark eyes. 'I know it was him, because we saw him through the Allerheiligen windows.'

'You can't have.'

'They're in the woods, by the Kreuzburg. There's a bit of land that belongs to the Reinartzes and there's a little church there, hidden away in the middle of the forest. Michel's father looks after it or something. And the glass is in the windows. Michel showed me. He took all the boards down and let the light in.' I was galloping on now, desperate to tell my story before Father Engels had another opportunity to interrupt me, hoping I might persuade him. 'There's Adam and Eve in the Garden of Eden, and somebody bathing in a river and a horrible one of soldiers killing babies. We were in the church looking at them and that was when we saw him, through the glass. He was moving along behind the windows, just like in the story about the abbot who died –'

'Enough!'

'– and we had to lock the door and not look at him, because otherwise, if we had looked –'

'*Enough!*' Now Father Engels was almost shouting.

I stopped, shocked at the vehemence in his voice.

'This is preposterous!' He slammed down a fist on the desktop. His handsome features were contorted with fury. At that moment he looked like Lucifer, an angel gone to the bad. With an effort he lowered his voice. 'This is an obvious fantasy.'

'It's not –'

'Don't interrupt. I don't know why you have chosen to come and see me with such a ridiculous tale, but I have no intention of listening to any more of it. I'm very sorry about your brother and I wish him a speedy recovery, but I think you might find something more useful to do than trying to draw attention to yourself with these stories.' He drew a deep breath and forced himself to lower his voice. 'If you know anything genuine about the attack on your brother or any other . . . crime . . . talk to the police. But if you have any sense you won't tell them a pack of lies about seeing a demon. Better still, talk to Frau Müller, the school counsellor.' He stood up and pointed at the door. 'I don't want to see you in here again.'

I got to my feet, hoisting my bag on to my shoulder. One

look at that thunderous expression told me that I would be wasting my time to argue any more. Without another word I slunk out of the room.

Further down the corridor, the school secretary was looking out of her door. Her glasses were, as usual, perched on the end of her nose, giving her ample opportunity to stare at me disapprovingly over them.

'Well,' she said as I passed, 'did you find Father Engels?'

She knew perfectly well that I had.

'No,' I said. 'He was out.'

CHAPTER FORTY-EIGHT

It was that conversation with Father Engels that made me do it. When I walked away from his office and past the curious gaze of the school secretary, I was defiant. I was concentrating on keeping my dignity. Going into my classroom, where the lesson was well under way and everyone looked up to see who was coming in late, I felt embarrassed. For a while, as I struggled to catch up with the exercise the class was doing, I actually felt detached from what had just happened. But as the morning progressed I started to feel angry.

It was not just the things he had said to me, even though it stung me to recall them. *Preposterous – an obvious fantasy – you might find something more useful to do than trying to draw attention to yourself.* I curled my hands into fists under the desk, digging my nails into my palms, as I thought about that. But what was worse was the way he had looked at me – the coldness, the irritation, finally the contempt. I thought I could see myself through his eyes – a silly girl with a ludicrous crush on someone, trying to attract attention with a melodramatic tale of murder and intrigue.

It was all so unfair. Who was I supposed to ask for help? Tuesday was useless – faced with a real problem she would probably need six months' therapy herself. My father would have liked to shovel everything on to her if he could. And Father Engels didn't just not believe me, he *despised* me.

I thought about that impossibly handsome face scowling at me and for the first time I understood why a vandal might want to destroy a work of art. I felt like punching that perfect nose, scratching at those gorgeous eyes. I wanted to mar the beauty that hid such coldness and arrogance. How could I have *loved* him? I thought of the hours I had spent dreaming of being with him, of seeing the soft sympathy in those dark eyes as I poured out my heart to him. All of it an illusion. I felt like killing him, then I felt like killing myself. It didn't seem possible to be this angry and not to explode or rupture something. The anger was like a toxin racing through my bloodstream, percolating through my whole body, poisoning it.

I don't know how I got through the rest of the morning. When the final bell rang at the end of the school day I was out of my chair and halfway through the door before the others had even collected their books up. Michel was just coming out of his classroom. I strode up to him and grabbed him by the arm.

'Let's go.'

He looked at me in surprise but didn't say anything. As we thundered down the staircase he was still trying to fit his right arm into his jacket while carrying his school bag. I didn't slow down.

'Where's the car?'

'Just round the corner. I got a really good space for once. What's the hurry?' he panted, trying to keep up with me as I stalked along.

'Nothing. I just want to get going.'

When we got to the car I threw my school bag into the back seat.

'Hurry up, can't you?'

Michel gunned the engine and pulled out of the space. Some of my classmates were coming towards us and someone waved. I slumped down in my seat and glared out of the side window.

'Bad morning?' asked Michel.

'No,' I said shortly.

'Well, what's –'

'Just drive.' I flipped the sun shield down, caught my own angry gaze in the mirror and flipped it up again.

It seemed to take forever to get out of Nordkirchen and into Baumgarten. Finally we were through the smaller town and on to the little road which led into the forest. I waited until we were actually on the pitted track which led to the castle, with the trees towering over our heads, and then I said, 'Stop. Right here.'

Michel slowed the car. 'What's the matter?'

'Just stop. Here.'

Obediently he braked.

'Turn off the road.'

There was a little side track, just wide enough for the car but deeply rutted. Michel looked at it dubiously.

'What for? We'll get stuck in there.'

'I don't care.'

'But –'

'Michel, *drive in there*!' I was almost shouting by this time. I slapped the dashboard with the flat of my hand. '*Just do it!*' I was drunk with rage; I didn't care whether he thought I was mad or not.

Michel turned the car on to the track. It bounced a couple of times on the ruts, then his foot slipped off the clutch and it stalled. We both felt the car roll a little. Michel sighed and put the handbrake on, then reached for the keys.

A second later I was virtually on his lap. Considering what he had done in the church in the woods, I was quite surprised to find Michel resisting me. He fought his way backwards out of my embrace, sheer astonishment spreading over a face that was now smeared with Tuesday's third-best lipgloss.

'What are you –'

I didn't give him time to finish the sentence. I pulled him towards me and kissed him again, locking my lips to his, raking my hands through his hair. This time Michel didn't try to fight me off; in fact he began to join in with a passion, sliding his arms around me.

When we came up for air he was looking at me with a kind of wonder. He touched my face very gently, as though he had wanted to do so for a long time but never dared.

I should have been honest with myself then, but I wasn't. Some kind of furious madness seemed to have possessed me. I pressed my mouth to Michel's again, clinging to him like a vampire. Father Engels's angry face flashed through my mind, but the thought of his contemptuous expression only seemed to spur me on. Illogically I kept thinking, *I'll show him. He's not so special*.

Rage dragged me down like an undertow, mixed with a kind of bitter joy. Michel found me attractive, oh yes, he did. Father Engels could go to hell. I dragged off my jacket, pulling the sleeves inside out in my haste. Already Michel's hands were sliding tentatively under my T-shirt. His touch on my bare skin was like the breath of a furnace.

I don't like to think how it would have ended if Michel hadn't said what he did.

'Lin . . .' he said. 'I – love you.'

'What?'

It took a moment for his words to sink in. I stopped trying to kiss him and pulled away, clawing my hair back from my face. Suddenly I was aware of the cool air on my bare arms.

'Oh, God,' I said.

Instantly his expression crumbled into hurt. He put out a hand and tried to touch my face, but I was already trying to back away. I didn't think I could stand to see that look on his face. What had I done? I could not think what to say or what to do to make it right again. The fury of a minute before had utterly passed and left me feeling cold and empty. I could think of nothing to do but to get away, to put as much space between us as possible. I fumbled for the door handle, avoiding his eyes.

'Lin? What's the matter?'

I yanked the door open and stumbled out of the car, clutching my jacket.

'Lin?'

I thought if I heard that pleading tone in his voice again I would go completely insane. I had left my bag on the back seat of Michel's car but I didn't care if I never saw it again. I slammed the door and cut off the beseeching voice mid-sentence. Then I began to run. I didn't think about where I was going; I simply ran into the forest. I left the track completely, crunching over piles of leaves and twigs, zigzagging around places where the brambles were too thick to negotiate, slipping a little where it was muddy but righting myself and carrying on, running until my heart was pounding and my chest felt as though it would burst.

I don't know if Michel tried to come after me on foot; I never looked back. At any rate after a few minutes I heard the distant sound of the car's engine starting far behind me. It coughed and died, then roared into life again; I suppose he had stalled it on the ruts. He had no hope of catching me now anyway, since it would be impossible for anyone to drive through this part of the forest. It was becoming more and more difficult to run through the thick undergrowth. Eventually I slowed to walking pace. There was a painful stitch in my side.

Up ahead I could see the castle tower through the trees. I stopped dead. If I went back now, with a red face and my hair a tangled mess, there would be questions. Worse, supposing Michel had driven round and was waiting for me? With a groan I sank down on to the mossy trunk of a fallen tree and put my head in my hands. That same thought kept going round and round my brain: *What have I done?* Just when I thought things could not get any worse, I had done something unthinkably terrible, and I had done it to the one person who had been trying to help me. The mere thought of what had happened in the car was so awful that I shied away from thinking about it.

A groan forced its way out, scouring my throat. I leaned further forward, hugging my knees, trying to draw myself into a ball. At that moment I wished I never had to go back to the castle, ever. Ru, Polly, my father and Tuesday . . . I couldn't protect all of them myself and I was worn out trying. Everything was wrong. A black cloud of self-loathing engulfed me. I had thought I was so clever, persuading Michel to show me the glass – investigating the scene of the attack on Ru – pumping Father Krause for information. But now the entire edifice had collapsed, as though it were a crumbling old tower whose last supporting beam had rotted through and brought the whole lot down into a heap of rubble. I didn't fully understand what had come over me in the car, but I knew one thing for certain: I had well and truly pressed the self-destruct button.

I hugged myself, gazing unseeingly at the silent ranks of tree trunks. Even the autumn sunlight seemed less bright, as though I was seeing it from the bottom of a deep, dark well. *It's too much*, I thought. It was as though we had been jinxed from the very first moment we had turned off the main road and driven into Niederburgheim. The moment I had stepped out of the car and walked through the fragrant grass to where Werner lay motionless underneath the apple tree, that was when it had all started going wrong. It was like some sort of curse.

That had been the day when I first saw Father Engels too. I remembered when he had opened the castle door and stepped out. That was the moment which had sown the seeds of today's disaster. If he had been old, or fat and jolly, or phenomenally ugly, I would probably never have given him a second thought. Those good looks were fatal; they could draw you in before you knew what was happening.

He's a devil, I thought bitterly, as I crouched there on the tree trunk, rocking myself in my misery, the memory of that handsome face distorted with anger tormenting me. *A devil.*

CHAPTER FORTY-NINE

I didn't expect Michel to pick me up on Wednesday morning. Nothing on earth could have induced me to give Tuesday and my father even a watered-down version of what had happened the day before, so I decided to get up early and make my own way to school. I thought that if I left half an hour earlier than usual and walked through the forest to the main road I might be able to pick up a public bus. The truth was, I didn't care much either way; being late for school was the least of my worries.

As I stood in front of the bathroom mirror listlessly brushing my hair, the disastrous scene with Father Engels kept running through my head – his angry face, my stumbling words. I felt sick thinking about it. I had told him everything. I had named the Kreuzburg and the Reinartz family – I had even described some of the scenes in the windows. What would he do with the information? He had seemed to disbelieve every word I had said; he had been furious at what he saw as my attention-seeking fantasies. Or was he angry because, like everyone else in Baumgarten, he thought the outsiders should be prevented from stirring up matters to which everyone else was happy to turn a blind eye? One thing I did know: whenever anyone had come close to the

Allerheiligen glass, it had led to disaster. If something else happened now, I would be to blame.

I drifted downstairs in a fog of misery, with no appetite for breakfast. I didn't know whether I would ever see my school bag again – if I were Michel I would probably have thrown it into the deepest part of the castle moat – so I grabbed a handful of my father's pens from the pine table and stuffed them into one of Tuesday's bags. There was nothing I could do about the neglected coursework; I would have to make up some excuse or other.

When I let myself out the sun was up but there was an autumn chill in the air. I hesitated outside the green gate. Almost certainly there was a quicker way through the woods than the one we usually drove, but the idea of getting lost among the trees, even with the sun up, was not a pleasant one. I thought of the bulky forms I had seen moving about in the forest sometimes as we drove to school. They were probably deer, but all the same . . .

In the end I took the normal route, Tuesday's bag thumping my shoulder blade as I hurried along, willing myself to be out on the main road before Michel could overtake me.

I almost made it; I could see the open stretch of meadow at the border of the forest when I heard the sound of a car engine behind me. I didn't look round. I pulled the hood of my jacket over my head and kept walking. The car was coming up very fast, and right until the last moment I thought that he would just drive past me and keep on going. Then I heard a squeal of brakes and half-turned in spite of myself. It was Michel, all right; I would have known that battered red Volkswagen anywhere.

'Lin!'

He was leaning out of the window, his dark hair falling over his eyes. I felt a fleeting impulse to walk on anyway, but then I relented. I could not imagine that he was going to say anything I would like to hear, but I was the one who was in the wrong, wasn't I? I didn't want to make it any worse. Unwillingly I retraced my steps until I was level with the car.

'Why didn't you wait?' said Michel. He sounded breathless.

'I don't know.'

'I went to the castle like normal and when you weren't outside I waited. Then it was getting a bit late, so I went and knocked.' He raised his eyebrows. 'Is your mother always like that in the morning?'

I didn't need to ask, *Like what?* I could imagine how Tuesday had reacted to having to get up and answer the door. I shrugged.

'Get in the car. Come on. We're going to be late already.'

I opened the passenger door and climbed in.

'Your bag's in the back,' said Michel.

I looked round. He had evidently picked up the books and pens which had spilt out when I threw it there.

I ran my hands through my hair. 'Look, Michel –'

'You shouldn't have walked,' he said. 'You'd never have made it to school in time. The bus which goes from the end of this road doesn't go to the school. You'd have had to walk the rest –'

'Michel, about yesterday . . .'

'I don't know why you didn't wait. Did you want the exercise or something?'

'No!' I realized I had raised my voice; he looked startled.

With an effort I made myself calm down. 'Look, I didn't think you'd want to pick me up today. Not after – you know, what happened yesterday.'

For a moment I thought he hadn't heard me. He was looking straight ahead, at the road, and not saying a thing. Then I saw that he was chewing his lower lip, and the faint red stain of a blush was creeping up his neck.

'I'm . . . I'm really sorry,' I tried, realizing how lame it sounded. 'I don't know what happened. I was upset. I just . . . went sort of mad. I'm sorry.'

'It's OK,' he said, but we both knew it wasn't.

I heard a sharp intake of breath, as though he was about to say something, but evidently he thought better of it. We drove on in silence for a while. I was gazing out of the window when I realized that I wasn't seeing anything at all; everything was a blur. I hadn't even been aware I was crying.

The car was slowing to a halt even though we were nowhere near the school. Michel pulled into an empty bus stop and put the brake on.

'Hey,' he said awkwardly.

I felt his hand tentatively touch my shoulder. I shook my head. The tears were coming faster and faster; I couldn't help letting out a sob.

'I'm sorry,' I choked out.

'That's OK,' he said.

He hadn't understood me; he thought I was saying sorry for what had happened the day before. But I was sorry for everything, for the whole horrible mess. For leaving poor Werner lying there in the grass, without even ringing the police. For fooling around in the church in the forest while someone was trying to spit my baby brother with a medieval spear. For making such an idiot of myself in front of Father Engels. The more I thought about it, the more I cried, until the tears scorched my eyes and my chest hurt from heaving.

Michel sat next to me for a little while without saying or doing anything. Then he reached over and put an arm around me. I pushed my face against the side of his neck and howled like a small child, until I had cried myself out and my eyes began to feel dry and itchy.

'Lin?' said Michel in my ear. 'There's a bus trying to get in here.'

In spite of my woe I peeped in the side mirror. He was right; a bus was looming up behind us, the bus driver grim-faced and impatient. The indicator was on and the next moment the horn sounded, twice.

'We'd better move,' said Michel. As we pulled out of the bus stop he said, 'Do you want to go to school?'

I shook my head.

'Then don't let's go,' he said. 'You can write one of your letters. Do you think you can forge my dad's handwriting too?'

I managed a weak laugh. 'I don't know. Tuesday's is so bad, anyone could do it.'

Michel patted his breast pocket. 'I've got ten euros. We can go to the drive-through and get some breakfast.'

'OK.'

I rubbed my face with my hands. I probably looked awful, but perhaps that was a good thing. If I looked horrible enough, I would lose my power to hurt Michel's feelings.

'Do you feel better?' he asked me.

'Well . . .' I shrugged.

'It's all right, you know,' he said, taking his eyes off the road for a moment to look at me. 'We'll sort it out somehow.'

'Yes,' I said, not wanting to contradict him. But there was still a heavy feeling in my chest, where the dark cancer of misery was growing. Whatever Michel said, I had a feeling this was beyond sorting out.

CHAPTER FIFTY

The rest of the week passed without incident. I went to school carrying the note I had carefully forged and did my best to look sickly while Frau Schäfer read it, her eyebrows raised. I spent the afternoons hanging around the castle, not wanting to leave Polly alone, even though she was distinctly offhand with me. Any remark which might conceivably have been the opening to a discussion about her eating problem was met with a wall of silence. We both knew that in another month she would have left for Italy and the topic would be closed. I fretted, waiting in vain for my father to say that he had spoken to Karl and Karl had suggested something . . . For the hundredth time I wished that Tuesday was the sort of person I could have talked to, but she was as irritable as a toddler who has missed its nap. She drank endless cups of herbal tea, roamed the house all day long with her little bottle of flower remedy clutched in her hand, and complained vociferously about everything from the non-existent mobile phone signal to Karl's lack of family spirit. Her patience ran thin with everyone, even Ru, who tapped into the current of bad feeling running through the house and became squally and fractious. Polly no longer seemed to have the energy to amuse him, so I did my best, but it was uphill work and my heart wasn't in it. All I wanted to do was be on my own and think about what I should do. I felt lonely, a little scared and most of all sad.

I look back on those few days now and realize that I did not know what it meant to be sad, to have regrets. I think that if I could have them back again, or one of them, or an hour, or even five minutes, I would try to speak to them – to my father, perhaps even to Tuesday, but most of all to Polly. I would try to say or do something – anything – which would make a difference. Supposing I had said to Polly, 'Let's wait until everyone else is out, then let's go, let's just go. Let's walk out of here and take the first train from Baumgarten. Let's go to Köln or Bonn and from there on to somewhere else. Anywhere. Let's just get away'?

I didn't do it though, and thinking about it now is like trying to talk to the ghosts of the past, or at least to one thin, sad ghost, the one who stands beside me sometimes in the hours before dawn, its eyes grave and reproachful.

CHAPTER FIFTY-ONE

By Saturday morning I had come to a decision. When I awoke it was still dark. I lay in the bed and watched the first grey light come seeping in at the edges of the curtains. Gradually the room took form around me – the furniture, the funny knick-knacks on the walls, Polly's sleeping body were outlined in the soft light of dawn. As the morning slowly brightened into focus, so did my resolve.

I slid out of bed, dressed silently and went downstairs. As usual the pine table was a panorama of empty wine glasses, dirty plates, books, papers and scattered pens. I cleared a patch of tabletop, took a sheet of paper from my father's jotter and wrote BACK SOON, LIN in capital letters using one of his markers. I weighted the note down with the salt cellar. Then I let myself out of the front door, closing it quietly behind me.

My heart was thumping as I worked my way carefully through the network of tracks which led towards the farm, taking care to follow the short cut Michel had shown me. If his father was up and about at this early hour I had no wish to be caught at the spot where we had met before. There was a tingling feeling, tight as a clenched fist, in my gut. *Bad idea*, said a voice at the back of my mind. I ignored it. This had to be the worst plan in the world, but I was going to carry it out anyway. The alternative was for me and my family to stay at the Kreuzburg like sitting ducks, waiting for the next attack. I knew with a chilling certainty that it would come. I remembered the Abraham and Isaac window, the great knife gripped in the hand of the patriarch, and shuddered.

For a long time all I could see were trees and the next curve of the track, but suddenly I glimpsed the wall and roof of the farm. A minute later I stumbled out of the forest and found myself in front of the wooden gate which led into the yard. It was closed. I approached it as stealthily as I could but all the same I heard something move inside, a sound which might have been the *clink* of a chain as it left the ground, pulling tight. There was a low growl from the other side of the gate.

I backed away. Was there another way into the farm? Treading carefully, I followed the wall. I turned a corner and there was a battered door, the paint peeling away in patches.

I lifted my hand, curling the fingers into a fist, getting ready to knock as loudly as I could, but then I hesitated. I wished I had tried to look through the keyhole of the gate, to see whether Michel's car was inside or not. I felt pretty sure that Michel's father would do nothing if Michel was there, but what if Michel was out? I let my hand drop to my side. I heard the sound of the dog barking from the courtyard, followed by a muffled bump from inside the house. A moment later there was a rattle on the other side of the door: someone was drawing back a bolt.

I took a step back. *I'm not ready*, I thought. I had no idea what I was going to say if Michel's father opened the door. Too late. The bolt slid back and the next moment the door was opened from within. For one long, horrible moment I thought it was Michel Reinartz Senior who was standing there in the dark passage, rubbing his eyes with one lean hand, his shoulder against the wall. Then I realized that it was not him at all, it was Michel, but I had little time to enjoy the feeling of relief that swept over me like an adrenalin rush. Michel's expression changed in an instant from one of sleepy bafflement to wide-awake alarm. He grabbed me by the shoulder, shoved me away from the door and closed it behind him with stealthy haste, as though he was afraid of disturbing a savage animal which slept within.

'What are you doing here?' he hissed.

'I have to see you.'

'Lin –' Michel looked distracted. 'Wait here. No –' He ran a hand through his hair so that it stood up in untidy spikes. 'Don't wait right here. You know the track to the castle?'

I nodded.

'Go down there. Just a hundred metres or so. And wait. OK?'

He turned to go back into the house and I saw that his feet were bare. He had only just got up. I glanced up at the house, wondering if anyone else was awake. I looked back and the door had closed quietly. I didn't waste any more time. I took the track he had indicated, half-ran and half-walked for about a hundred metres, until the wall of the farmhouse was hidden by the trees, and waited.

About five minutes later Michel appeared. He had put on an overshirt and boots, but his dark hair was still uncombed. I was uncomfortably reminded of his father's rough looks.

'Let's go,' he said, nodding at the track ahead.

I glanced back towards the farm.

'We can't take the car,' said Michel. 'I'd have to open the gates. The dog will go mad and Dad will hear.'

He was striding along so quickly that I had to trot to keep up. After a few minutes he judged we were well out of earshot of the farm.

'Here,' he said.

We turned off the path. There was a little picnic hut under the trees, a round construction with open sides and a thatched roof, and a bench which ran around the inside. Nobody had picnicked there for a very long time; we had to step over nettles and brambles to get inside, and the floor was littered with twigs and leaves. Michel sat down on the bench and I sat beside him.

'Michel –'

'Why did you come to the farm?' he said, interrupting me.

'I had to see you,' I said.

I saw the doubtful way he was looking at me and a horrible thought struck me. Did he think this was to do with what had happened the other day in his car? Did he think I had changed my mind – or worse, did he think I was messing around with him, leading him on for some unpleasant reason of my own? The more I tried to push the thought away, the worse I felt. It was the first time I had done this, sought Michel out, asked to see him. I could have waited until he picked me up on Monday morning – but my own desperation to do something had spurred me on. Now I could see that Michel might put quite a different interpretation on things. I moved along the bench a little, putting space between us. I could feel my cheeks burning and hoped I was not blushing. There was nothing for it but to push on.

'I couldn't sleep,' I said. 'I can't go on like this – we have

311

to do something. Either we go back there or we tell the police.'

I didn't have to say what I meant by *there*.

Michel let out a long breath. 'Lin, we can't tell the police.'

'Why not?'

'Because they'll think we're crazy.'

'We won't say anything about – you know, *him*. Bonschariant.' I brushed strands of dark hair back from my face. 'Look, we have to do *something*. My dad's been trying to find somewhere else for us to go, but the landlord won't let us off renting the castle. Tuesday's going mad – not that I care about that. I just don't feel safe, not after what happened to Ru. I feel like we're being watched all the time.' I saw a strange expression flicker across his face. 'What?' I said instantly.

'I get that feeling too.'

I eyed him warily, wondering whether he was trying to wind me up. 'Truly?'

He nodded. 'Not all the time. Just sometimes. It's like there's someone out here in the woods.'

'I know.'

Michel hadn't heard me. 'It's not just that. Someone tried to break into my car.'

'What, your old Volkswagen?'

I could hardly believe my ears. The car had an ancient tape deck which looked as though it had been manufactured round about the time Tuesday was still listening to ABBA and wearing flares, but otherwise there was nothing worth stealing.

'Yes,' he told me slightly defensively. 'The bonnet's scratched, like someone tried to lever it up. I think the dog

312

disturbed them. He's been barking a lot at night. Anyway I've started putting the car inside at night, in the courtyard.' He gave me a rueful half-smile. 'Took me hours to move enough stuff to make room for it.'

I pondered this. Perhaps Michel was imagining things with his car. It was such a rustbucket that I didn't see how he could pick out a few new scratches from the dozens of little scrapes and scuffs which adorned it. All the same, a whole new vista of unpleasant possibilities had opened up before me.

Herr Mahlberg, who had wanted to talk to my father about the Allerheiligen glass, was dead, and so was Werner, who might have talked about it too. Michel had done a whole lot more than just tell one of us about the glass – he had actually *shown* it to me. There was a cold and horrible logic to it. Of course he was in the firing line. I could not block out the vision which arose in my mind of something human-sized, with a dim intelligence below that of a man and the bloodlust of a wild animal, something with claws and fangs which scratched and gnawed at the empty car as a beast of prey might paw at an empty nest.

Don't be stupid. Demons don't tamper with car engines, I told myself, but there was scant comfort in the idea. Whoever had attacked Ru was quite solid and real enough to wield a spear, so why not a wrench or a screwdriver?

I huddled on the bench and looked surreptitiously at Michel's profile. I took in the firm line of his jaw, the fall of dark hair on his forehead, the lean lines of his shoulders and arms in the faded overshirt he was wearing. I thought briefly about Father Engels too. It was funny how I'd been blinded by one of them so that I hadn't even looked at the other. It had been like trying to listen to a ballad while someone was playing the 1812 Overture in your ear – it wasn't until the cannons and cymbals had died away that you'd even hear what was playing underneath.

I thought about the fight Michel had had with his father, about how he had refused to stop seeing me. The last faint traces of the fight were still there, in the yellowing line of old bruising under one eye. I remembered the time he had kissed me in the church. That memory made me run hot and cold with mixed pleasure and guilt. I knew how Michel felt about me. I was still deciding how I felt about him, but I also knew what I was going to ask him to do.

It wasn't fair; I was sure he'd do what I wanted, and it would probably be dangerous for both of us. But I was still going to ask.

CHAPTER FIFTY-TWO

'Let's go back to the church.'

He glanced at me.

'Not now. Later,' I said. 'When your dad's out.'

'Lin –'

'Michel, we have to.' I put a hand out tentatively and touched the bare skin of his arm just above the wrist. 'If we can't talk to the police, we have to go back there ourselves. We have to do something.'

'Like what? Make a bargain with him?'

'Actually, yes,' I said.

Silence. Then: 'That's crazy,' said Michel.

'I know.' We stared at each other.

'Look,' I said quickly, 'we can't leave. The landlord won't let us off and Tuesday's already asked Uncle Karl if we can stay with him. He said no. If we do nothing and something happens again . . .' I held out my hand, the thumb and forefinger a few centimetres apart. 'Dad said the spear missed Ru by this much. Next time . . .'

'Lin, whoever did that – he's dangerous.'

'So let's go to the police.'

We were going round in circles.

'No.'

'Why *not*?'

Michel didn't reply, but he didn't have to. I saw the answer in the way his eyes shifted away from me. He was really afraid that his father – or perhaps his father and his brother – would be implicated. *Dad had nothing to do with it*, he had said – but did he really believe it?

'Michel, we have to do something.' I raked my hands through my hair. 'You said yourself, you feel like someone's watching you. It could be you next, or me. If we don't go to the police, what *are* we going to do?'

Michel said nothing, but I could see from the expression on his face that he was weakening.

'All the attacks, they're based on the pictures in the glass,' I said. 'I didn't see it until the attack on Ru. Herr Mahlberg, that was the Naaman window. Your father's uncle, Werner, that was the one with Adam and Eve. It was the apple that made me think of it –'

'What apple?'

'The apple . . .' My voice trailed off. *Oh shit*. I put a hand over my eyes. 'Look, you can't tell anyone this, OK?'

Michel was staring at me.

'The day we came to Germany – the day we first met – we stopped in Niederburgheim to ask for directions and we saw him. Werner, I mean.'

'When? Was he still alive?'

'No.' I shut my eyes, not wanting to see Michel's face. 'He was dead.'

'Why didn't you tell me before?'

'We didn't tell *anyone*.' I opened my eyes and looked at Michel as earnestly as I could. 'You don't think we had anything to do with it? He was already dead when we found him.'

'But you didn't find him. The guy who worked with him did.'

'I guess that was later,' I said.

'But . . .'

'We didn't report it,' I said, interrupting him. 'Look, we didn't do anything to him. We thought – well, Dad thought – that he had probably just had an accident. And if we'd gone to the police we'd have spent hours and hours answering questions. So we just –'

'Just decided to drive away and leave him,' finished Michel.

'Well, I said we should report it,' I said defensively. 'But Dad –' I felt a twinge of guilt – 'Dad didn't want to.'

'Hmm,' said Michel. There was a very long silence as he considered what I had just told him. His face was grim. Finally he said, 'Your dad's got a cheek reporting my father to the police.'

Irrationally I felt a stab of irritation. I felt that I had crossed a line when I had blamed my father for abandoning Werner's body to the elements. I had trusted Michel; I had allied myself with him and not with my family. Now here he was, criticizing.

'Your dad threatened us,' I retorted angrily.

'He was scared.'

'*He* was scared?' I was so indignant that I lapsed into English. 'What do you think my family felt like? They'd never even met him before. He just came storming in like a maniac, with that – that *gorilla* of a brother of yours – and –' I realized from the expression on Michel's face that he was not following what I said at all. With an effort I made myself slow down and go back into German. 'Look, he really frightened them. Tuesday thought he was threatening to kill us.'

'He was scared for me,' said Michel. 'The ram's head –'

'Yes, where did he get the ram's head?' I demanded.

'He found it,' said Michel quietly. 'It was on the doorstep in the morning, when we got up.'

'He *found* it?' I was dumbfounded.

Michel nodded. 'That was why he went mad. He said it was a warning. He said I had to keep away from you, that if I hung around with you it would be dangerous.'

I stared at him. I had the sense of pieces of a jigsaw sliding together with the ponderous motion of tectonic plates.

'Abraham,' I said slowly.

'What?'

'Abraham and Isaac,' I said. I looked at Michel. 'He was right. It was a warning: *This time it was the ram, next time it'll be your son.*' I put my hands to my face and held them there, feeling the comforting warmth of my own breath on my fingers. 'Whoever left the ram's head on the step had seen the glass and they knew your father had seen it too.'

I looked out of the open side of the picnic hut, into the forest. In spite of the chill in the air, the day was brightening and sun was streaming down between the trees. I had the strangest sense of disconnection, as though I were sliding between two different worlds. In one of them the sun was shining and on the other side of the forest in Baumgarten shops and cafes were opening and people were doing ordinary stuff – walking the dog, shopping. In the other one anything could happen: legends could come to life; a killer could take inspiration from a medieval masterpiece and sculpt his own interpretation in the flesh of his victims. I felt as though something essential inside me was pulling apart, strands separating, ripping . . .

Michel was saying something. With an effort I made myself concentrate.

'He kept crying,' said Michel. 'It was weird.'

I agreed. Personally I would believe in weeping statues of the Virgin Mary before believing that tears ever came out of Michel's father's flinty eyes. I had no faith in his grief; I had seen the work of his fists.

'He said that he'd lost my mother and he wasn't going to lose me,' said Michel. 'He said he knew I'd been to the church . . .' He sighed. 'I guess I wasn't as careful as I thought I was when I put the boards back. He didn't seem to care much about that. He was worried that I was going to tell you or your father where the glass was. He said loads of crazy stuff. He said the glass was cursed.' He shook his head. 'And he kept saying the priest was right.'

'The *priest*?' There was a sickening lurch in the pit of my stomach. I could not hear that word without thinking of Father Engels, of his beautiful angry face, a memory which was inextricably entwined with a searing sense of shame. 'What did the priest have to do with it?'

'Dad went to see him after my mother died. I think he thought he shouldn't have shown her the glass and the church; maybe he shouldn't have brought her to live here at all. So he went and had a discussion with this priest, and the priest told him – he was right.'

'What do you mean?'

'He was right. It was the glass that was responsible for her death.'

'Who –' I could hardly bring myself to frame the question. 'Who was the priest?'

'He didn't say.'

319

I sat for a long time, just thinking. I thought about Father Engels, about the cold hard core which lay within that beautiful exterior. I thought about Michel's mother. I thought about Herr Mahlberg, who had written to my father, and Werner Heckmann, who could have told my father about the glass if he had lived. I thought about Michel's father crying and saying that he didn't want to lose Michel too. Michel's father was right; the Allerheiligen glass was cursed, and it seemed to me that we were part of the curse, my family and I. No one we touched was safe. If I asked Michel to help me, I was asking him to put himself deliberately in the line of fire.

'I'm sorry,' I said finally.

'What for?'

'I shouldn't have asked you to do this.'

Michel looked at me and his face was serious. 'You're not going back to the church on your own.'

I sighed. 'Michel, I have to do *something*. I have to try.'

'Then I'm coming with you.'

'No,' I said.

'Lin –'

'No. Really, no.'

'Lin, you need me to tell you when Dad's going to be away. And I'm not letting you go alone.'

I started to say that I didn't need Michel at all; I didn't need *anyone*. But the truth of it was, I *did* need him. I didn't really want to go back to the church on my own, to stand there in the dark with the smell of dust and decay and those mouldering crates, not knowing who or what would come to find me. I thought that I would feel a thousand times better if Michel was by my side.

I stood up. 'Can't we go *now*? Your father's not out yet, is he?'

Michel shook his head. 'I'm supposed to be helping him on the farm this weekend. I can't get away.'

He rose to his feet and for a moment we were standing very close to each other. It would have been quite natural to step a little closer, to touch his hand, to turn my face up to his, but I didn't. I knew that I was putting him in danger simply by being with him; I knew that what he was offering I had no right to demand. I was not going to pay for it with a Judas kiss.

I stepped away from him.

'Lin?' he said. 'Promise me you won't go there on your own.'

I looked him in the eyes. 'I promise,' I said.

CHAPTER FIFTY-THREE

Monday morning dawned clear and dry. When Michel arrived I was already waiting outside the gate, my bag over my shoulder.

We were halfway to school before he told me.

'My dad's gone to Prüm again.'

'What, today?'

He nodded. 'The rain caused a lot of damage on the farm. There's stuff he wants to get for the repairs.'

'Has your brother gone?'

'No, but he won't go into the forest. Lin, you know my brother's not – he's not quite like other people.'

I stared at him. 'What do you mean?'

Michel sighed. 'You'll see if you get to meet him. He won't bother us, don't worry.'

'Michel –'

'It's OK.'

I was tempted to probe further, but Michel was clearly disinclined to say anything else, and a more urgent consideration was filling my mental horizon.

'Then we can go to – you know?'

Michel nodded.

I bit my lip. 'Look . . . your dad, he's definitely gone, hasn't he? I mean, he couldn't just be –'

Michel was shaking his head. 'He's definitely gone. He's meeting someone in Lünebach at two o'clock.'

For a while we drove along without speaking. I don't know what was going through Michel's mind. I was wondering whether we were planning to do something heroic or something downright stupid. I had a nasty feeling that we were carrying on like two children trying to frighten off the night by waving a couple of sparklers at it. I was not sure whether I longed for the school day to end or for it to last forever.

I was still thinking about it when Michel pulled up at the school. For once there was a parking space free right outside the gates. Frau Schäfer was in for the surprise of her life: I was going to be on time.

'We should go in,' said Michel, glancing at his watch.

'I know,' I said, not moving.

Our eyes met. There were people walking down the street towards us, I knew that. The school bell was going to ring at any minute and the pavement was crowded with students, some of them from my year, probably from my actual class. None of it made the slightest difference. I leaned over and pulled Michel closer. Very deliberately I kissed him.

There was a thump on the window on my side of the car. The fat boy from my class was leering through the window at us, making the thumbs-up sign. There was a muffled cheer from someone behind him.

Michel himself was speechless and pink in the face, but I could see the corners of his mouth curling upwards. He still had that same radiant look on his face when we walked into school together.

I felt happy too. Something simple and wonderful had happened, and the burden of my woes was suddenly a little lighter. I had no idea that in six hours this was going to turn into the very worst day of my entire life.

CHAPTER FIFTY-FOUR

I had the first inkling that something was wrong when I was on my way to the last double lesson of the day. I was walking between classrooms when my mobile phone went off in the bottom of my bag. Normally I kept it switched off when I was in class; evidently this time I had forgotten. I fished it out, jabbed at the green button with my thumb and clamped it to my ear, hoping that none of the teachers would pass by and tell me off.

'Lin?' said my father's voice.

He spoke much too loudly as usual; it was as though he was shouting directly into my ear. I winced.

'Dad, I'm at school.'

'I know,' he said. 'Look, something's happened.'

'What?' I said, alarm instantly flooding through me.

'It's Tuesday. She's gone.'

'Gone?' Suddenly I actually felt weak, as though my legs would no longer carry me. There was a large window with a low wide sill; I went and sat on it. People walking past looked at me curiously. I ignored them. 'Dad? What happened? Where are you?'

'Baumgarten – there's a call box. She's just – gone. Went off this morning and took Ru with her.'

I let my head fall back against the windowpane and closed my eyes. I didn't know quite how to feel. I was shocked, but mixed with shock was a feeling of bitter satisfaction. It was as though I had always known that she would do it again.

'Lin?' My father's raised voice sounded tinnily from the mobile phone. 'Lin, are you still there?'

I didn't reply. In my mind's eye I could see Tuesday hurrying from the castle with Ru half-asleep in her arms. Settling Ru in his car seat and doing up the straps. Opening the boot to put a bag inside and closing it carefully so my father wouldn't hear. I could see her glancing back at the castle one last time, then climbing into the car and driving away, accelerating, putting as much space between herself and the Kreuzburg as she possibly could.

She's done it again.

Tuesday had run away once before, when Polly and I were little – old enough to understand that she had gone, but not old enough to understand why. Young enough to be terrified that our mother would never come back, that we would never see her again. An already untidy, disorganized family life had descended into chaos. My father had tried to jolly us along at first, to make it sound like tremendous fun to eat baked beans every night, to wear each other's things because he couldn't remember what belonged to whom. Eventually he had lost patience. He had work to do – important work, work which would make him famous. I never blamed *him* for not wanting to be bothered with two little girls – after all, our own mother had left us, hadn't she? All the same, I protested. Polly had become silent, a wraith with a thumb permanently in her mouth, even though she was too old for thumb-sucking. I had had tantrums.

In desperation my father had farmed us out to friends and relatives. He had even tried hiring a housekeeper, whom I had hated with a vengeance. Then one day Tuesday had come back. She had come back and the housekeeper was summarily dismissed. I had watched from my bedroom window as she walked down the garden path to the waiting taxi, with her parting shot ringing in my ears.

'You're no mother to those girls,' she had told Tuesday roundly. And I had believed her. I had never quite stopped watching Tuesday after that, waiting for signs that she was going to leave us.

At last, she's done it again.

'Lin?' I didn't realize I had spoken aloud.

'I'm here, Dad.' I sighed. 'She took Ru?'

'Yes.'

Should I be glad about that? I wondered. At least she hadn't abandoned him the way she had abandoned us. Perhaps she had learned something over the years. Or perhaps she loved him more than she had us.

'Where have they gone?'

'Karl's. She left a note.'

'But Uncle Karl said we couldn't go there,' I pointed out.

'Do you think that would stop her?' asked my father grimly. 'She said she's not staying at the castle any more. She thinks it's not safe.' I heard my father sigh into the phone and the line crackled. 'She took the car, obviously. I had to *walk* into Baumgarten. I'm going to try to hire a car, though God knows where –'

I interrupted him. 'Polly – where's Polly? Is she with you?'

'Well, no, she's still at the castle . . .' he began.

'Oh, *Dad*.' I could not keep the frustration out of my voice. 'You *promised* not to leave her there alone!'

'She was shut in her room. She wouldn't come out and I had to go.'

'Why was she shut in her room?' I could hear my own voice rising and with an effort I controlled myself.

'She had . . . We had a disagreement this morning.'

I didn't need to ask what it was about. 'You had a row?'

'Polly can be difficult, you know that.' My father's voice had taken on a defensive tone; he sounded like a little boy trying to cover up the fact that he had not done his homework.

'Dad, she's *ill*.'

'I know that, Lin.'

'And you *promised* not to leave her alone.'

The conversation was going round in circles. I listened to his protestations for half a minute more and then I told him I would be home in an hour and a half and hung up.

All through the last lesson I sat and fidgeted, unable to concentrate on what the teacher was saying. Polly would probably be fine, I told myself; she was not a little kid, and anyway she would not be on her own for long. All the same I could not stop thinking about her, stranded there in the castle, a little island in that vast expanse of forest. I imagined her coming downstairs, her anger fading, and finding the house empty. She would open the front door and look into the courtyard. She would see that she was quite alone and perhaps she would stand there for a while and listen. The breeze would be cool and sound would carry far through the crisp air: the crackle of bulky animal bodies moving through the thick undergrowth, the desolate cry of a bird of prey far above. If anyone – or anything – else were to approach the castle through the dense cover of trees, would she distinguish the stealthy movements of a killer from the natural sounds of the forest?

And so I squirmed in my seat and looked at my watch surreptitiously under the desk and counted the minutes until the bell rang. There was nothing else I could do, after all. I was dependent on Michel to run me back to the castle, so even if I had made some excuse myself and left the classroom early, I could not have got home without him. I told myself that then and I keep telling myself that now.

The moment the bell rang I was out of my seat, stuffing books and pens haphazardly into my bag. I ran for the door. Out in the corridor I paused. It was Monday, so Michel would be in the science lab. I was at the door before he emerged, and as soon as I saw him I grabbed his arm and tried to pull him along with me.

'What's the hurry?' he asked, struggling to fit a large file into his bag as he stumbled along beside me.

'It's Polly.'

'Your sister? What's the matter with her?'

'I don't know. I just have this really, really bad feeling.' I shook my hair out of my eyes. 'My stupid dad left her alone at the castle.'

'She'll be fine, Lin . . .'

'Maybe,' I said shortly. 'I just want to get back there, OK?'

CHAPTER FIFTY-FIVE

The journey back to the castle seemed to take forever. Anyone other than Michel would soon have become tired of me, the way I was squirming in my seat and rolling my eyes at slow-moving vehicles like a blue-rinsed back-seat driver. Every kilometre that crawled by was pure agony. As we entered Baumgarten a tractor pulled out in front of us, towing an enormous muddy trailer piled high with what looked like turnips. I gave a howl of frustration and slapped the dashboard with the flat of my hand.

'Calm down,' said Michel. 'Polly's fine.'

'You don't know that,' I snapped. I exhaled heavily. 'Look, I'm sorry, it's just I made Dad *promise* not to leave her there alone and he bloody did it anyway.'

Michel said nothing to this, but he pulled out into the middle of the road and peered around the tractor. He had to pull in again sharply; a moment later a bus thundered past.

'*Scheisse.*'

I laughed at that, but it wasn't really funny. I felt as though I might boil over into hysteria at any moment.

At long last we reached the turning on to the track which led into the woods. Michel went as fast as he could. The little Volkswagen lurched and bounced over ruts and potholes. As the trees sped past I wound down my window and stuck my head out, hoping to hear or sense something which would tell me that all was well – or at least the absence of anything which would tell me that it was not. I remembered the day my father and I had heard sirens as we drove down this very same track. It was not a comforting thought.

'Can't you go any faster?'

'Are you joking? We'll take off altogether.'

The moment the car screeched to a halt outside the castle I wrenched the door open and ran for the gate. It was closed. I dropped my school bag on the ground and grasped the handle with both hands. As I pushed the gate open, I heard Michel come up beside me.

'Polly?'

I stepped into the courtyard and looked around. The front door of the house was ajar. There was no sign of Polly and no sound other than ravens cawing overhead.

Michel touched me on the shoulder. 'She's probably in the house. Maybe she can't hear you from there.'

'Polly?'

My voice rose as I moved quickly over to the open door. I went inside. Everything looked perfectly normal: nothing overturned, nothing broken. There was a mug on the pine table, half-filled with what looked like herbal tea. A dining chair stood at an angle to the table, as though Polly had suddenly stood up. There was no sign of a struggle. So why did I have this overwhelming feeling that something was horribly wrong?

I moved slowly through each room, calling Polly's name. She was not in the kitchen. I touched the kettle; it still felt very slightly warm. I supposed Polly had made the tea an hour or so before. I turned around and went back into the living room.

'I'm going to try upstairs,' I told Michel.

'You want me to come?'

I nodded. It was a relief not to have to do it by myself, especially after what had happened to Ru. I didn't want to think of finding a scene like that one all on my own.

In the event we found nothing at all. The bedroom doors were closed; I opened all of them except Ru's, which was still sealed shut, but there was nobody there. The bathroom was also empty and rather cold. I touched the soap in the little dish by the sink; it was perfectly dry.

I clattered back down the stairs with Michel close behind me.

'*Polly?*'

'Maybe she went for a walk,' suggested Michel.

'She wouldn't do that.'

I stood there indecisively, looking at the abandoned cup of tea on the table. I knew Polly wouldn't have gone off on her own. Could my father have come back for her? Impossible – he didn't have the car. I slid my mobile phone out of my pocket and flipped it open, but of course there was no signal.

'Let's try outside.'

I stepped out of the front door and scanned the courtyard. There was no movement other than the restless wheeling of the ravens overhead, their harsh voices filling the air. I began to follow the thick yellow stone wall, as it ran away from the house and towards the square tower which had been the keep of the castle. Polly and I had explored the ruins not long after we arrived at the Kreuzburg, but we rarely strayed into them after that. If Ru had been older he might have liked to run about in them, waving a toy sword, but there was little to interest either of us and the tower was always locked. Still, I was running out of places to look.

It was not possible to see the foot of the tower from the courtyard. I had to go through a crumbling archway made of the same yellow stone and up a worn flight of stairs.

'*Polly!*' I shouted.

There was no reply.

I paused on the steps and called out her name again. '*Polly! You can come out now. It's not funny.*'

At the top of the steps I had to go through another archway and turn a corner into an inner courtyard where the tower stood. At first I thought there was nobody there. There was nothing moving in the courtyard other than clumps of weeds nodding gently in the breeze. The tower stood silent and uncompromisingly square, its ancient stones blurred and weathered by the passing of centuries. There was a thin band of blackness at the edge of the door, but at that moment I did not stop to think what it meant. The only sound was the crunch of gravel under my feet.

It was then that I saw her. For a moment I did not realize what I was seeing. At the foot of the tower there was something lying on the ground, something scarlet, an indistinct shape which might have been anything. I thought, *What's that lying on the ground?* But a horrid conviction was already forming in my brain. I took one unwilling step towards the tower and then another, my heart thumping and my breath shivering in my throat. One step closer, my eyes straining – then I was running towards her, stumbling, arms flailing, the breath streaming out of my lungs in one great throat-scouring scream.

'Polly! Polly!'

I fell to my knees beside her. My sister was sprawled on the cold earth, her face half-turned into it, her eyes half-open as though trying to take a sly peep through the strands of light hair which had fallen across them.

'Polly . . .'

I felt hollow inside. There was no known emotion which could encompass a discovery like this. My sister was dead. I knew it without touching her. Death was written in that frozen face, nestled into the unfeeling ground. It was in the sickening redness which matted her hair and stained the earth around her head like an obscene halo. Earth which shivered and glittered with tiny fragments of broken glass.

I stretched out a trembling hand and touched Polly's shoulder. I might have been touching a block of wood. She was not utterly cold yet, nor – thank God – was her body stiff, but there was an inertness about it which made my hand reluctant to linger there. For the first time I became aware of the cloth which shrouded her body. Polly – my Polly, not this inanimate thing which clutched the earth with frozen claws – liked to wear white, pink, shades of blue. She had nothing which was this strident scarlet, nothing in this heavy velvet which blurred the lines of her body as snow blurs the contours of a landscape. I lifted the edge of it; the material was worn and moth-eaten. I thought it might be a length of curtain. There were some like it in my parents' room.

I glanced at the tower door. Normally it was closed and locked. Now it stood open, the wood around the lock cloven into splinters. Someone had taken an axe to it. The implement still lay there on the stone lintel, a bright line of silver cut into the edge of the tarnished blade by the force of the blows.

I will never know how Polly's killer got her to the top of the tower. I can only hope that it was by deception, that she did not know what was going to happen until the last moment. But I fear she was dragged there, pleading for her life. Thin and weak as she was, she couldn't have fought him off. She was light enough from starving herself that he could have picked her up bodily and carried her inside.

My eyes burning with tears not yet shed, I gazed up at the tower looming above us. When they had reached the top, she must have known what was about to happen. Perhaps she had tried to fight for her life, but it would have taken more strength than she had left in that starved body. The killer had wrapped my sister in the scarlet cloth and bundled her over the parapet at the top. Then he had thrust her screaming and struggling into space. Down she had plummeted, the red cloth streaming behind her, until life had exploded out of her on the stones below. A sickly realization overwhelmed me. The Fall of the Angels: the killer had reproduced the scene with my sister's blood.

'*O Gott.*' Michel had come up beside me. 'Is she . . .'

I could see the legs of his blue jeans and his boots out of the corner of my eye but I didn't look up to meet his gaze. A hard resolve was growing inside me. I did not want to be swayed from what I intended to do.

I stood up. 'Yes, she's dead.' My voice had a curiously hard, flinty sound to it even to my own ears. 'Will you phone the police?'

I didn't bother asking him to phone for an ambulance, though I supposed they would send one anyway when he told them what had happened.

'What are you going to do?' asked Michel mistrustfully.

He must have read some secret determination in the way I failed to meet his gaze, the way I moved restlessly as though longing to be somewhere else.

I made myself look him in the eyes. 'I'm going to stay here with Polly.'

It would take him at least twenty minutes to drive to the farm, make the call and come back, I thought. Twenty minutes was a good enough head start. Let him come after me then – let the police come too, for all I cared – it would be time enough.

Michel looked reluctant, but there was no time for arguing.

'You're sure you'll be OK?' he asked.

I nodded. 'Just . . . go.'

I stood by my sister's body and watched him as he went back down the stairs and turned the corner. I waited as his footsteps faded into the distance. A minute more and I heard the sound of the car engine firing up. Michel had gone.

I went over to the open door of the tower and picked up the axe.

CHAPTER FIFTY-SIX

The axe in my hands, I half-ran and half-walked through the forest, the fevered panting of my breath loud in my ears and the undergrowth crackling under my feet. Brambles tore at the legs of my jeans and once I nearly slipped over on a patch of mud, but managed to right myself without losing momentum. I didn't waver for a moment. It was now or never. In an hour's time or maybe less, the castle and the surrounding woods would be crawling with police.

Very soon I reached the place where the wire fence was supposed to block the path. To my surprise it had still not been mended; in fact it had been cleared right away to the side of the track. Several deep ruts ran through the place where the fence should have prevented anyone passing. I could make no sense of this. I simply stepped over them and went on my way, further into the forest.

I had only been to the church once before and then I had had Michel as my guide. Now I was alone and might very easily have gone astray among the winding paths and criss-crossing tracks. I did not stop to think about this. I was committed. I strode along with confidence, hefting the axe, trusting that for once luck would be with me, and it was.

Another five minutes and I found myself at the edge of the clearing where the church stood.

I paused for a moment, looking at it. Here was the epicentre of the evil which had engulfed my family, the beating heart which pumped out its malevolence upon all whose lives it touched, from the abbot's beautiful niece in the sixteenth century to my poor sister, who lay broken at the foot of the tower. It seemed darkly miraculous to me that anyone could pass through this forest and not feel them, the vibrations which emanated from it, tainting the very air around it.

Tightening my grip on the axe handle, I was about to approach the church when I noticed something which made my heart lurch in my chest. The door was already open. I stared at it and then glanced about me, but there was no sign of movement anywhere other than the gentle swaying of tree branches. I swallowed. Was it possible that Michel Reinartz Senior had been here and had forgotten to lock the door when he left? It seemed unlikely – but then who knew what he might or might not do? He seemed like nothing more than a madman to me.

I waited. Still there was nothing. If Michel's father had been there, wouldn't that great monster of a dog of his have been there too, barking its hideous head off? Cautiously I began to walk towards the open door of the church, moving as quietly as I could and listening for the tiniest sound that would tell me if someone was there. As I approached I could see that the interior of the church was not the black pit it had been the last time I had visited; there was light inside. Someone must have removed the boards as well as opening the door.

This is a bad idea, Lin. Still I went carefully on, stepping over sticks and trying to tread on patches of grass or moss where my footfalls would be muffled. *Go back! Go back!* screamed a voice in my head, but I ignored it. I had come here to avenge my sister; let a hundred maniacs with savage dogs try to stop me, I was determined to carry out what I had come to do.

I reached the open door of the church and still there was no sign of life. I peered inside. The boards were down, all right. From here I could not see the glorious designs on the windows but I could see the rainbow streaks which striped the wooden pews inside and turned the dilapidated tiled floor into a jigsaw of colour. Well, that would make my task easier. I had no intention of leaving a single pane unbroken for the police – or my father – to find.

I stepped inside. It was cool in here and musty. Glancing down the aisle, I noticed something strange: those wooden crates, the ones which had played so unpleasantly on my imagination the last time I had been here, had vanished entirely. Now that I looked more closely, I could see streaks of dirt or rust on the worn tiles, as though something had been dragged out of the church, passing right over the spot where I now stood.

That moment of contemplation, as I stood there wondering what had become of the crates and who had taken them, was fatal. Distracted from my purpose, I did not realize that there was someone in the church with me until it was too late. Something hit the back of my head with the blinding force of the aneurysm that had felled Michel's mother and, groaning, I crumpled to the floor.

Chapter Fifty-seven

It is not as easy to knock someone out as you might think from reading books. There was no merciful descent into darkness. Pain exploded in my skull, a nuclear bomb which sent agonizing shockwaves shrilling through my brain, turning the world to a dizzying kaleidoscope of seething particles. Yet I was still conscious when I hit the floor. I rolled over on to my back, groping for the handle of the axe. Above me loomed a dark figure, blurred and indistinct. It seemed about three metres tall. I could make out no features; my vision swam nauseatingly, so that the figure seemed to sway and hover over me.

The axe, where was the axe? My hands flailed around wildly. By pure chance my fingers touched the wooden handle, but as they closed on it something came down with excruciating force on my hand and I let go. A scream burst from me, scouring my throat. From the explosion of pain in my hand, I guessed that something was broken, but there was no mercy. Someone grabbed my hands, causing a fresh supernova of agony in the injured one.

No, I tried to say, but what came out was the shriek of an animal in pain. Then I was being dragged along the floor, hauled by the arms. In some dim corner of my brain I knew that I should be struggling, fighting for my life, but the pain was so enormous, so nauseating, that it paralysed me. I squeezed my eyes shut. *Let it stop.* I thought I could feel the bones in the broken hand grinding together, like a bundle of splintering sticks. A bright flare of agony streaked up my arm. *Just let it stop – let it stop –*

Abruptly the grip on my hands was loosened. I slumped down, the hard cold edge of a stair biting into my ribs. I guessed I was lying on the steps which led to the altar. I cradled my broken hand, weeping with great choking sobs. How had it all gone wrong so quickly?

I could hear fleet footsteps on the tiles but I could not tell where my attacker was. Thunder still seemed to roll and crash in my head, disorienting me. There might have been one of them, or two, or more, closely clustered around me or darting about all over the church. I opened my eyes and the coloured light from the windows was dazzling. I could make out no one in the main part of the church. I shook my hair out of my eyes, blinked hard and looked again. Nothing.

The next moment I knew why. Someone was behind me, on the altar steps. I heard the infinitesimal sound of something scraping against the tiles. My mind made pictures of cloven hooves moving across the tiled floor, of upraised limbs which ended in yellowed talons, of sagging jaws lined with teeth as sharp as butcher's knives. Finally I had skidded off the edge of reality into a nightmare where a demon stalked his victims, his pitted reptilian skin tiger-striped by the coloured bands of light from the stained-glass windows. Windows of a church no longer sacred, a church which could offer me no salvation.

My heart pounding wildly, I struggled to sit up, the movement causing more sickening screams of protest from my injured hand. I was still trying to raise myself, my efforts staccato with panic, when someone did it for me. I was grasped firmly under the arms and hauled into a sitting position. At the first touch I felt a vertiginous thrill of shock, but a second later I realized what I was feeling. Hands. Whoever was dragging me up had hands. Not claws. Not the ragged talons of a demon.

When I was sitting up, my chest rising and falling as though I had run a sprint race, my hair hanging in tangled hanks over my eyes, he came round and squatted in front of me. I saw black first, the black garb of a priest, or a vampire, or a crow. Dark shoes, the arm of a black jacket. Then I looked up and saw a face I recognized.

He was looking at me with an expression which might have been friendly reassurance or might have been mild amusement.

'Father Krause,' I said in a weak voice. I felt a little dazed. What was he doing here? Dimly I was aware of his hands moving. He was holding something, turning it over in his fingers. There was a ripping sound and I realized that he must be holding bandages. He was going to splint my broken hand.

'Father Krause?' I said again. My voice was hoarse. I watched his strong fingers pulling at the end of the bandage and still it didn't occur to me to wonder how he had got here, how he could have known I needed help. 'Where is he?' I croaked.

'Where is who?' Father Krause asked me briskly.

I looked at him, shaking my head to try and clear it. My brain still felt as though it were filled with a thousand flies, all buzzing at once.

'Bonschariant,' I said.

'Bonschariant,' repeated Father Krause thoughtfully.

He lifted up my left hand, the unbroken one, by the wrist. The mild expression on his face never changed as he took hold of my other hand and yanked them both together. The pain was explosive.

When I had stopped screaming he said, quite calmly, 'He is in all of us.'

He held my two hands in one of his and with the other he began to wind something around my wrists. I saw now that it was tape, not bandages. I tried to pull my hands away, waking up to the reality of what was happening. I was too slow to see the blow coming until it was too late. My head ringing, I slumped back and let him finish the job.

Eventually he seemed satisfied. He got to his feet. 'Don't try to get up,' he said in a cold voice. 'I have the axe now, you know.'

He began to walk away from me, towards the door, where I knew the axe must still be lying. Panic was threatening to swamp me, but at least the clouds of grogginess were clearing away, driven back by the sharp need to survive. *Think, think!* shrieked a voice in my head. *Don't wait until he's got the axe! Do something!*

'What do you want?' I called out, cursing myself for the hoarse waver in my voice.

At first I thought he hadn't heard me, but then he came to a stop in the centre of the aisle. He turned slowly, and the smile he gave me was not pleasant to see. Coloured light from the windows tinted his skin red, so that he appeared to be grinning at me through a mask of blood.

'What do I *want*?' He paused as if considering. 'What I

want is for self-serving, greedy, ignorant outsiders to stay away. To stop plundering the church. To stop dragging the glory of God into the marketplace. *That* is what I want.' The complacent tone was gone; his voice was rising raggedly. 'I want that fool Mahlberg never to have written to your even bigger fool of a father. I want your father never to have come here. I want this treasure to stay where it belongs. I want you never to have seen it.' Now he was almost shouting. 'And if I can't have that, I want you gone. All of you. But most of all –' he took a step towards me – 'I want *you* gone. *You*, you interfering little slut.'

For a moment I thought he would stride back up the aisle and strike me, maybe carry on striking me this time, until I stopped moving. But he thought better of it. He went back to the doorway and leaned into the deep well of shadows behind the wooden door. There was a muffled clank as he picked something up.

My mind was racing, skittering around like a rat in a trap, trying to find a way out. How long would it take Michel to get to the farm and phone for the police? How long would it take them to arrive and to work out where I had gone? I looked at Father Krause, coming back up the aisle towards me, and I knew that however quick they were they would be too late.

He was carrying something in his hand, something which bumped against the end of a pew with a clank and a sound like liquid swilling around in a container. I began to scrabble with my feet, struggling to stand up, to put some space between me and him.

'Be still,' he barked at me.

He put the canister down on the tiles a few metres away

344

and there was a faint squeaking noise as he undid the cap. I began to detect a smell, a sharp stink which stung the nostrils. For one insane moment I thought of brimstone, the burning breath of the pit from which the demon Bonschariant had risen. The next second I realized what it was and why I had associated the smell with burning. Petrol. It was petrol.

'No!' I croaked.

My legs flailed uselessly as I tried to propel myself backwards, away from that poisonous stink. But Father Krause was inexorable. That unearthly calm had come over him again; he looked at me with that same cool, mild expression, like an entomologist watching the death throes of an insect in a killing-jar. Only the colours which dappled his face blurred and changed as he moved. He came over and delivered a kick to my hip which stopped my struggles immediately. Then he knelt by me on the floor and when he spoke his voice was almost gentle.

'Look,' he said, and he half-turned and pointed. 'That was Herr Mahlberg's window.' He indicated the depiction of Naaman submerged in the blue waters of the river. He smiled faintly and streaks of green and red danced across his features. 'That was the first. That was when I understood, when I knew what I had to do.'

He pointed next at the window showing Adam and Eve in the Garden of Eden. 'That one required perseverance.' He sounded almost proud. 'I waited for him in the orchard. The pattern had to be completed.'

Father Krause's gaze turned to the Fall of the Angels, the draperies streaming out behind the plummeting figures. 'That was your sister's window.' The satisfaction in his voice made me want to vomit.

'My sister didn't do anything to you,' I choked out.

'*Ich bin ein eifriger Gott, der die Missetat der Väter heimsucht über die Kinder ins dritte und vierte Glied.*'

I did not understand the whole of the quotation, but one phrase was crystal clear. The sins of the fathers. Those pale eyes were on me again.

'That is your window,' said Father Krause, and pointed.

I turned to look and a terrible groan forced its way from my lips. It was a Pentecost scene. Most of the window was filled with a crowd of figures representing the Apostles, bearded figures dressed in flowing robes in gorgeous colours – crimson, emerald green, cobalt blue. It was impossible to mistake the brilliance of Gerhard Remsich's work. Every upturned face had an individual expression and the distinguishing marks of its owner's character. My father would gladly have given ten years of his life to stand where I was now. But I was not admiring Gerhard Remsich's genius. I was staring at the corona of flame which surrounded every head. I was not the daughter of a medieval scholar for nothing: I knew what Remsich was showing. It was the moment when the Holy Spirit descended upon the Apostles like tongues of fire. This was what Father Krause planned for me: that my death should imitate Remsich's work, that I should die with my head engulfed in flames.

This time I managed to get to my feet. Father Krause could have kicked me a hundred times and I wouldn't have stopped fighting him. I was fighting Death, I knew; if I lost, my lifespan would be the time it took to strike a match. I swung my bound hands, heedless of the pain, desperate only to escape the far worse pain which awaited. Then I turned to run, and suddenly Father Krause's foot was in the way and I crashed on to the tiles.

The next second there was a knee in the middle of my back. I wallowed on the tiles like a landed fish, trying to throw him off, but it was no use. He had something in his hands, something red, and he was lunging at me, wrapping it around my head in stifling swathes. The world was reduced to blackness and the musty smell of old material – rotting tapestries and grave cloths. I was still struggling but now I was blind. It was difficult to draw breath. I began to think I would suffocate and I struggled ever more wildly, panicking.

'Stop!' thundered Father Krause. 'Stop or I burn you now.'

That was enough to make me freeze in terror, yet I knew better than to think that I could save myself simply by obeying. I was standing on the brink of the abyss, my thoughts wheeling like birds of prey at a cliff edge.

'Please,' I whispered into the musty cloth, 'don't do it.'

I couldn't say, *Don't burn me*. The bare thought made my flesh flinch away.

'I have to,' said a calm voice, very close by.

'Why?' My voice was hoarse with fear.

'To punish you.'

There was a finality about those words which struck me with such horror that for a moment I thought I would faint.

'What have I done?' I croaked, although I knew very well.

As long as we were talking, I could delay the evil moment, though I had no hope that it could be put off forever. The dread of that all-encompassing pain was so terrible that I would have given anything to put it off for another ten minutes, another five. Petrol fumes assailed my nostrils with their acrid stench. My eyes filled with hot tears.

'You were going to tell what you had found.'

'I wasn't, I won't,' I babbled, shaking my head frantically, though it was useless since it was enveloped in the dark cloth. 'I won't tell anyone, I promise.'

'It's too late,' said the voice. 'You and your father, you didn't stop searching when you discovered that Herr Mahlberg was dead. You didn't stop when your brother nearly died. You should have gone away then, but you didn't. And when your sister died, what did you do? You came here, as I knew you would, because you can't resist interfering.'

The next moment came the sound I had dreaded – the sound of liquid slopping out of its container. I felt it spilling on to my clothes and soaking into them. The wetness touched my skin. Another violent shake of the petrol can and it was vomiting out on to the cloth which shrouded my head. My eyes burned and as I shrieked out my terror I tasted petrol on my lips.

'Don't do it! Please don't do it!'

I kicked out with my feet but met empty air. The footsteps were retreating – to a safe distance from the coming conflagration, I realized. As I flailed about, my hand screamed with pain but I was almost past noticing it. The scent of petrol on the cloth around my head nearly sent me mad with terror. I thought, *I will die without ever seeing the light again*. On the heels of that thought came the even more horrible realization that I *would* see the light again – the light of my own burning. I might even see the dazzling colours of those stained-glass windows one last time when the flames seared the cloth away, but it would be the last thing I ever saw.

I had screamed myself hoarse. In a paroxysm of fear I collapsed back on to the floor and in the moment of silence which followed I heard the striking of a match.

CHAPTER FIFTY-EIGHT

In that moment I truly thought I was dead. The tiny tearing sound of the match running along the side of the matchbox was the sound of a guillotine blade descending. I scrabbled uselessly with my feet, but it was impossible to get up with my hands bound and my boots skidding in the stinking wetness on the tiles.

There was a low curse. The match had not lit, or else it had burned out immediately. Then there was a rattle as Father Krause slid the box open again to extract a second match.

At that moment there was a tremendous crash. It was unmistakably the sound of breaking glass; I could hear shards of it pattering on to the floor. Something heavy landed on the tiles close to me.

'*Bonschariant!*' shouted a voice I recognized at once as Michel's.

There was another ear-splitting crash and then a groan in return, the groan of someone who had been mortally wounded.

'No!'

Someone – it had to be Father Krause – was stumbling about, howling incoherently. I heard him stagger against one of the wooden pews.

'*Bonschariant!*' yelled Michel again. 'Come out!'

The cry that arose in response sounded barely human.

'Come out!' Michel's voice sounded closer now. I guessed that he had stepped up to the gaping hole in the window he had smashed. 'Come out or I'll smash every one of them!'

'I'll kill you!' screamed Father Krause in a voice that was thick with fury. The cool mildness had vanished altogether; this was not what he had planned.

'Come out here and try,' Michel shouted back.

I listened to this exchange in terrified bewilderment. What was Michel going to do if he got Father Krause outside? How could he possibly fight against someone with that single-minded intent to kill, that slavering desire for blood? Everything seemed mixed up in my head – Father Krause's warning about the power of demons, the shock of seeing my brother's bed with the spear running through it, Polly's fall from the top of the tower. I felt that I was going mad. Perhaps the sound of glass was not Michel breaking one of the windows at all; perhaps it was the sound of the Glass Demon freeing himself at last from his prison behind the panes, stepping out into the world through a shower of glittering glass splinters. He would destroy us all.

There was another almighty crash, followed by a roar of fury. I cringed. I could feel the end of a pew at my shoulder. With an effort I managed to wriggle between it and the pew in front. I had no idea where Father Krause was but I had some faint hope of hiding myself, of buying a little time and trying to free my hands. The reek of petrol made me want to vomit but I made a titanic effort to hold the feeling back, dreading the thought of throwing up into the thick material which swathed my face. I reached up and tried to pull it off my head, but pain flared instantly in my broken hand.

'Lin?' shouted Michel.

I dared not reply, afraid of attracting attention.

'Lin!' I could hear the bleakness in his voice. He thought I was already dead.

I heard the sounds of a series of mighty impacts. Glass rained down on the floor of the church. That was the end of one of Gerhard Remsich's masterworks, over four and a half centuries of history shivered into coloured fragments.

'Stop!' screamed a voice.

The smashing sounds ceased abruptly. I could hear Michel panting. He must be close to the window.

'Where's Lin?' he shouted.

I wanted to call out to him, to tell him that I was still alive, but I couldn't. I was paralysed with fear, terrified that a single word would bring down vengeance on my head. More than anything else, I did not want to hear that sound again, the tearing sound of a match striking against the side of the matchbox.

'She's in here.'

'Send her out!'

'You come in here.'

Don't do it, Michel, I prayed silently. *You don't know how strong he is*. I remembered the axe and a shiver ran through me. Where was it? If Father Krause had it, if he stood behind the door when Michel came in, just as he must have stood behind it waiting for me – what then? I imagined Michel stepping cautiously over the lintel, not seeing the figure that lurked in the shadows, the uplifted blade of the axe glinting silver in the gloom as it reached the top of its arc and began to descend with deadly force.

'Send her out or I'll break another window.'

There was a sharp hiss of anger at that.

'Michel Reinartz!' cried Father Krause. His voice was like the howl of the damned. It met with silence. 'Michel Reinartz! I know who you are.'

Michel did not reply, but there were no more sounds of breaking glass.

'You will die, just like your girlfriend.'

This provoked a reply. 'If you've hurt her, I swear I'll break every single window in the church.'

There was a scream of rage. Michel had finally provoked Father Krause into attacking. I heard him move away from me with a hurried tread towards the door of the church. I heard a clink as he picked up the axe, its head striking the tiles. Michel, who was almost certainly armed with nothing more dangerous than whatever bricks and stones he could find lying around the church, would stand no chance against someone wielding an axe.

I made another desperate attempt to pull the cloth off my head and this time I succeeded, though pain blazed an agonizing trail right up my arm. The light was blinding. I peered out around the end of the pew, but spots were dancing in front of my eyes. I could see a dark figure outlined against the bright rectangle of the doorway, the axe grasped in a clenched fist. The axe head struck the door frame with an ominous metallic sound and then Father Krause disappeared outside into the sunlight.

I struggled hard to get my legs under me. It was almost impossible to do so without putting any weight on my hands.

Still, I finally managed it, and by partially bracing myself against the pew I was able to get on to my knees and then to stand up. I was still holding on to the cloth. I looked at it now and saw that it was a piece of red velvet, torn across. *A piece of curtain*, I thought, and let it drop as though it were a venomous creature.

'Michel!' I screamed at the top of my voice.

My eyes were adjusting to the light and now I thought I could see him, a dark shape behind one of the unbroken windows, the one showing Naaman in the waters of the River Jordan. A sudden movement caught my eye and I turned to see a second shadow pass behind the window opposite, a brief glimpse of something black flitting past the scene of the raising of Lazarus.

'Lin?'

'Michel, he has an *axe*!'

'What?'

'He's got an *axe*!' I screamed at the top of my voice. I was almost sobbing in desperation, imagining Michel being hacked down where he stood because he was trying to listen to what I said instead of fleeing for his life. 'Run!' I shrieked.

I saw his silhouette behind the blue glass, but he was not moving. There was no sign of movement behind any of the other windows either and I realized with horror that this must mean that Father Krause had reached the end of the church, behind the altar. In another moment he would have rounded the corner and be bearing down on Michel, as inexorable as Michel's namesake, the Angel of Death.

'Run! Run!'

I looked about me wildly, scanning the floor and the pews for anything that I could use as a weapon. There was a large stone on the tiles, surrounded by shards of coloured glass. I had some vague idea of throwing it at the Naaman window, to try to distract the killer, to shock Michel into moving – anything rather than stand there and watch him cut down – but when I tried to lift it, it was impossible. My right hand was almost useless and the pain when I went to move it was dizzying.

Waves of nausea left me weak and trembling. I staggered against the end of the pew and attempted to steady myself without using my hands. Could I untie them? They were bound together with a heavy-duty vinyl tape, wound round and round my wrists. I knew before trying that it was useless to use my teeth on it, but I tried anyway, worrying at the tape while my gaze scanned the windows, praying that Michel would move in time when he saw who was coming for him around the end of the church, swinging the axe like a crazed headsman.

I was making no impression on the tape. I glanced around me, looking for anything sharp. The remains of the Garden of Eden window – the bottom edge was now a row of buckled lead cames and jagged spikes of glass like glittering fangs. I limped towards it on legs which felt as though they would give way under me at any moment.

Michel was shouting something. It sounded like, 'What?' His voice was hoarse and incredulous. He had not expected this from Father Krause any more than I had, any more than you expect a tame rabbit to turn and bite your hand to the bone.

I prayed that he would have the sense to run. Glancing round, I saw his silhouette move behind the Naaman window; he was backing away.

'What are you *doing*?'

I saw him move suddenly as something hit the stone window frame with a tremendous crunch. There was a howl from outside, but whether it was a cry of pain or anger I could not tell.

'Michel!' I screamed.

There was no reply. Sick to my stomach, I wondered whether he had been hit, but to my relief I saw him pound past the remains of the Adam and Eve window. Abandoning all pretence at making a stand, he was running for his life. A second later the dark shape that was Father Krause passed the same window at a fearful speed; he might be decades older than Michel, but rage was driving him on.

It was all too obvious what would happen. Michel could not run forever. His pursuer was strong and determined enough to lift a struggling teenage girl and hurl her to her death. He would have no trouble hunting Michel down, until Michel could run no further, and then – then, when he had dealt with Michel, he would come back for me, and with my hands tied I could do nothing to defend myself.

I staggered over to the broken window and reached up, straining to pull my wrists a few millimetres apart so that I could saw at the tape without cutting my own flesh. There was virtually no give in the tape; he had known what he was doing. I bit my lip and tried anyway, hooking the edge of the tape over the largest shard I could find, a great jagged tooth of yellow glass. Feverishly I worked at the tape, but in my haste I pulled too hard. The tip of the shard broke off, slashing deeply into the side of my thumb. Now there was blood flowing, making the glass and the tape slippery. Swearing under my breath, I gritted my teeth and hooked the torn edge of the tape over another of the wicked glass points. *Careful, careful*, I told myself through a fog of pain. *Cut an artery and you'll be dead before he comes looking for you.*

Sawing back and forth, I finally managed to cut halfway through the tape. Now there was a little more play in it and I was able to move my hands apart enough to slash at the tape without cutting myself. I glanced over my shoulder. Nothing moving: no sign of Michel or Father Krause. I turned back to the window and sawed through the last centimetre of tape. The injured hand was agony. It was swelling up nicely, the flesh blue and puffy. If I had waited any longer to cut the tape it would have been too tight around the swollen hand and I would probably have cut myself to ribbons.

No time to worry about that. *Think, think!* What could I use as a weapon? There were great shards of glass, wickedly sharp, scattered all over the floor but I doubted my ability to manipulate one of them with my left hand, even assuming I managed to get to close quarters. There were bricks and broken chunks of stone here and there, from Michel's assault on the window. I hefted one in my left hand. It felt like a pitiful defence against an axe.

The petrol can. It was lying there on its side in the aisle. I limped over and picked it up. It was nearly empty but it had a satisfyingly solid feel to it. It was metal, not plastic, and there was a handle I could curl my fingers through. It would have made an admirable weapon if I had been left-handed. Still, it would have to do. I grasped the handle in my left hand and tried taking a practice swing. Pitiful. I had barely enough power to swat a fly, let alone brain someone. I tried again, using the heel of the damaged hand to steady the can. A little better.

'*Michel!*' I yelled as loudly as I could. I willed him to answer me. 'Michel! In here!'

There was no reply, but a second later I saw him pounding past a window on the other side of the church.

'Michel!'

It was no use. Either he had not heard me or he was too focused on flight to take any notice. A second shape tore past the window: Father Krause. I thought he was gaining on Michel. I imagined the edge of the axe, the bright sharpness of the blade, carving great arcs out of the air. I remembered the crunch the axe had made when it hit the window frame. All it would take was for Michel to stumble, to fall, and he would be finished.

I looked up at the window closest to me, the one showing the Fall of the Angels. St Michael crowned the scene, over-topping the struggling group of winged creatures, driving the grinning demon with his crimson face earthwards with his spear. Sunlight shone through the pale glass of the saint's face, illuminating the finely painted features with pure white light, lending them a radiant otherworldly glow.

And in that moment I knew what I had to do.

Chapter Fifty-nine

I put down the petrol can and picked up the largest stone I could see. I gazed up at the Fall of the Angels, my skin bathed in the coloured light which streamed through the glass. Over four and a half centuries ago, a genius had made that glass, a genius whose work was so exceptional that people believed his skill came from the Devil. My father would have given anything to stand where I was standing now. Anything. Even the lives of his children. Deliberately I took aim.

It was a clumsy throw but it achieved what was intended. The stone caught the crimson face of the falling demon full on and shattered it into fragments, the leering features disappearing in an explosion of tiny shards which pattered down on to the floor like red rain.

'Hey!' I screamed at the top of my voice.

I picked up another stone. This time the placid face of an angel with a sword crashed out of existence. I stood there motionless, panting and listening, my gaze scanning the floor for something else to throw.

'Hey!' I shouted again. 'In here!'

A shape appeared behind the furthest window. I had no idea whether it was Michel or his pursuer. Swiftly I bent and picked up another stone. My eyes scanned the six unbroken windows. The faces of men and angels, of soldiers and saints, gazed down from the brilliantly coloured panes, their finely painted expressions unchanged for nearly five hundred years. It was impossible not to feel their ancient beauty. And yet I thought the Allerheiligen glass was beautiful in the same way that a great white shark is beautiful. Its history was one of obsession and death, as surely as if the flaming scarlet of the red panels had been painted in blood.

'Here!' I screamed, and flung the stone at the face of Abraham.

I heard the satisfying sound of glass breaking, shortly answered by a bellow from outside. The rage in that cry almost paralysed me for a moment. It sounded as though all that was human in Father Krause had been stripped away, baring a damned soul which howled and screeched in its agony.

Suddenly I doubted my ability to wound him at all, certainly not with a left-handed swipe with a petrol can. For a dizzying moment I thought I really might sink down there on the stained tiles and let him come for me.

'Lin!'

That was Michel. I heard the choke in his voice and realized that he was nearly at the end of his strength, almost speechless, panting from running.

'In here!' I screamed back.

Move! I urged myself. If I stood here doing nothing we were both finished. I swept the petrol can up from the floor, forming the fingers of my left hand into a fist around the handle. Then I moved as quickly as I could to the well of deep shadow behind the door. I braced the can against the heel of my right hand and slowly raised it.

There were noises outside. Footsteps, running footsteps, and the ragged panting of someone who was exhausted. I tightened my grip on the handle of the petrol can.

Oh, God, I thought suddenly. *Who's going to come in first?* If it was Michel, I had to wait for him to pass before taking a swing at Father Krause. If it was Father Krause – any hesitation and I would be lost. He would see me and I would be trapped there behind the door. He could cut me down as easily as a reaper scything wheat.

The sounds from outside were coming closer. I could hear someone stumbling towards the door, stones crunching under their feet. My fingers felt slick on the handle of the petrol can; my hands were sweating. No time to wipe them on my clothes.

Someone came hurtling through the doorway. At the last moment I managed to arrest the swing I had started, though the jerk sent a stab of pain through my injured hand. It was Michel, bent double, wheezing with exertion, still clutching a jagged stone like a talisman, as though it would provide any defence against an axe. He was ready to collapse.

There was no time to call out to him, and it would have given away my hiding-place. I saw him sprawl on the worn tiles, red-faced, his chest heaving, the perfect bait for the berserker who was raging up to the door. Now it all depended on me, on whether I could summon up the sheer strength to disable his pursuer.

Footsteps were approaching, heavy and ominous. I raised the petrol can again and as the demon who had clothed himself in the flesh of Father Krause came roaring through the doorway I swung it with all the force I could muster. With a dull thud the corner of the can met bone. He staggered, but did not fall. The axe was still clutched in his hand; I could see the whitened knuckles tight around it. In wild desperation I lifted the can and struck again, with a clanging impact which drove him to his knees. I think I was screaming, but the sound seemed to come from a long way off.

Michel was scrambling to his feet, the stone still in his hand. It seemed to take forever for him to cross the short distance from the spot where he had fallen to the place where I stood, sobbing, trying to take a third swing with the petrol can. With a great grunt of exertion he raised the stone. There was a sickening crunch as it made contact with Father Krause's skull, then, with a groan, the man slumped to the floor and the axe fell from his hand. As soon as I dared, I pushed it away with the toe of my boot.

I was looking at the back of Father Krause's head, at the bloody contusion matting the greying hair, gore already welling from it.

'Is he dead?' I tried to say, but nothing came out except the laboured whistling of my breath.

The petrol can slipped from my grasp and clanged on to the floor. I bent forward, my reeking hair falling over my face, and cradled my injured hand. Still I could not take my eyes off the body on the floor. I kept thinking, *He's going to get up again. He's going to get up again and lift the axe and –*

Michel was sitting on the floor, with the bloody stone still clutched in his fist. He was looking at it, at the red which stained its rough surface, with a kind of horrified fascination. He looked at me, looked back at the stone, then opened his fingers and let it fall on to the tiles. We stared at each other.

After a while Michel crawled over to the prone figure and,

with more bravery than I could have summoned up, grasped its black-clad shoulder and turned the body over. We gazed at the still face, blood streaking the skin like warpaint. Mercifully the eyes were closed.

'I couldn't believe it,' said Michel. 'When I saw him. Father Krause. How could it be him? He's just . . .'

His voice trailed off. I knew what he was thinking. Father Krause – he was just a geek. Just a sad little rabbity man, the sort of person who's more likely to bore you to death than anything. But he was wrong.

'He was a devil,' I said.

CHAPTER SIXTY

For a while we just stared at the body. Blood was slowly oozing out of the wounds Michel and I had inflicted on him, staining the tiles red. Blood that we had spilt.

'We killed someone,' I whispered.

Reaction was setting in; I was beginning to feel deathly cold. I could not seem to stop shivering.

'We had to,' said Michel.

He meant to sound firm, but there was something in his voice that made him sound as though he was trying to convince himself.

'Michel, I'm cold.' My teeth were chattering.

Michel crawled over to me and put his arms around me. For a while we clung to each other, my face buried in Michel's shoulder, but I could not dismiss the fear that Father Krause might somehow rise up and attack us again. When my eyes were not on him I could feel a prickling at the back of my neck, as though someone was watching me. I could not stop myself from peering around Michel to look at him.

'I didn't think you'd come in time,' I said.

'I didn't go back to the farm,' said Michel. 'I had this feeling . . .' There was a faint tone of accusation in his voice. 'I turned round and went back and you'd already gone. I knew what you were going to do. Why didn't you let me come with you?'

'I thought you'd stop me smashing them,' I said.

'I wouldn't –' began Michel, then stopped.

He had been going to say, *I wouldn't have stopped you*, but then he had realized that he probably would have. We both fell silent.

'You smell strange,' said Michel eventually. He touched my hair. 'It smells like . . . petrol.'

I didn't say anything.

'What was he going to do?' asked Michel, but I could tell from the note of incredulous horror in his voice that he had already guessed.

Very gently he pushed me away. He got to his feet, grasping the end of a pew for support, and took several steps down the aisle. He was looking at the Pentecost window – looking at it with the sick fascination of a bystander staring at a road accident. When he turned his face to me it was pale and shocked.

Standing up again gave me some trouble; my legs felt as though they would buckle under me at any moment. Still, by hanging on to the backs of the wooden pews I was able to make my way unsteadily to the spot where Michel was. I stood beside him, clutching his arm, and stared up at the window.

I looked at the brilliant colours, at the delicacy and precision of the brushwork on each upturned face. At the bright corona of flames surrounding each head.

I thought of my father, of the years he had spent dreaming of a discovery like this. The interviews he would give, the papers he would write, the inevitable coffee-table book crammed with full-colour photographs of the glass. I thought of him sailing into a future glittering with promise, and I saw him turn to us as he sailed away into the dazzling sunshine, turn and wave farewell.

And Polly? Polly would be left behind, frozen in a moment in time, a footnote in history. 'The tragic circumstances surrounding the discovery of the legendary Allerheiligen glass by Dr Oliver Fox . . .' That would be my sister's epitaph.

Carefully I disentangled my arm from Michel's. Then I stooped and picked something up from the tiled floor. It was a large chunk of stone. I took a step back, aimed and hurled it at the window as hard as I could. It made a sound like an explosion.

I took a step back, my boots crunching shards of glass, and bent to pick up another stone. It was awkward throwing with my left hand. I was not sure I could do this on my own.

'Help me,' I said, and threw the stone.

After a moment Michel joined me, scanning the tiled floor for anything he could throw. When we had used all the stones he had flung through the Adam and Eve window, we went outside and collected more.

A mighty crash and the Slaughter of the Innocents, the inspiration for the attack on Ru, was gone forever. Another explosive impact and Naaman, suspended in the blue water, had winked out of existence. *Crash!* went the depiction of Lazarus rising from his tomb which had inspired the desecration of the cemetery.

The coloured glass rained down, and there was an end of

King Herod, of Moses, of Isaac, of Michel's father's secret, of all my father's long-nurtured dreams.

And because we were intent on smashing the last of the windows, neither of us noticed until afterwards that Father Krause's body had gone.

CHAPTER SIXTY-ONE

Neither of us had the energy to react very much to the discovery. Michel put an arm round my shoulders and we stood staring at the blood congealing on the floor. There was absolute silence apart from the sound of our own breathing and distant birdsong from the forest outside. When either of us moved there was a crackle of broken glass underfoot. But there were no sounds of anyone else moving about in the church, no sounds of running footsteps receding into the distance. Father Krause had vanished. Later I remembered the day he had first come to call at the castle, how I had rushed outside with the forgotten card case and he had already gone. Evidently he knew the woods like the back of his hand. But at this moment I did not think about that. It seemed right, somehow, that he should vanish as though spirited away. I imagined him flying over the treetops as Bonschariant is supposed to have done, a snarl of frustrated malevolence distorting his face.

There was no point trying to lock the church again, or to put the boards back up on the remains of the windows. Michel took my hand in his and we walked out of the church and into the forest. Sunlight streamed down through the treetops. Far ahead of us a red squirrel suddenly ran on to the path, paused and then darted up the trunk of a tree. Otherwise we seemed to be the only living creatures in the forest. Strangely, I felt no fear. Father Krause could undoubtedly have ambushed us somewhere along the tortuous route back to the castle, but I instinctively felt that he had gone, that we would not see him again, and besides, I was too shocked and exhausted to care.

When we finally stepped out from under the trees and approached the castle, I was unsurprised to see blue lights flashing and what seemed to be an inordinate number of uniformed police everywhere. Someone saw us and shouted something, and then they were all running towards us. The flashing lights, the running, the shouting, seemed like a distant uproar, a tsunami perceived from the bottom of the sea. I drifted on my own undertow, not caring about any of it as long as I could keep Michel's hand in mine. I hung on to him as though my life depended on it.

Someone took us over to the ambulance that was parked outside the green gate. I knew what the ambulance was for and the waiting stretcher. Nobody had bothered to put my sister on the stretcher; there was no point. She would be photographed first, I supposed. I wondered if they had moved her or whether she was still lying in the same place, looking as though she had been frozen in the act of crawling across the hard earth.

The police did not leave us alone for a second. The two officers from Bonn who had questioned Tuesday at the castle that time appeared. I listened to their questions but found it difficult to formulate replies. The things they asked, about times and movements and sequences of events, seemed unrelated to what had happened. Even in my detached state, though, I could hear the suspicion fizzing in their voices. Who could blame them? They had a dead girl and two teenagers who had walked out of the forest with blood on their hands. Their suspicions grew when Michel and I managed – not very coherently – to communicate to them the fact that somewhere in the woods there was apparently another victim, an elderly man who (so they interpreted our wandering explanation) had been struck over the head and his body concealed.

A paramedic came out of the ambulance and examined my injured hand. While he was fixing up a support for my fingers there was a considerable amount of urgent conversation between him and Frau Ohlert, the blonde policewoman from Bonn. I was too exhausted to follow much of what was said, but I gathered that she wanted Michel and me to take the police back into the forest. She was pressing the paramedic to say that I was capable of doing it; she seemed to think that the 'other victim' might be found in time if we moved quickly enough. Michel tried to interject something at this point and earned himself a very evil look. Evidently Tuesday was no longer on the list of suspects; now we were.

While the discussion was still going on, my father came out of the castle, followed by another officer; clearly nobody was taking any chances. When he saw me he broke into a run, and I saw the looks which flashed between the policemen, the sudden alertness in their body language. They were half-expecting him to do something desperate – attack me, perhaps, or make a run for it into the forest. Everyone seemed confused about what was happening.

'Lin!' said my father. 'Thank God! When I found . . . I thought . . .'

He didn't say what he had thought. He began to put his

arms around me but I did not respond. My grip on Michel's hand tightened.

'What happened? Where have you been?'

The questions tumbled out of my father without leaving any space for me to reply. I saw that he was weeping. I let him hug me but I did not let go of Michel's hand. I stood passively, waiting for him to let me go. His tears meant nothing. If he had kept his promise, perhaps none of this would have happened.

Herr Schmitz, the policeman with the incongruous American accent, came over and began to talk to his partner, and then to ask questions. Gradually the story emerged, although what they made of it is hard to say. When Michel first mentioned the church in the woods they looked sceptical and when he told them about the windows expressions of frank incredulity crossed their faces. It was just the same with them as it was with Father Engels; they took us for a pair of attention-seeking fantasists. All the same, they had one dead body on their hands and apparently a second one somewhere in the woods. They continued to ask questions.

My father, listening to the tall policeman's occasional questions in English and doing his best to follow the conversations in German, slowly began to piece things together. His expression went from one of intense concentration to one of disbelief and then finally of terrible urgency. I knew what that look meant. Any minute now he would be interrupting Michel, wanting to know this and that about the glass, trying to establish whether it might really be what Michel said it was. I was standing there with a broken hand and reeking of petrol, his son had narrowly missed being spitted like a pig and he had found his eldest child lying dead inside the castle; in spite of all this he wanted to know whether the stained glass we were talking about was the real McCoy. The dead feeling I had inside seemed to sink further into me, as though something heavy were dragging me down. I could not even hate or pity him. I watched him with dull eyes and waited for the inevitable.

He insisted on going with us into the forest. He tried all the predictable arguments, about the unique importance of the Allerheiligen glass, the need for it to be properly assessed and so on. When this failed to make any impression, the police never having heard of Gerhard Remsich, he took another tack. I was his daughter and I was obviously traumatized and injured. He was not prepared to give his permission for the police to drag me about all over the forest unless he was allowed to accompany me. Never mind that I was old enough to be considered a suspect. He made it sound as though I was six years old.

In the end they buckled; it was the argument about not allowing his daughter to be led off into the woods that did it. We set off, with police both ahead of and behind us, not taking any chances. I stumbled along behind Michel, looking neither left nor right. The paramedic had given me something for my hand and the pure white agony which had been racking it had faded to a dull throb. My hair was sticking to the sides of my face. Every so often my father would get close to me and try to ask me something about the glass, but I ignored him and concentrated on putting one foot in front of the other.

We came to the place where the fence had been trodden down and the ground scarred with ruts, and a little later to the spot where we had to leave the path. I tried to ignore the fevered mutterings of my father at my shoulder, as though he were some tempting devil. A few minutes later we stepped into the clearing and saw the church.

CHAPTER SIXTY-TWO

'God in heaven,' said my father. 'It's true.' He took a couple of steps towards the church, but one of the policemen stopped him.

'Stay here, please,' he said gruffly in German.

'But –'

My father's German failed him as usual and he looked around for me, but I was not taking the bait. I stood by Michel and eyed the front of the church, shivering, wondering whether Father Krause still lurked somewhere within. He had grown in my imagination to such terrifying and diabolical proportions that even the presence of armed police did not make me feel safe.

My father stayed where he was, but he was visibly consumed with impatience, desperate to get into the church and see for himself. He came over to me and I could feel the excitement crackling all around him like static.

'Lin? Are you sure about what you saw?'

I just stared at him and felt for Michel's hand.

'Was there anything in the glass which would identify it? Any text? A name?'

I shook my head. If there had been anything, it was all gone now.

When he saw that there was nothing to be gained by questioning me, my father threw up his hands in a gesture of defeat, but he did not say anything.

The police were fanning out, surrounding the church on all sides. The word *Axt* drifted across to me. That was why they were being so cautious. From the incoherent account Michel and I had given them, they were not sure whether they were looking for a dead body or an armed one, very much alive.

The tall policeman from Bonn, Herr Schmitz, came over to where Michel and I were standing. I was glad it was him and not the blonde policewoman. In her icy blue eyes I read nothing but suspicion, but he was a little warmer, avuncular even. It did not occur to me that the two of them adopted these roles on purpose.

'This other person,' he said, not unkindly, 'where was he when you last saw him?'

'In . . .' I faltered. I pointed. 'In there . . .'

'Inside the church?'

I nodded.

'And he was injured? Or was he dead?'

'I don't know . . .' I shivered hopelessly. 'We thought he was dead . . . but then he was gone . . .'

'Fräulein Fox?' He sounded as though he was trying to talk someone back into consciousness. 'I need to know whether it's safe for us to go in there.'

'I don't know,' I repeated helplessly.

'Could he still be in there, this person?'

'Yes. I suppose so . . .'

He didn't ask me any further questions. It was not until very much later that I realized he probably wanted the full details properly recorded, not blurted out in the middle of a forest. Nobody knew yet what Father Krause was; they might have been looking for a murder victim.

The policeman moved away to confer with his partner, though one of the local officers stayed close to Michel and me. My father kept shooting glances at him and then at the church, as though calculating whether he could make it inside before anyone stopped him. The hunger in his stance was palpable; he was pointing like a gun dog. I looked at him and looked away. I felt slightly sick. Polly was *dead* and he still cared about the glass. He still wanted to be the first one to see it, the one to break the news.

The police had now encircled the church. I watched them without much interest. In spite of what I had said, I did not think that Father Krause might still be inside. The Allerheiligen glass had been the lodestone which drew him to the church, binding him to it as strongly as Bonschariant himself was bound in legend. Now the glass had been shattered I thought that the enchantment had been broken. When I had taken up the axe and marched into the forest, I had thought that at the first blow, when the glass had shivered into a million tiny fragments, Bonschariant would depart screeching into whatever dimension he had come from. I felt the same about Father Krause. I thought in my heart that he would never be seen again.

I watched two of the policemen cautiously approaching the door of the church. Everyone else had fallen silent. I could quite clearly hear the crunching of their boots on the stony earth. They disappeared into the church and for what seemed like an interminable length of time we heard nothing at all. At last one of them reappeared. The church was empty.

At this news there was a perceptible break in the tension which had filled the air. My father took the opportunity to move away from where we stood, with the policeman hovering a few metres away like a patient guard dog. The ground rose very slightly to the left of the church and my father began to walk slowly and self-consciously along the edge of the rise. *I'm not going anywhere*, said his body language. *I'm just stretching my legs*. The policeman glanced his way, but since he was obviously not heading straight for the church decided to let it go.

My father continued his crab-like scuttle along the higher ground. I could see that his face was always turned towards the church. He was eager for the moment when the south side of it would come into sight, when he would catch a glimpse of the windows, even from the outside. He would say, *Incredible, there must be eight different lights*, or, *Reticulated tracery windows, superb*, speaking to an imaginary audience of thrilled academics. I watched him step over a tree stump and stand still, staring. He stayed there for a long time. He never looked towards me, and as far as I could tell he never said a word, but his whole attitude was one of strained concentration. He took a step forward, down the bank, and then stopped. He put up a hand very slowly and began to rub his right eye, as though trying to clear blurred vision.

Then with a choked cry he was running towards the church at full tilt, running straight for the front door.

'*Halt!*' bawled someone, and then there was a confused chorus of voices all shouting at my father, who took not the slightest notice. If he had thought about it at all, he would have realized that they were armed, but I doubt it would have made any difference. At first they sounded irritated rather than threatening, but as my father neared the church door without any sign of slowing down they began to seem alarmed. Officers started to run towards him from all sides, the two officers from Bonn among them. Their faces were grim. Another few metres and my father would be in the church, trampling all over whatever evidence there was. He had taken them by surprise; I don't suppose they were used to having crime scenes contaminated by stampeding medievalists.

It is a tribute to my father's determination that he got into the church at all. The second police officer appeared in the doorway, summoned by the shouting outside, and my father simply shoved him aside.

There was a brief moment of silence as everyone gawped at what my father had done. Then a howl arose from inside the church, a cry that hacked through the air like an axe, hoarse and ragged. My father had seen what had become of the glass. For a second everybody froze. It was terrible, like the shrieking of a parent over a slain child.

Herr Schmitz was the first to collect himself. A moment later he had reached the door and began barking instructions at everyone else. I suppose he had foreseen that whatever had not been trodden underfoot by my father was about to be trampled by his fellow officers. He and the policeman who had just come out of the church went inside.

I did not go back into the church myself. I never went back into it. But I heard afterwards that the two policemen found my father kneeling on the tiled floor, raving like a madman. His hands were stained with red and he kept looking at them, then up at the ruins of the windows, and keening like a banshee. His hands were red with his own blood. The floor of the church was covered in tiny shards of stained glass, jagged and razor-sharp. My father had tried to take up handfuls of them, as though he could somehow summon back the form and light which had comprised Gerhard Remsich's masterwork before it ran through his fingers like sand. He kept trying to clutch at it, until Herr Schmitz and the other policeman hauled him away by force.

They dragged him out into the open air and Herr Schmitz shouted for someone to fetch the paramedic. The two of them were still holding on to him, but my father had stopped struggling. He stood between them with a stunned expression on his face. He kept looking at his hands, as though he did not understand what had happened to them. Perhaps he thought the magnificent crimson of the glass had somehow seeped into his fingers.

Michel moved closer and put an arm round my shoulders. Perhaps it was the movement which caught my father's eye; at any rate, he looked up and for a moment our eyes met. He gave a tiny start and realization flooded into that dazed expression. In his imagination he suddenly saw me swinging the axe, he heard the rain of glass pattering on to the church floor.

Even at that distance I could see the anguish and rage which blazed out of his eyes. One of them was rimmed with red; he had rubbed his face with his bloodied hands. It was like looking into a black hole, a ravening pit sucking everything in – light, understanding, forgiveness. I buried my face in Michel's shoulder. Bonschariant, if any such person had ever existed, had fled from the shattered remains of his home. But my father had still not cast out his demon.

CHAPTER SIXTY-THREE

Michel and I might have been in considerably deeper trouble if Father Krause had really vanished for good. If he had had the means to go right away, or if he had decided to destroy himself in some lonely spot and had never been found, our position would have been very difficult indeed. We had given conflicting accounts of our whereabouts when Ru was attacked and we had been the first to find Polly's body. In addition to these damning circumstances, there was the not insignificant matter of over a million euros' worth of art treasure reduced to a heap of glass splinters, and a third body apparently missing. As soon as my hand had been properly treated we could expect some very prolonged questioning from Herr Schmitz and his cold-eyed partner – and we had nothing to offer them except a tale which sounded as though it had come straight out of Grimm's. If I had not been so exhausted I would have been panicking. There was a very real possibility that Father Krause might have his revenge after all, if we bore the blame for his deeds.

By the end of my acquaintance with Herr Schmitz, however, I think he had a grudging admiration for Michel and me, although Frau Ohlert never did. Until the very last time I saw her, she was still eyeing me with a suspicious expression which said all too plainly that she thought we had got away with something. I never asked Herr Schmitz what would have happened to us if Father Krause had never been found, or what he had thought when he first assessed the events of that terrible afternoon. Some things it is better not to know.

CHAPTER SIXTY-FOUR

If you leave the Kreuzburg by the main track and drive straight out of the forest you will come to Baumgarten, but there is also a narrower, less well-known track, a track I had taken myself once before, which comes out at the village of Traubenheim. The spot where the track meets the main road is within a stone's throw of the railway station. The station itself consists of not much more than a pair of concrete platforms and signs with the name of the village. With no ticket office and no regular staff, in the middle of the day I should think there are rarely any passengers waiting. The platform is shielded from the road by a screen of tall trees. I am sure it would be quite possible for someone to slip out of the woods, step on to the platform and catch the first train to come along without ever being seen by a living soul. The northbound trains which pass the station at Traubenheim run towards Bonn and from there you can change and continue to Köln. From Köln you can go pretty much anywhere you like: Hamburg, Frankfurt, even over the border to Brussels or Paris.

I heard afterwards that Father Krause left the train at Köln's main station, where he crossed the Bahnhofsvorplatz and climbed the steps to the city's great Gothic cathedral, the Dom. The area is nearly always teeming with people and nobody seems to have taken any special notice of one dark-clad man of about sixty making his way to the cathedral's west door, even though he had several nasty-looking head wounds which were encrusted with dried blood. Perhaps they thought he was a vagrant who had fallen down dead drunk in the street somewhere. At any rate, no one accosted him. He entered the cathedral and walked down the nave towards the fourteenth-century stained-glass windows from which Sts Gereon and Maurice, Kunibert, Peter and Maternus gaze down upon the high altar.

He did not try to approach the high altar. In that case he would probably have drawn attention to himself much more quickly. Instead he stopped close to the *Vierungsaltar*, the altar which stands in the centre of the cross formed by the nave and transepts. He seems to have remained there for quite some time. Later, when the story had filtered out to the press, visitors to the Dom that day were falling over themselves to tell newspaper reporters and television crews that they had seen him standing there, staring fixedly at the great window in the south transept. More compelling than the tales related by media-happy tourists was the testimony of a local woman, Magdalena Fuchs, who had visited the cathedral to pray. Frau Fuchs said that Father Krause had accosted her as she passed him and had told her that the south window had been designed and made by an ancestor of his, Gerhard Remsich, in the sixteenth century. Frau Fuchs visited the cathedral so often that it is quite possible that she hardly noticed the individual subjects of the windows any more, but still this pronouncement surprised her: the design of the window in the south transept is an abstract one by a modern artist. She looked at the window, as if to confirm what she already knew, and then she looked at Father Krause and decided that it would be safer not to contradict him.

A little later one of the red-coated cathedral wardens noticed Father Krause in an agitated state, apparently attempting to approach other visitors, all of whom were swerving to give him a wide berth. I suspect that the warden nursed a secret desire to vent some of the irritation that had been building up after hours of shepherding gum-chewing tourists out of the building. At any rate, he went up to Father Krause and asked him in a very high-handed way what he was doing.

Opinion is divided about what happened next. Several witnesses swore that Father Krause cried out, '*Mein Haus soll ein Haus des Gebetes sein – ihr habt daraus eine Räuberhöhle gemacht!*' and threw himself on the warden with his fists flying. Others were equally ready to swear that the discussion had been peaceful until Father Krause suddenly took a large stone out of his coat pocket and aimed it at the south window. The warden tried to restrain him and took a blow to the head which cracked his skull. A woman who saw Father Krause standing over the warden's prone body with the bloody stone in his hand began to scream. One of the other wardens ran to call the police, but by the time they arrived Father Krause had been subdued, thanks to the intervention of two beefy tourists from Peoria.

Whatever really happened – whether an enraged killer would have had time to shout out, 'My house should be a house of prayer – you have made it a den of thieves' or not – the chunk of stone suggested that the window in the south transept had had a narrow escape.

Even now, I do not think that Father Krause will ever be called to account for what he did. He went before the courts and was declared *schuldunfähig* – that is, 'incapable of being guilty' – which is similar to being found not guilty by reason of insanity under British law. A lot of psychiatric terms were bandied about, all of which I took to mean that Herr Krause was, and continues to be, tormented by his own legion of demons.

The investigation into the events of that autumn never definitively proved that Herr Mahlberg's death was anything other than an accident, although the broken glass at this and the other murder scenes was noted. When asked about it, Herr Krause is said to have looked sly and said that it had been left by 'the Glass Demon'. Whether he believed this or not is unclear. I myself think that there remained quite enough cunning in that corrupted mind for him to have planted the glass fragments himself as a warning, knowing how it would be interpreted by both superstitious locals and experts on the Allerheiligen glass.

No connection was ever established between Herr Krause's family line and that of Gerhard Remsich. Herr Krause's family had been affluent in times gone by and a considerable amount of land had belonged to them, including the area of forest where the church stood and a long-vanished manor house whose foundations lie crumbling somewhere in the woods. All that remained by Herr Krause's time was the land where the church was concealed and the farm inhabited by the Reinartzes. Michel's father had leased both from Herr Krause on condition that he maintained the church in secret. It seems that as long as he did so, he was under no kind of threat from Herr Krause. Herr Krause himself had no means of maintaining it and he was content with the arrangement so long as it allowed him to do what he wished, which was to hug the secret of the glass to himself like an unscrupulous art collector hoarding a stolen masterpiece.

As for Michel's father, the farm was the ideal place for him to live with his two sons, Michel and Jörg. I had wondered about Jörg, about Michel's reluctance to talk about him, about the strange grimace Johanna had made when I asked her about him. *What's right with him?* she had said. Jörg had seemed elusive, even furtive – I had never seen anything of him myself apart from that glimpse of someone closing a window at the farm, as though hastily sealing himself in, out of my sight. I was not there the day Jörg and his father came to the castle, but Tuesday's description of Jörg's silence and the way he had spat on the floor suggested someone crude and menacing. Like everyone else in Baumgarten, I had jumped to conclusions.

Michel was right: his brother is not the same as most people, and hasn't been since birth. He probably won't ever be fully independent and he will probably continue to look at the world through the eyes of a child. All the same, he is fiercely loyal to his family. The day he and Michel Reinartz Senior stormed into the castle and threw their repulsive offering on to the dining table, he was simply following his father's lead. He himself is as harmless as a person can be – certainly less pernicious than the tongue-waggers who ill-judged him.

I wondered about Jörg's and Michel's mother – whether her interest in the glass and her belief that it should become public knowledge had led to her death. Michel said it hadn't.

'The police asked Dad a load of questions about that. But they think it really was an aneurysm.' He cleared his throat. 'They're sure enough that they're not going to – you know . . .'

I did know. It was not necessary to complete the sentence: *dig her up.*

'And the priest who told him that the glass was responsible for her death?'

Michel looked at me with his eyebrows raised.

'Father Krause,' I said, supplying the answer myself.

Thinking about it made me rather queasy. Even then, long before we had even dreamed of coming to the Eifel to look for the Allerheiligen glass, Bonschariant had claimed a victim for his own. So what if her death had been a random tragedy and not his work at all? You cannot expect a demon to play fair.

I still think about that, and about the morning Herr Krause called at the castle, ostensibly looking for my father but in reality probably coming to check that he had done his work thoroughly when he tried to spit my brother with a spear. Perhaps even coming to gloat. It makes me shudder, but not as much as the memory of him glancing around the room, his gaze dancing quickly from the table to the sideboard. At the time I had thought he was looking for evidence of my own transgressions, signs that I had been dabbling with the black arts. Now I think that perhaps he realized that I knew where the glass was, and he was looking for a weapon.

If Michel had not turned up at that precise moment, my parents would have come home a couple of hours later and found – what? There were so many ways in which Herr Krause could have made his point. I think again of the window depicting Abraham about to sacrifice Isaac, the patriarch standing there with a great knife held aloft, preparing to plunge it into his little son's body, and I feel faintly sick. At such times I am not sorry that those windows were destroyed.

CHAPTER SIXTY-FIVE

I did not see my father for a week. There was no question any more of staying at the castle. Uncle Karl appeared, summoned by the police or by my father, I can't say which, and took me back to Koblenz with him. I don't know where my father spent that week. Tuesday spoke to him by phone every day but always in hushed tones; occasionally she would look round to see whether I was anywhere in the vicinity. One time I asked her where he was and she simply said, 'Upset,' in an absent-minded voice. For once it seemed she was being tactful; personally I thought my father probably wanted to kill me.

The rest of the time Tuesday sat around doing very little, sometimes playing with Ru and very often crying, quietly and for a long time. I would go out most days, not with any particular aim but just to wander about in the fresh air, feeling my body moving and trying to let my mind freewheel for a while, and I would come back again an hour later and find that she was still sitting there with tears running down her face. It was hard to think of anything to say to her. I made her cups of tea, and sometimes I took Ru out for a couple of hours so that she could rest – not that she ever seemed to lie down or even relax. Polly was always between us, like a pale thin ghost, reproaching us with her absence. But we never spoke about her.

I remember one day towards the end of that week, when it began to rain before dawn and kept it up for hours, a long depressing downpour which pattered on to the windows and made the world outside run and blur as though we were seeing it through eyes brimming with tears. Uncle Karl's wife, Marion, had taken Ru and her own son, Johann, off somewhere for the day; I think she had no idea what to say to us either. I went to look for a coat. In spite of the weather the thought of being cooped up indoors was intolerable. I didn't bother asking Tuesday whether she wanted to come with me.

The only raincoat in the house was Tuesday's – predictably, it was more fashionable than functional, made of shiny black material with an elegant cut and a sash belt to nip in the waist. I looked at it for a few moments and then put it back into the wardrobe. I had no desire to steal Tuesday's clothes any more.

In the end I didn't bother with a coat at all. I just walked out into the rain and slammed the door behind me. It was a mild day, otherwise I would have frozen within five minutes. Eifel rain has a drenching quality; after barely a minute in it you might as well have emptied a bucket of water over yourself. It drove into my face like a hail of miniature fists and ran down the back of my neck. My clothes, rapidly soaked through, stuck to my skin like slime. I blinked hard and tried to drag wet strands of hair out of my eyes with dripping fingers. The sensation of rain streaming down my face made me gasp, but I didn't turn back. I strode out along pavements which turned into paths and then over grass which insinuated itself wetly against my ankles and soaked my shoes. The sky above was a great grey mass pressing down on me. I increased my pace. First I hurried, then I jogged and finally I broke into a run, hurling myself along, heedless of bushes and brambles which tore at my clothes as I passed.

I ran until I was utterly out of breath and was beginning to think that I might be sick. Then I came to a stop and stood there in the rain with my chest heaving and my limbs tingling. I put my head back and looked up. Nothing had changed. That fuzzy grey light still filled the whole sky like a creeping mould. The sun had vanished forever. My sister was still dead.

I walked home, and when I got inside I was not sure what to do with myself. Water was running off me in streams. I couldn't walk to the bedroom or the bathroom without leaving a dripping muddy trail behind me. I closed the door and stood on the doormat shivering. My teeth were beginning to chatter.

A door closed somewhere in the house and I heard footsteps – hesitant, slow footsteps. Tuesday appeared at the end of the hallway. Without her make-up, with her hair unbrushed, she looked younger and somehow smaller than she normally did. For the first time I realized that I was taller than she was. I began to think too that it must have hurt her whenever I said she wasn't my mother. It was certainly true that she wasn't the mother I had dreamed for myself, the warm, capable, endlessly understanding mother. But perhaps she hadn't expected me to turn out the way I did either.

Tuesday walked down the hallway towards me and, when she got to me, she put her arms round me. I was soaked to the skin, and pretty soon she must have been soaked too, but she still held on to me.

It's all my fault, I wanted to say. *I knew we were all in danger but I couldn't find the way to tell you.* Something was cracking inside me, as though someone had pushed a chisel into a rift in a stone and was hammering, hammering. *It was my fault for going to the church, for letting him see me in there. Polly would be alive if it weren't for me.* I wanted to tell Tuesday this, but all that came out were great racking sobs. I was gulping and coughing. Tears mingled with raindrops. I tasted salt on my lips.

Tuesday's shoulders were heaving; after a while I realized that she was crying too. 'I'm so sorry,' she kept saying. 'I'm so sorry.' She sounded as though she were choking. 'It's all my fault. I should have seen she was sick. I should – I should have stayed at home. I should never have left her.'

'It's not –' I began, and stopped. *It's not your fault,* I had been going to say. *You couldn't have known this would happen. And it wasn't you who killed her. It was that – devil.*

A weight was beginning to lift from me. I knew I would never be free from regrets about Polly's death. If I had insisted on going home earlier, regardless of what the school might have said – if I had told my father what I suspected, instead of keeping it all to myself – if I hadn't insisted that Michel take me to the church in the woods in the first place . . . But Tuesday was blaming herself, and I supposed my father was too. The truth was, none of us had intended this to happen, and none of us had taken Polly to the top of the tower and thrown her to her death. There was only one person responsible for that. I realized this at last, and it was a great relief.

I found that I was in control of myself again. I was no

longer choked by tears; I could speak. I put my arms around
Tuesday and let her cry.

'It's OK,' I murmured into her hair. 'It's OK, Mum. It's not
your fault.'

CHAPTER SIXTY-SIX

Eventually, of course, we were allowed home, although 'home' was hardly what it felt like when we finally arrived back in England. My father had managed to get the tenants out of our house and once the supposed sabbatical year had ended he would return to his old job. His dreams of becoming Professor Fox had evaporated and he himself was a broken man. I had the feeling that something inside him – guilt, or simple misery – took some strange satisfaction from the idea of knuckling under and working for the detested Lyle, now Professor of Medieval Studies. He saw himself as a bondsman tugging his forelock to the landowner, a dispossessed slave bowing to his master. I felt some dim understanding of this. After all, it was from him that I had inherited my own self-destruct button. In spite of this, we hardly ever spoke.

Sometimes we would be sharing a room, but not speaking – he would be writing, I reading, and I would look up to see him staring at me. Once or twice he said, 'Lin,' but then seemed to change his mind. I knew he was thinking about the Aller-heiligen glass, about the magnificent treasure he had so very nearly seen, but I could not bring myself to talk to him about it. We both knew very well that the only accessible place in which Gerhard Remsich's masterwork now existed was my memory, but my father hesitated to ask me and I could not bring myself to raise the topic with him. We might have carried on like that forever had it not been for Professor Lyle.

I met him one morning outside the Faculty of History. My father had given me a lift into the town centre and had then gone into the faculty building. This was ostensibly to read some obscure article, but more probably so that he could sit in a sunny corner of the library and ponder lost opportunities. I had some errands of my own to run and was supposed to be meeting a friend later.

I was trying to make up my mind which way to go first when someone said, 'It's Lindisfarne, isn't it?'

I scowled, feeling a stab of irritation so strong that it almost amounted to hate. I *detest* that name, and if I ever commit matricide it will be because Tuesday, in a fit of New Age madness, had seen fit to saddle me with it. She was welcome to name herself after days of the week or months of the year or anything else if she liked, but she could have given me a *normal* name.

'No,' I said shortly, before I had even taken a proper look at the speaker.

'Miss Fox? You are Miss Fox?'

I looked directly at him and realized that it was Professor Lyle. I had never met him before but his face had been splashed all over the university magazine when he got the appointment. I recognized that jowly and faux-jovial face without any trouble. I wondered what he wanted.

'I'm Lin Fox,' I said, in tones which clearly implied that I wouldn't have been Lin Fox if I could possibly have disobliged him.

'Oliver Fox's daughter, yes?'

I noticed he didn't say *Dr* Fox and guessed that he would have reduced my father's status to *Mr* if he had dared. I nodded curtly.

'I'd really like to talk to you. Would you care to come inside for a moment?'

I stared at him, wondering what he could possibly want to talk to me about.

'I don't think so.'

'Come, come,' he said in a jollying-along tone which made me feel as though I were about six years old. 'I won't bite you.'

Reluctantly I followed him inside. I took a swift look around but there was no sign of my father. Professor Lyle went through a couple of sets of double doors with me in tow and we found ourselves in a small, untidy office. He subsided into a chair behind the desk and waved me towards another. Then he sat for a moment, studying me and not saying anything.

I really hate that. I knew what he was doing; he was trying to put me on the defensive. I looked at my watch very ostentatiously.

'I'm meeting someone.'

He smiled faintly at this. 'Then I'll get to the point. Is your father planning to publish anything about the Allerheiligen stained-glass windows?'

'How should I know?' I glowered at him. 'He's more likely to tell you than me.'

Professor Lyle leaned forward. 'Ah, but he hasn't.'

'Well, what makes you think I'd know?'

'You've seen them. The windows, I mean. Haven't you?'

I nodded reluctantly.

'And I think I am right in saying that you are the *only* person who has seen them?'

'No, Michel – I mean, some people in Germany saw them too.'

'And these people, are any of them involved in this field?'

I couldn't imagine Michel Reinartz Senior taking time off from roaming the forest with his monstrous dog in order to write a monograph about medieval stained glass. I shook my head.

'Then I have a proposal for you.'

I stared at him. An inkling of his purpose was beginning to come to me. I wondered whether I should simply get up and walk out, but something kept me there in my seat.

'If your father is not going to write anything about the glass, tell *me* about it.' He studied my face, looking for my reaction, and then went on, 'I'm sure you realize – well, perhaps you don't – that the discovery of those windows would have been a sensation in the world of medieval studies. Something like finding the Holy Grail.'

He gave me a condescending smile. I didn't return it.

'Naturally I have no intention of impinging on your father's work,' said the professor smoothly. He raised a forefinger as though about to lecture me. 'But if he is *not* planning to write anything, well . . .' His eyebrows shot up. 'It would be nothing short of a crime if the academic world were deprived of whatever information is available – wouldn't it?'

I said nothing.

'It is, of course, a tragedy that the windows themselves were destroyed.' He gave no sign that he knew who had destroyed them or what the circumstances surrounding their destruction had been. His voice and demeanour were so calm that we might have been discussing some regrettable accident. He sat back suddenly, eyeing me. 'All that history – all that beauty – it doesn't have to be lost, you know. You're not studying at the moment, are you?' He didn't wait for a reply. 'You could come here . . . You could tell me as much as you can remember about the windows. You could draw them for me – the layout – as much as you can recall, and if you can't draw I'll get someone in who can do it for you. Like a police photofit,' he added jocosely. 'When the work is finished, I'll credit you, of course.'

I looked at him. I looked at his well-fed, self-satisfied face – the face of a man who is successful, a man who knows that he is going to get what he wants. I let him sit there for a while, thinking no doubt that I was awestruck by the generosity of his suggestion, savouring the moment of his triumph. Then I stood up.

'No, thanks,' I said. I hoisted my bag on to my shoulder and made for the door.

There was a stunned silence and then the scraping of chair legs on the floor as he stood up too.

'Lindisfarne! Lin –' He was around the desk remarkably nimbly for one so weighted down with his own dignity. I stepped back, thinking he might actually try to grab me by the arm. 'Think about this! Think –'

'I have thought about it,' I told him. 'And I've just remembered. My father *is* going to write a book about the glass after all.'

And with that I marched out of his office and fled down the hall. I've never felt bad about it. I could have forgiven him a lot, but I never forgive *anyone* for calling me Lindisfarne.

397

CHAPTER SIXTY-SEVEN

I didn't see my father during my precipitate flight from the Faculty of History, but by the time I got home late in the afternoon he was already back in his study. The door was closed. He liked to preserve the illusion that he was in there working away so furiously that no one could be allowed to disturb him, but after I had knocked and opened the door I was not surprised to see him sitting by the window, simply staring out at the sky.

'Dad?'

He looked at me a little vaguely, as though surprised to see me there. 'Is it dinnertime already?'

'No.' I slid into the room and shut the door behind me. 'I wanted to show you something.'

I went over to the desk. There was one drawer in which my father kept stationery – reams of paper for the printer, spare ballpoint pens, a battered stapler. I pulled the drawer open and began to rummage through it. I found what I wanted at the very bottom: a board-backed sketchpad. I put it on the desk and then I began to fish about in the mug he used to hold all his pens and pencils, looking for an HB pencil.

All this time my father said nothing. He did not ask me

why I was raiding his desk drawer instead of finding my own materials downstairs, or why I wanted the sketchpad in the first place. I had the impression that he was just waiting for me to go away again.

When I had what I needed, I fetched a chair from the other side of the room and seated myself at the desk. I opened the pad, smoothed back the cover and began to draw, slowly and carefully at first, but then with more confidence. Sometimes I had to stop and think a little, and once or twice I had to rub out details which looked wrong, but on the whole I was pleased with my work. It was a pale echo of Gerhard Remsich's genius, but I thought it would do.

I was puzzling over the spelling of NAAMAN when I heard my father heave himself out of his chair. He gave a heavy sigh; I supposed he was about to ask me why I couldn't go and do my sketching elsewhere. I looked up as he approached and I was struck by how old he seemed. He had begun to remind me of his own father, my grandfather. I put the pencil down and picked up the sketchpad. I held it so that he could see what I had drawn.

'It's the first one,' I said, and when he didn't reply I added, 'There are seven more.'

My father stepped forward and took the sketchpad from me. He studied the drawing for a long time. Still he didn't say anything. I began to feel uncomfortable and to wonder whether I was going to have to spell it out for him. *Look, I can draw all of the windows for you.* Or perhaps – perhaps I had got it completely wrong and I was just rubbing salt into the wound; perhaps he never wanted to hear the Allerheiligen glass mentioned again. Inwardly I cursed myself, but still I waited to hear what he would say.

Eventually he rubbed his face with his hand and said, 'This is . . . it? You can draw them?'

I nodded. 'That's the one of Naaman bathing in the River Jordan.'

'I can see that,' said my father with a slight touch of tartness. He gazed at the drawing. 'This might . . . can you remember the colours too? Can you draw all of them like this?'

'I think so,' I said.

I was tempted to blurt it all out at that point, to tell him of Professor Lyle's offer and to urge him to use the drawings himself, to write his own book before the subject could be snatched from under his nose by those less worthy to handle it. After all, my father had paid for his involvement with the Allerheiligen glass; Professor Lyle hadn't. With an effort I held my tongue. Let my father work it out for himself. I watched him studying the drawing, turning it this way and that, narrowing his eyes as though he were able to see right *through* the picture into some alternative reality where Gerhard Remsich's original masterwork still glowed with the tints of rubies and sapphires. I knew that eventually he would accept the task that was being offered to him.

'This . . .' he was saying to me. 'This, here in the background. This city. Or is it meant to be a castle? Naaman was the leader of the Syrian army, you know. Could it be a garrison?'

'I think it was a castle,' I started to say; the building or group of buildings had been too small to be a city. But my father was already launching into another torrent of questions.

400

'The waters of the River Jordan, here. Can you tell me *exactly* what colour they were? Blue, obviously, but were they cornflower blue? Greenish? Did they look turquoise?'

He put the sketchpad back down in front of me with a slap. 'No, forget that for a moment. We can discuss that later. Draw another one.'

I picked up the pencil and turned to a clean page. I had heard the eagerness in my father's voice; his old enthusiasm was seeping back in. I did not think that we would ever be the same with each other as we had been before. The fit was wrong – it felt like a tooth which has been knocked right out of its socket and put back in. It appeared to be as good as it ever was from the outside, but you would never dare bite on it again; you would know that one day it might have to come out for good. I would never look at my father again and see George Clooney, Sir Lancelot and Robin Hood all rolled into one. But I had helped to give my father back to himself and with that I was satisfied.

I frowned, adjusted my grip on the pencil and began to draw.

CHAPTER SIXTY-EIGHT

As for Michel, well, we write to each other: texts, emails, sometimes even postcards – his with hearty German scenes of half-timbered houses and forests on the front, mine with views of the spires and domes of the university city where I live. I like the postcards; I like to touch something which he has sent me.

I plan to see Michel again, very soon. My family and I are now firmly reinstated in Uncle Karl's good books. In fact I think he feels guilty about having even suspected any of us of involvement in the attack on Ru, not that he would ever admit it. At any rate he was happy to find somewhere for me to stay during the long summer holidays this year. Tuesday expressed astonishment that I would consider returning to the Eifel, but I told her I wanted to keep up my German fluency. Of course I didn't discuss the other reason with her, or with my father.

Not long ago I received the following email from Michel:

Hi, Lin
I just picked up your email – I had to go to the library.
If I check them at home Dad might see them.
    Of course I remember those wooden boxes, but I

don't know who took them from the church. My father says he didn't and I can't ask Father Krause. The police asked me if something had been removed from the church. I said no. I wasn't really thinking at the time – I was confused. Anyway they didn't ask me about it again. I don't think they were really interested. They had no way of knowing what was taken. It could have been old church furniture or something.

I only looked in one of the boxes. The others were held shut with metal bands, but the lid of this one was loose so I lifted it up and looked inside. At first all I could see was some material, like the stuff they make sacks out of. Something was wrapped up in it. I pulled the coverings off.

Did you guess what was in there? It was stained-glass windows. I couldn't really tell what they showed because of course the light wasn't shining through them. I could just see from the shape of the pieces of lead that there were figures. I tried to cover the glass up again, to make it look as though I had not opened the box.

So I guess we didn't destroy all of the Allerheiligen glass after all. There must be many more windows left other than the eight we broke . . .

The rest of the email was about other things. I didn't reply right away. I thought about it for several days and then last night I wrote back.

Hi, Michel
I read your last message about ten times. I can't believe you didn't tell me before what was in those boxes.

I had some really crazy ideas about them – you'd die laughing if I told you.

I'm feeling better now. I miss Polly so much. I don't think I'm ever going to get used to her being gone. But I can get through the day. The place where they put her is beautiful, really peaceful.

Tuesday and Dad finally agreed that I can come back to Germany in the summer. It took them a while to say yes, but I think now they can see that I'm OK, I'm not going to crack up or anything. My uncle Karl is organizing it – he knows some people in Nordkirchen and thinks I can stay with them. I'll send you the address as soon as I have it. I suppose I'll have to spend the first day with them, but then can you come and pick me up?

Look, those boxes, they can't be far away. The obvious place to hide them is somewhere in the forest or at the farm. Wouldn't it be cool if we were the ones to find them?

We could start by searching the farm. I guess we'll have to think how we can search without your father finding out. If there's nothing there we can try the forest. Maybe there's a hunter's hut or something. Father Krause can't have taken them far.

I really, really want us to be the ones who find the glass. Promise you'll help me look? And <u>don't tell anyone</u>.

I love you.

Lin

ACKNOWLEDGEMENTS

Once again I would like to thank Camilla Bolton of the Darley Anderson Agency for her enthusiasm, honesty and support. I would also like to thank Amanda Punter, Editorial Director at Puffin, and everyone else at Puffin and Penguin – it continues to be a pleasure to work with you, and a thrill to see that little penguin on the spines of my books!

A special thank-you is due to Polizeihauptkommissar Erich Trenz of the Bad Münstereifel police for answering my interminable questions about German police procedure, and to a German friend who kindly advised me on other aspects of German officialdom.

I would also like to mention the late Father Nikola Reinartz, whose articles about the lost stained glass of Steinfeld Abbey and descriptions of his correspondence with the late great Montague Rhodes James were a source of inspiration for this book.

Finally, a big thank-you to my husband, Gordon, for his moral support and the numerous cups of tea!

Meet the Author

Lin and her family move to Germany at the beginning of *The Glass Demon*. Did you have to research the area where the book is set?

I didn't have to do much research about the area itself because I lived in that part of Germany (the Eifel) for seven years, so I know it really well. I had already done a lot of research into castles and churches in the Eifel for some magazine articles I wrote several years ago. Truthfully, I didn't really think of it as 'research' – it was all so intriguing that I just had to find out more!

We've heard that the legend of the Allerheiligen stained glass was based on a true story. Can you tell us about it?

It's based on the true story of the Steinfeld stained glass. Steinfeld Abbey had a fabulous series of sixteenth-century stained-glass windows. Several times in their history they had to be taken out of the window frames and hidden, because there was a war on and they could have been damaged. In 1785 they were taken down for the last time, and when the abbey closed in 1802 they were sold and vanished altogether. For a century nobody knew where they were. In 1904 the famous ghost-story writer Montague Rhodes James was cataloguing the stained glass in the chapel of Ashridge House in Hertfordshire, and realized that most of it came from Steinfeld. The name of the abbey was written on one of the windows in Latin. He was inspired by the glass to write a story called 'The Treasure of Abbot Thomas', which is set in Steinfeld. A German priest called Father Nikola Reinartz heard about the story and when he was in England for a conference he contacted M. R. James to find out where the glass was. He was then able to visit it at Ashridge. He was thrilled that the lost glass had been found at last. The Steinfeld glass was eventually sold in the 1920s at Sotheby's for the equivalent of about £800,000 in modern money.

I found this story fascinating for several reasons. I would never have believed that something as fragile as stained glass could be taken out of the window frames and transported to another country without being broken. Also, I couldn't help thinking how amazing it would be if there were another set of priceless stained-glass windows still hidden somewhere, waiting to be found. That's what inspired the book!

In *The Glass Demon* and your first book, *The Vanishing of Katharina Linden*, you mix ordinary people and places with sinister human behaviour. What appeals to you in writing about crime?

Strangely enough, I didn't really set out to write 'crime' novels. I try to tell a story with interesting characters and exciting events. The people are just as important as the crimes. I love books and films with dramatic and thrilling events, but I think a lot of the excitement is lost if you aren't involved with the characters.

Do you use the names of real places in your books? Have you ever visited any of the German towns that you write about?

Normally I do use the names of real places – Bad Münstereifel, the town featured in *The Vanishing of Katharina Linden*, really exists (I lived there for seven years!), and all the street names are real ones. However, I departed from this approach a bit in *The Glass Demon* because a lot of the action takes place in a castle. Some Eifel castles, such as the ones at Dollendorf and Kronenburg, are ruined, and nobody lives there, but some are still inhabited. I wouldn't want anyone to read the book and think, *That's my home*, and perhaps be offended. So the castle in the book, the Kreuzburg, is a mixture of several different castles, and the place names are mostly imaginary ones.

Have you ever based a character on someone you know?

Funnily enough, I have based only one character on a real person, and that was Kate Kolvenbach, the mother of Pia Kolvenbach, heroine of *The Vanishing of Katharina Linden*. Just for fun, I based her on myself. She says a lot of things which I say when I'm feeling grumpy. When I came to submit the manuscript of the book to different agents, one of the first people who read it told me that he liked the book but that Pia's mother was a bitch!

Do you have any tips to becoming a successful writer?

Read as much as you can, experience as many different things as you can, and take an interest in human behaviour. Some people say, 'Write what you know,' but I write about murders without having committed one! However, the fact that I have travelled a lot and lived in different countries is hugely inspiring for me. It means that I can write confidently about unusual locations.

The other thing is just to keep writing – practice definitely makes perfect (or, at least, a lot better!).

Which authors did you love as a child? Did you have a favourite book?

I loved good old Victorian and Edwardian adventure stories. I inherited quite a lot of the books my parents had had as kids in the 1940s. I loved Sir Arthur Conan Doyle's *The Lost World*, but my hands-down favourite was *She* by H. Rider Haggard. It's about a lost kingdom in Africa, ruled by a queen who stays eternally young and beautiful. I liked the fact that the author went to the trouble of including documents in ancient Greek and Latin, giving clues to the location of the lost kingdom. The book also has a terrifically dramatic shock ending.

Which writers inspire you now?

I admire Anthony Trollope not only for his novels themselves but for his discipline. He aimed to write a set amount of words every day, in spite of the fact that he also had a job, often writing while travelling. Also he is credited with inventing the postbox. I think it's fantastic that he could be creative *and* practical!

For sheer grand-scale imagination I think the science-fiction writer Stephen Baxter is amazing. In one of his books he starts with the destruction of a planet and works up to a climax.

Are you writing anything at the moment?

Yes, I'm working on my third novel. It's also set in the Eifel region of Germany – it's a place I find very inspiring, because it is full of lonely pine forests and creepy old castles. I like to base my plots on real historical events and genuine folk legends, and in this case the story was inspired by the witch trials that took place in the Eifel in the sixteenth century. The heroine of this book is a bit different from Pia Kolvenbach (heroine of *The Vanishing of Katharina Linden*) and Lin Fox; she's very shy and one of the things she has to do in order to solve the mystery at the centre of the story is to discover her own inner strength. I'm enjoying seeing her do that!